Praise for

Four Sisters, All Queens

"In *Four Sisters, All Queens*, Sherry Jones tells an extraordinary story of four extraordinary women, all with royal destinies. In elegant but lively prose, she brings their triumphs and struggles to life."

—Susan Higginbotham, author of *Her Highness, the Traitor*

"The power of these four sisters, these intriguing women, commands every page as does Sherry Jones's exquisite and well-crafted narrative. Their particular experiences, so finely conveyed, offers a distinct glimpse into the full landscape of thirteenth-century Europe and the influence of its women."

—Donna Russo Morin, author of *The King's Agent*

"Sherry Jones brings medieval Europe to life through the extraordinary destinies of the 'ladies of Provence.' Queens, sisters, rivals . . . What a tale!"

—Catherine Delors, author of *Mistress of the Revolution* and *For the King*

"Sherry Jones bursts onto the medieval scene with this enthralling tale of four royal sisters vying for power. Engrossing and vividly rendered, the intrigue and splendor of thirteenth-century Europe are brought to life through the voices of these disparate women, each destined to take the throne and find herself in a dangerous struggle for dominance against her own kin. Family politics, forbidden passion, and heartbreaking sacrifice create a mesmerizing tableau of what it meant to be a queen."

—C. W. Gortner, author of *The Confessions of Catherine de Medici*, *The Tudor Secret*, and *The Last Queen*

———❖———

*"Many say that Richard of Cornwall, and not
Henry, is best suited to rule England," Uncle says.
"From what I have heard, Richard agrees."*

"That is treason! I would be more inclined to behead him than to befriend him."

"He could make life difficult for the king."

"Siblings fight." Eléonore shrugs. "What can one do about that?"

"You used to quarrel a bit with your sisters, as I recall. Especially Margi. You, of all people, ought to know how to smooth the ruffled feathers of rivalry."

Across the room, Richard has seen her looking at him. Holding his gaze, she gestures for her handmaid and gives her instructions. Then, with a lift of her skirts, she turns to leave the great hall.

"Where are you going, child?"

"To my chambers. I have summoned Richard of Cornwall, and now he must come to me. Such is the power of a queen."

Four Sisters, *All Queens*

SHERRY JONES

GALLERY BOOKS

New York   London   Toronto   Sydney   New Delhi

G

Gallery Books
A Division of Simon & Schuster, Inc.
1230 Avenue of the Americas
New York, NY 10020

Copyright © 2012 by Sherry Jones

First Gallery Books trade paperback edition May 2012

GALLERY BOOKS and colophon are trademarks of Simon & Schuster, Inc.

For information about special discounts for bulk purchases, please contact Simon & Schuster Special Sales at 1-866-506-1949 or business@simonandschuster.com.

The Simon & Schuster Speakers Bureau can bring authors to your live event. For more information or to book an event contact the Simon & Schuster Speakers Bureau at 1-866-248-3049 or visit our website at www.simonspeakers.com.

Designed by Leydiana Rodríguez-Ovalles

Manufactured in the United States of America

10 9 8 7 6 5 4 3 2 1

Library of Congress Cataloging-in-Publication Data

Jones, Sherry, 1961–
Four sisters, all queens / Sherry Jones. — 1st Gallery Books trade paperback ed.
p. cm.
1. Marguerite, Queen, consort of Louis IX, King of France, 1221–1295—Fiction. 2. Eléonore, of Provence, Queen, consort of Henry III, King of England, 1223 or 4–1291—Fiction. 3. Beatrice, of Provence, Queen of Sicily, consort of Charles I, King of Naples, 1234–1267. 4. Sanchia, of Provence, Queen, consort of Richard, King of the Romans, 1225–1261—Fiction. 5. Europe—History—476–1492—Fiction. I. Title.
PS3610.O6285F68 2012
813'.6—dc23   2011044484

ISBN 978-1-4516-3324-5
ISBN 978-1-4516-3325-2 (ebook)

For Natasha Kern:
literary agent, champion, inspiration, friend

Breathing do I draw that air to me
Which I feel coming from Provença
All that is thence so pleasureth me
That whenever I hear good speech of it
I listen a-laughing and straightaway
Demand for each word an hundred more,
So fair to me is the hearing.

—Peire Vidal, 1175–1205
from "The Song of Breath"
(as translated by Ezra Pound)

Europe in the
13th Century

Atlantic Ocean

NORWAY

SWEDEN

Baltic Sea

SCOTLAND

North Sea

DENMARK

POLAND

IRELAND

ENGLAND

WALES   Berkhamsted
Wallingford• •
London•

FLANDERS

GERMANY

NORMANDY   •Paris
BRITTANY   CHAMPAGNE

HUNGARY

POITOU   BURGUNDY
FRANCE
SAVOY
ANJOU
Toulouse   Tarascon• PROVENCE
GASCONY •   •Brignoles   ITALY
NAVARRE   LANGUEDOC   Marseille   PAPAL
STATES
ARAGON   Rome•   Capua
PORTUGAL   •Barcelona   •   •Taranto

CASTILLE

THE REGNO

SICILY

M e d i t e r r a n e a n   S e a

N
W   E
S

0   100   200 miles
0   200 kilometers

Map by Paul J. Pugliese

THE QUEENS AND THEIR FAMILIES

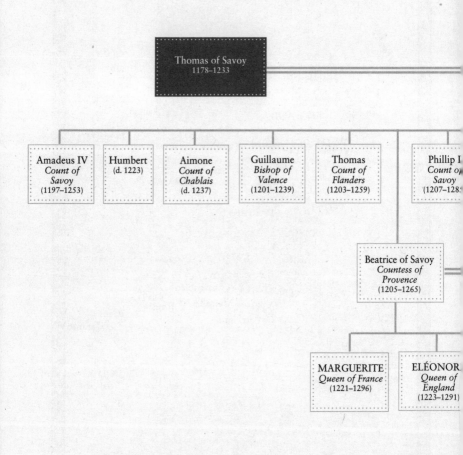

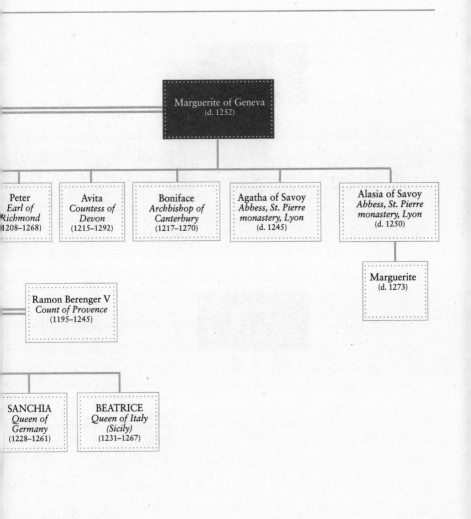

Peter
*Earl of
Richmond*
(1208–1268)

Avita
*Countess of
Devon*
(1215–1292)

Boniface
*Archbishop of
Canterbury*
(1217–1270)

Agatha of Savoy
*Abbess, St. Pierre
monastery, Lyon*
(d. 1245)

Alasia of Savoy
*Abbess, St. Pierre
monastery, Lyon*
(d. 1250)

Marguerite of Geneva
(d. 1252)

Marguerite
(d. 1273)

Ramon Berenger V
Count of Provence
(1195–1245)

SANCHIA
*Queen of
Germany*
(1228–1261)

BEATRICE
*Queen of Italy
(Sicily)*
(1231–1267)

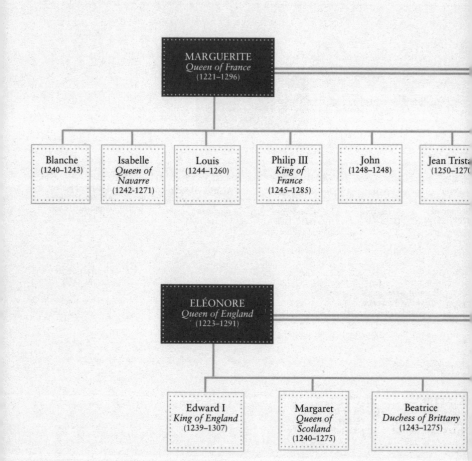

MARGUERITE
Queen of France
(1221–1296)

Blanche
(1240–1243)

Isabelle
Queen of Navarre
(1242-1271)

Louis
(1244–1260)

Philip III
King of France
(1245–1285)

John
(1248–1248)

Jean Trist
(1250–127(

ELÉONORE
Queen of England
(1223–1291)

Edward I
King of England
(1239–1307)

Margaret
Queen of Scotland
(1240–1275)

Beatrice
Duchess of Brittany
(1243–1275)

LOUIS IX
King of France
(1214–1270)

Peter
(1251–1284)

Blanche
(1253–1323)

Marguerite
Duchess of Brabant
(1254–1271)

Robert
Count of Clairmont
(1256–1318)

Agnes
*Duchess of
Burgundy*
(1260–1327)

HENRY III
King of England
(1207–1272)

Edmund
Duke of Lancaster
(1245–1296)

Katharine
(1253–1257)

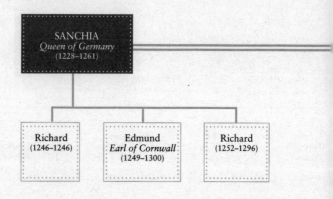

SANCHIA
Queen of Germany
(1228–1261)

Richard
(1246–1246)

Edmund
Earl of Cornwall
(1249–1300)

Richard
(1252–1296)

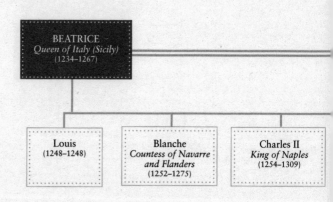

BEATRICE
Queen of Italy (Sicily)
(1234–1267)

Louis
(1248–1248)

Blanche
*Countess of Navarre
and Flanders*
(1252–1275)

Charles II
King of Naples
(1254–1309)

RICHARD OF
CORNWALL
King of Germany
(1209–1272)

CHARLES OF ANJOU
*King of Italy (Sicily), Naples,
Albania, and Jerusalem*
(1226–1285)

Philippe
*King of Thessalonica
Prince of Achaïea*
(1256–1277)

Robert
(1258–1265)

Isabella
(Elisabeth)
Queen of Hungary
(1261–1303)

THE FAMILY OF KING HENRY III (PLANTAGENET)

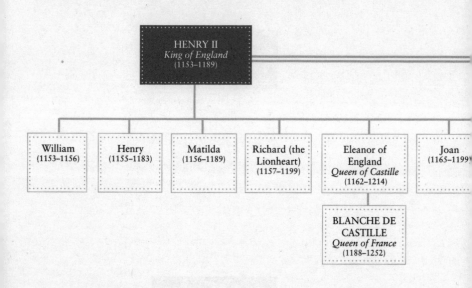

HENRY II
King of England
(1153–1189)

| William (1153–1156) | Henry (1155–1183) | Matilda (1156–1189) | Richard (the Lionheart) (1157–1199) | Eleanor of England *Queen of Castille* (1162–1214) | Joan (1165–1199 |

BLANCHE DE CASTILLE
Queen of France
(1188–1252)

Henry III's Lusignan Half-Siblings

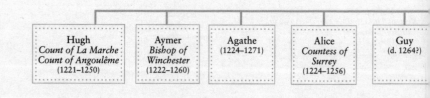

| Hugh *Count of La Marche Count of Angoulême* (1221–1250) | Aymer *Bishop of Winchester* (1222–1260) | Agathe (1224–1271) | Alice *Countess of Surrey* (1224–1256) | Guy (d. 1264?) |

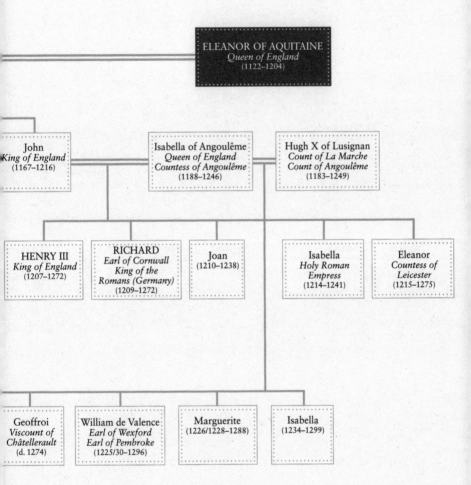

ELEANOR OF AQUITAINE
Queen of England
(1122–1204)

John
King of England
(1167–1216)

Isabella of Angoulême
Queen of England
Countess of Angoulême
(1188–1246)

Hugh X of Lusignan
Count of La Marche
Count of Angoulême
(1183–1249)

HENRY III
King of England
(1207–1272)

RICHARD
Earl of Cornwall
King of the
Romans (Germany)
(1209–1272)

Joan
(1210–1238)

Isabella
Holy Roman
Empress
(1214–1241)

Eleanor
Countess of
Leicester
(1215–1275)

Geoffroi
Viscount of
Châtellerault
(d. 1274)

William de Valence
Earl of Wexford
Earl of Pembroke
(1225/30–1296)

Marguerite
(1226/1228–1288)

Isabella
(1234–1299)

THE FAMILY OF LOUIS IX (CAPET)

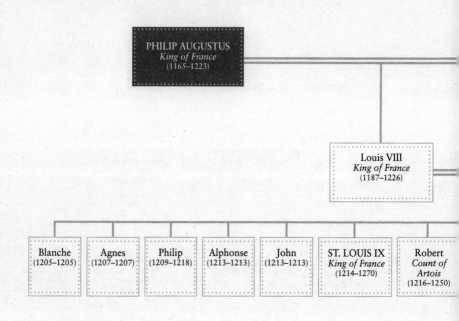

PHILIP AUGUSTUS
King of France
(1165–1223)

Louis VIII
King of France
(1187–1226)

Blanche
(1205–1205)

Agnes
(1207–1207)

Philip
(1209–1218)

Alphonse
(1213–1213)

John
(1213–1213)

ST. LOUIS IX
King of France
(1214–1270)

Robert
Count of Artois
(1216–1250)

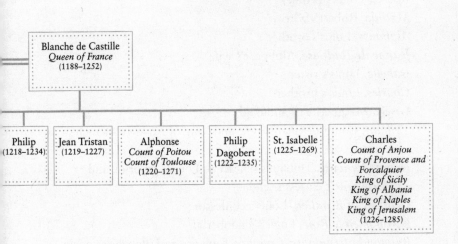

ISABEL OF HAINAULT
Queen of France
(1170–1190)

Blanche de Castille
Queen of France
(1188–1252)

Philip
(1218–1234)

Jean Tristan
(1219–1227)

Alphonse
Count of Poitou
Count of Toulouse
(1220–1271)

Philip
Dagobert
(1222–1235)

St. Isabelle
(1225–1269)

Charles
Count of Anjou
Count of Provence and
Forcalquier
King of Sicily
King of Albania
King of Naples
King of Jerusalem
(1226–1285)

THE COURT IN FRANCE

Marguerite de Provence, Queen Consort of France

Louis IX, King of France

Blanche, Isabelle, Louis, Philip, Jean Tristan, Peter, Blanche, Marguerite, Robert, Agnes, their children

Blanche de Castille, Queen Dowager of France

Isambour of Denmark, (formerly Ingeborg) Queen Dowager of France, widow of King Philip Augustus

Robert, Louis's brother

Matilda, Robert's wife

Alphonse, Louis's brother

Jeanne de Toulouse, Alphonse's wife

Isabelle, Louis's sister

Charles, Louis's brother

Gisele, Marguerite's handmaid

Thibaut, Count of Champagne and King of Navarre, Blanche's cousin

Jean de Joinville, Thibaut's seneschal, Louis's favorite, and Marguerite's closest friend

Geoffrey of Beaulieu, Louis's confessor

Bartolomeu le Roie, Louis's chamberlain

Raimond of Toulouse, Count of Toulouse and Blanche's cousin

Pierre Mauclerc, Count of Brittany, a leader of a thwarted rebellion against Louis

Hugh of Lusignan, Count of La Marche and Angoulême, husband of Queen Isabella of Angoulême, mother of King Henry III and leader, with Pierre of Brittany, of an attempt to overthrow King Louis

Isabella of Angoulême, King Henry III's mother, former Queen of England, now Countess of La Marche and Angoulême

St. Pol, Guy II of Châtillon, the Count of St. Pol and a fearsome knight

THE COURT IN ENGLAND

Eléonore of Provence, Queen Consort of England

Henry III, King of England

Edward, Margaret, Beatrice, Edmund, Katharine, their children

Guillaume of Savoy, Eléonore's uncle, bishop of Valence, prince-bishop of Liège

Thomas of Savoy, Eléonore's uncle, Count of Flanders

Peter of Savoy, Eléonore's uncle, Earl of Richmond, later Count of Savoy

Boniface of Savoy, archbishop of Canterbury

Eleanor Marshal, Henry's sister, Countess of Leicester

Simon de Montfort, Count of Leicester, Henry's seneschal, Eleanor Marshal's husband

Richard of Cornwall, Henry's brother, Earl of Cornwall

Margaret Biset, Eléonore's handmaid

Gilbert Marshal, Earl of Pembroke

Hubert de Burgh, Earl of Kent, justiciar of England and Ireland

Roger de Quincy, Earl of Winchester

Roger Mortimer, baron and ally to King Henry III

Dame Maud of Mortimer

Gilbert de Clare, Earl of Gloucester

John Maunsell, chancellor

Robert Walerand, chancellor

Hamo Lestrange, Roger Mortimer, Roger Leybourne, Henry of Almain, Edward's companions

Ebulo Montibus, protégé of Peter of Savoy, Eléonore's uncle, and companion to Edward

THE COURT IN PROVENCE

Beatrice of Savoy, Countess of Provence
Ramon Berenger, Count of Provence
Marguerite, Eléonore, Sanchia, Beatrice, their daughters
Romeo de Villeneuve, the count's seneschal (steward)
Madeleine, the girls' nursemaid
Gaston, the falconer
Sordel, a troubadour
Beatrice of Provence, Countess of Provence
Charles d'Anjou, Count of Provence

THE COURT IN CORNWALL

Sanchia of Provence, Queen of Germany, Countess of Cornwall
Richard of Cornwall, King of Germany, Count of Cornwall
Henry of Almain, Richard's son and heir
Edmund, Richard, Sanchia and Richard's children
Justine, Sanchia's handmaid
Mr. Arnold, Richard's seneschal
Abraham of Berkhamsted, collector of the Jewish tax
Floria, Abraham's wife
Joan de Valletort, Baroness of Tremberton, Richard's mistress

Prologue

I, BEATRICE OF SAVOY, am mother to four queens. What other woman in the history of the world could make this claim? None, I warrant, and none ever will.

Yes, I am boasting. Why shouldn't I? Do you think my daughters rose to such heights by happenstance? A woman achieves nothing in this man's world without careful plotting. I began scheming for my girls before I even held my eldest, Marguerite, in my arms.

Margi was no ordinary child. She spoke in sentences before her first birthday. But then, she is a Savoy, and we are no ordinary family. If we were, we would not have become guardians of the Alpine passes and rulers of an expanding domain, as well as friends of kings, emperors, and popes. How did we achieve such feats? Not by brutish battles and conquests, but with shrewd alliances and strategic marriages. My children, too, would marry well, I determined, and increase our family's influence as never before.

Here is how I fulfilled this vow: I raised my daughters as if they were sons.

Oh ho! I see shock on your face. Are you surprised also, then, to learn that I called them "boys"? Having taken my schooling alongside five of my eight brothers—in philosophy, Latin, astronomy, mathematics, logic, diplomacy, debate, hunting, archery, even swordplay—I recognized this: knowledge is the key to power. Why do you think men reserve it for themselves, leaving only fluff and nonsense for girls? What good to a girl are needlework, curtseying, drawing pictures, and feigning interest while a man prattles on and on about himself? These endeavors—the essence of feminine schooling—serve only to enhance men, and to diminish women. Wanting success for my girls, I taught them as though they were boys, endowing them with true power—the kind that comes from within.

When Margi was nearly of age, I enlisted my brothers to find a king for her to marry. Being Savoyards, we plotted. Amadeus, Guillaume, and Thomas praised her beauty, intelligence, and piety in courts near and far, and before every guest they entertained. Meanwhile, I charmed Sordel, the troubadour, to write a song in her honor, then paid him handsomely—with gold and, yes, kisses, but not the prize he preferred—to perform it before the French King Louis IX. Thusly captivated, the king sought Margi's hand—and before long, my four daughters were queens of the world.

I would have made them kings, if I could. Instead, I made them mothers of kings. It was the best I could do for them, and for the House of Savoy—for my family—now and in the future.

Family is everything. Nothing else matters. All other bonds may be broken—friendship, marriage, even queenship—except the ties that bind us to our relations. This is the second lesson I taught to my daughters: Family comes first. To my great sorrow, however, my words fell against their ears and bounced away, like seeds on a bed of stones.

If only they would heed my admonishments now, and help one another. Instead, they seem intent on tearing one another, and our family, apart. And I? I cajole, and advise, and lecture—and avert my gaze from them lest I cry a weak woman's tears. O, how it breaks my heart to see my girls suffer.

✦ *Marguerite* ✦

Four Sisters, All Queens

Aix-en-Provence, 1233

Twelve years old

𝒮HE TURNS SLOWLY around.

The great hall smolders, dimly aflame and smeared in an acrid haze. M. de Flagy holds a piece of white silk to his long nose and notes the cheap tallow candles, the stains on the tablecloth, the frayed cuffs of the countess's gloves. Before him, Marguerite turns slowly, stifling a yawn. She has taken the *monsieur* hawking and horseback riding, has performed a country dance on her vielle, sung three *chansons* by Bernard de Ventadour, defeated *monsieur* at chess, recited from Aristotle's new logic in the original Greek, and debated, in Latin, whether time has a beginning, she agreeing with The Philosopher that it does not, because God, the source of time, is eternal. M. de Flagy, seized by a fit of coughing, hurried from the hall and missed her father's challenge: Does time, then, have no ending? Does it exist in the realm of the eternal, or is time an earthly function? If earthly, then how could it be without beginning, God having created the Earth?

Now, for her final performance, Marguerite endures the stranger's gaze on her face, her hips, her bosom straining indecently against the too-small gown. As Queen of France, her *maire* has said, she would never wear ill-fitting clothes again.

His hand snakes out. "She appears to be perfect, but I have not inspected her teeth."

She steps back, out of his reach. "My teeth are strong, *monsieur*. And their bite is sharp."

Papa grins, but Mama is not laughing. Her eyes snap: *All I have taught you, for naught*! Marguerite's skin dampens; the room is suddenly too warm.

"She is but twelve years old," Mama says. "Her tongue is not yet tamed." The countess places a gloved hand on M. de Flagy's arm, dazzles him with her practiced smile. *Monsieur* bares his own stained and crooked teeth.

"Your daughter has spirit, *non*? *Très formidable*. If she marries King Louis, she will need it to contend with his mother." He winks at Marguerite. "*Ma belle,* you may need those sharp teeth, as well."

Music rises from the floor: rebec, guitarra morisca, pipes, small drums. A minstrel in bright clothing and a red beard sings the Kalenda Maya, meant to please the countess with its words of love for a different Beatrice—but, as she whispers to the visitor now, his grating voice only reminds her of another, more memorable, performance, when the composer Raimbaut de Vaqueiras sang it in this very hall. That was years ago, she does not add, before attacks and sieges depleted the treasury, when troubadours and trobairitz flocked to Provence for endless merrymaking, the wine flowed too abundantly to need mixing with water, and the hall glowed with the light of the finest beeswax candles.

When the song has screeched to its end, Mama hastens her to the nursery, giving her arm excited squeezes. "You have charmed him! Well done, Margi. As queen, you can save Provence."

The nurse, Madeleine, tuts over the hole in Marguerite's gown as she undresses her. Mama shrugs: Surely M. de Flagy did not notice such a tiny flaw. Yet her forehead wrinkles as her other daughters pile into a chair with her. She wants queenship for her daughter more than Marguerite wants it for herself.

"Was he looking at Margi's gown, or what was inside it?" Eléonore says. Too big for Mama's lap, she sprawls there, anyway, forcing Sanchia to the floor, at their mother's feet. Little Beatrice careens about on plump legs, snatching rushes from the floor and throwing them down, laughing each time as if she had done something clever.

Madeleine plaits Marguerite's hair while the countess tells her tales. "Your sister was as calm as the spring mist and as bold as Lancelot." Absently she caresses Sanchia's golden hair. "King Louis and his mother will hear only praise for Marguerite of Provence." Why, oh why didn't Marguerite bite the *monsieur*?

"I would make a better queen," Eléonore says. "I am stronger than Margi, and a faster runner. And I am a better huntsman."

And Eléonore *wants* to leave Provence. And she doesn't despise the French, as Marguerite does.

"Be patient, Elli!" Mama says. "You are only ten years old—too young for marriage."

Marguerite laughs. "Telling Elli to be patient is like commanding an ass to gallop."

"Mama! Did you hear her call me an ass?"

"You're as stubborn as one," Marguerite says.

"Why wouldn't I be stubborn, when I know I am right?"

"If you want to be a queen, Elli, you must learn to control yourself," Mama says. "In that regard, your sister is far ahead of you." She does not mention Marguerite's rude remark to M. de Flagy.

"Mama," Sanchia says, turning on the floor to tug at their mother's gown.

"Except when a tart riposte lands on her tongue. Then she cannot wait to spit it out," Eléonore says.

"How would you know the flavor of riposte?" Marguerite says. "Nothing but boasts ever land on your tongue. Apparently, you find them every bit as difficult to swallow."

"Mama." Sanchia tugs at the countess's gown again. "Is Elli going to be a queen, too?"

"Boys!" Mama's admonishment rankles Marguerite. Why must

she refer to them as boys? Does she wish they were sons instead of daughters? "The time for arguing—and for competing, Elli—has come to an end. Margi is poised to become a queen. And not just any queen, but Queen of France, the richest and most powerful of kingdoms. We must help her, not fight with her." The smile she sends to Marguerite is like a sunbeam. "And she will help us, in turn."

"But I like to fight with Margi," Eléonore says. "I always win."

"You wish that were so," Marguerite says.

"Your uncles and I used to fight, too," Mama says. "Since I married your *paire* and became Countess of Provence, we have worked together. That is the Savoy way. Now, with Margi's marriage to King Louis, the house of Savoy will rise like a shining star to the highest spot in the heavens. We shall rise with it, and all our family, and your children and grandchildren, if God is willing. If we help one another."

"Is Elli going to be a queen, too?" Sanchia says again.

"I shall be queen of the world!" Eléonore wriggles out of Mama's lap and lands on her feet. "I won't be content with a kingdom as small as France. I'll have an empire." She folds her arms across her chest. "And, don't worry, Mama, I'll give castles and lordships to all my family."

Marguerite laughs. "And who will be your emperor? Will you join the harem of Stupor Mundi?" Astonishment of the World: It is a fitting title for Frederick II, whose blasphemous remarks—calling Christ a deceiver!—and worldly lifestyle have made the pope of Rome's jaw drop in not only astonishment, but outrage.

"Whichever king I marry will become great. I will make sure of it."

"Are you going to make Elli a queen, too, Mama?" Sanchia says.

"Not I, but your uncle Guillaume," Mama says. Eléonore gasps. Mama smiles. "He and Romeo foresee crowns on all your heads. They have sworn to make it so."

"Four sisters, all queens!" Eléonore dances about. "Who has ever heard of such a thing?"

"*Three* sisters," says Sanchia. Worry wizens her eight-year-old face. "I'm going to take my vows at Ganagobie." Eléonore rolls her eyes: Sanchia has talked of nothing else since last month, when Mama's cousin Garsende joined the Ganagobie cloister in a ceremony so moving, it made even Mama cry.

"My pious little peapod, as gentle as a newborn lamb," Mama says to Sanchia. "You would make a splendid nun, were you plain or deformed." Sanchia has hair the color of spun starlight, eyes as black as the night sky, a dimple in her chin, and a mouth like ripe cherries. To hide such beauty would be a shame, Mama says, for it would certainly attract a fortuitous marriage.

"Erase all selfish thoughts from your heads," Mama says now. "Family comes first. As women—and as queens—your loyalties must lie with your sisters, your uncles, and your parents. We are your foundation. We are your strength."

She is speaking to Marguerite, who looks down at her hands. Does Mama know of the pain that stabs Marguerite's chest when she thinks of leaving Provence? Most likely, she does not care. The Count of Toulouse lurks ever like a shadow over their door, ready to strike. He would take for himself the flowering fields, the shining mountains, the glittering shores of Provence—and the star of Savoy would drop lower in the sky than ever before.

"In our world, fortunes are gained and lost in the blink of an eye." Mama snaps her fingers. "As you've seen, to rule even a small county such as Provence brings peril. Think of the difficulties when you are a queen, and far from home! Danger lurks not only outside your domain, but also within, even in your own court. Women envy you, especially if you are beautiful. Men resent your power over them, especially if you come from a foreign land. This is why you need your family's help."

"When I am queen, I won't need anyone's help," Eléonore says.

"Have you forgotten your lessons?" Lately, Mama has been teaching Marguerite and Eléonore about ancient queens. "Even Cleopatra needed help. Without Caesar, she would have lost the throne."

"Cleopatra." Eléonore snorts. "She used her woman's charms to get what she wanted. We wouldn't need to do that. We have the 'minds of men.'" It's the phrase that Mama uses to brag about their rigorous schooling. Marguerite thinks of M. de Flagy staring with hungry eyes at her bosom, then disappearing as she discussed Aristotle.

"You're no Cleopatra, not with that flat chest," she says to Eléonore. "But you could be Artemisia. The warrior queen, remember? She had a 'brave spirit and manly daring.'"

"That is our Eléonore, full of manly daring," Mama says.

Eléonore struts about like a proud knight, wielding an imaginary sword.

"Which queen would I be?" Sanchia says, caught up in the game.

"That's easy: Helena of Constantinople," Eléonore says. "She became a saint."

"I say Elen Luyddog," Marguerite says. "A Welsh princess who became Empress of Rome. She went home after her husband died and converted everyone to the Christian faith."

"I would not mind being a queen if I could use my powers for the Lord," Sanchia says in her soft voice.

"I'd use my powers to help my family." Eléonore looks at Mama with shining eyes, having caught the beam of her approval for a moment, at least.

"I would hope to rule wisely," Marguerite says. "That is all that one can ask, I think."

"You are like the Queen of Sheba, then," Mama says. "She told her people, 'I am smitten with the love of wisdom . . . for wisdom is far better than treasure of gold and silver.'"

Marguerite feels herself blush. If Mama knew her true feelings, would she still consider her wise?

"'I am only wise insofar as what I don't know, I don't think I know,'" she says, quoting Socrates.

"Wisdom is a noble goal," Mama says. "The pursuit of a lifetime."

"Margi will need a lifetime to attain it," Eléonore teases.

"What about Beatrice, Mama?" Sanchia says. "What queen is she most like?"

"A queen bee, always buzzing about," Mama says. Beatrice careens toward the doorway, as she does every night. Madeleine snatches her up, exclaiming—as she does every night—and Beatrice begins, predictably, to whine for Papa.

"Bedtime must be at hand." Papa walks in; Beatrice wriggles free from the nurse's grip and runs to him. He scoops her up and kisses her cheeks as she protests. She does not want to go to bed. She wants, she says, to stay up with Papa.

"I am going to play chess with Sordel. He likes to cheat, and I like to win. That is too much excitement for a little girl."

"I don't care. I want to come." She nestles her curly head against his shoulder.

"Do you promise to be good, and sit in my lap and not move?" She nods. "Then you may come with me." Madeleine plants her hands on her hips as he walks out with her; she has told her lord—how many times?—that baby Beatrice needs her sleep, that she will be tired tomorrow, and ornery. But there is no telling him anything when it comes to Beatrice.

"Beatrice uses her charms to get what she wants," Eléonore whispers later, as she and Marguerite lie in bed with the sleeping Sanchia. "*She* is like Cleopatra."

"I hope you are wrong," Marguerite says. "Remember what happened to Cleopatra's sisters."

Eléonore bares her teeth. Looking like a gargoyle in the moonlight, she lifts her index finger and draws it slowly across her throat.

❖ *Marguerite* ❖

The Light of Destiny

Brignoles, 1234

Thirteen years old

THE FALCON HOVERS, its eye piercing through the trees and the long grass, abiding on invisible currents, waiting. Then: the sudden stoop, the scurry on the ground, the swoop and upward soar, talons clutching a fat hare. "I won!" Marguerite shouts.

"You did not." Eléonore turns to the falconer. "Gaston. Tell her! My hawk had already exhausted that hare."

From the château they hear their names. They race down the hill, mouths watering. Yesterday's dinner consisted of brown bread, cheese, and a few leaves of the spring's first lettuces; for today, they have been promised raspberries and a fish from the pond. Eléonore reaches the château first, as always. In the glow of victory she doesn't notice Mama's glare at her tunic, torn and dirtied in her rolling down the hill this morning. Or, more likely, she pretends not to notice.

The girls sit at the raised table at the front of the great hall, on their mother's side. Beside her, Papa talks intently with Uncle Guillaume and Romeo, arrived today after a visit to the French court. Marguerite catches her uncle's eye, but his wink doesn't tell her whether he has brought a marriage proposal. On the floor, minstrels play pipes and drums while jongleurs stand on their heads and turn cartwheels in bright short tunics and hose. At the tables behind them, knights jostle for seats closest to the front, while troubadours elbow one another and make sport of them. Papa's favorite, the red-haired troublemaker Bertran d'Alamanon, scribbles a verse on his hand and shows it to the fat Sordel, who holds his belly as if bracing for the shock of a full meal.

"The King of France wants Margi," Uncle Guillaume is saying to Papa, holding up a hand to stop the servant's watering his wine. "The man they sent here last winter took back a glowing report."

"'A girl of pretty face but prettier faith,'" Romeo quotes, then beams as proudly as if he had invented the phrase.

Pretty faith? Her religious landscape is strewn with the burned and decapitated bodies of the Cathars, some of them poets. Labeled heretics for criticizing the pope of Rome. Slaughtered by the French. Her faith is a drop of blood on the tip of a sword, unglimpsed by M. de Flagy's eyes as they admired her chest.

"But you said his report was glowing," Papa says. "That tribute sounds lukewarm, no? As if our beautiful Margi were a plain-face destined for the convent."

"That is exactly what we want the White Queen to think." Uncle Guillaume quaffs his wine and gestures for more. "Blanche de Castille does not allow beautiful women in her court."

A shout rises from the floor. The servants in their unbleached tunics and linen caps have entered the great hall bearing covered trays, which they place first on the count and countess's table. Anticipating raspberries, Eléonore reaches for the plate before the cover is lifted. Marguerite kicks her. "Uncle is here! Remember your manners," she whispers.

Eléonore's hand falls away as Mama lifts the lid. Each round plate holds a dollop of cheese, a loaf of brown bread, scraggly bits of greens. Mama clenches her teeth so tightly, the slightest jostle might snap off her head.

"What is this?"

The servant clears his throat. Cheese, he says, and bread. And some early lettuce from the garden.

"We were promised raspberries," Eleanor says. "And fish."

The countess shushes her, but the servant responds: No rain has fallen in weeks. The trout pond is drying up; the fish have died. The garden is wilting for want of moisture, in spite of daily waterings. As for the raspberries, the birds have attacked the canes and eaten all the fruit. Except for milk and wheat, the pantry is bare—and there is no money with which to replenish it.

The countess stands. "This will not do. Girls, go and tell your maids to pack your belongings. We shall dine this evening in Brignoles."

❦

*T*HE VERY THOUGHT of peaches makes Marguerite's mouth feel ripe and lush—and Brignoles makes her think of peaches, which drip sweetly from the trees there. The season is too young for them now, but other deliciousness awaits, for the rain and sun fall in perfect balance in Brignoles, bringing a bounty of vegetables and fruits all around the year. Beside her in the carriage, Eléonore tosses small stones onto the seat, playing at dice. Opposite them, Sanchia presses her cheek against Mama's arm, unheeded as Mama sings to the baby:

> When fresh breezes gather,
> That from your country rise,
> I seem to feel no other
> Air but that of Paradise.

Brignoles belongs to Mama, its town, its orchards, its square, its white palace all given by Papa as a wedding gift. Marguerite hums Bernard de Ventadour's *chanson* and closes her eyes, feeling the fresh breeze on her face. Which of Provence's treasures does she love most? Moustiers, with its rugged cliffs of rock, so thrilling to climb? She thinks of the lavender-scrubbed hills in Aix, where she and her sister have raced on horseback many times, kicking up fragrance; the fruit trees in Brignoles, not only peach but plum, from which she has gorged, and sickened herself; the blue-lapped Marseille shores, where Papa would bury his girls in sand from the neck down, then fashion for them mermaid's tails; the Alps ringing the Provençal border like a strand of diamonds, in whose foothills she and Eléonore discovered a secret cave, filled with wondrous formations, where they pretended to be fairies. But no—her favorite has to be Tarascon, on the broad plain of the ribboning Rhône, the mighty fortress whose carved statues and gargoyles seem to spring to life in the moonlight (the fanciful Eléonore swears that they do), and where the troubadours and trobairitz fill the gardens with song. At Tarascon, they know, they are safe from harm, for no siege by mortals—by Toulouse—could penetrate its fortified walls.

He wants her. Soon King Louis of France will send a marriage proposal, and her life in Provence will end—for now. When Papa dies (in many years, please God), she will become Countess of Provence, and she can move between her county and her kingdom, caring for one, enduring the other. Until then, France will seem a purgatory and her life a dreary waiting. Provence is the realm of all her happinesses.

"Mama," Sanchia says, "Margi is crying."

Mama stops bouncing the baby.

"I love Provence," Marguerite says.

The countess sighs, and gives Marguerite what she and Eléonore call her Smile of Infinite Patience. "Of course you love Provence. We are the envy of the world. But your family needs you in France."

"Mama," Marguerite says, "I have been thinking. In Paris, I would be far away. Couldn't I help Provence more as its countess than as queen of another country?"

Her *maire*'s laugh is mirthless, as if Marguerite were a jongleur who kept dropping the balls.

"Do you think you could bring peace to Provence, and accomplish what your parents have not? Would you be like Cleopatra and charm the emperor into sending help? Perhaps he will invite you into his harem. Frederick loves pretty faces." Marguerite's cheeks burn.

"Or maybe you could impress the pope with your pretty faith, and convince him to crush the heretic Raimond of Toulouse like an ant." Having chastised her, Mama has stopped laughing. "Would you be willing to pay the price that Rome demands—fees; knights and foot-soldiers for the pope's battles; the loss of our independence?"

Eléonore's cry pulls Marguerite's attention to the sere fields outside. A peacock faces the carriage with its tail spread, looking as proud as if it had won it in a contest. Her hand closes around one of Elli's pebbles; she hurls it at the bird.

"You missed, as usual," Eléonore says. "Don't be shy: Throw harder. Like this." She leans over her sister to take aim with the second stone—and sends the bird off, squawking, in a flurry of blue.

⬩—❊—⬩

THE PALACE STAFF greets them at the door, then resumes setting up tables and benches in the great hall and setting down tableclothes, knives, spoons, and goblets. Shouts rise to the ceiling, and laughter. The aroma of roasted meat rumbles Marguerite's stomach. Papa accompanies his knights and their horses to the livery stables. Mama, in the nursery, oversees the unpacking of the girls' bedding and clothes. While the nurse consoles the crying Beatrice (awakened from a too-short nap), and Sanchia holds onto Mama's skirts, Marguerite and Eléonore slip into the great hall.

"Let's go to the kitchen," Marguerite says. "Someone is sure to give us a bite of something."

"If not, we'll steal it." Eléonore's voice trills low with the excitement of thievery.

A man runs in, seeking Papa. The Count of Toulouse approaches with fifty men, on horses and in full armor. They have been spied in the forest, building a siege engine.

"A siege now, when supplies are so short? We will starve," Mama says. She sends Madeleine, with Marguerite's sisters, to the tower. Marguerite remains, Mama's shadow since her twelfth birthday, when she began preparing to rule Provence—and, these last months, France.

"Fetch the count's armor," Mama orders Papa's chamberlain. "Fetch the count," she tells Romeo, before rushing off to the kitchen with Marguerite.

"Our men will need nourishment to fight," she says. She steps into the kitchen, claps her hands, cries, "Hurry! Hurry! Or we will be lost." Marguerite stares at the mutton and trout, olives, cheese, lettuces, baby artichokes, warm breads, and—yes—raspberries. She swallows the water pooling in her mouth, dances one way, then the next to avoid being overrun by servants snatching up the dishes of meats, fish, fowl, and vegetables, baskets of fruit, and flagons of wine. Her mother's voice blares like a trumpet over the cacophony of running feet, clattering dishes and silverware, knife blades scraping against whetstones. Mama thrusts a platter of roast mutton into Marguerite's hands. She blinks: is she a servant?

"Take it," her mother says. Marguerite scurries out into the hall and places the platter before a group of knights who are already stuffing themselves, then hastens to join her *paire* at the head table. No sooner does she pick up a leg of guinea hen, though, than do trumpets announce the sighting of Toulouse and his army.

Papa leaps up and, donning his helmet, races out the door, shouting, followed by shouting men. While the hall empties, Marguerite follows her mother up the winding stone stairs. In the dim tower Madeleine holds Beatrice on her lap and feeds her bits of bread and meat while Sanchia sits on a stool and whimpers, her food untouched.

"You must eat," Marguerite tells her. "What if the baby needs you? What if Mama does? How will you be useful if you have no strength?"

Mama stands at the tower wall, peering through a notch. Marguerite, too, watches as Papa and his men thunder across the drawbridge and pour onto the field. Toulouse's knights scatter, except for those pulling a trebuchet and others dragging a felled tree to use as a battering ram. All wear battle gear, some in mail and others in the new plate armor that the Count of Provence cannot afford.

"Look at the puny size of Toulouse's force," Eléonore scoffs.

"They did not expect to find us here," Marguerite says. "They had thought to conquer an empty castle."

"Very astute, Margi," Mama says.

"Anyone could have guessed that," Eléonore says.

Up goes the red flag of Toulouse with its distinctive, twelve-pointed cross. Up goes the gold-and-red striped Provençal standard. As the horses make their initial charge, Marguerite grips the window ledge, bracing for the crash. Her father rides before his men, his lance lifted high. But the clash is not to come. Already Toulouse's men are turning away, abandoning the trebuchet on its cart, dropping the battering ram.

"Hit him, Papa! Knock him down!" Eléonore shouts. Marguerite holds her breath. Riding straight for the Count of Toulouse, their *paire* smacks his lance at his opponent's chest—a solid blow, but Toulouse is ready. He deflects the blow with his shield and smashes his lance into Papa's stomach, knocking him to the ground. Eléonore's shriek echoes off the walls. Marguerite's heart clatters, a stone in a rolling drum, as Papa staggers to his feet. Toulouse hurls himself down and a hand-to-hand fight begins, both men thrusting and slicing and clashing their heavy swords.

Even a renowned swordsman such as Papa cannot defeat plate armor, which resists his every blow. After a time, his movements grow sluggish, his swordplay clumsy. His chest rises and falls, and he stumbles. Toulouse lifts his sword; her father's cut follows a moment too late, and the blade falls across his shoulders, knocking him to the dust.

"Papa!" Tears fill Marguerite's eyes. Elli screams. Sanchia buries her face in Mama's skirt. Mama's pale lips move in silent prayer. Then comes God's answer: a foot soldier rushes to Papa's aid—but Toulouse strikes him down with a blow to the neck. Next comes Romeo on his horse, a red feather in his helmet and a lance under his arm—but Toulouse leaps onto a horse and rides away, followed by his knights. The battle is finished.

Marguerite hurries downstairs with her mother and Eléonore, gripping her sister's hand as if to hold herself upright. Papa may be dead. *Please God, no.* Her chest tightens, crimping her breath. His kind face, his laughter-crinkled eyes, the large nose she loved to tweak (making him sound like a honking goose as he talked), swim now before her tearing eyes. What did he say to her last night? *You will always be a queen in my eyes, no matter what King Louis decides.*

How great is the space between one heartbeat and the next? For Marguerite, time stretches into infinity as she stands at the door with her Mama and Eléonore, waiting for Papa. Unwanted thoughts intrude. If Papa dies, what will happen to her? Would she yet go to France, or would she remain in Provence to take his place? As if anyone could take her Papa's place.

At last two men bear Papa through the château door, into the great hall, and up the stairs to his chamber. Marguerite stretches her neck, looking for signs of life. His grunts of pain reassure her as she slips into his chambers where he lies on his bed, soaking his bedclothes in blood, his blanched face gaping and popeyed. His arm hangs next to his body like a door that has fallen off its hinge. Mama goes to his side.

"I will be fine," Papa rasps. His skin is as pale as a bleached skull, as if all his blood had drained through his wound. Mama grips his good hand as the healer eases his shoulder back into its socket.

"This is why you must go to France," Mama says to Marguerite. "These attacks against Provence must end."

Romeo strides in. What are the losses? Papa wants to know.

Five men wounded, he says. One killed.

"It could have been you!" Mama's sob twists like a shriek in the wind. Marguerite turns away, unable to bear her mother's tears.

"I will not die at Toulouse's hand. God loves me too much for that," the count says.

"God loves the heretic Toulouse more, it seems," Mama says. "Perhaps our Lord does not realize that he is excommunicated. Or maybe he does not care."

"Hush! The priest might hear you." Papa closes his eyes. "Father Austerc is on his way to administer the final unction."

"No! Papa!" Eléonore flings herself over him, protecting him from unction—or death. The count laughs, but Mama's glare is a knife cutting short Marguerite's giggles.

"Ramon, these attacks must stop. If you are killed, we lose Provence. And Toulouse is draining our treasury with these constant battles. We have only a few days' worth of food here. Our children are as thin as twigs, Elli has to wear Margi's used clothing, and the servants are grumbling because they have not been paid."

"The knights complain, as well, but what are we to do? We cannot surrender Provence, so we must fight."

Mama lifts her eyebrows at Marguerite, as if she had just won a bet or a dinnertime debate. "Now do you see? Like it or not, you must go to Paris," she says. "Until you take the crown from Blanche de Castille, Provence will remain in danger. Your family will be in danger. The White Queen waits like a hawk to swoop down and snatch us away. Only you can save us from her clutches."

Marguerite meets her *maire*'s gaze, but cannot hold it for long. The light of destiny being too bright for her to bear, she closes her eyes.

———

"TEN THOUSAND MARKS!" The count slumps in his throne when the French emissaries have gone to bathe and prepare for the meal that Romeo has promised, somehow, to provide to them. "The White Queen cannot be serious."

"Of course she is serious," Mama says. "She knows how much we have spent fighting her cousin Toulouse. The more she weakens Provence, the more easily France can swallow us up."

"It is no use." Marguerite's hopes soar: The white sands of Marseille, she thinks. The fragrance of rosemary. The summer sun. "We cannot afford this dowry."

"We must afford it," Mama says.

Papa rakes his fingers through his hair. He gives his eldest daughter a wan smile. "Margi, we should have sent you to Paris with Romeo. If King Louis had even one glimpse of you, *he* would be paying *us* for your hand. As it is, I do not see how . . . I am sorry, child. You will not be a queen, after all."

Marguerite, sitting on a divan by the window, rises to move to his side. She slides her arms around his neck, kisses his cheek. "I am not disappointed, Papa. Didn't you know? I would rather remain here with you."

"And your father would rather keep you nearby." Romeo struts in, tossing his curls. "But you must think of the future, my lord, not only for Margi's sake. Make a queen of her, and I can make queens of them all."

"You, Romeo? Or my brother Guillaume?" Mama purses her lips, not liking to see her family's contributions ignored.

"Think of the glory that would follow, like ripples in a pond, to all your generations," he says. "Your daughters and granddaughters, queens! Your grandsons, princes and kings! You must not let a temporary shortage of coins stand in your way."

"True, but—"

"I knew you would agree!" He rubs his hands together. "I have just told the French that you agree to the dowry. They have already left for Paris." The mystery of how to feed them thusly solved, he bows, his lips twitching in self-congratulation.

"By God's head, Romeo, you will ruin me." Papa leaps up. "You have given Queen Blanche the perfect excuse to invade—to collect the debt we will not be able to pay."

"My lord, you are a noble warrior and a prince of poets, but you lack imagination in matters of money. You must leave the financing to me."

The marriage price came as no surprise to Romeo. He had expected it to be even higher. After taking Normandy, Anjou, and Aquitaine away from England, France has risen in wealth and power to become one of the greatest kingdoms in the world. When Queen Blanche named her terms, he never hesitated, but rode straight to Savoy to ask for money from Mama's brothers Guillaume and Thomas. In exchange, he promised them bright futures in the French court. He also solicited two thousand marks from the archbishop of Aix. "He does not want to lose his independence any more than you want to lose yours."

"You are still a long way from ten thousand," Marguerite points out.

Romeo shrugs. "The count may lack cash, but he does have land. We need only to pledge it, and castles, for the dowry. Tarascon is desirable, being so recently fortified. Since Margi will inherit Provence, you lose nothing—but you gain the allegiance of France."

Mama rises and, her eyes soft with pride, enfolds Marguerite in her arms.

"Queen of France," she says. "My little girl."

She inhales Mama's perfume and presses her face against her breast, hoping tears won't stain her mother's silk tunic.

❧ *Marguerite* ❧
Country Bumpkin
Sens, 1234

*T*HE FANFARE OF trumpets startles her awake—that, and her carriage's sudden stop. She lifts her head from Aimée's lap. Outside the window: Uncle Guillaume's thickly bearded face.

"Are we in Sens?" Has she slept for so long?

"Not yet. But your husband cannot wait for us to arrive, it seems." He beams. "King Louis approaches, my dear."

Aimée snaps the curtain shut. Her fingers fly about her mistress's head, tucking her loose hair into a crespine (for she is married now, already given by proxy to King Louis by Papa), tying a yellow barbette under her chin, topping her with a scalloped fillet. "You'll not be caught by surprise as long as I serve you," she says, dabbing red ochre onto Marguerite's lips. From outside, fanfare. Marguerite lifts the curtain, sees Provençal horses bearing red-and-gold-striped banners and, in the distance, cathedral spires. Her time is nearly at hand. She takes a deep breath.

Guillaume raps again. "Will you keep His Grace waiting?"

"Go. Hurry!" Aimée pushes her out the door. "Go and charm your king, and save us all."

She takes her uncle's proffered hand and steps down to the

ground. "I don't know who is more excited about this meeting, you or Aimée."

"I think the king outshines us both."

Marguerite sees him—and gasps.

"I agree, *ma chère*, but of course you will not laugh," Uncle Guillaume murmurs.

She is permitted to smile, however, and she does so, as broadly as her mouth will stretch as she glances into his eyes and then away, not letting her gaze linger on his mail suit of dazzling, eye-popping gold.

"My lord." She curtseys deeply.

"Please do not be intimidated. I have dressed to impress you, but I am only a humble man under this armor."

"A most dazzling man, my lord." His eyes are a shade of blue she has not seen in eyes. They ask questions to which Marguerite has no answers. She has questions of her own, but now is not the time—not until she has won his affection.

Light bounces off his suit and across her eyes. She averts her gaze. He moves toward her.

"You are far more beautiful than anyone has said." He stands so close that Marguerite can feel the sun's reflection off his suit. Her breath catches in her throat. "M. de Flagy did not describe you fully."

"'*Singing proves merely valueless/ If the song moves not from the heart,*'" she sings softly.

The king blinks in confusion. "Pardon?"

"By Bernard de Ventadour, my lord." He knits his brow. "Do not mind me. I have recently awakened from dreams peopled by troubadours, and filled with song."

"Troubadours?" His face smoothes out, relieved. "Ask Mama. She knows all about them." Does the White Queen share Marguerite's love for song, then? If so, befriending her may not be so difficult.

A young man and a boy approach. As they bow, the king introduces them: his brothers—Robert, tall and broad-shouldered, the quintessential courtly knight except for his smirk; and Alphonse, small and dark-haired, blinking with purpose.

"Welcome to France, my lady." Robert bows. "We hope you will enjoy our brother's company more than we do."

Alphonse sniggers. "Yes, please keep him amused. We are tired of hiding and running away from him."

The king creases his forehead. She turns to present her uncles. "I believe you are acquainted with Guillaume, the archbishop-elect of Valence, and Thomas, the Count of Piedmont."

"Who does not know the men of Savoy?" The king smiles as her uncles kneel before him. "The Holy Roman Emperor is said to keep your counsel these days," he says to Guillaume.

"I dined with him a fortnight ago, my lord," Guillaume says, standing. "And the pope of Rome the week before that. It would please me greatly to share my insights with you—"

"Yes, of course, you must speak to my mother." Louis turns to Marguerite. "Shall we proceed to Sens, my lady? Mama waits to receive you there."

He takes her hand and, bowing, kisses the air above it. Marguerite's skin tingles as if he had touched her with his lips. He turns and strides to his horse, his brothers behind him. Beside her, Uncle Thomas arches an eyebrow and Guillaume shrugs.

"The king has no interest in policy making," Guillaume says as the men escort her back to her carriage. "Can we blame him? Tomorrow is his wedding day."

"He is enchanted by his new bride." Thomas winks. "As is every man in his entourage. Did you note how they stared at you, Margi?"

"And you are not even wearing a gold suit," Guillaume says.

Marguerite's legs ache from the long hours of sitting. She longs to walk, but of course she cannot, for the crowd that has gathered along the roadside would suck her into itself, consuming her. Outstretched hands make her want to shrink back, but smiles and shouts hold her in the window of her carriage. *"Vive la reine!"* Goosebumps tickle her arms. *"Vive la reine Marguerite!"*

She ventures a wave, uncertain how to respond to these Franks and poor villeins, barefoot and dirty in their coarse clothing, fresh from work in the fields. A girl hands her a bundle of wildflowers; she crushes them against her nose as though they were fragrant roses. She blows a kiss to the girl; the people cheer. Standing so close, can they hear her thoughts? Pollen itches her nose, but she suppresses a sneeze for fear of spitting on them.

The path to Sens grows more clotted as the procession nears the city. People swarm the bridge, leaving little room for the carriage. At times it stops altogether, allowing hands to reach her window. "They will tear you apart with their love," Aimée says. Marguerite lifts her hands, touches fingers and palms in passing, accepts the prayers and good wishes of her people.

"How pretty she is! She and the king will make handsome heirs."

"Shh! Do not talk so about our queen."

"And see? You are making her blush."

In the crush, the spires of the Sens cathedral disappear from view, but a blast of trumpets announces its imminence. Her pulse flutters in time to the rat-a-tat of drums. So much depends on her success here. If she fails to stop Toulouse, her family may be lost—and so may be Provence, lost to that greedy tyrant, her people and her lands torn apart like a hind overcome by hounds.

The carriage passes under the jutting upper stories of tall houses which block the last light of the now-waning day, but no matter: Lighted candles ensconced on the outside walls illuminate the way and highlight the red, green, and blue banners and fragrant garlands of flowers draped over windows and doorways. "*Vive la reine!*" people continue to cry, but the shouts subside as the ragged and frayed tunics of the peasantry and the pale linens of the townspeople give way to colorful silks, velvet and fur, gold buttons, glittering jewels. These are the barons of France and their families, too refined to shout, too elegant to do more than smile and wave—if that. For at least one in their midst does neither, but watches her with contempt on his soft, almost womanly, face.

Toulouse.

She ducks behind the curtain. Why has he come to Paris? Not to congratulate her on her marriage, surely; not to bow before her tomorrow, when she takes the crown. Whatever his mission, it cannot bode well for Provence.

The carriage halts at the cathedral grounds. Myriad candles and torches illuminate the festive scene: horses munching from oats poured onto the grass; silk-clad men and women drinking from under shelters of branches and leaves; the cathedral, its spires piercing the night sky, its enormous rose window overlooking the sculptured saints lining the path to its door. Perfumes scent the air, and horse dung and burning tallow. Laughter and music weave an intricate dance under the peeping stars; a baby cries; horses whinny and nicker. Uncle Guillaume opens the carriage door and beckons her forth. Aimée hands her a mantle; she pulls it close. The air is cool for May—but this is not Provence.

The king's smile makes her forget the chill. Her hand in the crook of his arm, they pass a mélange of faces—friendly, curious, bland, sullen—before stepping into a white palace beside the cathedral. These, the king tells her, are the archbishop's apartments, given up for their use.

Up a set of stairs, then into a lamplit room. On the walls: a tapestry of gold, red, and saffron hexagons from Outremer; another depicting the crucified Christ, tears like diamonds on his cheeks. Carpets pad the floor in red and blue. Green velvet curtains hang at the windows. Gold and sandalwood perfume the air. She detects a faint fragrance of rose as well. Sumptuousness stretches like a cat in her lap. Her father's household was never so luxuriant.

"Behold my mother." Louis murmurs as if this were the cathedral. Marguerite blinks, adjusting her senses: the flickering light, the music of the vielle—and the woman with the snow-white face on the red velvet throne. When her sight returns, she moves across the room to kneel at the feet of Blanche de Castille, the legendary White Queen.

She extends her hand, allowing Marguerite to kiss her heavy gold ring. "I am deeply honored, my lady." Marguerite's hand trembles as she touches the cool fingers. "You are much acclaimed in my home of Provence."

Blanche de Castille gives an indelicate snort and looks away, as if bored. Louis helps Marguerite to stand.

"Your home is in France now." The queen mother's voice holds a chill, like the night air. "The people of France are your people."

Marguerite tries not to stare. This is the woman of whose beauty the troubadours sing? Her shaved hairline makes her forehead seem to bulge, ledge-like, over her eyes. The paste covering her face and throat renders her a White Queen, indeed.

She clears her throat. "And as queen, I only hope I can serve the French people as well as you have done."

"M. de Flagy told me that you are a good girl." The White Queen's voice has softened. "I can see that he was correct. We are going to get along very well."

"It is my fervent wish."

Her blue-gray eyes, the "eyes of vair" praised in many a song, peruse Marguerite from head to feet and back up again, as did M. de Flagy's, but without the leer.

"The problem is, *ma chère,* you do not look French. Your skin is as brown as a peasant's, exposed to the sun during your rambles in the southern fields, I presume. Your hairline encroaches most unattractively onto your forehead, and your gown looks thin and garishly dyed. You remind me of one of those vulgar flowers that grow in the South, or of a common servant prancing about in her mistress's clothes."

"Yes, my lady." Heat rises in her face.

"But these superficial flaws are easily remedied. I will send someone over in the morning, before the wedding ceremony, to pluck your forehead and to help you with your makeup. I will also provide you with a wedding gown, for I am sure the one you have brought is inadequate."

From outside, shouts: *Where is our new queen? We want the queen!* The queen mother's smile disappears.

"That is all for now. Louis, my love"—her voice becomes a

caress—"you are in demand. Go and present your little wife to the people, then send her to her room to rest. I will wait for you here, darling. We have matters of the kingdom to discuss."

"Yes, Mama." The king kisses her hand, then offers Marguerite his arm. When they turn to leave, she remembers her uncles, standing in the doorway and waiting for their introductions.

She turns back to the White Queen. "My lady, may I present my guardians, my uncles Guillaume and Thomas of Savoy? They have come to pay their respects."

The White Queen heaves a sigh, as if exhausted by the short meeting with Marguerite. "Not tonight. Tomorrow. I have had my fill of country bumpkins for one day."

Tears spring to her eyes. "Yes, my lady." As they start to walk away, the queen speaks her name.

"You may call me 'Mama.' I have only one daughter, and she is a silly child. It may please me to have a girl in the household with some sense in her head. As long as it has not gone *to* your head."

"Yes, Mama," Marguerite says. And walks out of the room with her husband, the king, her emotions whirling like bees around a vulgar flower.

———◆———

*O*UTSIDE, WHEN THEY emerge: Cheers and a burst of music. Jongleurs hurl sticks of fire; a golden goblet, filled to the brim with wine, finds its way into her hand. The king leads her beneath a spreading oak, up onto a platform ringed with candles; their light, reflected in his gold mail, makes him look aflame. *"Vive la nouvelle reine!"* people shout. *"Vive Marguerite!"*

The king gestures toward the goblet. She drinks the sour stuff—not Languedoc wine, to be certain. But she squelches her distaste and lifts her cup to toast her new countrymen and women, soon to be her subjects.

"Vive la France!" she cries. The crowd's response rolls like thunder over the lawn. The king's eyes shine as he accepts the goblet from her.

Two men ascend the steps, carrying a large trunk. From it they pull gifts, which the king presents to her: two new leather saddles; a golden bridle; a necklace dripping with diamonds and rubies; a bejeweled tiara, and, the *pièce de résistance,* a cloak of rich sable with fifteen gold buttons, each inscribed with the fleur-de-lis, the symbol of France, and sparkling with sapphires. Gasps and murmurs swirl as he drapes the soft fur over her shoulders, then fastens the buttons one by one.

"How beautiful she is!"

"See the roses in her cheeks—so delicate and feminine."

"Only the best for our King Louis, *non?*"

The king hands the goblet to her; she drinks again, more deeply now, her blood warmed by the adoration, the cloak, or the wine—or all three. Then music begins anew, and the crowd begins to dance.

Her husband leaps to the grass, then turns toward her with arms outstretched. Marguerite leans in; he grasps her at the waist and twirls her down, sets her before him, she laughing, knowing the stars do not twinkle more brightly in the sky than do her eyes, and he gazing at her as though she were a gift he cannot wait to unwrap.

The music and the crowd sweep them along as if they were petals on a summer breeze, whirling them in a circle of dancers, his hand squeezing hers as they step and turn, his eyes never leaving her face even when his arm surrounds her waist and he swings her around. They laugh as the dance grows more frenzied, dizzy with the joy of being alive and young and together, until a small man with a balding head and shifting eyes taps on the king's shoulder.

"Pardon, my lady," he says, bowing before turning to Louis. "Your Grace, the queen reminds you that she is waiting." Marguerite's gaze follows the king's to see the queen mother silhouetted in an upstairs window, looking over the festivities. Beside her, a familiar paunch-bellied figure with overlong hair: Raimond of Toulouse. Louis drops her hand as though caught in an indecent act.

"It is late." He averts his eyes. His shoulders sag. "Let me show you to your room."

He strides away so briskly that she must trot to keep pace, back into the palace, up the stairs, past the royal quarters to another set of rooms. He leads her through the door where her uncles sit at a table by a fireplace and sup on fish and vegetables. They leap to their feet, Guillaume nearly knocking over his goblet of wine.

"I have kept your niece too long. She must be tired and hungry." Louis's words tumble out. His hands clench and unclench at his sides. "Is everything to your liking? Are your rooms comfortable? Then I must leave you and attend to business. Good night, gentlemen." He lifts her hand to his lips but he barely glances at her; his thoughts have already gone elsewhere, and then, just as abruptly, so has he.

Aimée brings over a chair and sets it at the table, facing the fire. Marguerite plops down, feeling like a sail that has lost its wind. This apartment is smaller than the royal quarters, and filled with wall sconces of shimmering gold and statues: grotesque heads of saints lining the ceiling, and, in the corner, a statue of a nude man with private parts so lifelike she blushes and tries not to look. Uncle Guillaume offers her wine, but she declines. "Dreadful stuff, anyway," Thomas mutters.

"The king left hastily." Guillaume peers at her from under his thick brows.

"His mother called," she says. She does not mention Toulouse, dreading their response. They might want to know why she did not join the meeting—why she did not at least try. How could she tell them of the White Queen's cold demeanor, of her condescending remarks? *Country bumpkin.*

"Have you heard the tales about the White Queen and her son?" Uncle Guillaume dips his bread in his wine. "I never believed them, but now I wonder . . ."

"She said she needs to talk with him about matters concerning the kingdom." Marguerite closes her eyes.

"On the eve of his wedding? They must be urgent matters, indeed."

"Or maybe she is a mother who clings to her son. King Louis is the very image of his father," Thomas says. "Blanche's passion for her husband was widely known."

"Uncle!" She opens her eyes.

Guillaume grins. "Perhaps the son fills certain . . . *needs* that the husband once did. He adores her, for one thing."

"And yet she would have sold him to gain a kingdom." Thomas tells the tale: Blanche's husband, Louis VIII—heir to the French throne—answered the English barons' call to revolt against the English King John. They promised to award the crown to Prince Louis. Blanche urged him to go, although his father, King Philip Augustus, argued against it. The parochial English would never allow a Frenchman to rule, he insisted. *Their tyrant vanquished, they will remember their hatred against France—and turn against you next.* Prince Louis went anyway, but King John proved a cunning and brutal opponent. When Louis sent home for more funds, King Philip refused to pay. But Blanche, ambitious from the start, was determined to become England's queen. If he would not send Louis the money he needed, she threatened, she would sell her children—his grandchildren—to raise the sum.

"She would have done it," Thomas said. "The White Queen will stop at nothing to obtain what she wants."

"She is passionate," Marguerite says. "What is wrong with that?"

Her uncles grin. "We shall ask you that question in a few weeks," Guillaume says.

After supper, the queen mother's tailor, a fussy man whose wrists stick out from his too-short sleeves, measures her for her wedding gown. As Aimée prepares her later for bed, unlacing her tunic, helping her into her robe, and combing and plaiting her hair, she spills over with questions. Did the king please her? Does Marguerite like his mother? Which of her gifts did she treasure most? Is she excited about tomorrow's wedding? Marguerite says nothing and, always sensitive to her moods, the handmaid grows quiet.

Yet she ponders the questions, and her answers. What does she think of her husband? He seems kind, he appears handsome, and he dances well. He knows nothing of poetry, and his riposte is not as clever as she has hoped, but perhaps he was nervous today. His mother made a stronger impression—a number of them, in fact, and all contradictory.

Every woman hopes to win her husband's love, but you have an added task: charming his mother. Although King Louis is now nineteen years of age, Blanche still rules France—and, from what Marguerite has seen, she rules her son, as well. She, not Louis, gives money and men to Toulouse for the raids on her father's castles. She is the reason why Provence suffers—why Papa suffers. To help her family—and to save Provence—Marguerite must befriend the White Queen.

Laughter floats upward from the lawn, and more music. Marguerite moves to the window for one last look at the festivities: the jongleurs doing handsprings and flips, rehearsing for tomorrow's celebration; children chasing one another, darting in and out of the makeshift shelters; servants rushing about with filled goblets for their masters and mistresses; dancers whirling and spinning.

Below her window, onlookers clap in time to the music as a couple turns before them, fleet-footed and lithe, gazing into each other's faces with delight. She watches for a while, wishing she had a rose or a token to toss down to the dancing couple. After a while, the song ends and they fall apart, panting and laughing, the woman's hand on the man's arm in an intimate caress. How lovely to be in love! Marguerite smiles—but her smile freezes when she recognizes the pair. Louis, dressed now in a red tunic and mantle, and his mother exchange a kiss, then join hands for another dance.

❖ *Marguerite* ❖

A Perfect and Holy Union

Sens, 1234

*W*HITE-FACED WOMEN DISTURB her sleep, clamping fingers of bone around her throat, pressing her into her pillow—*Hold still, you stupid bumpkin*—flashing long, curved knives, scraping their blades across her eyebrows, her forehead, her scalp. She awakens with a start, her pulse thumping like the foot of a hare. She snatches her hand mirror from the table, sees herself looking back, unmolested. It was only a dream. Then she sees the statue in the corner and remembers why she is here, and her heart begins to race again.

The lamps are already lit. Aimée, dressed in a tunic of pale rose, bustles about, bringing Marguerite's gown in from the garderobe ("Today is your wedding day," she purrs, as if Marguerite needed reminding), setting out a sop for her breakfast, pulling back the bedcovers and bidding her to rise for the prayer service, although the sun has not even begun to think about doing so.

"Is God awake at this ungodly hour?" she wonders as her handmaid combs her hair.

"I don't know, my lady, but the French certainly are." Outside, the chapel bells ring. A moment later, Uncle Guillaume is at the door, eyes puffy. It is time, he says, for prayer.

"At this hour, one wonders what there is to say to God," he grumbles.

"*Who ever did penance employ before he sinned?*" Marguerite sings. Fully awake now, she feels filled-with-air light, as if she might float like a bubble to the ceiling.

"Your King Louis, that is who," Uncle Thomas says as he joins them for the walk across the dew-damp grass. "Our friend Bertran d'Alamanon must have seen into the future when he wrote those lines."

"Or he knew the king's mother," Marguerite says.

"Perhaps. But Blanche was not always such a model of piety," Guillaume says.

How the rumors flew after Louis's father died! The most popular—and tenacious—tale involved Blanche and the handsome papal legate, and an illegitimate pregnancy. Blanche finally stilled the wagging tongues by stripping off her clothes before the barons' council to show her flat stomach.

"No one would start such a rumor today," Thomas says. "Blanche de Castille has transformed herself into a veritable Virgin Mother." By donning the mantle of a stern prioress, she avoided both scandal and marriage—and saved the throne for herself. Prising it away from her will be Marguerite's task.

The chapel is surprisingly full when they enter, of bleary-eyed barons and their rumpled wives, servants asleep on their feet, prelates fairly bouncing with zeal for God and their king—and, standing in the front, her husband and mother-in-law to be. Louis gives her a shy smile while his mother presses her lips together, disapproving of her late entrance. Marguerite smiles in reply, still thinking of Blanche in her underwear before the barons' council. Who else on earth would dare? Tomorrow, Marguerite will arrive on time.

After the service, she at last introduces the uncles to Blanche, who bats her lashes as though she had not recently snubbed them. "I did not see either of you at our festivities last night," she simpers. "But you must have been resting after your long journey. A dance today? But of course, *monsieurs*. I have had so many requests already, but I will certainly fit you in. You men of Savoy are renowned for grace and charm."

"Blanche is beautiful, but brittle about the edges," Thomas remarks later, as he and Guillaume lounge in their apartment. "One can see why she never remarried."

"Do not underestimate the White Queen, my brother: She has never lacked suitors. She simply loves power too much to share it with a husband. Or with her son, I hear."

Aimée, styling Marguerite's hair for the wedding, works silently so that they can listen.

"Let us hope that she can relinquish her power when the time comes," Thomas says.

"She will have no choice. Margi's coronation is tomorrow. The entire kingdom will know our niece as the new queen."

"And if she does not? Will Margi be able to stop Toulouse? Ramon's health cannot withstand these attacks for much longer. Our sister says he collapsed on the journey home after signing the *verba de praesenti* for Margi's marriage."

Marguerite gasps. "Papa! Is it serious?"

"According to your mother, no. She blames fatigue, and your father's sorrow over losing you to France. But as you know, his heart's beat has become uncertain and erratic of late. He will not withstand many more weeks of battle. You must stanch the flow of French *livres* into Toulouse's coffers, my dear."

"Stopping Toulouse will be my first priority." Along with producing heirs: a queen consort's primary role is that of mother, not ruler, her mama has taught. "But I would appreciate any help you might provide."

"Perhaps your handsome uncle Guillaume will revive his once-formidable seduction skills in order to win her favor."

Guillaume laughs. "Charming the ladies is your specialty, Thomas, not mine."

"I saw how the king looks at you, lady," Aimée murmurs to Marguerite. "You will soon win his heart and then he will listen only to you, no matter what his mother desires."

That time cannot come soon enough. After this morning's prayer service she spied Toulouse lurking about the cathedral door—waiting for Blanche, no doubt. What did they discuss last night? Did he request more money, or troops, or weapons with which to attack Provence? When she is queen, will he dare to approach her for help? Let him try! She'll send him home with a drooping scabbard and an empty purse.

Aimée laces up the gown that Blanche has sent—lovelier, indeed, than the one she has brought from home—a confection of saffron silk with a cream surcoat embroidered in gold thread, and a green-and-gold mantle trimmed with ermine. Over her dark hair, worn loose for the ceremony, she lays a fine net woven with diamonds, rubies, and emeralds. Before her uncles, she turns slowly around. "*Trop belle!*" they exclaim from their cushioned chairs, over their brandies. "*Madame, nous sommes enchantés.*"

Is she going to faint? She takes long, deep breaths, calming herself as she walks arm in arm with the uncles, across the lawn and through the gathered crowd of nobles. "What an elegant young lady the countryside has produced!" she hears someone murmur. "She looks as lovely as her namesake, the daisy."

"Lift your head," Uncle Guillaume urges. "Walk like a queen."

Her step falters nonetheless as she forces herself to meet the curious stares, noting the nobles' shimmering silks and swirling taffetas, their glittering jewelry—and their narrowed, scrutinizing eyes.

"See how happy she is to marry our king."

"Who wouldn't smile to trade Provence for Paris?"

True to the queen mother's word, the women wear ghostly white faces and rouged lips under cleanly plucked, prominent foreheads. How rustic she must appear with her golden complexion, inherited from her Aragonian father, and her simple necklace of pearls. She turned away the queen mother's man today with his pot of pale paste and his curved blade. And yet: *La reine belle jeune*, they call her, the beautiful young queen.

Queen Blanche, standing near the gate where the ceremony will begin, watches her approach with glinting eyes. Marguerite kneels before her to kiss her ring. "Mama," she murmurs, but the word weights her tongue like a stone.

"I hope you will consider me a daughter from this day forward, and your humble servant," she says. Blanche's stern gaze softens— until the murmurs begin again.

"How gracious! The 'daughter' outshines the 'mother' in disposition as well as beauty."

"Blanche was never so sweet, not even as a child, I'll wager."

"Was the White Queen ever a child?"

The queen mother's hand stiffens. She withdraws it from Marguerite's grasp.

But King Louis takes both her hands in his own as he kisses her. In his many, colorful robes, he reminds Marguerite of a peacock in full display. Today, though, he wears no gold except his crown and his fair hair curling softly about his chin.

"I hope the festivities did not keep you awake," he says.

"No, my lord, I slept deeply."

He grimaces. "I, too, wished to retire early, but my barons insisted that I rejoin them in the merrymaking."

"I saw you dancing with the queen mother."

"Thanks be to God for sending her out with me. It was Mama who prised me from the nobles' grip. Otherwise, they might have danced me through today's morning prayers."

The archbishop emerges, clad in cloth as fine as the king's and of the richest red, his chubby face shining under his broad-brimmed cap, his hands cradling an open book. He bows to them, then begins the ceremony atop the cathedral steps: the confirmation that they are both of age and not too closely related; and that they and their parents consent to the marriage. The wedding vows. The incensing and blessing of the bridal ring. Louis's voice coarsens as he slips the ring over each of her fingers—"In the name of the Father, the Son, and the Holy Ghost"—before landing on the fourth. The archbishop intones a prayer, then leads them into the cathedral. She walks without feeling the ground, as if her feet were too light to touch the earth, catching her breath at the grandeur of God's house: the high, narrow arches overhead, the statues of saints lining the walls, the light flooding the altar from the high windows, the splendid rose-shaped window over the entry whose stained glass sends colors floating down like petals.

Once everyone has wedged into the cathedral and quieted at last, the archbishop celebrates the mass, offering communion to the wedding couple, lighting candles, and saying prayers.

"Wife, be good to your husband," he says. "Submit to him in all things, for that is the will of God." What of submission to one's mother-in-law? Is that God's will, as well?

The archbishop kisses Louis on the mouth: the kiss of peace. Louis gives it, in turn, to Marguerite. His lips feel strange, but not unpleasant. When it ends, she wants another, as if his kisses were sweets; she imagines sliding her arms around his neck and pulling him closer. But of course she does not. Now is not the time for more kissing, but it will come soon enough.

The archbishop pronounces them husband and wife. Louis grasps her hand, his expression eager, and the room fills with shouts and cheers—but before they step down from the altar, the queen mother steps forward and whispers to the archbishop. He nods and lifts his hands, silencing the crowd.

"I had almost forgotten an important addition to this ceremony," he says. The White Queen beams at Louis as if she has just given him a golden horse to match his shiny mail suit. "For a perfect and holy union, the Church exhorts the newly wedded couple to delay the consummation."

Exclamations and chatter arise, prompting the archbishop to call for silence. Then he turns to Louis and Marguerite.

"Cleanse your souls with prayer for three nights before uniting your bodies," he says. "When you join together in holy matrimony, you also join with God. Your purified state may please our Lord, the better for you to produce an heir to the throne."

Louis's expression darkens—but then the queen mother cries out, "Praise be to the Lord," and soon everyone is praising God, and Louis's frown turns, again, to a shy grin. Marguerite's smile feels like a fragile ribbon that has been pasted to her face. After all the blessings, anointings, and prayers, aren't she and the king pure enough? How much sin can one soul hold? How much scrubbing does it need to be considered clean?

"*Vive le roi!*" the crowd cries. "*Vive la reine!*" Louis bows to her, and she to him, and he squeezes her hands affectionately, the way he did last night as they danced. They turn to face their cheering, adoring audience.

"*Vive la reine!*" Marguerite's heart seems to leap about. She came to win the love of her husband and his mother, but behold the people—*her* people—embracing her so ardently. Perhaps she will enjoy being Queen of France, after all.

⊰ *Marguerite* ⊱
The Weight of Rule
Sens, 1234

*A*FTER THE DAY'S excitement, she feels content to rest on her knees in the chapel, by her husband's side, and thank the Lord for his blessings. Then the archbishop gives his instructions: They are to begin with the Pater Noster, followed by the Ave Maria. Next come the Credo and the seven Penitential Psalms, then silent prayer and contemplation. The cycle begins anew every hour.

"And are we to sleep between the Pater Noster and the Ave Maria, or during the silent prayer?" she asks.

The archbishop regards her for a long moment—unused to questions from women, apparently, since he doesn't answer hers. "Isn't that what you wished, Your Grace?" he says to Louis. "A ritual of prayer to last until the morning?"

"Do not fret, my bride." Louis's voice sounds far away, as if he had already crossed into the shadowy world of credos and penances. "The Lord will sustain us through the night."

Marguerite closes her eyes, imagines a bed, imagines herself lying down in it, sinking in softness, burrowing in quilts. Today she became the bride of the King of France. She had a royal wedding and a magnificent feast with course upon course heralded by trumpets: a pie from which songbirds flew; a gold-beaked swan roasted and refitted in its feathered coat; a pudding of cherries sprinkled with rose petals, and an endless stream of sycophants filling her time with gratuities and expecting inanities in return. Afterward, minstrels and jongleurs performed under the arbor. And, through it all, the appraising eye of Blanche, whose frown deepened with every compliment paid to Marguerite. When troubadours from her father's court performed a sequence of songs in her honor, Blanche's face turned bright red under her white makeup.

"The White Queen covets all the praise in her court," Uncle Guillaume said. "Have you noted the paucity of women? She employs only a few female servants, and all are either old or plain."

Thomas laughed. "I do not envy Margi."

At this moment, she does not envy herself. If the queen mother resents compliments given on her wedding day, how will she react when Marguerite dons the crown of France? All of France will honor her then. Without adequate sleep, how will she forbear her mother-in-law's acerbic comments, her droll sarcasms? How will she make a good impression, and gain her respect? Yet she must do as Louis wishes. He is her husband, after all—and he is the king.

Yet not even the king can stop her thoughts from roaming as she prays.

Was that a smirk on Blanche's mouth today when her young son Charles snatched a piece of meat from Marguerite's fingers? And then the little beast stuck out his tongue and declared that she was too petite to be a queen. "You look like my sister's queen-doll, only not as pretty," he said for all to hear. Blanche never uttered a word of reprimand, but hid a smile behind her hand.

Marguerite would have used her hand for a different purpose—but instead she ignored him. Reacting would only increase his enjoyment, as she knows from experience with Beatrice. Of course, no child of the Count and Countess of Provence, even one as spoiled as Beatrice, would behave so rudely.

The manners are despicable here. During silent contemplation, she composes a letter to Eléonore. *I saw a nobleman blow his nose in the tablecloth. I heard the queen mother's ladies-in-waiting tell bawdy jokes about my husband and the washerwoman. Their own king! Even the troubadours lack refinement. While ours in Provence sing the* chansons de gestes *of knights and chivalric deeds, these poets fawn over the queen mother—while she dimples like a girl and pretends to blush.*

A slow ache spreads through her knees, then a tingling, then numbness. Her head slumps forward; she jerks awake and resumes her prayers. *Pater noster, qui es in caelis, sanctificetur Nomen tuum.* Blanche indulged the impudent Charles, yet snapped irritably at the nine-year-old Isabelle. "I am going to marry Jesus," the child said to Marguerite, her face as earnest as a martyr's.

"The nunneries are filled with wives for our savior," Blanche said. "You are my only daughter, and you will marry to benefit France."

Isabelle's smile held the secret of a child determined to have her way. "I have heard that you love the poets," she said to Marguerite. "Do you know this song? '*Amongst others I feign the status quo, while the day seems tedium congealed.*'"

Quoting Arnaut! Were Isabelle older, this alone would bind them in friendship. And yet—who else in this court would suffice? For all the love poured upon her during her wedding ceremony, the nobles' wives held themselves aloof during the feast. Is it because she hails from the south—a country bumpkin—or because she is going to be queen? Perhaps, after all these years of Blanche's rule, the French are unaccustomed to friendly queens.

Without Aimée, she would be bereft. Her handmaid is her only tie, now, to Provence. Memories rise: The music her family made together. Marguerite playing the vielle. Her father striking his dulcimer. Eléonore on drums. Mama's riddles at table, the slant of her eyes as she offered clues, her mysterious smile as Marguerite and Eléonore shouted their answers while Sanchia cringed in the corner, afraid she would be called upon—and then, more often than not, solved the riddle. And the hunts, grand affairs with thirty or forty men and women and nearly as many dogs. The fragrance of lavender wafting up from the trampling hooves; the apricots, peaches, cherries and tangerines dangling ripe from the trees; the jump and wriggle and strain of the dogs at their leashes. And always Eléonore's shout as she raced ahead with her bow, eager to be the one to fell the deer. The troubadours and trobairitz, new ones arriving at court every day, it seemed, bringing new songs.

> *I see scarlet, green, blue, white, yellow*
> *Garden, close, hill, valley and field,*
> *And songs of birds echo and ring*
> *In sweet accord, at evening and dawn.*

She can hear their song, the song of Provence. The harp and vielle rise up in accompaniment, and the voices of Papa and Mama singing along while she and Elli link arms to dance, spinning faster and faster until, exhausted, they fall to the floor, laughing, dizzy with music and happiness . . .

Marguerite. Marguerite!

She opens her eyes. Louis's frowning face hovers above. "Are the prayers finished?"

"You fell asleep." He averts his gaze, as though embarrassed to look at her. "You must confess this sin tomorrow."

"I was afraid that might happen." She gives a little laugh. "Forgive me." She shakes her head, but the music that lulled her to sleep continues to play.

"It is not my forgiveness that you must seek, but that of our Lord."

Is sleeping now a sin, also? "I will. But for tonight, I must go to bed. My journey from Provence was very long." Louis's mouth droops. "Yet—I do not want to disappoint you."

"I do not lament for myself, but for you." He helps her to her feet. "To be unable to sustain your prayers for even two hours . . . but you will become stronger, in time."

"And you? Will you come and sleep?"

"I do not desire sleep. I have spent many nights with our Lord in prayer, and he protects me against that temptation."

Later, in bed, Marguerite ponders again the strange notions of God in her new kingdom. Sleep, a temptation? Is it another of God's tests, like the fruit tree in the Garden, to give us bodies in need of rest and then to punish us for sleeping? She snuggles into the mattress Louis and Blanche have provided for her, down deep under their tempting gifts of furs, linen sheets, and an embroidered quilt. *Forgive me, Father,* she prays, but she forgets what she is supposed to have done as she plucks a peach from the tree and takes a bite of Provence.

———◆———

$\mathcal{S}$HE BECOMES QUEEN of France in a gown of silk spun with gold—another gift from Blanche, who apparently nurtures a fondness for shiny clothes—and a face and neck covered in white makeup, and lips so darkly ochred they appear bruised. Her second day in Paris, and already she is transformed. Yet the capitulation is not complete: she declined the razor's edge.

"You do not look like yourself, my lady." Aimée's voice holds a tinge of disapproval. Marguerite, looking in her mirror, can only agree. From inside the glass, Blanche de Castille stares back at her. When she accepts the crown today, she will be another White Queen. No matter: she came to Louis as her true self for their wedding, but as Queen of France she will wear whatever mask is required. She only hopes her mother-in-law will welcome the change.

She enters the cathedral through the back, avoiding the onlookers already crowding the floor, and finds Louis kneeling before the altar in his gold chain mail suit. His knees must be made of plate armor. His eyes widen at the sight of her so altered—but, already an expert in the art of diplomacy, he tucks his startled expression behind a smile.

He pushes himself to standing in increments, weighted by the suit. "I was just praying for you, and voilà," he says, "you appear."

"What did you request for me, my lord? Courage, I hope—and makeup that doesn't smear when I cry."

He clears his throat. "I prayed for your forgiveness. For falling asleep last night."

"Oh, that!" She laughs. "I had forgotten all about it."

"And I asked that God might strengthen you for tonight's prayers."

"I hope he doesn't wait until then to provide me with strength. Otherwise, I may collapse of fright during the ceremony."

"Fright? Of whom, the Count of Champagne? Old Queen Isambour?" Dare she mention Raimond of Toulouse? But no—the music has begun. "Grab hold of me if you feel yourself falling," Louis says. "I'll hold you steady."

She takes his arm and he leads her to a platform on one side of the choir. He bows, then takes his place opposite her. Golden thrones encrusted with jewels and cushioned with silk glimmer between them, on the choir stage. Ribbons and banners streaming from the rafters lend a festive and colorful air, even more so than at yesterday's wedding—and the crowd is larger, too, filling every space with men and women and children who stare at her and yet, because of the paint, do not see her. *Breathe,* Mama always said. She does, and is calmed by the fragrance of incense mingling with the perfume of lilies filling the chapel, and the faint warm scent of fire from the thousands upon thousands of burning candles. The entire room shimmers, as though they were in a jewelry box.

Spectators continue to stream in: nobles in the front, towns-people in the middle, servants and villeins in the back, spilling out the doorway, standing on tiptoe, stretching their necks. Excited talk and laughter careen about the room. Then the archbishop ascends the platform and the room grows silent except for the clanging of a bell.

Her gaze drops to the front row, where her uncles grin proudly at her. If only her parents could be present—but they dared not leave Provence to the mercy of Toulouse's marauding knights. When he has ceased his attacks, perhaps they might visit her in Paris. Papa would be impressed to see her on the French throne—and if he had any qualms about her ability to govern Provence someday, they would surely disappear.

Papa. She imagines his proud gaze as the archbishop anoints her with blessed oil and presents her with a golden scepter—but then all else is forgotten, even her father, as the monks chant their ethereal song and the king's nobles—Hugh, Count of Lusignan, Pierre, Count of Brittany, and Thibaut, Count of Champagne—struggle up the steps bearing an enormous gold crown. The archbishop utters a blessing and they lift the crown to Marguerite's head, then hold it there, supporting it with their hands. His Grace turns and, waving incense, leads them to the center platform, where Louis stands before his throne. Noblewomen descend on her like a flock of solicitous birds, straightening her skirts as she sits beside her husband, barons holding up her crown and Louis's, too—the weight of rule being too great, it seems, for anyone to bear alone.

The air thickens, warmed by the breath and blood of one thousand onlookers. Perspiration beads on Marguerite's brow and upper lip but she dares not remove it with her handkerchief or even a gloved finger for fear of smudging the paste on her face. As queen, she must always maintain the appearance, at least, of dignity.

As the archbishop conducts the mass, she peruses the crowd. Soon she will be responsible for these, her subjects, and many more. Her uncles reminded her last night of the duties of a queen: to intercede for those accused of crimes, asking the king for mercy; to administer the kingdom's finances, furnish the royal palaces, and arrange advantageous marriages for the sons and daughters of the barons; and to advise the king in matters of war and peace—including, she vows, a peace treaty with Provence. She may rule from time to time, when Louis leaves the kingdom. And she will, if God please, provide heirs to the throne—which, in France, means sons.

At ceremony's end, the barons remove the heavy crowns from hers and Louis's heads and the archbishop replaces them with smaller ones. She stands, and the entire room seems to shift as the people sink to their knees and bow their heads to her. Tears track the pale landscape of her face but Marguerite no longer cares. These are her people. *Dear God, help me to rule wisely.* She thinks of the Queen of Sheba, craving wisdom, seeking it like light.

Beside her, Louis raises his scepter. *"Vive la reine!"* he calls.

"Vive la reine!" The crowd chants in unison, rising to its feet. All the nobles—her uncles, Raimond of Toulouse, the Count of Champagne, Louis's brothers, and hundreds more—all have bowed to her except two: Isambour of Denmark, Philip Augustus's first queen, pinching her wrinkled mouth into a dour smile; and, beside her, Blanche, who watches the ceremony with dull eyes, but does not bend her knee. No matter. Her mother-in-law might not bow to her—yet—but she must defer. Marguerite is now the Queen of France.

The ceremony ended, the barons shepherd the crowd outdoors for the royal almsgiving. Blanche approaches. Louis hastens down the choir steps to her, leaving Marguerite to trail after him. His mother kisses him on the mouth more fervently than his wife has been able to do—and then graces Marguerite with a limp handshake.

"I see that you have adopted the French fashion," she says.

"The makeup feels strange, but the gown is glorious," she says. "Do you approve, Queen Mother?"

Blanche sweeps her appraising glance from Marguerite's crown to her shoes, and back again. Her eyes glint like glass, though her smile is broad. "The saying is true, apparently," she says. "One cannot fashion a silk purse from a sow's ear. You will always be a country girl to me."

Heat floods Marguerite's face, but the White Queen cannot tell. Or so she hopes. "And to me, you will always be the dowager queen," she says. "Although your rule is ending, I hope that Louis and I will be able to rely on your advice."

The White Queen's gaze pierces, ruthless. "Do not fret, child. I don't plan to leave you, or the throne."

"Will a single chair accommodate us both, then?" Marguerite forces a laugh.

"Didn't Louis tell you? He has had a new throne fashioned for you. The three of us shall sit together. And"—she flashes a triumphant smile—"he vowed to regard my counsel above all others'."

She sends Louis a querulous look. "Is this so, my lord?"

"Today the Lord has blessed our kingdom with two queens," he says. "One to enrich our heart with affection and heirs"—he squeezes her hand—"and one"—he takes his mother's hand, as well—"to conduct our business with wisdom and experience."

The blast of trumpets interrupts their talk. Excitement leaps from Louis's face like light from a flame. "And now, my new queen, comes the best part of our work," he says as he leads Marguerite outdoors.

On the lawn, it seems as if they have stepped into another world—out of the light and into shadow. Peasants crowd the square, their tunics theadbare, their feet unshod, their hands outstretched. Again she feels thankful for the mask upon her face, the feel of the thick paste reminding her to hold her expression still against the smells of rotting teeth and unwashed bodies. She wills herself not to shrink back from the grasping hands that might tear her dress or snatch her golden crown away. Yet when she presses a silver coin into an old man's palm, his shout of thanks makes her smile and reach for another coin. Louis, too, smiles as he distributes coins that, in his world, are spent as carelessly as stones tossed into a stream.

Two men push through the crowd, bearing a woman on a stretcher. She lies gasping and pale. Bulges as large as hen's eggs protrude from her neck. Lord Peter, the Count of Brittany, draws his sword as if to fend off her sickness, but Louis calms him with a touch of his hand. He steps over to the poor woman. "My wife has scrofula, Your Grace," one of the stretcher-bearers says. "I beg you to heal her."

"Not I, but the Lord." Louis gestures to the archbishop, who squeezes through the roiling crowds, grasping his prayer book. Louis places his hands on the afflicted woman's neck. She closes her eyes, sighing, while the archbishop intones a Latin prayer.

"You are healed," Louis says, and gives the husband two pieces of silver.

Marguerite stares at the scene, dumbstruck. The King of France's piety is widely known, but—this? "Praise the Lord!" Blanche cries. Marguerite's muscles tense; she wants to run—but she turns away from the weeping family, from their ecstatic kisses and shouts, and walks, moving slowly against the crush, handing coins along the way. Aimée follows: is she unwell? A headache, she claims, and heads for the palace to rest before the feast, and to ponder the vaunted pride of the man she has married.

———◆———

"*I*S THE WOMAN truly healed?" she asks Louis later, sitting with him at a banquet table under the trees. "Have you driven away her sickness with your hands?"

He looks at her in surprise. "Not I, but the Lord Jesus Christ."

"Does Jesus Christ work miracles through your hands, then? Has he given you special healing powers?"

"Your question disturbs me," he says with a frown. "Does that diseased peasant, cursed with the lowest birth, have more faith than her exalted queen?" Marguerite's face burns as if warmed by the very fires of hell.

On her right, the elderly Isambour of Denmark gives an ungraceful snort. "If our king is such a worker of miracles, why doesn't he raise his mother from the dead?"

Marguerite bursts into laughter, then looks around to see who might have heard. Fortunately, Louis is occupied with his sister Isabelle, while the rest of the diners watch and laugh as a minstrel plays the recorder and breaks wind in rhythmic accompaniment.

Encouraged by Marguerite's reaction, Isambour winks. "Perhaps Louis's mind is a bit muddled on the day after his wedding. Did you keep him awake too long last night?"

"Not I, my lady. Louis spent the night in prayer."

She snorts again. "Whose idea was that? Blanche's, I bet."

"The archbishop suggested it. At the wedding?"

She nods. "That would have occurred during my nap. Celebrations of the mass always put me to sleep. But that delay-the-consummation folly most certainly originated with Blanche."

She prods Marguerite with a long fingernail. "Be on your watch where that woman is concerned. She has enjoyed the comforts of Louis the Son ever since Louis the Father died. Ten years! And I doubt that she will give him up."

"She invited me to call her 'Mama.'"

"Have you ever seen a lion smile? It is not a smile at all, but a baring of teeth before the final pounce."

A song springs to Marguerite's lips.

"Waters that slide calmly by
Drown more than those that roar and sigh.
They deceive who seem so fair,
Oh, be wary of the debonair."

"I know well the songs of Ventadorn," Isambour says, nodding. "Hugues de Saint Circq used to sing them for me when he came to our court. He was a lovely man, handsome if you like little dark Italians, which I do. My husband treated me cruelly, but he at least sent the trouvères to amuse me."

Marguerite knows her story well, how King Philip petitioned for an annulment the day after he married Isambour. Rumors abound: He could not perform the consummation act; her brother, the King of Denmark, broke his promise to renounce his claims to the throne of England; he discovered a penis under Isambour's clothes. Whatever the reason, when the pope refused to annul, Philip locked Isambour away.

"Like a caged bird," she says, "singing was all I had."

"Music is the language of angels, they say."

"A love for music will avail you little in King Louis's court, unless you sing the psalms. When his mother dies, I wager, he'll prohibit all entertainment except those gloomy monks' chants. Blanche might have done so herself, if not for the trouvères' flattery."

A growl startles them both. They turn to see Louis, slumped in his seat, snoring as if there were a contest for it in the tournament. A smile twitches his lips.

"Of whom does he dream?" Queen Isambour said. "His bride or his mother?"

"Neither, is my guess. After a night on his knees in the chapel, I think he dreams of his bed."

"Do not be so certain. Blanche has a strong hold on her eldest son. I do not envy any woman Louis would marry, for his mother will not easily let him go." She prods Marguerite's arm with her fingernail again. "Pray to your name-saint that you will produce an heir soon. The White Queen won't relinquish her son—or her power, which she loves more—until that day."

Trumpets sound, startling Louis awake. At the tables next to theirs, servants lift the covers from platters of food and twenty peasants fall upon the roast meats, bread, and fruit that Louis has provided for them.

"Pearls before swine," Isambour says with a sniff. "A complete waste of France's money. Do you know how much beggars earn in a day?"

"They seem to have very little," Marguerite says.

"That's because they squander it on wine and gamble the rest away." She squints at Blanche, who is making her way toward them, having spent the last hour conferring with the Count of Toulouse. "Is that the White Bitch now? Suddenly, I feel in need of a nap."

A manservant helps her to untangle herself from the bench. Marguerite kisses her ring. "Remember what I said, dear. Have a son and your troubles will be over."

As soon as she is gone, Blanche slips into her empty seat. "How awful for you to be seated beside that feeble-brained crone for so long," she says to Marguerite. "Isambour talks more quickly than her mind can think. And yet you are still awake! I thought she might put you to sleep, especially after your long night of prayer."

"If only I could boast of that feat." Marguerite giggles. "I was so tired from my travels and the long day that I fell asleep on the chapel floor last night."

"And you find that amusing? I had been told that you were a pious girl." She sinks her teeth into a chicken leg and tears the meat away.

"*Sans doute*, I would have preferred to pray all night with Louis." Marguerite lifts the tablecloth to wipe her lips. "But, as Ventadorn wrote, '*I' has no power over 'I'*.'"

"Yes, and did he not also write, '*A fool fears not till he is in distress?*' Our Lord's displeasure is no occasion for laughter." She arises and, with a final, cold glance at Marguerite, bends to greet her newly wakened son with a kiss and the soft, delighted voice of a mother cooing to her infant.

— ✦ —

AFTER TWO MORE days of revelry and two more nights of prayer—dread, not of God's wrath but of white-faced queens, keeps her from falling asleep on the chapel floor again—she slumbers in spite of the jostle and shift of her carriage, sinking into the fur-covered cushions, pressing her cheek against Aimée's lap as though they were the swaying arms of a nurse rocking her to oblivion.

Not long after she awakens, the carriage halts outside a large, plain château. "Fontainebleau," Uncle Guillaume announces as he escorts her forth. "The White Queen prefers to rest here tonight."

The gathered crowd erupts into cheers, tossing flowers to Marguerite and calling her name. Louis offers her his arm. With musicians before them and the queen mother behind, she walks in a rain of petals through a stone gate, past a line of servants standing at attention, and into the great hall, bedecked with colorful banners and bejeweled tapestries and filled with long, linen-covered tables and benches. Louis leads her up onto a dais and they take seats at the table with Blanche, while the rest sit according to their rank.

Servants scurry in bearing great platters of food: duckling, carp, venison, lettuces, cheese, cooked apples, foie gras, olives, raspberries, and bread—and pouring wine into goblets with pitchers of water set alongside for mixing. Louis hands her their golden goblet and watches her drink; she returns it with lowered eyes. Tonight they will spend their first night together as husband and wife—on their backs in the marriage bed instead of on their knees in the chapel.

Her stomach flutters, causing her to pick at her meal although she has not eaten all day. Coming from a home where food was scarce, she is accustomed to hunger. Louis, too, eats little, and grins much. When the musicians begin to play, he leans toward her. He is tired, he says, of music and crowds. Would she welcome a tour of the château and grounds? The gardens are most impressive.

They step into the courtyard and it is as he said: cherry trees blossom wantonly, filling the air with fragrance, and lilies bloom around a burbling fountain.

"This fountain seemed much larger when I was small," Louis says. "I remember hiding behind it. Now I see why I was so easily found."

"From whom would little Prince Louis have hidden?"

He grimaces. "My tutor. I had neglected my studies. His beatings were quite severe."

"What a pity!" She reaches up to stroke his cheek. "A good teacher would have inspired you instead of beating you."

"Oh, but I was a very sinful child. I was much more interested in chasing frogs and torturing beetles than reading my psalter." He sighs. "Think of my poor mother, trying to bring up an unruly boy while ruling a kingdom of malcontents. I caused her much woe— until my fourteenth birthday. On that day Mama appointed M. de Flagy to me, a true gift from God. His daily whippings helped me to mend my ways."

Marguerite gasps. "Daily whippings! You poor boy."

"It is not so serious as that." He plucks a blossom and tucks it into her crespine. "But I did not bring you into these beautiful gardens to discuss my tutors. I had hoped for a kiss under these trees from my lovely wife."

He brushes her cheek with his lips. His breath is hot on her face. His heart thumps against her chest.

"You are lovely." He kisses her on the mouth, gently at first, as if he can feel her pulse, too, racing in her breast. At last, when she winds her arms around his neck, delighting in the taste and feel of him, his kiss deepens.

"I cannot wait to join our bodies," he murmurs. "I pray that the priests will bless our marriage bed soon."

"Soon enough, my son." Blanche's voice is a lance piercing their privacy—or their illusion of it. "First, however, we must discuss affairs of the kingdom."

Louis stiffens. His hands fall from Marguerite's body. Blanche's face holds disgust, as though she had found them naked and fornicating on the lawn.

"Your presence is required in my chambers, Louis. If you are not too busy."

What "affairs of the kingdom" cannot wait until tomorrow? This is the life of a queen, Marguerite supposes: no time to call one's own, ever subservient to the people's needs. She had thought that, as queen, she would have control over her life as well as the lives of others. Now, after three days of fulfilling others' desires while putting off her own, she thinks the opposite may be true.

Inside the great hall the music continues, but the diners, weary after days of travel and revelry, are dispersing. Marguerite nods to her uncles, across the room, talking together and glancing at her. Blanche speaks to Louis but Marguerite cannot hear her over the din. They pass through the great hall and up the stairs to the queen's chambers, where Raimond of Toulouse awaits outside the door, flanked by palace guards.

The White Queen greets her cousin with a kiss. "Your presence is not needed here," she says to Marguerite. "I will have one of the guards show you to your chambers. I know how you love your sleep."

"But . . . I am the queen, *ma mère*. I would like to participate." She hopes the quavering in her voice is not detectable. Blanche arches her brows at Louis: *Do you see what I mean about her?* He averts his gaze from Marguerite, refusing to meet her eyes.

"These are delicate negotiations," he says.

"And I am your queen. I want to be included."

An uncomfortable silence follows.

"Perhaps you can be of use to us," Blanche says at last. "My cousin Toulouse says that your father has taken a number of French knights as hostages. He demands an exorbitant ransom for their release. How much influence can you wield with him?"

"If Raimond of Toulouse will agree to stop attacking our castles, I think my father would reduce the ransom," she says.

"*Our* castles? Is your allegiance yet with Provence, then?" The White Queen turns to Louis. "Do you agree with me now?" His gaze droops. "Louis, I will see you inside. Marguerite, enjoy your rest."

When she has gone, Marguerite knits her brows. "Am I Queen of France, or is she?"

"It is . . . complicated. You would do well, I think, to avoid this meeting. Toulouse is temperamental and vindictive. One errant word from you might worsen matters—for all."

"But didn't you marry me for my ties to Provence? Doesn't your mother want an alliance with my father?"

"That will come in time," Louis said. "You must be patient. For now, it is best that you keep yourself apart from the situation. Mama and I must consider Toulouse's proposal carefully and do what is best for France."

"What is he proposing? Some bold new plan for ruining my family, no doubt."

"I cannot discuss it with you now." He holds both her hands. "Please, darling, wait for me in your chambers. The priests are blessing the nuptial bed even now, and I will join you soon." He pecks her on the forehead with lips like a smooth stone, then steps into his mother's chambers. Marguerite wants to follow, but a guard blocks her way. She heads into the great hall, where her uncles wait for the bed-blessing ceremony with several men:

Odo, the abbot of St. Denis; the red-faced Count Enguerrand of Coucy, the noble she saw blowing his nose in the tablecloth during the wedding feast; Louis's uncle Philip Hurepel, who once fought Blanche for the kingdom and lost; Thibaut of Champagne; and still others. Her uncles pull her aside.

"Why aren't you in the meeting with Toulouse?" Uncle Guillaume demands. "We hear he is plotting to invade Provence yet again, and with a greater force than before."

"Blanche barred me. She said my connections to Provence would upset the 'delicate' discussions."

"I knew it!" Thomas says. "Blanche will not give up her power so easily."

"You must be stronger, Margi," Uncle Guillaume says. "Otherwise, we have married you to France in vain."

"I welcome your advice, Uncle. Or perhaps you would care to provide an example, and force your way into the meeting? It is taking place in the queen mother's chambers."

Thomas grins. "Margi, you remind me more of your mother with each passing day."

"You have our sister's wit," Guillaume says, "but are you as discerning as she? How will Louis and Blanche respond to Toulouse's request? How should they respond?"

She ponders for a moment. "I think," she says, hesitating, "that the White Queen will say no. Toulouse has her affection, but she will not help him. For one thing, the pope of Rome is indebted to my father for supporting him during the Albigensian raids. France does not want to fight the Church."

It was the one policy of her father's with which she disagreed. How could he allow the Church to attack his people? Why would he aid the pope of Rome by granting his troops safe passage to Languedoc? "We know the Cathars," she argued, "and they are not heretics."

"We know nothing," her father had responded, "except that the pope is winning his war against the Holy Roman Emperor. His power grows daily. If we refuse him now, he may refuse us someday when we need his help." Now, however, when they do need his help, Papa will not request it. Favors from the Church, he fears, might come at too high a price.

"Also," she tells her uncles, "the Holy Roman Emperor now supports Toulouse. Blanche would not want to join that alliance." In the bitter fight between the pope and the emperor, France has managed to remain neutral.

"Well spoken, Margi," Uncle Thomas says. "Do you see, brother? We will leave France in very good hands."

"But you've only just arrived," she says with a little laugh. "You're to become advisers to the crown, remember?"

"Your mother-in-law is not interested in our advice," Thomas says. "She is sending us home."

"Home! But that is impossible. There must be a mistake." Her head begins to ache.

"There is no mistake." Uncle Guillaume places his hands on her shoulders. "All who accompanied you from Provence must return in the morning. Blanche commanded it today."

"All?" Marguerite's voice falters. "Even Aimée?"

"Blanche has appointed new ladies-in-waiting for you, probably daughters of the barons who are friendly to her," Thomas says. "They will certainly spy for her."

"Try not to cry, my dear." Guillaume kisses her tears. "It is most unqueenly, and your subjects are watching."

"I do not care," she says as she dries her eyes. "I can't lose you. Uncles! You, at least, must stay with me. My parents would want it."

"There is nothing we can do," Thomas says. "The White Queen has spoken, and the king has concurred. None of us, not even Guillaume or I, will be allowed to enter Paris with you. It is why we stopped in Fontainebleau for the night. We leave for Provence tomorrow."

⇒ *Eléonore* ⇐

A Fickle King
Canterbury, 1236
Thirteen years old

*B*Y GOD'S HEAD, he is an old man.

His eyes crinkle as he smiles at her—not just crinkles but lines, deeply etched, eroded by time. Old. If his face were a rock, she could use those lines for climbing, and those in his forehead, too, to boost herself to the top of his head. Up and over his crown, holding onto the emeralds and rubies. He extends a hand to help her from the carriage. Russet hair curls along the backs of his fingers. Old. A shudder runs through her.

"You are shivering." He removes his outer mantle, green velvet lined with fur, and places it on her shoulders. "January is our most inclement month. And February."

"It is never this cold in Provence," she says as he fastens the clasp at her throat. "Not in Aix, or Marseille." The skin around his left eye slumps like marzipan left in the sun to melt. He appears sad. She wishes she hadn't shuddered.

"You'll think the climate here atrocious," he says. "Complaining about the weather is a favorite English pastime, and with good reason. There." He smoothes the fur, crushing her new gown, a gift from Margi. "Is that better? Good. Welcome to England."

She remembers her uncle's instructions, and drops into a bow. "I am delighted, Your Grace," she says. "I have looked forward to this day all my life."

Uncle Guillaume's advice prods her. *Do not appear too eager, lest he lose interest in you. King Henry is notoriously fickle.*

"I mean—I have long wanted to visit your kingdom."

Canterbury, he says, is one of England's most popular destinations. His voice sounds slightly gruff, an old man's voice. "You are aware of the pilgrims who journey here year-round?" Knights serving King Henry's grandfather, Henry II, assassinated the saint Thomas à Becket in this very chapel, he says as they walk toward the magnificent cathedral. A line of barons, ladies, priests, monks, merchants and peasants, bearing candlesticks, jewels, goblets, robes, and other precious gifts as well as donkeys, horses, several goats, chickens, and a gaggle of honking, screeching children snakes its way across the plaza and through the chapel doors. "A mere visit to his shrine, it is said, will cure any illness."

Eléonore wonders why the king has never sought a cure there for his drooping eye. And does he always talk so much? Perhaps he is nervous, too. She smiles, reminding herself of her goal—capturing the king's fancy and holding it until she is queen—and changes the subject to one that she knows they both enjoy.

"Have you been to Glastonbury, my lord?"

His smile broadens. "King Arthur is a hero of mine. Even if he is only a myth."

"A myth? My lord, no! He was as real as you or I." Her eyes shine with the fires of Camelot. "Monmouth's *History* is a bit fanciful, I admit."

"And what of Lancelot? Is he Chrétien de Troyes's invention, or did Monmouth omit him from his account?"

"I have not read it, my lord, but have heard parts of it recited in my father's court." Toulouse's attacks have increased, not diminished, since Marguerite's wedding to King Louis. The count can barely afford to feed his court, let alone buy books.

"We have Chrétien's book at Westminster. Fully illuminated. It shall be my wedding gift to you."

"My lord!" She wants to squeal and jump about, but he is twenty-eight, a grown man. *You must act his age, not your own.* "But—I have nothing for you."

"Heirs to the throne will be gift enough." She stiffens. "Forgive me for frightening you. I forget the difference in our ages." His eye seems to droop more than ever now that his smile has gone. "I can imagine how I must appear to you."

Eléonore stops and lays her palm against his cheek, touching the place where it sags. She searches for some kind thing to say that would bring his smile back.

"A youth of such unparalleled courage and generosity, joined with that sweetness of temper and innate goodness, as granted him universal love."

"That is from Monmouth, isn't it?" He scowls. "Are we back to Arthur now?"

"No, my lord, I am answering your question. That is how you appear to me. As generous and courageous as King Arthur."

"Do you think so?"

"Indeed I do."

The corners of his mouth twitch.

"And as sweet-tempered," she adds.

"Sweet-tempered! My dear, you must tell my sister," he says, then throws back his head and lets out a mighty roar—of laughter.

In the next moment they are stepping into the cathedral. The making of heirs is forgotten amid the fanfare of trumpets, the servants bowing—to her!—the appraising stares of some nobles, the shouts and cheers from others, the lofty choir with its series of pointed arches ascending like stairs to heaven, and the glimmer of a starry sky's worth of candles flickering on the walls and on every surface. The cathedral shimmers as if bathed in fairy dust.

Uncle approaches and Eléonore introduces him. "A most illustrious house, Savoy," King Henry says.

"More so than ever, now that our Eléonore joins her sister in marrying a powerful king," Uncle says. "My sincere compliments, Your Grace. I attended King Louis IX's wedding to our Margi, and it was a lackluster affair compared to this." He makes a sweeping gesture. "Canterbury Cathedral is transformed!"

Pleasure writes itself on the king's face. "Could I have arrayed the very stars throughout the chapel, they would pale against the beauty of my bride-to-be." His eyes caress her face. Eléonore leans toward him, her heart unfurling like a slowly blooming rose.

"You will find our Elli to be a woman of stout heart, loyal and bold, an excellent companion," Uncle says. "And she can ride, shoot, and spar as well as any man."

"Do you enjoy the hunt, then?" King Henry looks as though he has shucked an oyster and found a pearl.

"I enjoy winning," she says, grinning at him.

"A brilliant match," the king says to Uncle. "Delightful."

"Yes, truly, Your Grace. And, as you may know, it was I who arranged this marriage. If you will grant me an audience for even a short while, I can provide many more ideas for increasing England's stature."

"Henry, what are you doing?" A tall woman with hair the color of russet, like the king's, rushes over and takes Eléonore's hands into her own. "Your bride has traveled across the sea and, today, all the way from Dover. My dear, you look tired."

Eléonore yawns. "A drink of water would put me in the right."

"Nonsense!" The woman places an arm around her shoulders. "Oblivious as usual, Henry. Are you going to give your young bride some nourishment, or let her faint away here on the floor?"

Uncle's petition forgotten, the king and his sister Eleanor Marshal lead the party into the monastery, where a great banquet awaits. Servants bring washing cloths and bowls of water, gourds of Henry's favorite wine from the Loire Valley, bread, and dishes of meat, fish, and cheese.

"Ours must seem a bland diet compared to the fare in Provence," Eleanor Marshal says. She eyes Eléonore's gown. "Our fashions pale in comparison, as well, it appears."

Marguerite had this gown made for her, a confection of purple silk with silver lace, on Eléonore's stop in Paris. *You cannot greet the King of England in your clothes from Provence. They will think you a simple country bumpkin.* Judging from the out-of-date gowns she is seeing here—trailing tippets! wimples!—Eléonore thinks her sister need not have gone to the expense.

"I can make anything you own into something equally beautiful," she offers, eyeing her sister-in-law's austere gray tunic and surcoat. "After wearing my sister's castoffs all my life, I became a proficient seamstress."

Eleanor Marshal shakes her head. "I took a vow of chastity when my husband died. Dressing to allure would gain me nothing."

"A vow of chastity? Why? You could marry any man you choose."

"A woman, choose? Things *must* be different in Provence." Her laugh is wry. "I was given in marriage to an old man. For the sake of the kingdom, they said. May the Lord spare me from that fate a second time."

A striking man with wavy, jet-black hair and blue eyes refills the king's water pitcher. Eléonore catches her breath at his smile.

"Simon de Montfort, from France," Eleanor Marshal whispers. "Have you ever seen a more handsome fellow? And he speaks so eloquently. Henry adores him."

A shout rings out, and the clatter of horses' hooves. "More visitors?" Henry says. "My God. Interrupting our meal."

A servant appears. "The Count of Ponthieu, Your Grace, with his daughter, Joan." Murmurs fill the hall.

The king scowls. "Ponthieu? What? Impudence."

Through the windows Eléonore sees a man in armor pulling a woman to the door, where a row of knights stands on guard. She hears the clang of swords and the clatter of a blade to the stones. She cranes her neck to see the fight. "Let them enter," King Henry grumbles.

Moments later the Count of Ponthieu stands before them, his helmet under one arm, his daughter beside him, sullenness puckering her face. She is tall, with hair as sleek and shiny as sable—drawing

Henry's eye. Eléonore remembers Uncle's warning: *King Henry is notoriously fickle. You must captivate him now, or he may change his mind before the wedding.*

"I came to discern whether the rumors are true," the count says, fingering a mole on the side of his nose. "Now, Your Grace, I must ask: How can you marry this one"—he gestures toward Eléonore—"when you are already married to this one?"

Gasps fill the hall. Joan of Ponthieu shoots a defiant gaze at Eléonore, as though she would challenge her to a duel. Eléonore's blood quickens. The skinny waif would not stand a chance.

"But Sir Simon, you know the betrothal has been contested," Henry says. Eléonore's pulse thuds in her ears. Her King Henry, already promised to another? Why has no one told her? She turns accusing eyes to Uncle.

"Until the matter is settled, Your Grace, you are still bound to my daughter," the count says.

"We are too closely related." Henry's voice rises. "I expressed this concern from the beginning, Lord Ponthieu, but you pressed me to move forward. You said you held influence with the pope."

"And I do," the count said. "But not as great an influence, it seems, as Queen Blanche."

"To hell with that woman!" Henry cries. "Does she think she rules the world?" Eléonore frowns. Would King Henry prefer to marry this girl? His face pinkens, and the muscles in his neck bulge.

Eléonore reaches over and touches his arm. "Breathe," she whispers. Her mother's advice, and most beneficial.

Henry takes a deep breath before continuing. "The White Queen aims to withhold from me the lands France stole from my father. Ponthieu is too close to Normandy for her comfort. And she has Pope Gregory's ear. If she wants him to annul our contract, he will do so."

"I am willing to wait for his ruling. My daughter's honor hangs in the balance, as does that of your new intended bride."

"I have waited long enough for marriage!" Henry bangs a fist on the table. "It might be years before he decides." He turns wild eyes to Eléonore.

Uncle rises from his seat. "Your Grace, I have information that can help in this matter. If you will meet with me privately."

"I do not see how involving other parties would be beneficial," the count says.

"Quiet!" Henry roars. "I have not given either of you permission to speak."

With a trembling hand he touches the platter of food in front of them. She watches, fascinated. Will he hurl it at the count, or at her uncle? Uncle, back in his seat, mouths a command to her: *Do something.*

Joan smiles at Henry, aiming to beguile him with her buxom figure. Eléonore places a hand on her own, still-flat, chest. Should she intervene, or would she only agitate Henry more? His eyes linger on Joan of Ponthieu, the forbidden fruit. He licks his lips. Eléonore leans toward him.

"My lord," she whispers.

He draws his gaze away from her competitor. She places her hand on his, possessing him.

"Our meal is interrupted, as you noted. May we dine, and then discuss this matter? I have traveled so far today." She gives him the wide-eyed look that always melted Papa's resolve. Joan of Ponthieu might have the body, but Eléonore has the heart-shaped face, the long lashes, the perfect smile. And, at the moment, she has the King of England's full attention.

"Of course," Henry says. His smile is the sun emerging from behind the clouds. He claps his hands, and servants come running. "Set up tables for the count and his entourage," he commands. "We will meet in my chambers once the feast is finished."

"And my uncle, too?" she murmurs. "He met with the White Queen during our visit to Paris. He spent quite a lot of time with her."

"We do desire the attendance of the bishop-elect of Valence," Henry says. "We are most eager to hear your news, sir."

Eléonore sends a look of triumph to Uncle, whose grin is as satisfied as if he had already filled his belly.

❧ *Eléonore* ❧

Ruffled Feathers
Westminster, 1236

Before the coronation, she sits in her chambers, thumbing through the *Lancelot du Lac* Henry had given her the previous day; and writing to Marguerite about their journey to Glastonbury. *They were real! Arthur, the great king who fought off the Saxons and brought peace to England; the Round Table and its knights; the Lady of the Lake; the magical sword; the wise Merlin; the noble and pious Guinevere—they are all real, as I have argued. The monks told of a leaden cross bearing their names and bones buried under a tree.* Eléonore could not contain her excitement: proof at last! But she had not seen the artifacts. The monks have reburied them, and stand vigil day and night to guard them against robbers.

Henry promised to build a shrine in their chapel if they will let me carry the relics in a special ceremony, she writes. *He is the most generous man I could ever imagine. Perhaps, in time, I will not shrink from his caress.*

She strikes out this last line. What does Marguerite know about a man's caress? King Louis is young and handsome, unlike Henry, but his mother keeps him from her. After two years of marriage, they have not been able to consummate, she whispered to Eléonore in Paris last month. Henry, on the other hand, has no difficulties in the marriage bed. The problems are all Eléonore's.

She cannot bear to look at him, at his drooping eyelid, at the hair blanketing his chest, his back, his neck, his feet. He reminds her of an ape, even in the dark or especially so, when she cannot see his gentle eyes but can only feel his hair scratching against her smooth body. When he kisses her, his beard tickles her skin, filling her with revulsion. She knows the quantity of hair has nothing to do with his age, but she cannot help thinking, *Old.*

"My lady, His Grace has come to see you," Margaret says. She turns the letter on its face and rises to greet him, sweet Henry, smiling shyly after their night together. He has a gift for her, he says, and takes her by the hand.

"Not another gift! Henry, this is too much." In the six days since their wedding he has given her a belt with a diamond-studded holster and matching dagger; cloth of taffeta, velvet, and the finest silk woven with gold thread; a ring in the shape of a lion—the Plantagenet symbol—with emerald eyes; necklaces, bracelets, cups and, best of all, books: his copy of *The Great Books of Romances,* a psalter, a book of hours, a bestiary, and a collection of songs from Provence, all gilded and illuminated in rich colors as well as silver and gold.

"Nothing but the best for my queen," he says, as they step into the great hall and she sees the palfrey, a beautiful dappled mare with a yellow mane wearing a saddle with stirrups of gold. She will look splendid riding it in today's procession, he says.

She strokes the horse's cheek and murmurs to her. *Sweet baby.* If only Henry's hair felt as soft, or if only her heart were. His smile is indulgent: he hopes those are tears of joy? She nods, blinking and turning away from him, hating to lie.

He is trying to buy her affection. The adornments and entertainments at their wedding ceremony will be the talk of Canterbury for many years. Her coronation is sure to be equally opulent. Already she has seen lions in cages, dancing girls in exotic costumes, and a cake as big as a house that surely contains something fanciful within.

"It thrills my soul to bring you happiness," Henry says, pulling her close for a kiss that she must return, and eagerly.

"I am happy," she says, laughing, wiping her mouth quickly against her sleeve. "So you can stop spending the kingdom's treasury, if that is what it is for."

"It is—but there are other reasons to put on a spectacle today." He helps her onto the horse and she walks the beauty around the hall. The Count of Ponthieu, he tells her, has been granted an audience with the pope. He will argue that their marriage is invalid and that Eléonore is not the true Queen of England.

"Ponthieu? I thought he had given up this fight," she says, dismounting. "What about the White Queen? Didn't she attack him?"

"Blanche, too, thought Ponthieu had given up. His reputation for obstinacy appears well deserved." Someday, they may need the barons to attest that they paid homage to Eléonore as queen. "I have planned an event that they will not forget."

THE ENTIRE CITY of London, it seems, has come to the procession, all dressed in their finest garments and ornaments: thousands lining the streets to gawk at the three hundred sixty knights and nobles on splendidly bedecked horses, each carrying a gold or silver goblet for the feast; at their king, in his purple, green, and red silks and plush furs; and, most of all, at Eléonore, who sits high on her horse in a dusty rose gown, mantle of gold and ermine, and glittering necklace of rubies—another gift from Henry—and tries not to shiver in the January chill although she has never felt so cold. Already the Earl of Norfolk has been heard to complain about the king's giving them an "alien" queen. Only an hour from gaining the crown, she does not want to remind the English that she is, as Norfolk (preposterously) said, "nearly French." Everything must be perfect on this day, and the English, so often conquered in the past, deplore the very idea of foreign rule.

Her hopes for perfection soon fly apart, however, when the

heavy cathedral doors open with a mighty crash during the coronation ceremony. The Count of Ponthieu runs down the aisle, cutting through the crowd with his sword. A woman shrieks; a child begins to scream, nicked on the shoulder by the blade. Henry, sitting on the throne beside Eléonore, leaps to his feet. "Seize him!" he shouts.

It takes four strong knights to subdue him bodily—but they cannot silence him. "This coronation is illegal, for they are not truly married," he cries, struggling against his captors. "It is a travesty and a sham. The king has already betrothed himself to my daughter."

The archbishop sets down the incense. "This is a grave allegation. Where is your proof?"

The count waves a parchment. "Here is the *verba de praesenti* he signed with my seneschal, naming Joan as his wife."

Eléonore stares at the man who may or may not be her husband. He signed a *verba de praesenti*? Is she an adulteress, then? She scans the crowd for Uncle, finds him through her tears.

Uncle steps forward to address the archbishop. "We have already dealt with this . . . most delicate situation at Canterbury, before the wedding." The marriage to Joan is invalid, he says, because of a prior agreement the count signed with Queen Blanche of France.

"He lost a battle with the French, but she allowed him to keep his lands and castles in exchange for the right to choose his daughter's husband. Since the queen is contesting the *verba de praesenti* before the pope of Rome, it obviously violates this agreement."

"And we are too closely related," Henry says. "Cousins in the fourth degree."

"My lady, since you are most affected by these charges, I ask what you desire." The archbishop turns to Eléonore, his expression grave. "If Pope Gregory rules in the king's favor, then nothing will change. But should he rule for the Count of Ponthieu, he will annul your marriage. You will lose everything—and your children will be considered illegitimate. They will inherit nothing."

Eléonore's racing pulse sends her to her feet. Lose everything—when she stands on the cusp of having it all? Her children illegitimate? She is only the daughter of an impoverished count. What sort of future could she make for them?

The cathedral is hushed with expectation. All eyes are on her, waiting for her to do something, to say—what? She needs time to think. Her pounding heart urges her to flee, to escape from these eyes, this terrible pressure, this husband who has humiliated her so. He signed a *verba de praesenti*. Why didn't he tell her? Under Eléonore's accusing glare, he seems to crumple. His eye droops so sadly, it might slide off his face completely. He has never looked so old—or so pitiful.

"I only wanted a family," he murmurs, so low that no one else hears. "With you, Eléonore."

Tears spring to her eyes. In seven days with Henry, she has seen only kindness, generosity, and passion. *My lion,* she called him. But even a lion has weaknesses: Henry's is a yearning for the family he never had.

She reaches over and slips her hand into his. Her thumb slides over the hair on his fingers, hair like the silk on a baby's head. Standing with him, she looks out at the people who would call her queen. What kind of queen would she be, to shrink from this small test? She narrows her eyes at the Count of Ponthieu, still and subdued but his eyes defiant. She thinks of Margi, who, as the Queen of France, may help her to defeat him. A frisson of excitement shivers through her. Eléonore always did love a contest.

—◦•◦—

AFTER THE CEREMONY, Gilbert Marshal, the Earl of Pembroke, waves a wand to clear a path for Henry and Eléonore from the chapel to the banquet hall, while nobles of the Cinque Ports carry silken cloths lined with silver bells on their lance tips to shelter the royal heads. The nobles vied for this privilege, as have others serving the royal couple during the feast—including Simon de Montfort.

"Will the Count of Ponthieu feast with us today?" he asks Henry, a twinkle in his eyes. "Shall I add a drop or two of something to his hand-washing water? A tincture of spiderwort to hasten his digestion of the meal?"

Uncle, awarded a seat at the king's table for his help with Ponthieu, gestures toward the young man.

"See how skillfully Leicester comports himself?" he says to Eléonore. "Take note, as well, of your husband's delighted response. Simon de Montfort is a shrewd and ambitious man. You should befriend him."

She smiles broadly as Montfort offers her the basin. "To what do I owe the honor of being served by you today, *monsieur*? This has been the Earl of Norfolk's task."

His intimate gaze sends a ripple down Eléonore's spine. "The English nobles do love money, my lady."

She plunges her hands into the water, then dries them on the towel he provides. "You paid Norfolk? How much?"

"Not nearly enough for the privilege of serving the world's most beautiful queen."

She reaches into the pouch on her girdle and pulls out several coins. "Would this be adequate recompense?"

His gaze flickers over the silver. Ah! He, too, loves money. "Please take this, *monsieur,* as my gift."

"Thank you, my lady, but I cannot—"

"Shh! Do not let the king hear you refuse his queen's gift, *monsieur*. He has a terrible temper."

He accepts the coins, kisses them, and tucks them into his pouch. "I will sew them into my chemise, to wear next to my heart."

"If he does sew them in, they won't remain there for long," Uncle says when he is gone. "The Earl of Leicester is in dire need of an income."

Simon, being a younger son of the Count of Montfort, seemed destined for the clergy, Uncle tells her. But he had other ambitions. He talked his eldest brother into signing over the rights to the earldom of Leicester, then traveled to England and petitioned Ranulf, the Earl of Chester—Leicester's custodian—to turn the title and lands over to him. Soon he had won Ranulf's affection, and Leicester, too.

"Simon arrived at the court five years ago under Ranulf's sponsorship, and has remained here ever since," Uncle says. "He continually gains influence over the king and the court."

"He must be glib-tongued, indeed," Eléonore said.

"See how easily he extracted coins from you."

Eléonore grins. "You advised me to befriend him, didn't you?"

"And you used a most expedient method. Leicester's castle was abandoned for many years, and is in ill repair. The earl needs an income—a substantial one—if he is going to rebuild it."

"He needs to marry an heiress."

"It is his only recourse. Unfortunately, heiresses are scarce these days. And Montfort has little to offer except good looks and a golden tongue."

❦

*S*EATED BEFORE THE scowling barons' council, Henry gives Eléonore a look as if to say, *do you see what I must endure?*

He clears his throat, tries again. As ruler over Germany and Italy, the Holy Roman Emperor is a valuable friend to England, he says. The fifty or so barons, seated in the great hall before them, begin to mutter. Some fold their arms across their chests.

"The pope is more powerful, and he hates Frederick," says the gray-bearded Earl of Kent. "Why not follow the example of the French king, and remain neutral in their dispute?" He shakes his shaggy head. "As your former guardian, Henry, I thought that I had taught you to choose more wisely."

"You are not my guardian now, Sir Hubert, but my royal subject," Henry snaps. "And you are to address me as such."

He is losing his temper again. It is time for Eléonore to step in.

"The king has already pledged the dowry for his sister's marriage to the emperor," she says. "He did so in good faith, certain that you would recognize the value of having Frederick for an ally. Was he wrong?"

"He was wrong to pledge a dowry that he could not pay," the Earl of Kent grumbles.

"So you think the alliance is without value?" she asks.

He bunches up his face. "I did not say that, my lady."

"How much is it worth, then? Five thousand silver marks?"

"Certainly—"

"Ten thousand? Twenty? Or perhaps we should ask how much we would spend to defend ourselves should the emperor attack? Because if we do not pay, he will attack."

Gilbert Marshal, Earl of Pembroke, stands to speak. "Do not forget, Your Grace: Your authority depends on your barons' submission. We are loath to submit to another increase in taxes. What happened to the portion you took from us so recently? Wasn't that supposed to pay the empress's dowry?"

"Spent on the king's wedding to a foreigner, and her coronation, no doubt," Roger de Quincy, the Earl of Winchester, says. "Thirty thousand dishes served at the feast, I was told."

"That is a gross exaggeration!" Henry's voice rises. "As for my queen being a 'foreigner,' I wonder which of you has only English blood in his veins."

"You ought to know, having bled us nearly to death to fund your follies," Sir Hubert grumbles.

Simon de Montfort leans against a far wall, insouciant and grinning. "Ideas become follies when the bill comes due," he says. "This council supported an alliance with Frederick when the king proposed it."

"That was two years ago," the Earl of Winchester says with a sniff. "And he may have discussed the marriage proposal with us, but he gave the Lady Isabella's hand before we voted."

"Is it my fault that the emperor grew tired of waiting?" Henry says, looking to Montfort as though he, and not Henry, were king. "While the barons deliberated, he would have married someone else."

"A council this large cannot meet more often than it does. We have our own affairs to conduct," says Simon. "Our king must sometimes make decisions in haste, without our approval. Had he a smaller group to advise him, however, this would not be the case."

Having given Henry an entrée to announce his Council of Twelve, Montfort retreats back into the shadows, forgotten by all except Eléonore. Her sister-in-law is right: he is an extraordinarily handsome man. Only his eyes disturb the perfection—not their shape or color so much as their expression. Something hard lurks within. Something cold.

The council sits wordless as Henry announces the names of those he has selected to serve. The Earl of Winchester's name is not on the list; neither is Gilbert Marshal's, nor Hubert de Burgh's. Henry has chosen men who fully support him—with Uncle Guillaume to lead them.

As soon as he finishes his list, Roger de Quincy begins to shout. "The king's insolence knows no bounds! First he forces upon us a foreign queen with no dowry and no lands, and now he elevates her foreign uncle above us."

"Sir Roger, we will send you to the jail if you insult our queen again," Henry roars. "As for her uncle, Guillaume of Savoy has served us well."

"He has convinced you to violate your oath of marriage to Joan of Ponthieu, and damn the consequences," the Earl of Kent says. "He has given to you, instead, the daughter of an impoverished foreigner with neither power nor influence to benefit England."

"And now we hear that you have put Richmond in his care," the Earl of Winchester says. "Any one of us might have performed that service for you. But we are not exotic enough, being mere Englishmen."

Eléonore can restrain herself no longer. "Tell me, Sir Roger—have you been entertained in the emperor's palace? How often do you dine with the pope? Can you walk into the French court unannounced and be granted an immediate audience before the king?"

Roger clenches his jaw. "The kings of France have invaded our borders and robbed us of lands belonging to our fathers. I cannot imagine why I should wish to pay homage there."

"Your lack of imagination is why you need my uncle to guide you," Eléonore says. "He has more expertise in world affairs—and more ideas for how to increase England's influence—than all the men in this room combined."

"And his loyalty? Where does it lie? With England, or with Savoy?" This from the Earl of Pembroke.

"Your sister is Queen of France," Kent says. "To whom are you loyal, O queen?"

Eléonore's face grows hot. "My loyalty is, and ever will be, to my husband."

"Enough!" Henry cries. He leaps up from his throne, his hand on the hilt of his sword as if he might need to fight his way out of the room. His eyes look wild and desperate, like a trapped animal's.

Simon de Montfort steps forth again, into the thick of the fray. He bows to Henry and Eléonore and then to the nobles, whose agitation has all but drowned out the king's shout.

"My lords. My king and queen." He kisses Eléonore's ring, sending a shiver up her arm. "Not all are so fortunate to be born in England." His voice rings out over the crowd, subduing it. "I hail from France, as you know. And yes, our queen and her uncle have come to us from afar. But I speak for us all, I believe, when I say that, when first we glimpsed England's green pastures and rolling hills, our hearts became captive to this fair isle. We are as English as if we had been born here—indeed, more so, since we chose this as our home instead of having it chosen for us by the accident of our birth."

"He makes a good point," Gilbert Marshal says.

"The wedding and coronation ceremonies we have all enjoyed— yes, *monsieurs,* enjoyed greatly—were necessary to demonstrate England's power. I assure you: France was watching. The White Queen observes all that we do. The moment she thinks we are weak, *pom!*" He smacks a fist into his hand. "She is like a serpent, lying in the grass at England's feet, waiting to strike."

"The king has done well to demonstrate his wealth with these feasts," he says. "The whole world is now in awe of England's splendor—and the king's own subjects, having been fêted and fed, will not soon forget his generosity. A united England is a strong England."

Eléonore sees her opening, and takes it. In like fashion, she says, "All will know if England fails to provide the dowry owed to the Holy Roman Emperor. We must give, gentlemen, in order to receive. If we want the honor and glory due the most powerful nation in the world—if we want to *be* that nation—we must pay the price. Can we afford it? Here is a better question to ponder: can we afford not to pay?"

She was never as powerful a speaker as Margi, never as quick of mind or tongue. But today she has found her voice—and she sees, at last, the value of all those cursed lessons in rhetoric. The barons agree—by a narrow vote, yet they agree—to levy a tax on their tenants one more time, and no one mentions "foreigners" again at all.

When Uncle enters the room, however, she takes note of the dark glances directed his way. The barons do not yet realize his value to them—to England. Living on an island, they forget that they are part of a larger world. They cannot see beyond their purses. England will never regain its former glory if such narrow minds prevail.

She embraces her uncle, wishing she could protect him from sour remarks. "Do not listen to these men," she murmurs. "They are like children, bickering over who is English, and who is not."

"Heed your own advice, my lady." He chuckles. "Be of good cheer! Think of all that was accomplished today. I became head of the king's council. And you discovered who among the barons is your friend, and who is not."

"Yes. All despise me except Simon de Montfort."

"And what a splendid champion for you! Your little gift to him has come back to you in full measure. But if you want to help your husband succeed, you will need more supporters in this court. What of that most wealthy and powerful of men, who never said a word today?" He nods toward Henry's brother, fair-haired and broad-shouldered and splendidly dressed, as always, in a red surcoat and ermine mantle.

"Richard of Cornwall has amassed more money and lands than almost any other man alive," he says. "Many say that he, and not Henry, is best suited to rule England. From what I have heard, Richard agrees."

"That is treason! I would be more inclined to behead him than to befriend him."

"Your husband feels quite the opposite." This is true, Eléonore knows. Arrogant and greedy though Richard may be, he is Henry's only brother.

"He could make life difficult for the king. And their relationship is far from perfect. They have quarreled bitterly in the past."

"Siblings fight." Eléonore shrugs. "What can one do about that?"

"You used to quarrel quite a bit with your sisters, as I recall. Especially Margi. You, of all people, ought to know how to smooth the ruffled feathers of rivalry."

Across the room, Richard has seen her looking at him. Holding his gaze with her own, she gestures for Margaret Biset, her handmaid, and gives her instructions. Then, with a lift of her skirts, she turns to leave the great hall.

"Where are you going, child?"

"To my chambers. I have summoned Richard of Cornwall, and now he must come to me. Such is the power of a queen." She lowers her voice. "If he's as confident as you say, then he'll have many opinions regarding today's meeting. And I shall listen to them all, with utter delight."

❧ *Marguerite* ❧

A Woman's Heart

Pontoise, 1237

Sixteen years old

*T*HEY MEET BEHIND hedges, in dark passageways, underground in the cellar where the royal wine is stored—but eyes—*her* eyes—are always there, watching. They ride into the woods but the groomsman comes along: *The White Queen would have my head if anything happened to Your Majesties.* They try the obvious meeting place—Marguerite's chambers, or Louis's—but Blanche appears within minutes, a veritable hound on her son's trail. Louis has a visitor, or an urgent matter to address; or a meeting scheduled at this very moment—did he forget? Marguerite, never summoned, never acknowledged, might as well be invisible except for Blanche's look of triumph as she pulls the blushing Louis from her arms.

"Ruling a kingdom is a demanding task," the queen mother says. "We have no time for frivolous pursuits."

"Why can't you simply tell her 'no'?" Marguerite pleads. At first, Louis asked for patience, offered promises. Now, in their second year of marriage, he clenches his jaw and reminds her that he is in charge of an entire kingdom. *Who is in charge?* she wants to ask.

"Your son appeared to me in a dream," she whispers to Louis

one night, just before he drifts off to sleep. "He is waiting to come into the world."

This tale appeals to his sense of the mystical. He sits up in bed: "By God, he will not have to wait long." He takes her into his arms and kisses her fervently—but, once again, cannot finish what he has begun—cannot, really, even begin. "The day's events have used my strength," he says.

"Then we must meet during the day."

"My mother will never allow it. She says the day is for duty and the night, for pleasure."

"Producing heirs isn't one of our duties?" Ah, she has him there.

"But how? Servants and courtiers are everywhere. Someone would tell Mama."

"We need secret signs, you and I," she sings. *"Boldness fails, so let cunning try!"*

She hovers like the hawk, biding her time. A trouvére comes forth with a new song for the White Queen. Marguerite slips out of her throne, unnoticed by the enraptured Blanche. She hands a servant a note for Louis, then steps into the garden. When he appears, they slip behind a row of tall hedges. He draws her close— *my beautiful wife*—and kisses her as though his life depended on her breath. He tastes of strawberries, his favorite fruit. His hands move like slow riders over her body's terrain. The two of them fall, sighing, into the fragrant grass, slide tunics up and leggings down. His skin smells of cinnamon and camphor; his hipbones make a hollow into which he pulls her, his breath panting and hot on her throat.

"He stepped out here a few moments ago." His mother's voice quivers like a drawn blade, cutting between them.

"I saw no one, my lady," a man answers. "His Grace must have continued into the bathing rooms."

"I am not going to follow him in there, am I? Why don't you go and see if the king is bathing? Report to me in my chambers if you do not find him, or send him to me if you do."

The voices fade. Marguerite lifts her tunic again. "Hurry."

But Louis cannot. "*Merde*. My mother—"

She makes herself kiss him. "Don't worry. We have all our lives to make an heir."

"We will not have to wait that long." He pulls her close. His heart knocks against her chest. Soon they stand and dress, she adjusting his mantle, he tying her sleeves.

"We will have many children, I promise," he whispers. Something crunches under her foot. She has stepped into a bed of irises: the flower of France. She reaches down and tries to stand them up, but their stalks are broken, their petals crushed.

———— ❦ ————

AND THEN THEY are on the move again, headed for Pontoise, north of the city, favored by the Emperor Baldwin of Constantinople, for its baths on the shore of the river Oise. The emperor will arrive today with an urgent petition, but has kept its subject a secret. "Money, most likely. I doubt you'll be needed," Blanche says to Marguerite. "Why don't you play with Isabelle today?"

But Isabelle is not feeling well, so Marguerite sends her to bed and instead is directing the chamberlains and chambermaids preparing her rooms—hanging clothes, setting up her bed, arranging her favorite chair by a sunny window—when she hears a knocking. She turns and opens a door—and sees Louis, beckoning her into a stairwell.

His kiss dizzies her; his arm around her waist steadies her. With his free hand he unlaces her tunic and slips his hands inside to caress her.

"My room is directly above," he whispers. "My queen, we have found our place."

Desire surges through her, pumping like blood—but a knock interrupts, from the door at the top of the stair. Louis's chamberlain opens it: "The queen approaches," he rasps. Louis runs up the steps. Tugging at her gown, she wonders: *Who* is Louis's queen?

She throws open the door to her chambers, stomps inside. She calls her ladies' names—Gisele, Bernadette, Amelie—her voice ringing like a trumpet's call. The women buzz around her, pulling off her tunic and hose, sliding her red gown over her head, clasping a mantle of vair about her throat, folding her hair into a crespine of gold, pinning on her crown. In the mirror, she sees a queen. Now it is time to behave like one. And then she is striding into the great hall, where a small, slight young man stretches open hands toward Louis and Blanche.

"Without France's help, cousin, these relics may be lost forever," he says. His pointed little beard lends poignancy to his chin— indeed, gives him a chin at all. He reminds Marguerite of a rat. A royal rat, in purple and gold with a red mantle, and a crown whose excess of jewels nearly obscure the gold. The man stops speaking as she walks to the dais and sits on her throne, at Louis's left-hand side—Blanche is on the right. A smiling Louis introduces her to Baldwin, the Emperor of Constantinople.

"What a surprise to see you here, daughter," Blanche says. Her voice sounds pinched, as if she were holding her nose. "Did you grow tired of playing with Isabelle?"

"I have just returned from comforting the poor child. She has not seen her mother in several days, and is sick with longing. You will find her in her bed, crying for you."

All eyes turn to Blanche, whose blush bleeds from the edges of her white mask. As she must know, Isabelle has taken to her bed with stomach pains. Several days earlier the girl asked Blanche for alms to give to the poor, but Blanche did not respond. Now the girl refuses to eat until her mother sends money.

"I shall go to her in time," Blanche says.

"She is quite ill. She says that only you can cure her," Marguerite says.

"Please, Mother, do not feel pressed to remain with us," Louis says.

"And insult our visitor?" She smiles at the emperor, who lowers his eyes like a bashful lover. "I want to hear his petition."

"Dear Mother, your devotion to our kingdom is impressive," Louis says. "Yet you have taught us well. We can surely judge this matter."

"Yes, Mother, I am here to advise the king." Marguerite reaches over to give Louis's hand an affectionate squeeze.

Overruled, Blanche stands. Her cold glance lifts the hair on Marguerite's arms. The emperor bows as she steps off the platform with a swish of her skirt. He then turns to Louis.

"If we lose these items to the Venetians, who knows what will happen to them? The merchants there think only of money, and would no doubt sell them for the highest price—even if it came from a Jew."

Louis pales. "God forgive us if we allowed such a thing to come to pass. A Jew, acquire the holy relics of Christ! They who sent our Savior to his death? They would destroy them as evidence of their sin."

"Relics of Christ!" Marguerite catches her breath. "Which ones?"

The emperor pauses, looks around as if fearing he might be overheard. "The Crown of Thorns."

Louis crosses himself.

"But why would you sell such a priceless item?" Marguerite says.

"The Roman Empire is in tatters. So many sieges and conquests. Constantinople is all that remains. My father lost much land."

In the fight to regain his territory, the emperor borrowed heavily from Venice. As security for the loan, he gave up the Crown of Thorns. "The doge of Venice will sell it if I don't repay him soon. I am in agony over it. After many long nights of prayer, the Lord has sent me to offer it to you."

"Praise God for this opportunity! He has chosen to glorify France." Louis's eyes seem to glow. "We must not fail him."

"How much will it cost?" Marguerite says.

"The Lord has willed it." Louis frowns at her. "France is destined to own this relic."

"If that is so, then why pay for it? Won't it come to us no matter what we do?"

"We have decided!" He pounds his fist on the arm of his throne, glaring at her. "France will pay the price and rescue the crown."

"Thank you, Your Grace." The emperor's mouth twitches as he bows. "The Christian world is beholden to you."

When Baldwin has gone to his chambers, she turns to Louis. "Why didn't you negotiate a price? Who knows how much the emperor has invested?"

"You should not have interfered. This matter is greater than money."

"But how do you know the relic is authentic? Anyone could fashion such a crown and call it Christ's."

"First you argue with me in the presence of the emperor, and now you question my judgment?" His raised voice draws the eyes of all in the room—the guards, the servants, those awaiting their turn to petition the king and queen. "You, a mere child from the country, with no knowledge or experience in these matters."

Heat floods her face. "I have questioned nothing except the claims of our petitioner, who rules an empire in dire need of funds. Were your mother here, she would have voiced the same concerns."

"You are not my mother." His mouth trembles. "You are nothing like her."

"That is a pity, I suppose." She stands and smoothes her skirt. "Otherwise, I might be carrying your child." She steps down from the platform and leaves the great hall without even a glance back at him.

———

THE CUP QUAKES in her hand. She longs to hurl it against the wall, if only for the clang it would make. Instead, she sits at her desk and scribbles a furious letter to Eléonore that she will not send. No one here would deliver it unread.

I have never felt so alone.

For three years she has lived in isolation. She has not a single friend in the court; all, including her ladies-in-waiting, report to Blanche.

I have no one with whom to talk, no one with whom to laugh.

If only the queen mother had not sent all her companions away at Fontainebleau. She longs for Aimée, for her uncles and her parents, for the debates at table that made up so much of her youth in Provence. No doubt she could learn more there than here, where Blanche shuns her from the daily discussions in her chambers and Louis chastises her for offering opinions.

Louis is like a ghost, seeming not even to see me sometimes, and, when I complain, looking as if he wished he could not hear me.

His mother's contempt toward Marguerite is beginning to affect him. That was clear today. Only by bearing him a son will she gain his respect.

I must make a friend in this court, not only for my sanity but also for my security—someone who can help me achieve the impossible task of giving my husband an heir.

But—who? Who can absolve Louis of the shame his mother has inflicted? Who can give him permission to desire his wife?

How is it that Louis "heals" others of their illnesses but cannot heal himself? Of course, only God can work such wonders. Perhaps I need a miracle.

She puts down her quill and gazes out the window, over the broad river valley. The silvered skein of water, the velvet landscape, the slow birds tilting their wings like sails: Didn't God create all of this? Didn't he implant his son into the womb of a virgin? Giving Louis desire for her should be no great task. Perhaps she needs only to ask.

A knock sounds at the inner door, so soft she almost doesn't hear it. In the far corner, her ladies talk and embroider. She pulls the curtain around her bed as if planning a nap, hiding the door from their view, then pulls it open.

Louis has folded his hands as if in prayer. "I should not have spoken to you so harshly."

"Make love to me now," she murmurs, "and all will be forgiven."

She beckons him into her bed, then whispers that she will return in a moment.

"I want soft music to lull me to sleep today," she says to her ladies. Soon a lute player is plucking out a soft tune in their corner.

She and Louis will not be heard. She slips into bed beside her husband.

"My dear, sweet beloved," he murmurs as they disrobe each other. "You are too good for me, Marguerite. Oh, so good."

"Shhh! Quiet—do you want to be discovered?"

"I don't care. Let them hear. Aren't we husband and wife?"

How readily God has answered her prayer. Indeed, she did not pray, but only thought of it. Now, lying under Louis, she thinks of giving thanks—but that thought is interrupted by a knock.

"Your Grace!" The cry comes from within the staircase. "The queen mother approaches."

Louis curses, leaps from the bed, pulls up his hose, and disappears. Marguerite lies still and throbbing, her heart thumping with excitement. They came so close this time.

"Where is she?" Blanche's voice cuts through the folds of her curtain before her scorn-filled face appears at the foot of Marguerite's bed.

"Sleeping at this hour? Are you ill?"

"No, only tired." *Of you.*

"And no wonder, you poor child!" Her smile twists. "Giving my son such intelligent advice must have required all your mental faculties."

Marguerite closes her eyes.

"What could you have been thinking, you foolish girl? Allowing him to pledge to pay any price, no matter how high, for that relic?"

"I am sure you know, Mother, that one does not 'allow' my husband to do anything. He has his own will."

"He would have listened to me. But I was not there—and why? Because you concocted a tale to be rid of me."

She sits up. "That is quite a costly gown to wear to bed," Blanche says. "But, judging from today's debacle, you have little sense of the value of money."

"Judging from your misplaced anger, you have little sense of your son."

"He is bewitched by you. You, who need only flutter your

eyelashes to bring him running to your bed. Such pretty eyes you have! How unfortunate that nothing lies behind them except a need for attention."

"And you have a black hole where your heart should be."

"A weak woman's heart has no place in the ruling of a kingdom."

"What would you know of a woman's heart?" Marguerite leaps out of bed and stands to face her, eye-to-eye. "You have had no consideration for mine. You've sent away everyone I care about and denied me the love of my husband."

"What is the matter, dear? Has my son been neglecting you?" Malice glints her eyes. "Don't worry. You'll be reunited with your country bumpkin family very soon."

"Are we traveling to Provence?"

"Not 'we,' my dear. I harbor no fondness for the smell of goats or the feel of dirt under my fingernails. You, however, seem destined to return to your precious Provence."

"I don't understand."

"Haven't you heard? Our subjects are beginning to talk. You have been married three years to the king, and still no heirs. If you don't conceive a child soon, we'll have to annul your marriage.

"Why the tears, dear? This is nothing personal. If you cannot perform your duty to France, then someone else must. Johanna, Countess of Flanders, is seeking a husband, we hear. She will not tarry long—and we covet her wealthy county for our own."

⇥ *Marguerite* ⇤
Endless Songs of Love
Paris, 1237

*R*ICHART DE SEMILLI stands before her, singing his *Par amors ferai chanson* while Marguerite stifles a yawn. "That is enough," she says. "You may go."

"You are as difficult to please as ever, I see." Uncle Guillaume steps into her chambers as the unfortunate trouvère steps out. She exclaims with pleasure and leans into his silken embrace; he is so rich, he even smells of gold.

"The French bore me with their endless songs of love, love, love," she says. "I am sick of love."

"You would prefer Hue de la Ferté's *sirventois*, I presume. Especially those he wrote against the White Queen."

"Ferté! How I mourned his death. I had hoped to bring him to Paris." She laughs. "His songs would have sent Blanche far away."

"Has she been hard on you, my dear? You look as if you have not slept in weeks. And you have grown even thinner since I last saw you. Are you eating?"

"Not as well as you," she teases. Uncle Guillaume has gained so much favor with King Henry that he now holds the second-highest position in the English court. Being the king's chief adviser has enriched him with land, titles, and daily meals at the royal table.

"One cannot dine on English food for long without increasing the waistline." Uncle Guillaume pats his stomach. "Meat and more meat, and all smothered in a greasy sauce." He smacks his lips. "I have grown fond of greasy sauce."

He hands her a packet of letters from Eléonore, apologizing: They are quite old. He tarried long on his visit to Uncle Thomas in Savoy. "But I carry an interesting proposal to London. It may soften the English barons' rancor toward me."

"I received a letter from Mama yesterday." She breaks open the first seal. "She wrote of difficulties in London."

"King Henry's love for me has caused your sister much misfortune. The barons whisper against Elli whenever he gives me a gift. Which is often."

"Have you considered declining his gifts?"

"And insult my king?" He grins. "His Grace enjoys giving to me. His face lights up like a child's at Christmas." He settles himself on the divan while she reads.

"I envy Elli," she says as she reads. "Facing down disgruntled barons would be a trifling task compared to keeping one's marriage from being annulled."

"Annulled? Louis is smitten with you."

"His mother is not." She drops the letter to the table by her side. "She wields her power like a noose, strangling Louis's appetite for me. If I don't conceive a child soon, she says, she will send me to Provence and marry him to the countess Johanna."

"That cannot be." William pulls out a handkerchief and dabs at his face. "This is disturbing news, Margi. Very upsetting. Provence needs you on the throne."

"I have done little for Provence, I'm afraid."

"You do not know that." He tucks his handkerchief into his sleeve. "Without your influence, might Toulouse have taken your father's castles? His attacks have not ceased, but they have subsided."

She hides her surprise. Has Toulouse run out of funds? Is he injured? Whatever the reason for his retreat, it has nothing to do with her.

"Simon de Montfort aims to spoil the queen mother's plans, at any rate," she says. According to Eléonore, he has proposed to Johanna of Flanders who, enthralled, has agreed to marry this in the spring.

The creases deepen in her uncle's forehead. "Blanche must hear of this! The English king's seneschal, the Count of Flanders? Normandy is on the border—too close for the White Queen's comfort." He brightens. "No need to worry, my dear. The White Queen will block that alliance."

"But Uncle, that is the very circumstance I dread. An unmarried Johanna of Flanders is as tempting to Blanche as mouse to a cat."

"Have you seen the countess? Quite plain. She resembles a mouse, in fact. Your husband would not choose her over you."

"Dear uncle, do you still not understand? Louis has no choice. Blanche chooses for him."

He waves his hand. "I can provide her with a different alternative. Fear not: when I leave the queen mother's chambers today, Johanna of Flanders will pose a threat to you no more."

⤞ *Eléonore* ⤝

The Taste of Treachery

London, 1237

Fourteen years old

$\mathscr{S}$IMON DE MONTFORT bursts into Eléonore's chambers unannounced, causing her to prick her finger with her sewing needle and drop the peacock feathers she is affixing to a new hat.

"Allow me," he says, and drops to his knees, presses her finger to his lips, and kisses away the drop of blood. His eyes hold anger, and a glint of mockery. Red smears his upper lip.

"Treachery cannot be tasted, after all," he says. "If so, your blood would surely hold a bitter edge."

She tucks the lines into her memory: They are perfect for the song she is writing. But petulance, not poetry, is Simon's reason for being here—indeed, his reason for being at all, she has learned. She pulls tight the cord of self-control, hiding her annoyance.

She stands. "Apparently, I have offended you."

"You have injured me, and deprived my future," he says. "I thought we were friends."

"So we are."

"Snatching away my bride-to-be and giving her to your uncle is hardly the act of a friend."

Eléonore gasps. "My uncle?" Guillaume, marry? Has he renounced his bishopric? "You must be mistaken."

"If only I were. But Johanna is quite clear." He pulls a letter from the pouch on his belt. "Thomas of Savoy is nearer my age and experienced in government, and he has the approval of the French queen," he reads. "We announced our betrothal yesterday, and will be married before Christmas."

Thomas. Of course. He and Johanna will make a perfect match. Both tall, fair-haired, and prone to bouts of laughter, they could almost be brother and sister. Both are noted diplomats, respected by barons, kings, and clergy. And Johanna, like Thomas, adores dogs, horses, and everything to do with the hunt.

"You did this," Simon says. He crushes the letter in his fist.

"I had nothing to do with it. I am as surprised as you."

"No one but you knew of our plans."

"But why would I interfere?"

"Yes, why? Out of jealousy, to think of me with another woman?"

Eléonore forgets, for one moment, that she is queen; she drops her gaze like a shy girl. In fact, she dreaded his marriage to Johanna, not out of jealousy but because it would take him far away from the English court.

"Or perhaps you think Thomas of Savoy would be more useful in your pursuit of Normandy," he says. "Yet he is also uncle to the Queen of France, and would be as likely to help her as you."

Eléonore thinks of her letter to Marguerite, telling her of Simon and Johanna's plan. She only wanted to reassure her sister—how cruel of the White Queen to taunt her with threats of an annulment!—but now she wonders: did Margi use the letter to advance her own interests?

"In Flanders, I could have helped King Henry regain those lands, and their riches, taken so unfairly from England," Simon says.

"I know! I wanted that."

"But not enough to keep our secret."

"Simon, I only told my sister because—"

"Aha! You admit it! You told the French queen of my plans."

"Yes!" Eléonore's eyes fill with tears. "The queen mother threatened to annul my sister's marriage, and to marry King Louis to Johanna. I was trying to console her."

"She used your news to prove her loyalty to France—and to betray you."

Dear sister, I cannot believe you would do such a thing. Please tell me it is not so!

Eléonore remembers herself. "This is a family matter. I will not discuss it with you."

"I am not a member of your clan, so my welfare is not your concern?"

"You know that is not true." He turns to leave. "Simon, wait. Simon! I command you to come back this instant."

He whirls around and drops to his knees before her, his cap in his hand, his eyes downcast. "You summoned me, my lady?"

"Cease this mockery," she snaps. "Stand before me, Simon."

He obeys, but still will not meet her eyes. "I apologize for what has happened," she says. "I betrayed you, although I did not mean to. Your friendship means everything to me."

Now he looks at her. "You might make amends."

"How? I will do anything in my power."

He shows his perfect teeth. "You can find another wife for me," he says. "Someone as good as Johanna of Flanders, or better. Someone very rich."

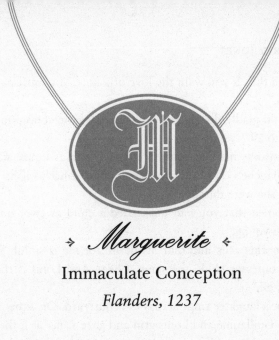

⤜ *Marguerite* ⤛
Immaculate Conception
Flanders, 1237

No one is happier than Marguerite at the wedding of her uncle Thomas to Johanna of Flanders—except, perhaps, Uncle Guillaume, who has at last gained the favor of the White Queen. Blanche seats him next to her during the banquet and flirts and laughs as though they are old friends, while he glows with anticipation over the lands and titles that will surely follow.

Marguerite smiles, as well, at the table with the new Count of Flanders and his wife. Gone is this threat to her marriage, at least. But today she has another reason to smile, as well: Mama has come, with Sanchia—tall for her age, extraordinarily pretty, and very shy—and they sit by Marguerite's side.

"Behold Thomas's dazed expression," Mama says, watching him dance with his bride. "If I did not know my brother better, I might think he were in love."

"Louis used to gaze at me like that," Marguerite says.

She has not seen Mama in three years. Did she expect sympathy? How forgetful of her. Mama looks pointedly at her flat belly.

"Nothing is without its cost, Marguerite," she says. "I have taught you this. If you want the love of a king, you must pay for it with heirs."

"I would gladly do so, Mother, if immaculate conception were available to all."

Mama raises her eyebrows. She peers over at Louis, who has gone to Blanche's table and now leans toward her as if he were a plant and she were the sun.

"I assumed that you had miscarried a child or two, since you married so young."

"His mother tells him that his desire for me is sinful. She has paid his confessor to do the same, I hear. And Louis is the most pious of men."

Blanche's laughter rings across the courtyard. On either side of her, Uncle Guillaume and Louis grin and gaze at her as if they were competing suitors. Mama's face flushes. Marguerite looks down at her lap, where she has clenched her hands so tightly that her wedding ring cuts into her fingers.

"This will not do," Mama says. "This will not do at all."

———◆———

$\mathcal{S}$OON UNCLE GUILLAUME has the promotion he has earned with his clever scheme to block Simon de Montfort from becoming the next Count of Flanders.

"I am to become both prince and bishop of Liège," he exults to Marguerite and her mother once they have all returned to Paris. "The queen—sorry, Margi, I mean the queen mother—has suggested my election and the Holy Roman Emperor has approved it. By God! I am a wealthy man."

Eléonore will be jealous. Not only has Uncle thwarted England's hopes for an advantage on the Norman border, he has now become a member of the French court. *You should see our uncle strut about like a proud cock,* Marguerite writes to her. And she cannot resist adding, *yet, even in his excitement, he is grateful to me for this new honor.*

It is a pitiful lie. Yet how can she tell the truth to Eléonore, of all people? While Marguerite fights to sit on her throne, her sister freely awards English lands, titles, and prosperous marriages to their relatives. Uncles Peter and Boniface returned home from King Henry's court laden with gold and promises—Richmond for Uncle Peter, the archbishopric of Canterbury for Uncle Boniface. Meanwhile Marguerite has not even a handmaid in whom she can trust. Why did she confide her troubles to her sister? She cringes to think how superior Eléonore must feel—until she reminds herself: Provence will someday be hers.

Eléonore, of course, has her own struggles. Like Marguerite, she has not yet borne a child. And her life in England is far from ideal. *The English barons talk against me, calling me a 'foreigner' and our father a 'minor count,' but I do not care,* she has written. *With Henry's blessing I shall surround myself with family who will buffer me from my enemies like the walls of a fortified castle.*

Marguerite wishes she enjoyed such protection. Should Blanche talk Louis into annulling their marriage, who would advocate for her? Not even Uncle Guillaume would be able to help, in spite of his new title. Mama, on the other hand, is here now—and determined to do what she can for Marguerite.

On her last evening in Paris, Mama meets with the White Queen in her chambers. She returns to Marguerite wearing a gold necklace—Blanche's gift—and eyes as hard as flint.

"Blanche de Castille wants you out," she announces, as if imparting new information.

Marguerite sighs. "She has disliked me since our first meeting. If I knew why, I would try to change her opinion."

"You would need to lose all your teeth and hair, grow enormously fat, and become as dull-witted as that poor girl Isabelle for her opinion of you to improve. Blanche does not dislike you; she fears you."

"Fears me?" Marguerite laughs. "The little country bumpkin with dirt under her nails and not a lick of sense?"

"If you fit that description, you might be pregnant now." When Blanche sent M. de Flagy to their castle in Aix, he sought—and found—in her the qualities that Blanche and Louis wanted. Her "pretty face" brightened Louis's spirit, but her "prettier faith" delighted the White Queen.

"She relied on your piety to bend you to her will," Mama says. "But she did not envision your beauty. And she did not anticipate your intelligence."

Blanche sought a wife for Louis to keep him out of mischief and to bear him sons. She never intended to compete for admirers; nor did she plan to share her power as queen.

Mama glances over at the ladies-in-waiting, who sit in their corner, feigning oblivion. "I need fresh air," she says. "Let's go to the gardens for a mother-daughter stroll."

The ladies lay down their needlework and stand, ready to join them, but Mama waves them aside. "You may remain here. Your queen has all the service she needs from her doting mother."

"But we must accompany her at all times," Gisele says. "The White Queen has commanded it."

Mama gives her the warmest of smiles. "Don't you think our Laughing Knight will adore this one?" she says to Marguerite. "And Pierre of Aix for you, and Hugh of Tarascon for you," she says to the others. A retinue of knights from Provence will soon arrive to escort Mama home tomorrow—and they will attend a feast in the countess's honor tonight.

"The men of Provence are not only the most handsome men in the world, they are also the most exhilarating dancers you can imagine," the countess tells the maids.

Excited chatter fills the room. Marguerite forgotten for the moment, Mama tucks her hand under her daughter's arm and walks her into the gardens. There, with her head close to Marguerite's, she tells her how to win Louis's body at last—by starting with his soul.

→ Éléonore ←

Scandal and Mutiny

London, 1238

Fifteen years old

ÉLÉONORE YEARNS TO be there. She is not invited, however.
Worse: she has been told to stay away.

"Already the barons point the finger at you for every unpopular
decision that I make," Henry said. "We can't have them blaming
you for this marriage, as well."

They might easily do so. Eleanor Marshal is, after all, her
dearest friend, and Simon de Montfort is, famously, the queen's
champion. ("Her Lancelot," some call him, winking sly.) Today,
while she paces in the great hall, fingering her rosary beads and
praying, the two are exchanging their vows in secret before the
Westminster chaplain. Henry, who will place the bride's hands
into the groom's, is the only witness—or so they hope. Richard of
Cornwall, having learned of the wedding, races toward London
even now. *Slow his journey, O Lord.* Should God refuse her
request, she must make sure that he does not reach the chapel until
after the ceremony is complete. Her friendship with Simon, her
only ally at court, depends on this marriage.

"My lady." The young knight bows tremulously, as though
afraid she might strike him. She is not the one he fears, however.

Richard has arrived, and waits impatiently for permission to enter the castle. Delay him, Eléonore tells the skittish youth, for as long as possible.

But Richard will not be kept waiting, not today. In the next moment he storms into the great hall, his hand on the hilt of his sword. *Breathe.* She greets him with a kiss which he does not return.

"Where are they?" he growls.

"Who?" she asks.

He narrows his eyes at her. His jaw tics. "In Henry's chapel," he guesses. One look at her face and he laughs without mirth, then starts toward the stairs.

"Dear brother, no man may enter the palace bearing weapons, as you know," she says. "I must ask you to leave yours with our guards."

He grimaces, but he removes the scabbard and sword from his belt, hands them to the young knight, then refastens the belt around his waist. She would block his way as he marches toward the stairs, but he dances around her to charge up the steps.

"Where are you going?" she cries, but he runs toward the chapel where, at this moment, the nuptial couple stands amid the gorgeous wall hangings of embroidered green and blue and the saints' relics and speak their breathless promises to love, honor, and obey. Simon cradles Eleanor's hands in his, as if they were a cherished gift. She gazes into his eyes with utter, breathless love. By the time they kneel before the chaplain for the celebration of mass, emotion has overcome Henry; tears drip from his chin as he bows his head and sends fervent prayers to Mary, the Mother of God, for the couple's happiness. And then Richard, followed by Eléonore, bursts into the room.

"In God's name, am I too late?" he cries.

"You are not too late, Sir Richard, to offer your good wishes to your sister and to me." Simon beams as though the Earl of Cornwall had stopped in to celebrate.

"By God, I would not believe this folly had I not seen it myself."

Richard glares at Henry. Dust covers his tunic and riding boots and reddens his eyes, lending him a grim, wild look. "Did you not send me home just hours ago? Even as you kissed me farewell, you harbored this secret in your heart. God! How I wish you were not my king, for I would cut out your deceitful tongue."

Two of Henry's guards step forward with their blades drawn, but the king waves them back. "Our sister wished for a private wedding," he says, averting his gaze.

"Why would she wish for that?"

"We knew you would object," Eleanor says.

"To such a fine match?" Richard's laugh cracks. "The king's sister and a French dandy with only a crumbling manor to his name? I cannot imagine why anyone would protest."

"Now, see here, Sir Richard—" Simon begins.

"I see much, Sir Simon. I see that you have insinuated yourself into my sister's heart for your own gain." He glances at the chaplain and presses his mouth shut. Clerics love to spread tales.

"Richard! Your quarrel is with me, not with my husband," Eleanor de Montfort says. "I chose Simon of my own volition."

"That is not a choice for you to make. Your duty is to enhance our kingdom, not to satisfy your own desires." He glares at Henry. "I should have been consulted about this marriage. But it is not too late. What has been done, can be undone."

He turns to leave, but Eléonore stops him. "Stay, Richard, and celebrate with us. Simon and your sister love each other. Doesn't Eleanor deserve some happiness in life?"

"She married our Lord Jesus Christ seven years ago. She deserves the nunnery," he says. "Her seducer, Simon de Montfort, deserves to burn in hell—and he will, if I have to spend every coin in my treasury to make it so."

No MUSIC PLEASES the ear so well as the clink of silver. It is a tune that Richard of Cornwall plays very well, having so much of it in his purse. His song enchants the archbishop of Westminster into declaring the marriage invalid. It marches the people of London to the palace, where they shout out of tune, demanding the heads of those associated with the scandal. It stirs the indignation of the barons, who send their most pugnacious member—and, heretofore, an admirer of Simon's—to protest the match.

Roger de Quincy, the Earl of Winchester, rides into London in typically dramatic fashion, galloping through the streets as though racing to a fire, kicking up clouds of dust, and shouting for all to clear the way or be trampled under his horse's hooves. He marches into the palace in his battle armor, including a silly peacock plume atop his helmet, and sings Richard's song of discord.

"The barons of England are outraged over the travesty that occurred, with the king's blessing, on the sixth of January," he says. "We demand that the marriage of the lady Eleanor Marshal, Countess of Pembroke, to Simon de Montfort, a Frenchman"—his lips curl—"be nullified at once. Else, we must insist that the king abdicate the throne."

Henry's face reddens. "On what grounds?"

"Henry is God's chosen monarch," Eléonore says. *Breathe.* "Our Lord placed him on the throne, and only our Lord can displace him."

"Well may he do so. The clergy stand with us on this matter. I have brought a petition to that effect, signed by England's most prestigious barons and our exalted bishops."

"What arrogance!" Henry leaps to his feet. "I would like to see you try to remove me."

De Quincy's jaw tics. "By conducting this marriage in secret, you have broken your pledge to consult the barons' privy council. This is a grave offense."

"The people of London would not support mutiny against their king," Eléonore says. "They love Henry." And yet she needs Simon and Eleanor's love in this conniving court. She peers within for a solution, sees its rippling image, amorphous and shifting, as on a dark pool.

"Without the support of your barons, you cannot rule," the earl says. "And we will not support this union of our English princess with French nobility. Think of it, Your Grace! Should you perish, Simon de Montfort might claim the throne. And if he sired a son? England would be lost forever."

"And the sun might fail to rise tomorrow and the world would perish," Eléonore snaps. "You forget the king's brother. Richard of Cornwall holds a stronger claim to the throne than do the Montforts."

"I have forgotten nothing, my lady. But the complexities of this situation are too great for a foreigner to grasp. And I did not ride all this way to discuss the succession to the throne."

"What have you come to discuss?" Henry asks.

"The marriage of the Countess of Pembroke to the Earl of Leicester cannot stand. The barons of England have not given their permission for it, and will not do so."

"Permission?" Henry barrels toward the little man, who stands his ground—for a moment.

With the tip of his long index finger, Henry prods the earl's collarbone. "Pray tell me, Winchester, under whose authority do you hold your lands and titles? Mine, that is whose." The baron steps backward, but Henry advances.

"Under whose authority do I hold the kingdom? As the queen has already pointed out, none other than God has given it to me." He punches his own chest. "As God's anointed king, I will arrange any marriage that pleases me, your permission be damned."

His red face, his wild eyes, the veins bulging in his neck and on his forehead: Henry reminds Eléonore of a snarling beast. She would shrink back in fear if she didn't know the gentleness beneath that fury. Might he someday unleash it against her? But—no. Henry would not.

The Earl of Winchester, too, seems surprised by the king's attack. He dances backward before tripping and nearly falling to the floor.

"That will teach you to harass your king," Henry says. Winchester looks as though he'd like to stab him in the back.

"You seem to forget, my lord, how you depend on your barons' support," he says. "I pray that you will come to your senses soon. For, by refusing to accede to our demands, you have placed your throne, and your person, at great risk. Were I you, I would gird myself for war."

"*R*UBBISH," ELÉONORE SAYS when Roger de Quincy has gone. Surely he exaggerates the barons' wrath. After all, Eleanor Montfort is the youngest of Henry's siblings, and a woman; her offspring would lay no claim to the English throne. They must placate the barons, she tells Henry, and protect Simon.

"You need only apologize, and the matter will resolve itself," she says.

Henry thrusts out his lower lip, reminding Eléonore of her sister Beatrice, who crashes around breaking things when she doesn't get what she wants. "Apologize to that sniveler Winchester, with his peacock's feather? He should be grateful that we didn't throw him into the Tower."

Who is the peacock? Eléonore wants to say. Who is the sniveler? "I agree, he is tedious," she says. "Perhaps we should inform him of your sister's condition."

"Risk my sister's honor? You surprise me, Eléonore."

She raises her brows. Cannot the Earl of Winchester count to nine? When the child is born, the entire kingdom will know the truth. "An apology seems our only recourse, then. A few words on your part, a minor puffing of the earl's chest. A small price to pay for your sister's happiness." And for Simon de Montfort's friendship, she might add. Considering the barons' grumbling against "aliens" and "foreigners," Eléonore may need Simon's support in the future.

Henry looks at her as if she had spoken in a strange tongue. "A king does not apologize to his vassals. We must convey strength, Eléonore, never weakness. Disaster would ensue, otherwise. Usurpers always await, coveting our thrones."

If her years in Provence taught her anything, it is this: Real strength lies not in denying one's deficiencies, but in admitting them. For once, though, she keeps an opinion to herself.

———◆——————

*T*HE CROWD HAS grown larger every day. Now, little more than a week after the Montforts' wedding, thousands press against the castle gates, waving torches, hurling rocks, brandishing fists. "Send the foreigners home!" they cry, forgetting that their great-grandparents came from Normandy, or Germany, or Wales. The Earl of Winchester, whose ancestors were Scottish, has smashed all his casks of French wine, declaring that only "fine British ales" will be served at his table. Immediately the guest list for his feast celebrating St. David of Scotland shrank to only a few friends.

"Damned be Simon de Montfort," Henry rages to Eléonore in her chambers as her tailors fit her for a new Parisian gown. "Damn him and his ambition! Always grasping for what is above him. I would have given him anything except my sister, for the love of God."

"But you did give him your sister." Eléonore turns, her arms spread. "Not for the love of God, but for the love of your sister."

"Yes, but what about the love of Henry? Simon's ambition knows no bounds. Next he might try to take the throne."

"Nonsense." She turns again. "Not only is Simon your brother-in-law, but he is also French. And, as we can hear so clearly at this moment, the French are unpopular in England."

"I wish they would stop that noise." Henry stomps over to a window and slams the shutters shut. "Shouting for Simon's head, and on what grounds? He has done nothing without my consent."

"Be grateful that they are not demanding your head, then."

Uncle Guillaume enters, newly arrived from Uncle Thomas's wedding, ready to embrace Eléonore but for the pins at her waist and sides. Henry kisses him as if he were a long-lost brother, so pleased to see his friend that he doesn't notice his somber expression.

"No one is calling for your head today, Your Grace, but they may be soon," Uncle says. "Your brother wields much influence in England."

"His purse wields much influence, you mean," Eléonore says.

"Do you think that Richard is behind this?" Henry gestures toward the window. "And over such a trifling matter?"

Uncle folds his arms over his chest. "Some say the Earl of Cornwall fancies himself the next king."

"He has always thought himself more capable of ruling," Henry says. "He has told me so many times."

Her pins removed, Eléonore steps down from the stool. "Money matters to Richard, not power. He already has the wealth of a king, without the hardships."

"As king, he would lose that wealth," Henry says. "Gascony alone would suck it like marrow from his bones."

"He claims to have lost much of his fortune already." Uncle moves to a window to look down upon the jeering crowd. "All the barons have suffered since the pope's legate arrived, demanding coins for the next campaign in Outremer."

"I would not listen to those mutterers." Henry steps before him to shutter that window, as well. "Ottobuono is a good man."

"He reminds me of a serpent," Eléonore says. "His eyes look sly, and he is always darting out his tongue."

"Like a serpent, he has a poisonous bite." Uncle reaches out a hand as if to push the shutter open again, but thinks better of it. "Let anyone refuse to pay, and he is soon hit with an interdict. Pope Gregory excommunicated Roger de Quincy, I hear."

"A penalty well deserved, no doubt," Henry says with a snort.

"Try telling that to his villeins. With the churches closed, who will bury their dead? Who will conduct their weddings? Who will baptize their infants, or perform their last rites? Lords have been murdered over less."

"Eleanor's wedding to Simon is only an excuse for rebellion," Eléonore says.

"The barons want Otto sent back to Rome, but Henry has refused. Perhaps they think Richard would comply."

"Richard would not do this to me." Henry opens the shutters again, looks out at his shouting subjects. "He can be arrogant, even avaricious, but we are brothers."

"But—haven't you heard?" Uncle stares at him. "No, I suppose not. If not for my knights, I would not have penetrated this crowd. I cannot imagine that messengers are getting through." His furrowed brow portends bad news. Eléonore clutches Henry's arm, bracing him—and herself.

"I landed at the Cinque Ports yesterday," he says. "The Earl Richard of Cornwall was there, hiring mercenaries."

Henry's jaw drops. "For what purpose?"

"To attack you, my lord. They say that Sir Richard intends to seize the crown."

"Impossible!" Henry looks as if he might be sick. "Not Richard. My God. Mutiny? And then what—imprison me in the Tower? Have me hanged? All because I didn't ask his permission before giving our sister's hand?" He looks as if he had wandered off the road spinning fancies and now surveyed a strange and bleak horizon. "If only he knew the truth. But then he might attack Simon, instead."

"He doesn't want to attack anyone," Eléonore says. "Richard isn't a warrior, remember?" Henry has told her the stories: How, as a youth, Richard shied from fencing lessons. He avoids tournaments, even as a spectator: The sight of blood sickens him. He is known not as a fighter but as a negotiator, preferring talk to battle.

"And yet he killed one of his servants a few years ago," Henry says. "Caught him in his treasury, stuffing a sack with coins. Ran him through with his sword. Richard loves money more than he loves his soul."

"Then we know what we must do."

"I do not want to fight against him, and I will not imprison him," Henry says. "Our kinship means something to *me*, at least."

"We don't need to fight Richard if he can be bought," Eléonore says. "We need only discover his price—and then, no matter how much it hurts, we must pay it."

❧ *Marguerite* ❧

A New Jerusalem

Sens, 1239

Eighteen years old

HEAVY WITH COINS and hope, Marguerite's purse thumps against her thigh as she walks. Sunlight streams through the high windows, illuminating the long aisle of the Notre Dame Cathedral. At the end waits Father Geoffrey of Beaulieu, his round face pink and sweating, his hand moist as he kisses Marguerite's ring.

"The king speaks of you with the utmost love," she says, even as she wonders which of her secrets Louis has confided in the private recesses of the confessional. "If you love King Louis, too, then you must help him."

The Father smiles, but his gaze seems out of focus, as though a competing voice clamored for his attention. She opens her purse and pours silver into his hands. "I'd like to make an offering to my name-saint, Marguerite." The patron saint of pregnancy. "Will you help me, Father?"

The clouds clear from his eyes. He looks at the coins, licks his lips. "You say the king is having difficulties? He has not spoken of it. Come, my lady. Sit in my inner sanctum and tell me how I can help."

What she asks for, sipping fine Languedoc wine with the Father amid red-curtained walls hung with gilded crosses, is not much. A few words. A nudging of Louis in her direction. A reminder that God has blessed their marriage and their marriage bed, and that the union of husband and wife carries no sin.

"He desires only to please our Lord." And his mother. She puts down her wine, its taste grown suddenly bitter.

Father Geoffrey lifts his nose. His nostrils flare. Sniffing for scandal, perhaps. Marguerite slides more coins across the table. He lowers his nose.

"Nothing pleases God more than heirs to his anointed king." He scoops the money off the table and into the pouch at his waist. "I will remind His Grace of this fact tonight, after prayers."

As she is bidding farewell, a young man in cleric's robes bursts through the door. "*Père! Père!* A most wonderful thing!" He stops at the sight of his queen and, blushing, drops to one knee. Her ladies-in-waiting are searching for her, he says.

"They are preparing for the journey even now," he says as he stands. His face gleams pinkly, as if he had been running. "The king has given orders to depart as soon as possible. May we go, Father?"

Marguerite arranges her face, hiding her surprise. "I have spent much more time here than I intended," she says. "Forgive me, Father. I must hasten away."

"But—to where, my lady? Where are you and King Louis taking us?" the priest says. Noting her blank stare, he turns to his clerk, who is hopping from foot to foot.

"To Villeneuve-l'Archevêque, Father," the youth squeals. "The Emperor of Constantinople awaits us there—with the Holy Crown of Thorns!"

———◆———

A MOUSE SQUEAKS, and then is silent—awed, perhaps, by the golden box on the table. Standing under the high arches in the chapel where she and Louis married, Marguerite can hardly breathe. It is the same with everyone; no one makes a sound—not

Louis nor his mother, not the grinning Robert, Alphonse, nor the little tyrant Charles, who hides behind his mother's skirt and sticks out his tongue at Marguerite; not Isabelle, whose protruding eyes glow like a bride's; not Thibaut, the Count of Champagne, standing scandalously close to his beloved Blanche who, for once, allows him to touch her sleeve; not the Count of Brittany, nor Hugh of Lusignan or the hundreds of nobility, clergy, monks, and nuns gathered here; not the archbishop of Sens, who prolongs the excitement with his long contemplation of the box, his hands folded before him. Why does he tarry? Marguerite longs to lunge forward and lift the lid. Will angels sing? Will the chapel fill with light? Will she be transformed at the sight of the Holy Crown of Thorns?

The archbishop chants the liturgy. He waves incense, as if the relics were not already blessed enough. The cathedral bells ring. He places his hands on the lid, then pauses, checking the seals to make sure they are intact. He, for one, revels in the drama. Marguerite grits her teeth and prays for patience. The Crown will appear in God's time. Will it be stained with Christ's blood? She imagines his anguish as the sharp thorns pierced his scalp, sending blood in rivulets down his face like the tears streaming down her cheeks now. *Our Father, who art in heaven, hallowed be thy name.* She will faint if he delays any longer. And then, as if he had heard her thoughts, the archbishop lifts the lid, oh, so slowly, revealing the box's contents. Marguerite's hands fly to her throat.

What Crown? What thorns? All she sees are a few straggly rushes, arranged in a circle on a velvet cloth. Has her eyesight left her? She looks at the others around the table, who blink and squint and frown. Thibaut shakes his head as if to clear the clouds from his vision. A laugh forms inside Marguerite's mouth. Louis will be livid. For this forgery, France paid thirteeen thousand pieces of gold.

Beside her, a cry. The queen mother, as pale as a corpse, slumps toward the floor. While Robert and Alphonse revive her, Marguerite sends a look of sympathy to Louis—who leans over the weeds with his hands clasped and his face toward the heavens, as enraptured as if Jesus were descending through the ceiling.

"I see him!" he gasps. "On the Cross, sighing and bleeding, dying for my sins. My Lord! Oh, my poor, suffering Christ."

Blanche, too, begins to moan and sway in the arms of her sons, her face wet with tears. "I see him, too!" she sobs. "He walks among us." She grabs Charles and pulls him to her breast, clutching his hair. "Don't look, darling! The wounds in his hands are bleeding, his head bleeds, his holy blood is everywhere. Mother Mary! Pray for us sinners." Around her, others weep and exclaim, crying Jesus's name and praising God, until the chapel fills with shouts, sobs, and moans of rapture.

Marguerite rocks in silent mirth, struggling to hold in her laughter. Is she the only one here who sees? The thing is a mockery. The emperor Baldwin has made a fool of France in order to replenish his empty coffers. Surely the archbishop must realize—but, no, he continues to chant his Latin liturgy and wave his scepter, his eyes closed.

Louis strips off his mantles; Robert follows. And then, as if they had planned it, they remove their shoes, their hose, their tunics and belts and rings, and fall to their knees wearing nothing but undertunics—Robert's of fine bleached linen and Louis's of goats' hair. Around the collar, Louis's skin puffs and oozes, scabrous and swollen, irritated by the hair; as he lifts his hands to the heavens, he reveals long, gashlike streaks of red on his forearms. Marguerite looks away, wishing she could disappear, while the others stare at the naked, suffering body of her husband who has, once again, put himself in the place of the Lord.

The crowd murmurs in surprise as the brothers stand. A few fall to their knees in awe: exactly the sort of encouragement Louis does not need. Beside him, Robert resembles a plucked chicken, bony legs and feet protruding from his undertunic. His face, too, glistens with pious tears, as if he had not last week dumped garbage from a high window onto the departing Count of Champagne's head, then filled the Fontainebleau castle with squeals of laughter. Thibaut,

meanwhile, clutches the White Queen's arm as though afraid she—
or he—might fall through the floor.

Extending the dubious box before him, Louis steps down from
the high altar, his expression as tragic as if the Lord's pierced and
flagellated body lay within. Robert walks with him toward the
cathedral door, his gaze shifting from the trembling gold box to
the ecstatic crowd pushing against the royal guards with arms
outstretched, striving to touch the relic. The queen mother, flanked
by Alphonse and the florid Thibaut, shoves her way in front of
Marguerite, leaving her at the rear of the procession with the
elderly Queen Isambour.

"Imagine how our poor Lord must feel," Isambour says, noticing her flush. "He died on the cross, but the glory goes to Blanche."

What can Marguerite do but walk with her head high, like the
queen she is? She turns from side to side, looking from one face to
another, but all eyes stare at the box, the barefoot king, the hysteri-
cal Blanche. Almost all eyes.

There: A youth meets her gaze. He is younger than she, not
quite a man, and richly attired in blue and gold, the colors of
Champagne. His eyes dance. He knows. Marguerite has to glance
away or else burst into laughter.

Outside, hysteria. Townspeople in linen and fine scarlet cloth;
prostitutes in their yellow hoods; mothers with their children;
beggars in rags—all jostle for a glimpse of the so-called crown,
trampling, in their frenzy, those unlucky enough to fall. The guards
swat grasping hands away from the royal family, but an old man
crawls, unnoticed, to Louis's feet and clutches one of his ankles.

A knight presses the tip of his sword against the poor man's
hand, pricking the thin skin—but in the next moment, Louis hands
the box to Robert and snatches the weapon away. The old man
cowers, arms crossed over his head. Louis tosses the sword to the
ground and kneels beside him.

"What do you need, friend?"

"I am ill, my lord. I suffer with every breath. Please help me."

Louis lays his hands on the man's head. Marguerite turns away, resisting the urge to flee this blasphemy. Instead, she steps into the royal carriage to wait for her husband, away from the nonsense a tangle of dusty weeds has inspired. Yet—how Louis shines. Marguerite hasn't seen so much life in his sleep-starved eyes since their wedding day. Soon, with Father's Geoffrey's encouragement, he may regain his vitality in other ways, too. Marguerite smooths her skirt, reddens her lips, and waits.

When the carriage door opens, Blanche folds herself into the seat. "Louis and Robert will carry the Crown to Paris—on foot," she says, smiling as proudly as if the idea were hers, which it probably was.

"They are walking? That will take more than a week." What fools the French are, as gullible as children! Marguerite might laugh except for her mother-in-law's cold stare and the realization that she must wait even longer to conceive her child.

"I don't expect to see them for two weeks. Their feet are quite tender."

"They will walk barefoot?"

"What are a few blisters compared to the pain our Lord endured on the road to Calvary?" Blanche's eyes fill with tears. "Jesus was whipped, mocked, and pushed to the ground, all while carrying his cross on his back, all while the Crown of Thorns cut into his scalp."

Marguerite looks out the window, sees Louis and Robert making their halting way down the rocky road, Louis's face alight with rapture, Robert's smile a grimace.

"The very Crown of Thorns that Louis holds in his hands today," Blanche presses.

Marguerite can hold her tongue no longer. "The crown in Louis's hands would not dent an unbaked loaf of bread, let alone draw a man's blood."

Blanche gasps. "Do you doubt the word of God?"

"I doubt the word of Baldwin. Haven't you wondered, Queen Mother? About the thorns? Our crown has none. Where are they?"

"The thorns were removed before the crown came to France,"

she says. "For safekeeping. They touched the blood of Christ, and must not float about unprotected."

"What did France purchase, then, with her silver?"

"Prestige, you silly girl. Glory. The honor of possessing the most important of our Lord's relics." Her tone softens. "Soon we will own a piece of the True Cross, as well. The Emperor agreed today to sell his fragment to France."

Marguerite knows better than to roll her eyes. Antagonizing Blanche will only cause her to tarry. "I'm sure we will be leaving soon, Queen Mother," she says. "Mustn't you hasten to your carriage?"

"I will ride with you," Blanche says. "We have matters to discuss."

"I didn't think you were interested in anything I have to say, my dear mother-in-law." Marguerite summons her sweetest tone.

"I thought we might discuss your childlessness, and France's need for an heir."

Marguerite fumbles behind her back for the door latch. Perhaps she will walk with Louis. She would rather trek barefoot to Paris than listen to Blanche's harangues. Alas, the carriage begins to move.

Blanche removes her crown and places it on the seat between them. As she speaks, she traces its points with the tips of her fingers.

"You are eighteen years of age, married five years. And still not a single pregnancy."

Marguerite looks out the window. How she longs to hurl herself out onto the road.

"Barrenness is a woman's worst fate. I do pity you." Blanche sighs. "But it must be the Lord's will. You are not as pious as M. de Flagy said. Not a good match for my Louis, I fear."

Marguerite's face grows hot. The countryside moves past at an excruciatingly slow rate. Shouting, sobbing, praying people line the road, but their noise is not, unfortunately, loud enough to drown her mother-in-law's words.

"No response from the Queen of Riposte?" Blanche smirks. "I know this must be difficult for you—but do try to consider

France's interests above your own. For the sake of our country, you must admit defeat. I sent a letter to the pope this morning, asking him to annul your marriage."

≈━◆━≈

As BLANCHE PREDICTED, Louis and Robert arrive in Paris exactly two weeks after beginning their long walk, their clothes stinking, their legs covered in filth. Robert's undertunic sags about his knees, his body having grown even thinner; Marguerite can see the shape of his skull in his sunken face. Louis's feet are cracked and swollen, yet he steps as jauntily as if he had danced on a cloud all the way home. His eyes seem to crackle with an internal fire. "Darling," he says when she greets him in the great hall. He holds out his arms to her but his eyes wander, seeking Blanche.

He smells, inexplicably, of cabbage. She deftly avoids his embrace by clasping his hands and leading him up the stairs and onto the balcony, where a ceremony is planned. Marguerite wears a saffron tunic and no jewelry except her crown, striking a balance between queenly elegance and the simplicity the occasion demands. Their audience swarms over the plaza, all the way to the Cathédrale Notre Dame de Paris, where workers building the western towers shoo the revelers from the scaffolding. Those near the palace cry out, their faces radiant and eager. Louis kisses Marguerite, evincing cheers, then lifts the box for all to see. His odor forgotten, Marguerite dimples at the warmth in his eyes. This is not the Louis she left behind in Sens. She turns to his confessor, standing just below; Father Geoffrey winks at her.

And then, when it seems the shouts cannot increase, Blanche steps onto the balcony in an undyed tunic and white wimple, her face clean of makeup. Marguerite cannot help staring: Blanche is quite old—her white paste does hide wrinkles—but still lovely. No wonder she was once renowned for her beauty. And yet she is still the same White Queen. The crowd roars; she flings out her arms to embrace her sons, pulling them to the fore—and shunting Marguerite aside.

"As mother to your most pious king, I can well imagine the Virgin Mary's sorrow as her son Jesus suffered on the cross," Blanche cries. "The Holy Crown of Thorns reminds us of her pain as well as his, endured for our sins." Marguerite presses her lips together, or else her jaw would drop. In comparing herself to the Holy Mother, Blanche has sunk to new depths. She looks down at her yellow gown, so ostentatious next to the queen mother's attire that it might as well be made of pure gold.

"My son and I purchased this Crown, and the fragment of the True Cross soon to arrive, for the many blessings they will bring to France," Blanche says. "They add to the glory of our country, and make of Paris a new Jerusalem."

A new Jerusalem! The woman is brilliant. Is this the same Blanche who railed at her over the relic's price? Now, apparently, the Crown of Thorns is the best bargain the kingdom has ever struck—and Blanche and Louis are to be thanked.

And Marguerite is diminished, shoved aside, and publicly so. Everyone saw Blanche step in front of her, and watched as Marguerite shrank back like a chastened child. In the past, the White Queen concealed her disdain behind false smiles and solicitous words, but today she shows the world that she reigns as queen, and that Marguerite is nothing.

Marguerite heads to her chambers in a blur, suppressing her tears. On her desk she finds a letter from Eléonore, announcing—oh, how cruel!—that she has given birth to a son.

We have named him Edward, after Edward the Confessor. He is a beautiful baby, strong and healthy.

Tears blur her letter of congratulations, smudging the ink. She throws the quill across the room. How triumphant Eléonore must feel! Yet, were this a contest, her sister would hold an unfair advantage: No jealous mother-in-law thwarts Elli's success. Henry's mother, Isabella of Angoulême, lives across the channel, now Countess of Lusignan. If only Blanche would move away, too.

Marguerite lies on her bed. Her future now rests in the hands of Pope Gregory—who wants more than ever to please Blanche.

His war against the Holy Roman Emperor relies on France's support. Her father's help against the Cathars means nothing to Pope Gregory now, for Papa cannot spare a single knight to fight Frederick for him. The pope will grant the White Queen's request. Toulouse will take Provence and exile her parents, or imprison them. Eléonore, disinherited, will lose what little respect she has gained in England. Sanchia and Beatrice will not marry kings; they will be fortunate to be paired with minor counts. She has failed her family utterly.

Exhausted by her tears, Marguerite falls into a deep and dreamless slumber. She awakens to a face above her own and a hand on her mouth, stifling her startled cry.

"Shhh," Louis whispers. "Make no sound, or your maids may run to awaken my mother. It is time, Marguerite! In the midst of my prayers with Father Geoffrey, the Lord spoke to me this night. Praise be to God! He is ready to bless us with heirs."

⤳ *Sanchia* ⤲

The Curse of Beauty

Aix-en-Provence, 1239

Eleven years old

RAIMOND OF TOULOUSE licks his lips. Sanchia bursts into tears. Mama frowns, but she only cries harder. "You are eleven years old—nearly a woman," Mama said as she dragged her away from her game of Fox and Geese with Beatrice. "If your sisters endured this test, so can you."

But she is not her sisters. Marguerite and Eléonore wanted to be queens. And Raimond of Toulouse is no king, but an ugly man with greedy eyes. She covers her chest with one arm but Mama shakes her head. She stares at her mother. Is this the ogre who attacked their château in Aix while Mama lay within, giving birth to Sanchia and praying for God's protection? "Toulouse frightened the wits out of Sanchia," Eléonore used to snicker.

She is not as stupid as they think. She might not be witty, but she does have wits. When Papa danced in joy over the salt mines Romeo opened, Sanchia chewed her nails. Salt is exceedingly costly, being rare. "Now everyone will want to conquer us," she fretted. Papa laughed at her, but what happened? Stupor Mundi sent troops to attack them, and the White Queen sent Toulouse to marry Sanchia. Blanche de Castille wants Provence more than ever, but she can't pay for Raimond's attacks now because her treasury is bare. The French spent all their *livres* on the Crown of Thorns and the True Cross.

She cannot marry anyone; she has told Mama this. She is already married to Jesus. She promised herself to him in a beautiful dream. No one believes her, though. Last month, she asked her parents again to let her join the convent, but Mama laughed. "Your beauty is your curse," she said. Sanchia couldn't agree more. With so many men wanting her hand, she cannot possibly hide herself away. Family comes before everything, no matter what Sanchia desires. Family, Mama said, comes first.

Romeo and Uncle Guillaume want to make a queen of her, like her sisters. But marriageable kings are scarce. For that favor, at least, she thanks God. She has visited Margi's court, and Elli's. How she would hate that life, all slippery words and watchful eyes! Queens have little time in which to play the harp, or paint landscapes, or even to pray. Privacy is only a dream. And queens may not be shy.

Nothing is shy about Raimond of Toulouse, who has brought a marriage contract even though he is already married. "I have asked the pope for an annulment," he says, picking his teeth with a long fingernail. "Twenty years is long enough to wait for a son."

Papa doubts that the pope will grant Toulouse's request, and so he signed the marriage agreement with a smile, thinking of the peace it would bring. Toulouse will stop his attacks now. In celebration, the men drank a bottle of wine. Then, wiping his mouth with his sleeve, Toulouse asked to view Sanchia.

"A man desires to see the goods before he makes the purchase," he slurred.

Now, as she stands before him, the count exclaims loudly, making her flinch, "What a beauty!" He opens his arms. "Come here, sweetheart. Let's find out if you're as soft as you look."

Sanchia whimpers. Mama steps in front of her. "Forbear from

laying hands on our daughter, I pray. You are yet a married man."

Toulouse's cheeks burn a furious red. "You dare to chastise me? By God, I could crush you all like ants."

"If you could, you would have done it by now," Mama says. She holds Sanchia's hand. "And if you were to attack us again, you would lose the prize of Provence."

Toulouse bares his dirty teeth. Sanchia's stomach churns. *Please take me to heaven now, oh please please . . .*

"I wouldn't risk this sweet treasure," he says. "We will meet again, darling, and soon." He stands and walks out of the castle.

Sanchia falls to her knees before her Papa. "Please don't make me marry him," she says. "I will die."

He pats her head. "Not to worry. You will not marry Toulouse, no matter what he thinks. And, with no more wars to drain our treasury, I will be able to amass a proper dowry for you and your husband—whomever that might be."

⤳ *Eléonore* ⤳

Sacrificial Lambs

London, 1239

Sixteen years old

$\mathcal{S}$HE RESEMBLES A sunlit cloud, Marguerite says, jealousy pinching her tone, as Eléonore turns before the mirror in her gown of creamy silk, pearls, and gold thread, and shimmering undertunic of pale saffron. She feels like a cloud, too, filled with light, glowing about the edges. Her skin tingles; her blood hums in her veins.

Today is the most important day of her life. Moments from now, the entire kingdom—indeed, all the world—will honor her. At last, after three years of doubt, the dark cloud under which she married Henry will roll away. The barons will cease their mumurs against her. The taint of illegitimacy will fade, and the Count of Ponthieu will seek another match for his daughter Joan. Eléonore has given the king an heir, the kingdom a prince. She is, at last, England's undisputed queen.

"Are the pearls in my hair too much adornment? I hope Edward doesn't cry during the service—he has been quite fussy lately. Margi, where are my slippers? No, these are gold. I want the white ones. Help me with this clasp? My hands are shaking."

"Breathe," Marguerite says, sounding like their mother. Uncle Thomas would have brought Mama today, but Papa has fallen ill again, his heart a clanging bell under the strain of Toulouse's newly redoubled attacks. Marguerite, for all her efforts, has not been able to stop them. Until she gives King Louis an heir, she has no power in France. In spite of herself, a frisson of triumph trills through Eléonore at the sight of her sister's face drawn, like a hound's, to a jealous point.

"Afraid the Count of Ponthieu will come charging in again?" Marguerite says. "He can't harm you now." So why does she quiver on the walk to the cathedral as if the devil awaited within?

Her ladies—Marguerite, Eleanor de Montfort, Margaret Biset, and the countess Dame Maud of Mortimer—surround and guide her, and a retinue of knights guards her (or tries to) from the crush of villeins and townspeople eager, it seems, to tear her apart. A woman's hand snatches at her skirt, trying to tear off its pearls. Another grasps her hair, knocking her crown askew. "Knights! Are you sleeping?" shrieks the Dame Maud as she knocks the offenders aside with her fist. In fact, the knights are too few to stanch this roil. Eléonore struggles for breath as the crowd presses in until, giving up all semblance of dignity, she lifts up her skirts and runs. My God! Are these the same Londoners who, only a year ago, screamed for hers and Henry's heads because they'd married the king's sister to a Frenchman? How fickle is the love of the English.

At the cathedral door the bishop of Winchester waits to bless her, his smile as calm as if only the two of them stood on the stair. He hands her a candle and spreads a piece of purple velvet at her feet on which to kneel, then sprinkles her with holy water. "Lo, children are an heritage of the Lord, and the fruit of the womb is his reward," he intones.

She is blessed: No bishop need tell her this. Already she gives thanks every day for Henry. He has won her heart completely with his goodness and his keen intelligence—and with his love. When she miscarried their first child, he comforted her, telling her that God had another, better soul waiting to be born to the throne. And yet, had she never conceived another, he would not have set her aside. "I will never forsake you, my dear," he said. His words return to her now, as she steps into the splendor that he has commanded in her honor.

The cathedral is a flickering fairyland, alight with the flames of so many candles that it looks as if the night sky had been turned upside down and the stars shaken into it. White silk drapes the ceiling and walls, fairly glowing in all that light. A choir of monks sings a haunting melody; young novices chime bells. Frankincense from Outremer exudes its expensive perfume of spice and pine. The women follow Eléonore through the crowded cathedral, nobles dropping to their knees as they pass, to the cloth-draped Offertory table at the front of the chapel. Marguerite presents a miniature of the madonna in gold, and the others fill the table with equally exquisite gifts: an illuminated psalter, acquired from a monastery in Northumbria; a child's rattle, encrusted in jewels; a basket of ripe fruit, sending up the fragrance of tangerines like a breeze.

They await the celebration of the mass on a cushioned pew. Across the room, Henry's brow furrows and his jaw tics as he listens to Uncle Thomas. His face reddens. His drooping eye twitches. What could Uncle say to anger Henry so? Perhaps he has decided to ally Flanders with France instead of England. Henry covets his county as a launching point for an invasion of Normandy—which will never happen, of course, until his barons agree to pay the costs.

After the mass, the women step back across the lawn to the palace, where a feast awaits. "The king looks strangely unhappy for a man who has just sired an heir to the throne," the Dame Maud says, arching her brows at Eleanor de Montfort as if she were the reason why.

Eleanor takes no heed. She scans the crowd for Simon, due any moment from Rome, where he went to ask Pope Gregory to free her from her chastity vow and legitimize their marriage. Whether the pope agreed no one knows, for Simon sent no messengers ahead of him.

"To sway the pope, one needs money," Eleanor says. Her laugh sounds forced. "We have none, not until Henry gives to me my marriage dower." Which, Eléonore knows, is nearly two years late—but, thanks to the intransigent barons, Henry's coffers are as empty as Simon's.

Minstrels sing St. Godric's "Virgin Saint Mary" and servants have just presented her favorite dish, a salmon and fruit pie, when a herald announces the arrival of Simon de Montfort. Eléonore nearly leaps up from her seat, then feels Marguerite's eyes on her and settles quickly down again. She cannot help staring at him, however, as he enfolds his wife in his arms, looking more handsome than ever after six months away. Eléonore had almost forgotten the flecked blue of his eyes, like robin's eggs, but his smile has haunted her dreams. He meets her gaze as he kisses Eleanor's hair, spurring an erratic knocking in her chest.

Eleanor leads Simon to the royal table, where he kneels in homage before his king and queen. Pleasantries form on Eléonore's lips but they drop away at the sight of Henry's scowl and his face on the verge of bursting into flame.

"I bring good news from Rome," Montfort says. "The pope has released my wife, your sister, from her vow of chastity."

A cheer arises from the surrounding tables and Eleanor Montfort, her face shining, embraces her husband again. Henry's shade of red brightens even more. "At what price?" he snarls.

The room grows quiet. Simon clears his throat.

"Forgive me, Your Grace, I do not understand your question. Our son, your nephew, is now legitimized—"

"At what price?" Henry says, more loudly this time.

"I—I paid what was necessary to secure your sister's future—"

"Her future? As the wife of an impoverished foreigner?"

A maelstrom of questions spins and whirls in Eléonore's mind, chief among them being *why Henry is so angry?*; quickly followed by *must he confront Simon here and now?* This is supposed to be her day. And, when did Henry start to use the word "foreigner" to describe Simon? He sounds like his barons, who use the word to describe Eléonore—while wearing a sneer. It is as if Englishness were everything—in spite of the horrible weather, the bad food, the pasty complexions and the crude, garbled language.

Simon's jaw drops open at the insult, but his wife appears undaunted.

"Henry, we are here to celebrate your queen and your new son," she says. "Why don't we discuss this tomorrow?"

"Because we wish to discuss it now." He never moves his glare from Simon de Montfort's bewildered face. "How much did you pay, Simon? We demand to know!"

"Stupidity," Simon mumbles.

Henry pounds the tabletop with his fist, clattering the dishes, making Eléonore jump. "Speak so that we can hear you!"

"I said that His Grace would not want the details of our agreement to be made public. I am loath to displease him."

"And what of displeasing your king? Is that not a concern?"

Eléonore touches Henry's arm, hoping her soft touch will calm him. "Perhaps your sister is right," she says softly. "Let this wait until another time."

"If you want to please us," Henry says to Simon, "you will give us two thousand silver marks."

"Henry." Eleanor Montfort's tone is stern. "You know we do not have it. We are still waiting for my dower from you."

"And you will wait even longer now that your husband owes us this enormous sum."

Simon snorts and shakes his head, curls his lips. Murmurs ripple through the hall. Henry's eyes bulge, his pupils now tiny points. He bares his teeth. Eléonore cannot tear her eyes from him. Soon, he will be frothing at the mouth. She must find a way to calm him.

"Something amuses you, Sir Simon?" the king says with a sneer.

"Forgive me, Your Grace." Simon bows his head, hiding his scorn. "I do not recall incurring any debt from you. I think the opposite is the case. My wife has waited nearly two years for the dower that you promised upon our wedding."

"Wedding? There was no wedding, only a secret marriage made in haste to avoid scandal!" Henry shouts. Dread gathers like storm clouds in her belly. Henry must be stopped before he says too much—but how? In their years together she has not found an effective remedy for his temper. "You seduced our sister under our nose, with one goal—to increase your wealth and stature."

Through the hall, gasps fly upward like shot arrows. Eleanor Montfort's face turns as red as Henry's. Under the table, Eléonore clasps her fingers together so tightly she winces against the pain.

"We risked everything to cover up your indiscretion," Henry rages. "We married you in secret, knowing it would incur the wrath of our brother"—Richard of Cornwall, dark and clenched, glowers from the front table—"and our barons, who would have wed her to one of their sons. And how do you repay us?"

Simon drops to one knee and slaps his hand to his chest. "With my loyalty and my love, my lord. As ever."

"Is it loyalty, or treason, to promise that the king will guarantee your debts? Because the Count of Flanders brings word that you have done so."

Simon knits his brows at Uncle, in the seat of honor beside the king.

"King Louis of France has sent me to collect the two thousand silver marks you borrowed," Uncle Thomas says. "Didn't you swear that King Henry would repay it?"

Simon's smile quavers as he rises. "Yes, I did make the pledge. But you told me, Your Grace, that you would give any amount for our cause."

"I never did."

"Don't you remember?" Simon sounds as guileless as a pleading boy. "You predicted that the pope of Rome would command a high price to legitimize our marriage—as, indeed, he did—and you vowed that England would pay it."

"After extorting it from your lords, no doubt!" Roger de Quincy stands, his large moustache twitching. "Your Grace, I demand an explanation."

"Treasonous lies," Henry says, and orders the Earl of Winchester to sit. "Sir Simon, I command you to the Tower this day. You will remain there until you pay your debt." Eléonore jumps up, losing her composure at last.

"By God's head, let us have peace," she says to Henry. Tears fill her eyes as she gazes at Simon, whose complexion has lost all color. "As your queen, it is my right to intervene. I beg clemency for our brother-in-law, my lord. On this, my special day, I pray you will honor my request."

Her voice pleads, but her eyes warn him. He has already gone too far. Now is the time to relent.

Henry drops his head, suddenly sheepish. "As our queen wishes."

"Then we will leave you to celebrate in peace." Eleanor Montfort smoothes her skirt. "First, however, I must make a correction."

"You need say nothing, sister. You are the innocent, the victim of this treasure-seeker's lust and ambition."

"No, brother, you are wrong." She lifts her chin and turns to face the room.

"Simon did not seduce me," she announces. "I was not an innocent young girl when we met, but an experienced widow. I fell in love with him the moment we met, and have loved him for years." She turns to Henry, who is now the slack-jawed one. "I seduced Simon, and not the other way around."

She takes her husband's arm. They stand for a moment like statues, looking straight ahead, avoiding the myriad eyes upon them. Then, together, they march out of the great hall, mount their horses and gallop away, leaving Westminster in a cloud of dust and exclamations.

<hr/>

*S*CHEMERS—THERE ARE SO many—watch and whisper as she nibbles the meat from the bones of a lark. Coming to Simon's defense did not endear her to the nobility. Nor did it help her to do so, for he is gone, and her dear sister-in-law, too, leaving Eléonore alone to face the English wolves and their fangs dripping with insinuation.

"You must be furious," Marguerite whispers. But she is wrong. The old Eléonore would be fuming—but she and Henry cannot *both* stomp their feet like little children, or they will accomplish nothing.

She sets down her bird and wipes her fingers on the tablecloth.

"He is passionate, my Henry." She smiles, remembering last night, his hot mouth, his hard body. "I would despise a dull man."

"But you're in love with Simon."

She arches her brows at her sister. "As you have seen, we have our share of scandal in this court. Let's not add to it with fruitless speculation." She lowers her voice. "It is Richard whom I wish to discuss."

"Your husband's brother? Elli! You have managed to shock even me."

"Not for myself. Really, Margi! For Sanchia."

Richard has taken the cross, she tells her, and plans to leave for the Holy Land next spring with Thibaut. "We must tell Mama to invite him to Provence on his way. But—we mustn't tell her why." Richard is too recently a widower, and, faced with Mama's ambition, would close himself like a tortoise against her.

"Richard of Cornwall, campaigning in Outremer?" Marguerite smirks. "But he will ruin his silks and pointed shoes, and muss his careful hair."

"Not so careful these days. His wife's death has left him in disarray, not to mention despondency. I'm sure he hopes to die in Jerusalem so he can join her in heaven."

"After a long purification in purgatory. You know what they say about rich men and the eyes of needles."

"He does love money. And beautiful women. Isabel Marshal was extraordinary. But she would have faded like an old bloom next to Sanchia."

"Like that old bloom, Sanchia would fall apart in Toulouse's hands," Marguerite says. "You and I must save her, Elli, I agree. I can't imagine what Papa was thinking."

He was thinking of stopping Toulouse's attacks, and nothing more. He told their *maire* that the marriage would never happen, that Toulouse would never get his annulment. But instead of rejecting his petition, the pope has called for a hearing. If he grants Toulouse his wish, Sanchia will be his, and Provence will be free of his tyranny at last. Sanchia, however, will suffer for the rest of her life—a sacrificial lamb, like her beloved Christ.

Back in Eléonore's chambers, the sisters plan. First, they send a letter to Pope Gregory, asking him to deny Toulouse's annulment request. *We protest his casting out a long-faithful wife simply because she has produced a daughter instead of a son*, their letter reads. *Let not the vows of marriage, sanctified by the Church, be forsaken lightly.*

Next, Eléonore arranges for Richard to sail to Outremer from her father's port in Marseille, and asks him to deliver a package to Sanchia on the way. "Make certain you place it in her hands," she tells him. "There are secrets in these letters, between sisters, that no other eyes should see."

It will be a perfect match. Sanchia, who would rather marry a toad than the Count of Toulouse, will swoon over the charming Richard. And, with the Earl of Cornwall's wealth to protect her family, Toulouse will never attack Provence again. Everyone will be happy except Raimond of Toulouse—which makes the sisters' plan even more delectable.

⇥ *Sanchia* ⇤

The Company of Young Girls

Marseille, 1240

Twelve years old

SANCHIA PRESSES HER knees into the floor. If only it weren't so smooth. She wants sharp stones to cut her flesh, so that God might take pity on her.

I want only to serve you. Release me from these marriage bonds, O Lord. Send me to a convent, I pray, or take me to you now. The pope has heard Raimond of Toulouse's plea for annulment. "A very effective speech," Romeo said when he returned from Rome, making Sanchia's heart skip not one beat, but two. Making her faint, almost. She thought she might be dying of fright. She hoped for it. But, no. The Lord wants her to live. He must have a purpose in mind for her. Is she selfish to wish for death instead of marriage to Toulouse? *Forgive me, O Lord. I submit to your will.*

As she wipes her tears and struggles to her feet, Mama appears. An English visitor has come—with gifts from Eléonore to be given only to her. An hour later, freshly bathed and wearing a gown of yellow linen sewn with pearls, Sanchia stands in the great hall before the brother of the English king. His eyes move like dancers, now on her face, now on her hair, now on her bosom. When he hands her a package from Eléonore, he leans in as if she were a fragrant flower.

"The queen has sent letters, and a fabric embroidered with roses. To match the roses in your cheeks, no doubt," he says. He leans closer to hear her stammered thanks. Heat rises from his skin. His mouth looks soft and full, like a woman's. He smells of oranges.

He smiles at Mama, who blushes like a girl. "Will your lovely daughter dine with us tonight?" Sanchia's stomach forms knots.

Mama's laugh breaks like a bubble. "She's only a child, Lord Cornwall—too young for adult conversation."

"I see." He crinkles his eyes at Sanchia. "Perhaps a dance later? After the meal."

"Mama, I am not a baby," she says as her *maire* escorts her to the nursery. "Elli and Margi both married kings when they were twelve."

"Age means one thing to one girl, and something else to another," Mama says. She lifts her eyebrows. "Did you desire to dine with the Earl of Cornwall? What would you talk about? He is a worldly man, while you fear your own shadow."

"We could talk about Outremer," she says. How she would love to travel to Jerusalem, and walk in the Lord's footsteps.

"What do you know about Outremer?" Mama says, frowning. "If you had tended to your lessons, you might have something interesting to say. As it is, you would only bore him with your ignorance."

She leaves her in the nursery and hurries back to the great hall, to take for herself the seat that the Earl of Cornwall offered to Sanchia.

Mama is so witty and charming, everyone says so. But soon a servant comes to the nursery to fetch Sanchia back to the great hall. She hopes she will not be asked to perform for their guest. Margi used to entertain on the vielle, making Mama proud—but, as Mama says, she is not Margi. She plays the harp only for herself, and for the Lord. When others listen, her fingers turn to sticks.

In the hall, a minstrel performs the Kalenda Maya—again. Sanchia can almost hear Mama telling the earl that "the great troubadour Raimbaut de Vaqueiras performed this song in this very hall." She always says this as proudly as if Raimbaut had written the song for her, instead of for a different Beatrice. But Mama is almost as fanciful as Eléonore sometimes.

She awaits Sanchia on the floor, wearing a smile that looks painted on. The Earl Richard has asked again to dance with Sanchia, she says. "Neither your Papa nor I can hold his attention for long. He wants only the company of young girls today."

"But—what will I say to him?" She tries to pull her hand from her mother's grasp. Mama tightens her grip.

"Do you think he requested you for conversation?" Mama says with a laugh.

As they step up to the table, Papa is offering to escort the earl to the shrine of Saint Giles for blessings before he embarks on his journey. The earl sits up and fixes his eye on her, as if he were a bird and she were a wriggling worm. She steps back, behind her mother, but Mama nudges her forward.

"Our daughter is exceedingly shy," Mama says.

"The Queen of England's sister, shy?" He grins. Sanchia cringes. Why must everyone compare her to her sisters?

"Her bashfulness confounds us all," Mama says. Her voice slurs a little, as if she needed a nap. She holds out her goblet for more wine. "Her sisters excel at riposte and debate."

"And yet her beauty outshines theirs," the earl says. He chases her eyes with his, as if they were playing cat-and-mouse.

"Do not be afraid of me," he says. His voice sounds warm, and her arms feel cold in this large hall. "Forgive my boldness, but you remind me, somehow, of Isabel, the beloved wife I so recently lost." His voice cracks, as though he might cry. The Lord has sent him, she thinks, for her to console. "I would derive comfort from a dance, if you would do me the honor."

Moments later she twirls in the earl's arms, blushing and tongue-tied and avoiding his stares until, at last, he starts to talk about the Promised Land. "I leave tomorrow, not knowing whether sickness, disease, imprisonment, or death awaits me," he says. "Nor did I care, until today."

"May Our Lord guide and protect you," she says. "I will remember you in my prayers."

She whirls away, looking up at her parents. Watching them watch her, and knowing what their smiles say. Romeo watches, too, and whispers to Papa. She can read his lips in part. "Not a king," he is saying. "Very wealthy."

The dance finished, the earl lingers on the floor with her. "You must not marry the Count of Toulouse," he says. "Wait for me. I will come back for you."

He tucks her hand into the crook of his arm and returns her to the table. His smile billows like a sail. "Your daughter has captured my heart," he tells Papa. "I would take her away with me, if I could."

Mama, pinkening as though she were the object of Cornwall's desire, murmurs that, as the earl surely knows, Sanchia is engaged to Raimond of Toulouse.

Richard of Cornwall laughs. "That eunich, who hides his inability to sire sons beneath the skirts of his wife?" Papa frowns, having fathered only girls. The earl slaps his back. "Leave Toulouse to me, my lord. If it is a breeder he desires, Pope Gregory will find him another. I would make your daughter my most prized possession, the envy of every woman from Ireland to Outremer."

In the nursery, Sanchia walks in circles, wondering what has happened. She prayed to be released from marriage, yet now another suitor vies for her hand. "Is anyone listening?" she whispers. And then rushes to the chapel to fall on her knees and beg forgiveness for her moment of doubt until her voice becomes a rasp and no one can hear her at all.

⟶ *Marguerite* ⟵

The Jaws of Death

Paris, 1240

Nineteen years old

To bear a child, it is said, is to pass through the jaws of death—as if death were like Jonah's whale, waiting to swallow a woman at the moment of her life-giving. But death is no passive creature. On the day that Marguerite bears her long-wished-for child, death is a monster ripping her with ruthless claws. Death seizes her like the teeth of a lion and shakes her, splintering her thoughts. Hands pull the infant from her body but later she will remember only her screams, said to send horses stampeding through the city. "Call the queen mother," Gisele says, but Marguerite moans for Louis, her only friend in this cold place. His hand soothes her hot brow; his prayers gather her back to herself.

Then she hears the monster speak, and its voice is a woman's. "Louis! Are you here yet again? The Emperor of Constantinople has brought the fragment of Our Lord's cross. You must come at once. Come now, Louis. He is waiting. You can do nothing here, anyway."

She feels his fingers slip away, as her life wants to do. "No!" she cries, and opens her eyes to see Blanche plucking Louis from her bed. Marguerite's shout—really a feeble croak, although it seems to her that she snarls like a tigress—goes unheeded, although Louis turns to her, hesitant. Marguerite summons her strength.

"Mother-in-law, why are you here?" she wails. Blanche's eyes, red-rimmed against the white of her makeup, stare as if Marguerite were a ghost. "Haven't you done enough harm?"

"She is delirious," Blanche says. "Her life is in God's hands now. Come, darling. The business of your kingdom awaits." Louis kisses Marguerite's hand and lays it across her chest as though she had already left this world.

"Hateful woman! Murderess! Deceiver!" Blanche, both hands grasping Louis's arm, urges him out the door. "Where is your Christian love? You have kept my husband from me for four years, and now you take him again, in the hour of my trial. Why? Are you jealous? Do you want him for yourself?"

The room buzzes with murmurs. My God, how many have come to watch her die? No—not that—they came for a birth. Her baby . . .

"She is delirious," Blanche says again.

"And yet she speaks the truth," Gisele murmurs. She slips her hand into Marguerite's.

"You accused me of barrenness, when you are the empty one," Marguerite says to Blanche. "Louis! Please don't go, or I will die."

Blanche never turns around, but Louis does. She imagines, for a moment, that he will rush back to her side and grasp both her hands in his own, forsaking his mother at last. Instead, he seems unable to choose between them, at least at first. His eyes look to Blanche, beseeching, apologetic. She turns on one heel and marches from the room. Only then does he slowly—hesitantly—return to her bed.

"How is our child, my lord?" she asks when he has sat beside her again. "Is he well?"

He heaves a great sigh. His mouth sags at the corners. "What, is something amiss?" Marguerite's voice rises. "Oh, God, no!"

"All is well, my lady." Gisele's soft voice soothes her even as Louis's eyes well with tears. "Your baby suckles at the nurse's teat, as healthy as can be."

"Praise be to God, then." Marguerite squeezes Louis's hand. "Have you seen him, my lord? Is he a wondrous prince?"

"You have borne me a girl," he says, his mouth tight with the effort of smiling.

"A girl!" A sweet ache spreads through her bones. She lifts her gaze to Gisele. "I want to see her."

"I will go and fetch her now, my lady."

"You are disappointed," she says to Louis. A tear slips down his cheek. Marguerite squeezes his hand again, thinking to console him, but no words will come. A boy would have been Louis's, but a girl is all hers. At last, someone for her to love in this friendless court.

A baby's cry rings through the castle, the sweetest song ever to Marguerite's ears. She feels a warm rush in her breasts and then sees, in Gisele's arms, a perfect little babe with a head full of dark down. "Sweet darling," she murmurs, drawing her baby close. The infant clutches at her mother's breast with greedy hands and opens her mouth like a bird's.

"My lady, we have a wet nurse for that," Gisele says as Marguerite tries to latch the baby onto her nipple.

"Excellent! Have her come and show me how to do this." Then, as her baby suckles, she gazes into her bright eyes, thanking God and the saints for her good fortune. Her love is a river of milk, rushing through her blood and into the body of this perfect little being. Even the brisk step of Blanche reentering the room cannot stop the flow.

"Your country bumpkin upbringing is showing again," she drawls. "How crude, to bare your breast before God and all!"

"But see how beautiful she is, Queen Mother," Marguerite says. Blanche's appraising eye remains cold. Marguerite casts about for some way to appease her. The White Queen's affection will be crucial to her daughter's happiness.

"Babies all look like rats at this age," Blanche sniffs. "And France still lacks an heir to the throne."

"I see no resemblance to rats, but to me—for she has my dark hair, as you can see—and to you. See how blue her eyes are!"

"All babies are born with blue eyes." Yet she moves a little closer to the bed. Marguerite slips her finger into her baby's mouth to detach her from her nipple, then holds her out for the queen mother's inspection.

"But hers are especially blue—the very shade of her *grand-mère*'s eyes. Would you like to see for yourself?" Blanche stiffens as if she might refuse, but how could she with her son looking on? Then, as she folds the baby into her arms, the child belches and spits a stream of watery white milk onto the queen mother's gown.

Gisele gasps. "Let me get a towel for you, my lady. Oh, my, what a bad girl to spit up on your *grand-mère*!"

"Those are bad manners, indeed," Blanche says. But she speaks in a cooing tone, and tickles her granddaughter under the chin. "We will have to teach you better, won't we? Yes, we will! Yes, yes, yes, little— What have you named her?"

"We would have named a son Louis," Louis says. "But a girl? We had not even thought of it."

"I had," Marguerite says. "Of course, the two of you would need to agree."

"You're not going to name her Eléonore, I hope." Blanche's lips twist as if the name made her mouth hurt. "Sister or not, she is the Queen of England—our enemy. They are preparing even now to invade our lands."

"I desire not to honor England, but France," Marguerite says. She takes her girl back into her arms, strokes her soft cheek with the back of her finger. "With your permission, Queen Mother, I would name her Blanche."

———◆———

*M*ARGUERITE BLINKS HER eyes, wondering if she has fallen asleep on the long ride to Saumur and now dreams of barons carrying mattresses and chairs from the castle and tossing them like refuse into wagons outdoors. As her carriage draws closer, she begins to laugh. Not barons, but servants perform the task of clearing out the castle for Louis's brother Alphonse. And yet—is this a dream? A man missing all his teeth wears a tunic of red silk embroidered with gold lions as he ties a rope across the bulging wagon's cargo; a boy wearing a green-and-yellow-striped mantle lined with vair runs into and out of the stone château, dragging the valuable cape on the ground as he helps other exquisitely dressed servants load trunks, tapestries, carpets, clothing, candlesticks, plates, cups of gold and silver, jewels, and other items. These wagons, Louis says, leave today for the Earl Richard of Cornwall's castle at Wallingford, in England. The items, including the clothing on the servants' backs, belong to the earl—who, when he left for Outremer a month ago, counted the castle as his own, as well.

"He will be furious," Louis says with a grin. "But by the time he returns, Alphonse will possess Poitou. Lord Cornwall cannot regain it without a battle, which he will never wage, not with his baby-soft hands."

Such is the Earl of Cornwall's reward for doing the Lord's work in Outremer. Louis may be right. Richard would not go to war over Poitou, no matter how outraged he might feel. Henry and Eléonore, on the other hand, will be furious. They will certainly amass an army to retaliate. King John let the French take Normandy without so much as a whimper of protest; Henry, still ashamed of his father's inaction, will certainly fight for Poitou, tiny and insignificant though it be.

Does Eléonore know what is happening today? Louis intends to knight his brother Alphonse and to name him as the new Count of Poitou. The celebratory feast will cost twice as much as hers and Louis's wedding, for he and his mother intend to display France's wealth and power to all the world.

The urge to write to her sister nags like an itch between Marguerite's shoulder blades, insistent yet impossible to satisfy. If only she had someone in this court with whom to talk—someone who could advise her, whom she could trust with her confidences.

I beseech you, Virgin Mother, send me a friend. She cannot even write to her mother for advice, for who would deliver her letter without reading it and reporting to Blanche? Turning to Eléonore is, of course, out of the question. But—no matter. Word of this transgression will reach Westminster soon enough. Marguerite hopes her sister will know that she had nothing to do with it.

Perhaps Blanche desires a war with England. She certainly has gone out of her way to insult King Henry's mother. Isabella and her husband Hugh de Lusignan are Count and Countess of La Marche, an area encircled by Poitou. Whereas Henry, a king, was Isabella's lord before, she now must pay homage to Alphonse, a mere count. "I am a former Queen of England," she has been heard to say. "I bend my knee to no one."

"That harlot? She has bent both knees for lesser men than my son," Blanche says with a coarse laugh as they step into the castle. Marguerite wishes she would speak discreetly. Servants talk, and if Henry hears her insults against his mother, he will be even more inclined to attack. As Queen Consort of France, Marguerite does hold some power. She must use it to prevent a war, if she can.

Her first opportunity comes very soon. While she and Blanche sit in the baths, having the dust of their journey sponged from their bodies, Gisele enters with an announcement: Hugh and Isabella have arrived, and request an audience with the King and Queen of France.

Marguerite stands, splashing water onto the floor. "Sit down," Blanche says. She waves her hand languidly. "Our journey has been long, while they live a short ride away from here. It will not harm them to wait until we have refreshed ourselves."

Then, after their bath, Blanche yawns. She must have a nap. Go, Marguerite says, seeing her chance to avoid trouble. She will greet the count and countess herself. Blanche, however, commands her chamberlain to see them to their rooms—with a message that the queen will not receive them today. Marguerite wants to argue, but she cannot in the presence of servants.

"It is my place, as mother to the French king, to greet the

English king's mother," Blanche says. "I will receive her in my own time. But I feel a headache coming, and I need to lie down. The countess will have to wait until tomorrow for her audience with me."

No, she will not, Marguerite decides.

"I hear that Queen Isabella is much agitated by your refusal to receive her," her confessor, Guillaume de Saint-Pathus, says as he escorts her to the feasting tent. "She is known for her passionate temper, and may not be easily soothed."

Marguerite intends to try. When she meets Queen Isabella today, she will apologize for the delay and invite her to her chambers after the day's festivities. If, by doing so, she angers the White Queen, so be it. Queen Isabella must know that one of them, at least, respects her person and her position.

At the head table, Marguerite watches as the palace lawn fills with nobles and villeins come to honor the new count. Isabella is not among them. The great barons Humbert of Beaujeu, Enguerrand of Coucy, and Archibald of Bourbon enter with their wives, all bedecked in colorful silks, flanked by rows of knights, and accompanied by fanfare. Beside her, Louis wears a shimmering tunic in the blue he loves with gold fleur-de-lis, and mantles of purple and red, lined with mink—as well as an ugly cap of plain cotton.

"The cap is incongruous, don't you think?" she says as he sits. "You are the king." And she is the queen. Has Louis forgotten both their places?

"It pleases the Lord for us to humbly serve." On his plate lies a single piece of coarse brown bread.

Asceticism seems out of place here. With the money spent on this feast, she and Louis could feed everyone in France for a year. Servants rush about with platters bearing the sweetest of fruits and the choicest of meats—including, at the head table, peacocks skinned and roasted, then re-dressed in their feathers of brilliant blue, their tails spread like beautiful fans behind them. The aromas of imported, costly spices—cinnamon and mace, galangal and cardamom—swirl through the air. Musicians perform in clusters—inside the tent, which is so vast that the notes from one group fade before they can clash with others, and outside, where jongleurs and acrobats and dancers flip and twirl and spin in dizzying motion. Beyond them, on the green, knights practice for the afternoon jousting tournament. Like a stream reflecting the hues of spring, the guests flow past the table in their brilliant finery, come to pay homage to Alphonse. Most opulently dressed of all—even more so than Louis—is Thibaut, not only Count of Champagne but also, now, King of Navarre, glowing from head to toe in shades of purple—and pouting to find his beloved Blanche absent from the festivities.

"Never fear, cousin," Louis says, scratching his chest, always itching from his goat's-hair shirt. "You know Mama adores a fête. Nothing would keep her away today."

Indeed. Before Thibaut turns away, the trumpets' blare announces the entrance of the Queen of France—a tribute they have already paid to Marguerite. The gathering sinks to its knees as Blanche makes a truly royal entrance, rustling in silk and diamonds. Marguerite can only marvel at the quick recovery from her debilitating headache.

"My lady, I wrote many poems in your honor while I was in Palestine," Thibaut gushes when Blanche stops for his kiss. At least he accomplished something in Outremer besides losing every battle, and most spectacularly: fifty-seven of his knights captured, many from France. He should be in Palestine now, working for their release, but he ran away, instead, leaving Richard of Cornwall to clean up after him. The earl arrived to find the expedition in ruins, a truce with the Saracen sultans begun but never finished, and the men of France and its surrounding counties locked away and in chains. In Thibaut's absence, Richard negotiated a pact with the sultans and freed the French prisoners. *Be forewarned,* Eléonore wrote. *Richard will expect a reward from King Louis.*

And how prettily Cornwall will be paid for his efforts! Marguerite has said nothing to Louis or Blanche about the debacle; as far as she can tell, Thibaut hasn't mentioned it, either. As a simpering minstrel sings the King of Navarre's new song, Marguerite imagines the uproar to come. See how Thibaut struts, the valiant warrior! Meanwhile, the real hero can expect a slap in the face when he returns home.

A pair of dark eyes among Thibaut's knights catches her gaze, and the face of a youth so familiar, she almost returns his smile. His look is so intent, he seems to read her thoughts. But—who is he? The answer whispers itself but she misses it amid the song of Thibaut's yearning to hold his "Lady" in his arms.

When the last notes of the minstrel's flute have faded, Thibaut bows to his Lady and then, with a flourish of his hand, to Marguerite. He has not forgotten her, "the fairest daisy of them all," he says. He turns to the youth.

"May I introduce Sir Jean de Joinville," Thibaut says, "my seneschal, as was his father, and a most talented wielder of sword and lance. He will compete in my lady's honor today, as your champion."

"And please accept my offer to serve you at table," the young man says. "Your every wish would be my desire."

He kneels before her and kisses her ring, and she remembers: this is the boy who, in the Sens cathedral, shared her amusement over the so-called Crown of Thorns and the hysteria it inspired. He is a boy no more, but a tall and confident young man with soft brown hair and eyes the color of honey. Heat falls over her like a shower of sparks as he climbs to the royal table to pour water into her cup.

"Pouring water seems a tedious task for an accomplished knight," she says.

"The King of Navarre exaggerates my martial prowess. I have never competed in the joust before today."

"Some champion you will prove to be, then."

"I hear that you prefer poetry to tournaments, anyway."

She looks at him askance. "*You* are not going to warble now about your love for some unattainable 'Lady,' I hope."

"*Au contraire*. I have instead fashioned a response to the King of Navarre's verse. For your ears only."

He leans in close, ostensibly to pour wine into her water, and murmurs:

Sir, you have done well
To gaze on your beloved;
Your fat and puffy belly
Would prevent you reaching her.

Her delight peals like a bell through the tent, attracting startled glances, for who has heard her laugh since she arrived in Paris? For this alone the young knight deserves a token: her favorite necklace, a shell cross on a silver chain, will be his reward. Wanting to escape the curious glances of the gossiping court, she hurries up the stairs to her chambers to retrieve the gift—but is stopped by murmurs from inside a darkened room.

"Please, darling, once more before I die. I risked my life in Palestine; doesn't that demonstrate my worthiness to you?"

"You left our knights for an Englishman to rescue. That demonstrates nothing but ineptitude. And do not call me 'darling.'" It is Blanche's voice. Marguerite holds her breath.

"What more must I do to prove my love? My poems in your honor are sung throughout the land. I even killed for your sake."

"Hush! Thibaut, I told you never to speak of that again."

"What, do you fear we will be heard? The entire hall feasts on stuffed peacock, while I wish only to feast on your charms."

"Stop! Thibaut, unhand me at once."

"I beg you to cease this terrible abuse. Why did you mislead me so, even beguiling me to kill your husband, if you never wanted my love?"

"Be quiet, you simpleton! Do you want to hang?"

"You wanted to rule France, and you have done it thanks to me. And how have you repaid me? With utter coldness. But oh, my love! It only makes me desire you more."

"I have had enough."

"But where are you going, my darling?"

"To rejoin the feast before you send us both to the gallows."

Marguerite flees back to the great hall so lightly her feet barely touch the floor, loath to be discovered spying on their tête-à-tête. She barely tastes the food placed before her, grits her teeth against the chatter and the clank of dishes and cups and the constant whine of the music all drowning out the remembered voices of Blanche and Thibaut and her own thoughts swirling and spinning like leaves in a storm.

The rumors about Blanche are true. She deflected them so cleverly all those years ago with her dramatic appearance before the barons' council, when she yanked off her tunic and stood practically naked to prove that she was not pregnant. In their astonishment, they forgot that she was also accused of conspiring to kill her husband. In the midst of the king's siege of the rebellious city of Avignon, Thibaut departed with his knights and foot soldiers, saying they had served their obligatory forty days. King Louis VIII died two months later, supposedly of dysentery—but some speculated that Thibaut had poisoned his wine before he left for home.

Her new knowledge presses like a too-tight cap against her temples, making her head throb. She should do something, tell someone—but whom? Louis would never accept her word over his mother's. Who else would believe her? She wishes, again, for a friend. Blanche's ferocious power has the entire court frightened into submission. Were she to tell what she knows, she would be branded a liar and booted out of France, with Blanche delivering the first kick.

And yet—this secret may benefit her someday. When she has had a son and annulling her marriage is no longer a threat, she may exchange this bit of knowledge for something from Blanche. Something big. The shiver that runs through her feels as pleasurable as a lover's hands.

And then her attention is required. Sir Hugh, the Count of

Lusignan, has approached the table with his hat in his hand, here to pledge his loyalty to Alphonse—alone. "Where is your wife?" Blanche demands.

"Queen Isabella will not attend the ceremonies until my lady has received her."

"Ridiculous. We are here to establish our son Alphonse as lord of Poitou. When you have both pledged yourself to him, then we may welcome you."

"Isabella is a queen," Hugh says.

"A former queen."

"As are you, yet you bend your knee to no man."

"Save our holy father and his blessed son."

"So you understand Queen Isabella's position, *non*? Surely you do not expect her to kneel before your son."

"Indeed I do. We are in France, not England, and I am queen here."

Former queen, Marguerite wants to say. "Sir Hugh, please tell the Queen Mother Isabella that Marguerite, the Queen of France, will receive her tomorrow," she says. "She may come to my chambers in the morning, after matins."

Blanche's back stiffens. Louis frowns and scratches his stomach. Hugh de Lusignan takes a step away.

"Excuse me, Sir Hugh. I think you are forgetting something." Louis scratches his neck. Has he acquired fleas?

The Count of Lusignan turns slowly back around, then kneels before Alphonse and, in a near whisper, pledges to serve him. Blanche's glare tells Marguerite that she has erred, and grievously so. It is all she can do not to laugh out loud.

Jean de Joinville sidles over with her finger bowl. "Well done, my lady," he says in a low voice as she washes. "You have reminded us all who is the true Queen of France."

"If only the king would keep the fact in mind."

"A king has many facts to remember. Perhaps he only needs reminding from time to time."

On his other side, Louis asks for the washing bowl. "Sir Jean, do you always smile?" This from a man who has forgotten, lately, how to do so.

"Your Grace, I have no reason to frown. But the Queen Marguerite has increased my joy by consenting to let me serve as her champion. Have you ever seen a more beautiful queen? And her intelligence is beyond compare." His eyes caress her as though they were lovers, causing her to blush.

"I hear that you are a student of theology and philosophy," Louis says without looking at Marguerite. "Why don't you come to court in Paris and join my discussions? We host the brightest scholars from the university. You may remain for as long as you wish."

Marguerite looks only at her food. Jean de Joinville, in Paris! The Virgin has answered her prayer. As he and Louis plan his visit, she eats greedily, tearing her bird apart with her teeth, suddenly ravenous with hunger.

⥤ *Eléonore* ⥢

The Storm and Its Omens

Bordeaux, 1242

Nineteen years old

*T*HE WIND SHRIEKS in their ears, pummels their sails, battles the King of England's ships in an unfair attack, for there is no fighting the wind with saber or lance. The ship heaves and bucks as if they sailed in the belly of a retching sea monster. Henry cannot even get out of bed. His servants run to the rail, royal vomit sloshing in their clay vessels. Everyone is sick: Richard of Cornwall; the fearsome Roger, Baron of Mortimer; Uncle Peter; Simon de Montfort, restored to Henry's favor for aiding Richard in Outremer. These are the mighty warriors who would overthrow the King of France, brought to their knees before they even reach the shore.

Not so Eléonore. Perhaps her oversized belly prevents her from seasickness—but then, what of the Earl of Gloucester, whose girth is greater? His agonized groans compete with the storm's howl. Perhaps the child she carries calms her. In her berth, she cradles her womb and sings a lullabye. *Lullay lullow, lullay lully . . .*

Shouts, curses. The mainsail rips. Eléonore, peering out onto the deck, watches the sailors struggle to take it down while holding on to anything they can grab. Behind her, the cook pulls on a surcoat and steps past her, going to fight the storm. He speaks rapidly, gesturing toward the sky. Eléonore who speaks almost no English, recognizes one word: "God." God has sent the storm, apparently, and the sailors are not the only ones who think so. Even Simon de Montfort mentioned an *avertissement,* a warning, as the clouds gathered like dark fists overhead.

Eléonore crosses herself. Might this storm indeed portend disaster? Conquering Poitou will be difficult, especially with only three hundred men. But what else are they to do? Poitou belongs by right to England, with Richard as its count. They cannot do nothing while Blanche gives it to her son. They must fight back, or the arrogant White Queen will take Gascony next. That must not happen. Indeed, Eléonore and Henry have agreed, it will not. Gascony belongs to Edward.

And yet—three hundred is a paltry force. Henry could not muster a greater army without levying another tax, which the barons refused to pay. England, they pointed out, has a standing truce with France—which the French king (or his queen mother, more likely) has broken. Still the magnates refused.

"How does England profit from these overseas ventures?" sneered the powerful Earl of Gloucester, who holds no lands across the channel and so has nothing there for which to fight. Until now, Eléonore agreed with him. But Blanche de Castille must be stopped. Not only has she humiliated Marguerite—that *chienne!*— but now she threatens Edward's future, as well.

Henry has explained to the barons many times why England needs Poitou. The kingdom has already lost Normandy, Anjou, and Aquitaine—three territories on the French coast. Without Poitou and Gascony, where on the continent would England land its ships? Trade would become most difficult. England would be diminished.

But the barons' council refused to pay a single mark. "Damned shortsighted," Henry huffed later in his chambers, to Eléonore and Richard. "A pity that I must heed the edicts of fools."

The French king has none of these concerns. Without the

Magna Carta tying his hands, he governs his kingdom as he—and his mother—desire. As a result, France is expanding, swallowing everything around it to become the most powerful nation on the continent. "That position should be England's, if not for my father's weakness," he says. Which weakness he is speaking of, he does not say: King John's lust for the beautiful Isabella of Angoulême, which caused him to lose his lands to France, or his failure to take back those lands?

Some of the barons are calling this a woman's battle. "They blame our mother," Richard told Henry. The whole world knows, by now, how Queen Blanche snubbed Isabella during Alphonse's feast. In outrage, Isabella rode to the château which Alphonse had provided for her and her husband, and set it on fire.

"They blame Queen Isabella? Instead of Blanche?" Eléonore said. Which of the barons would not avenge such an insult as Isabella bore? Which of them would not fight for his son's honor, as she is doing?

"They say she seduced our father, she seduced the Count of La Marche, and now she seduces you, Henry."

Henry reddened. "Charter or no charter, I don't need the barons' permission to travel over the sea and take what is mine." He brandished his most recent letter from Hugh of Lusignan. The rebel forces have amassed, many thousands from Poitou, Gascony, Anjou, Aquitaine. Never mind the paucity of English warriors: Henry need only bring money. *All are eager to serve you, now and after our victory,* he wrote. *We cannot lose.*

Bring money. This request seems simple enough for a wealthy kingdom such as England. Then Richard calculates the costs: Ships. Crews. Horses. Men. Food. Weapons. Armor. Housing. Bribes. The sum is staggering—forty thousand pounds, two times the amount collected in the last English levy.

"Without the barons' aid, how will we afford to go?" Eléonore asked. "Where will we find the funds?"

"I'll take it from the Jews," Henry said, giving her a surprised look. "Of course."

After the storm has subsided, she lies in bed, one hand on her jumping womb—a boy in there, surely—and one hand gripping her mattress, as if the ship had not ceased its violent plummeting. Henry wants to take not only Poitou, but all the lands his father lost. To do so, he will need to usurp the French crown completely. Should he succeed, what would become of Marguerite? Would Henry protect her from the terrible, dank Gascon jails? She is one reason Eléonore has come, heavy with child and foreboding. Sanchia is the other.

Toulouse's marriage is annulled, one of Pope Gregory's final acts. Now the pope is dead, and Toulouse has sent for Sanchia. *I can do nothing,* Marguerite has written. She has no power to stop the marriage, especially with no pope to hear an appeal. Richard of Cornwall is their sister's only hope.

Richard, however, has been away for two years. After rescuing the French army from prison in Outremer—while the French were taking over his castle—he took advantage of his new "hero" status to increase his stature in the world. Not only did he pay homage to Pope Gregory in Rome, but he also visited the Holy Roman Emperor in Sicily, where Saracen dancing girls entertained him for months. Sanchia's beauty, once so entrancing, has faded from his memory—but that is going to change very soon.

The baby kicks again, harder this time, looking for a way out. As impatient as its mother. Eléonore smiles. *Tarry a while longer, little one. You have a very important role in my scheme, but you must make your appearance at the crucial time.*

———◆———

$\mathcal{I}$F GASCONY'S JAILS are notoriously grim, its people are even more so. Its lush landscape, mild climate, and meandering river ought to produce gentle, cheerful folk, as in Provence, but here no one smiles. Even the castle staff greets the royal party with downturned mouths and looks askance.

"They resent you," Simon tells them. "The Gascons do not want to be ruled from across the sea. They want to shape their own destiny." Coming from France as he does, Simon knows Gascony better than Henry, who has relied on seneschals to administer it for him.

"Silliness," Henry snaps. "Destiny is God's to determine." And God has given Gascony to England, which intends to keep it. When Prince Edward comes of age, he will become its duke, and the duchy's income will be his—enabling him to care for his wife and family until he becomes king.

Simon's knowledge of the French is one reason Henry recruited him for this campaign. After fleeing England he lived in his family's manor in Montfort-l'Amaury, near Paris, and became a companion to King Louis. To Henry's irritation, he demures when asked for the French king's secrets.

"Would he confide in me, your vassal?" Simon's exaggerated shrug tells Eléonore the answer is "yes."

After a few sunny days in Bordeaux, the Gascon capital, the storm and its omens have faded from memory. Henry and Richard wave jauntily as they depart for battle, as though on a pleasure excursion. They are confident of victory, and why not? Practically all of southern France waits at Taillebourg to fight with them. Eléonore and Eleanor Montfort wave good-bye while their toddling children play at their feet, bumping into their mothers' shins and evading their nurses' grasping hands. On his horse, Henry leads the procession in full regalia—tunic and fur-lined mantles of colorful silk, golden crown—and holds his sword high. Before him, heralds blow trumpets and pipes, and tap drums to announce his approach along streets that are virtually empty. Except for a few curious onlookers, the disgruntled citizens of Bordeaux have chosen to stay at home today, "extracting the sticks from their bottoms, one hopes," Eleanor Montfort says. She glances at the Gascon servants nearby, but they pretend not to hear.

"These Gascons have no sense of humor," she declares. "Of course, the truth is painful."

In the pleasure of her sister-in-law's company, Eléonore forgets, for a moment, her fears for Henry's safety. Yet she cannot set aside her anxieties about Sanchia, whom Raimond of Toulouse has twice tried to abduct.

Abhorring the marriage as much as her daughters, Mama delays. *We do not wish to send her now,* the Countess Beatrice has written. *She has reached the age of womanhood, but Sanchia is still a child.* Toulouse doesn't care about her readiness for married life. He craves the prize of her exotic, golden-haired beauty, and of her presumably fertile womb.

When the warriors have disappeared into the trees and the notes of the trumpets have dwindled, Eléonore feels a touch on her shoulder.

"They have gone at last," Uncle Peter says, rubbing his hands together. "I am off to Provence, my dear, to execute our plan. Trust me. I visited Sanchia only two months ago. She is more stunning than ever before. One glimpse of her, and Richard of Cornwall will beg for her hand."

→ *Sanchia* ←

A Piece of Ripe Fruit

Aix-en-Provence, 1243

Fifteen years old

THE SKY'S BLUE is so deep, she wants to dive into it and swim around. How many months has it been since she was allowed to leave the château? Not that she minds being inside. She prefers her clean, safe home to dirt, thorns, and insects—and strange men lurking about the grounds, waiting to steal her away. Today, though, she must be out, for her kitten has escaped. Beatrice let her go, cook said. Now poor Poivre is lost and Beatrice won't help find her.

"It was an accident," her little sister said (with a wicked grin). "She followed me out the door, and I couldn't catch her." How she lies! Satan has wormed his way into Beatrice's heart. Her sister has tormented the kitten since Sanchia got her, a gift from Papa "to console you in your confinement," he said. She will ask the saints to erase Beatrice's jealousy—after she rescues Poivre from the dangers of the wild.

"Poivre!" she cries, for, although she knows that kittens do not answer to their names, her cat is very intelligent. Poivre might come bounding up at the sound of Sanchia's voice, for she knows it well, having been sung to, read to, and cooed over by her mistress every day for the last week. "Come to me, darling! Your mama is worrying about you." Her kitten might be snatched away by a hawk (her eyes fill with tears at the thought), or eaten by a boar. The woods are full of danger, and not just for kittens.

A movement catches her eye, and a flash of white in the long grass at the edge of the willow grove. She runs, singing, her *petit chou* is safe, and as she nears the grove she sees her kitten in the grass, pouncing on crickets. Sanchia's laugh is a sparkling brook, but Poivre, who hates the water, scampers into the woods.

She stops at the forest's edge. Her *paire* warned her to stay near the château. Vicious creatures live in the woods, wolves and snakes and nasty, mean boars. "Come back, Poivre, or you will be eaten!" Her plea bounces from tree to tree but Poivre does not return.

A rattle of wheels turns her head—the carriage is almost upon her—Raimond of Toulouse leans out the window, his arms outstretched. "I have come for you at last, my lovely!" His wicked laughter chases her as she runs, not toward home as she knows she should go, but into the trees, where it is dark and he may lose her, where she may hide from his fat belly and wrinkled hands and eyes that stare through her clothes. Who cares about wild animals? She would rather be gored by a boar than snatched away by him.

And then tree trunks surround her, and leaves, and there is no direction but up. She turns around and around, dizzying herself. Every tree looks the same. Where is home? She grasps a limb and tries to climb, but her arms are weak and the bark scratches her soft hands.

"I have you now." The count grabs her legs and yanks her down to the ground. Sanchia struggles in his arms, trying to scream but she doesn't know how. A mewing sound is all she can make, like her kitten, as she twists under him. His hands move over, then under, her clothes, from one forbidden spot to another. His breath is hot on her neck, followed by his wet mouth. One of his hands clamps between her legs, pressing her into the ground but not far enough, unfortunately, to bury her. *Forgive me, O Lord.*

"What do you think, my wife? This is a romantic spot to con-summate our marriage, no?" She cries out. He covers her mouth with one hand and begins pulling up her skirt, panting slowly, as if pacing himself in a long race. His fingers tickle like the feet of an insect. She kicks, smashing her heel against his shin. He yelps, then laughs. "At home," he says, "I will tie you to the bed."

Then he flies up and away, his mouth an O of astonishment; not flying, but lifted by Romeo, who holds a rapier to his throat, his nostrils flaring as though the scent of blood were already ris-ing from the count's body. His weight gone, she feels as light as a song, and then she is running without seeming to touch the ground, speeding toward home and her *maire* supervising the servants load-ing trunks, baskets, and beds onto a carriage.

"Mama," she says between gulps of air, "the Count of Toulouse is here."

"He is too late!" Mama sings. Her barbette and coif give her an impish look. "Climb in, darling. A much better husband awaits you in Bordeaux."

"Mama, he tried to steal me again."

Creases appear between her mother's eyes. "Raimond of Tou-louse is a toad, and not nearly as wealthy as the Earl of Cornwall. We must hurry! Your uncle Peter says the earl never tarries long in one place. Climb into the carriage, darling. Your clothes are packed. Madeleine will be out with Beatrice in a moment."

"Romeo is bringing the count—"

"Let your papa deal with him." The countess claps her hands. "Hurry! The sooner we leave, the better for you. We must take ad-vantage of this time with no pope. Your papa can nullify the mar-riage contract Pope Gregory approved and sign a new one for you before a new pope is elected, without repercussions." Her mother smiles at the horizon as if it held a beautiful rainbow. "Remember how the earl gazed upon you? As if you were a piece of ripe fruit, or a bag full of gold."

Sanchia shivers, remembering his lips parted in astonishment, his constant exclamations over her beauty, his age-roughened hands in hers as they danced. But at least he handled her delicately. She shivers.

"Toulouse touched me, Mama. In bad places." Sanchia begins to cry. "Do you think Jesus would still want me?"

The countess opens her arms, but her embrace is brief, almost furtive. "Poor thing, everyone wants you. Ah, no, here comes Romeo with Toulouse. Quiet, my bird, we do not want him to guess where we are going, lest he ride after us and ruin all. Madeleine! Madeleine—where is she? Oh, here. Hurry!"

Madeleine steps out onto the lawn with a steering hand on the crown of Beatrice's sullen head. "Pardon, Madame, the little princess here put water on her hair and destroyed the curls I made. So it is not my fault that she resembles a drowned cat."

"Beatrice, why?" their mother asks. "Don't you want to look your best for the English king?"

"Curls are stupid," Beatrice says.

A horse nickers. Just at the bottom of the hill, Romeo rides slowly toward them with Raimond of Toulouse walking beside, his bound wrists tied to the saddle. "Let us go. Now!" The countess takes Sanchia's arm, as if she were unable to find the carriage without her mother's help.

"Where are we going, Mama?"

"To see your sister Elli in Bordeaux, and her new baby girl." From inside the carriage, Uncle Peter extends a hand to help Sanchia inside. He has such big teeth, and he shows them all the time, even today at dinner when he told Mama and Papa about a war between England and France.

"This could divide the family," Mama said. "I cannot believe that Elli and Margi would allow it."

The danger of that is past, Uncle Peter said. England was promised an easy victory, but France had already won the war before King Henry's ships landed. When he and his troops arrived at the battlefield the French fighters were waiting. They almost captured King Henry, but the Earl Richard saved him. When Uncle Peter said this, Mama beamed with pride at Sanchia.

"Queen Blanche must be crowing like the cock she is," Papa said.

"She predicted that the English dogs would slink home with their tails between their legs," Uncle Peter said. "And she was right." Beatrice made a funny drawing, a dog with a drooping eye and a crown eating from a dish in the shape of France.

The carriage begins to move. Mama pushes her down, telling her to hide, that Raimond of Toulouse must not see her or he will try to follow them. She lays her head in Mama's lap and thinks of the Earl Richard, the way his eyes followed her like, yes, a dog.

Only when the carriage is far from the château does Mama allow her to sit up. "If we are lucky, you will see the Earl of Cornwall again. Would it please you? It will surely please him. But we must hurry, or he will sail for home before we arrive."

"I hope he has gone," Sanchia says. "I don't want to see him."

"Nonsense! Of course you do. You don't want to marry Raimond of Toulouse, do you? Of course not. Richard of Cornwall is your only hope, child. No need to look so frightened! You are more beautiful than ever before. The moment the Earl Richard glimpses you, he will fall to his knees and beg for your hand—and you will be free of Toulouse at last."

❧ Eléonore ❧

Gascony Is Edward's

Bordeaux, 1243

Twenty years old

*S*HE ARISES BEFORE the sun, before the cock's first crow, before her handmaid has even dressed herself. She still hasn't regained all her strength, but there is work to do and Henry is not going to do it, not in his state.

"Slowly, my lady," tuts Margaret Biset, who knows nothing about moving slowly, even at her age. "You do not want to tempt the devil." Six weeks have passed since her labor, six weeks since she nearly bled to death, yet her handmaid still coddles her. The wet nurse enters with the infant Margaret in her arms and Eléonore stops to cuddle her, dodging her tiny fists as she covers her girl's sweet face with kisses.

"Your *grand-maire* arrives today, little one," she says, laughing as the baby grabs hold of her nose. "All the way from Provence, just to see you." Not precisely true, but no one—not even Margaret Biset—must know the real reason for the visit. If Eléonore's plot is discovered, all will be lost. Sanchia will be lost.

As her handmaid dresses her in a simple gown of pale linen— on this day, she wants only to fade beside Sanchia—she sends a servant to discern Richard's whereabouts, then consults with the head cook about today's feast. Disgusted by Henry's tears, Richard had planned to sail for Cornwall today. Eléonore begged him to remain, offering trout stuffed with hazelnuts and his favorite German brandy at the feast—but he would promise nothing. She must find him lest he slip away.

Her handmaid clucks her tongue when the cook has gone. "Supervising the kitchen staff is no job for a queen," she mutters.

Eléonore laughs. "What would you have me do? We've hardly any servants left."

"I only think the king—" Margaret presses her mouth shut. Eléonore can guess what she would say: that Henry ought to take care of these matters so his wife can fully recover. But Henry cannot think of anything or anyone now except his own humiliation. Her task would be easier had her cousin not fired so many of their servants. But neither could they stay. Even while Eléonore's screams of labor rang through the castle, the Gascon servants barred the midwife from her chambers—hoping, no doubt, that she and the baby would die. Then Eléonore's cousin Gaston de Béarn, a local viscount, arrived in time to save them both, pushing past his countrymen muttering "traitor" to usher the midwife into her room.

"I abhor English rule as vehemently as any Gascon," he said to her later, smoothing his green silk tunic, stroking his mustache. "But you and I are family. The same blood runs in our veins." He then summoned the most renowned healer in Bordeaux for her, and found a wet nurse to suckle the baby. When he left, Eléonore promised never to forget what he had done.

"I may remind you of that promise someday," he said.

Her crown in place, she visits Henry in his chambers. He slumps on his bed as if broken, wiping tears as Richard and Uncle Peter politely look away—and Simon paces the floor.

"I might be in chains now, or even killed." Henry's monotone reminds Eleanor of a winter wind. "If not for you, brother."

"You have only yourself to blame," Simon says. "If you had listened to me, we might have prevailed."

"With three hundred men? The French force numbered in the thousands," Richard says.

"But—didn't the Count of La Marche bring more men?" Eléonore sits beside her husband on his bed.

"His letter promised troops from Angoulême, Poitou, even Gascony." Henry's voice quavers like an old man's. "Now he denies it. Says he never wrote a letter."

"I told you he was unreliable." Simon stops his pacing to glare at Henry. "Hugh of Lusignan has rebelled against King Louis before, and failed spectacularly."

"As we have now done, as well." The room falls silent as they ponder their loss. Henry fought with his barons, alienating them, and squeezed money from his Jews, depleting revenues he may need for some other cause. They sailed through terrifying storms. She nearly died giving birth in a hostile land. It was all, all for naught.

"You should have listened to me, and brought more troops," Simon says. "But you preferred the false promises of a deceptive woman."

"We don't know—" Henry begins, but Simon cuts him off with a sardonic laugh.

"You would know if you opened your eyes. Isabella of Angoulême wrote that letter, and signed her husband's name to it. She is to blame for our failure, and her conniving, scheming—"

"That is enough!" Henry's roar has returned. "How dare you degrade my mother?"

"How dare you degrade your kingdom? You should have listened to me. My father was a great warrior, while you—you're just another battlefield bungler. Like Charles the Simple."

Henry stands, raises a fist. "I could have you imprisoned for that."

"For telling the truth? Forgive me, I had forgotten that you prefer lies."

"Get out of my sight." Tears fill Henry's eyes. "Get out, now! Or lose your tongue. Treason!" His shouts bring men running in, who escort the red-faced Simon from the room.

"The Earl of Leicester has now accused me of weakness and simple-mindedness." Henry's voice breaks. "But he has never even met my mother. He doesn't know her."

"She is cunning," Richard says. "And she may have written the letters calling us here. We would not be the first men she has tricked. Such are the ways of women." Eléonore holds her tongue, or she would leap to Queen Isabella's defense. Who, man or woman, would not have done the same—or more—for a son? Without land, without money, a man is nothing.

Why, she asks, did Hugh of Lusignan challenge the French without an ample force? "You wrote him, Henry, of your difficulties recruiting troops."

"He and Pierre of Brittany had amassed a large army," Richard says. "But Brittany coveted the throne for himself. He didn't know the King of England had been summoned. When he found out that we were coming, he withdrew—and took most of the troops with him."

"As we prayed for our lives at sea, Hugh and my mother were already pledging allegiance to King Louis," Henry says. He slumps onto the bed again, covers his face with his hands. "When we reached Taillebourg, the French were waiting for us."

"How dreadful!" Eléonore takes his hand. He gives her a little squeeze, his eyes moist. "How did you get away?"

"By the grace of God, and the talents of my brother."

"The men I rescued from prison in Outremer were the same men leading the French forces," Richard says. "They allowed us to escape."

Henry withdraws his hand from Eléonore's. "If not for Richard, you might be a widow."

Eléonore doubts this; surely the French king would have ransomed Henry rather than kill him. Yet there is no denying the importance of what Richard has done. "How can we repay you?" Eléonore asks, sure he will think of a way.

Richard smiles. "My brother has already given me more than enough."

"Oh?" Eléonore smiles, too, knowing how easily Richard can coax gifts from Henry. "What did you give him, Henry? Not our first-born child, I hope?" She keeps her tone light.

"Nothing that drastic," Henry says. "A small gift, really, for such a great favor."

"Now you are being humble," Richard says. "Gascony is hardly a 'small gift.'"

"I failed to regain Poitou for you. Gascony is just recompense."

"Gascony?" Eléonore's pulse skips. "Edward's Gascony?"

Henry titters and pats her hand. "All of England will belong to Edward. Why does he need Gascony?"

Eléonore can think of many answers to his question: Because the income will benefit him when his barons say "no" to his requests. Because once Gascony has passed out of their hands, they will not get it back. Because Edward will need an income while he waits to become king. Because the more lands and titles he owns, the better the marriage they can make for him. Because Richard is already wealthier than anyone else in England.

But she says none of these things. Because Richard, at this moment, looks happier than Eléonore has seen him since before his wife died. Such is the power of money to soothe a man's troubled soul—and just in time for Sanchia's arrival.

When Richard has gone, Henry crumples into Eléonore's arms. "I have failed, my dear, and most spectacularly. Poitou is lost. How will I face my people now? How will I face my barons?"

As Eléonore strokes his back and murmurs consolations, she gazes into a mirror on the opposite wall and thinks of Gascony. "You will face them with pride, after you have won the hearts of the Gascons. Our barons who own land in Gascony will be most grateful. Think of it, Henry! We will return to England in glory, reveling in our success."

"But Gascony is Richard's. Not England's."

"You must take it back from him."

"What? Impossible."

"Not impossible. You are the king. You can do what you desire."

"Eléonore. You do not know. We need Richard."

"And we shall have him. My mother and sisters arrive soon. When Richard beholds the legendary beauty Sanchia of Provence, he will give anything to marry her—including Gascony."

⇥ *Sanchia* ⇤

Sister to the Queen

London, 1243

Fifteen years old

HE IS NOT a handsome man. Nor is he a king. But he is the brother of a king, and his eyes watch Sanchia every moment. With him, she feels as if she were on a stage, putting on a dazzling show.

On the steps of the Westminster Cathedral, her hand trembles as he slides the ring onto her finger. The aroma of frankincense fills her nose and mouth, gagging her. She is married now, like it or not. *Forgive me, Jesus.* But at least he is not Raimond of Toulouse.

She glances shyly at him. He smiles. It is a nice smile, even if it does crinkle his eyes. He is quite old, nearly twenty years older than she, but she doesn't mind. "Till death do us part," she says. If he dies first, she can enter the convent.

They finish their vows, then follow the archbishop into the cathedral. Richard tucks her hand into the crook of his arm. "You are beautiful," he whispers as they walk. "Ravishing."

She does not even blush. All her life, people have praised her beauty. "Golden girl," Mama used to call her. Sordel wrote songs for her. Whenever her tutor scolded her for neglecting her work, Madeleine would wipe Sanchia's tears and say, "A beauty such as you will not need Latin to please her husband."

(Her father never praised her at all. "Everyone says Sanchia is prettier than me," she overheard Beatrice tell him once. "What do you think, Papa?"

"All my girls are beauties," Papa said. "But—may I tell you a secret, little one? I have never cared for fair hair.")

The Earl of Cornwall's compliments are different, though. He regards her breathlessly, as though she were a sculpture or painting from which he cannot tear his gaze, like the rose garden painted on the walls of Eléonore's chambers in the Tower of London. Sanchia once spent an entire afternoon lost in those roses, imagining herself walking with Jesus in that garden, dreaming of the flowers' fragrance.

"He worships you," Eléonore said this morning as the maids dressed Sanchia in her wedding gown—made by Eléonore's tailor, of green silk with a blue velvet surcoat—the most beautiful garment she has ever worn. "I have never seen a man so smitten. Of course, Richard loves nothing more than women."

"Except for money," Marguerite said drily. "But he was mad for his first wife, I hear. She was renowned as a great beauty."

"If he were not so rich, no woman would look at him," Beatrice said. She sat at a dressing table trying on Eléonore's jewels and crowns, imagining herself as a queen—in spite of Marguerite's glances of irritation. "His eyes pop out like a toad's."

"Was he kind to his wife?" Sanchia said. "He seems harsh at times. When he is annoyed, he grinds his teeth together, as though he might bite."

"At least he will not drool on you like Toulouse." Beatrice drops a necklace on the dressing table, dislodging an emerald from its setting.

Marguerite snatches up the necklace. "This is not a conversation for unmarried girls."

"She is eleven," Sanchia said, seeing Beatrice's pout. "Nearly marriageable." But Marguerite sent her off to the nursery, "where there are toys more suitable for you to play with." The look in Beatrice's eyes said revenge. Sanchia must placate her later, or she will ruin this day.

"I would prefer a gentle man," Sanchia said to her sisters. "Someone younger would be nice, too."

"I felt the same way with Henry, at first," Eléonore said. "But I came to love him. You might do the same. Richard can be charming."

"Not as charming as Jesus."

Marguerite bursts into laughter. "Yes, the Romans *loved* Jesus."

"Sister," Eléonore says to her. "Be kind."

Heat spreads through Sanchia's face. Sometimes she wonders if Margi even believes in God, the way she talks, the way she laughs at everything, even King Louis, whom everyone calls "the most pious king." She defends the Cathars, too, even though they are going to hell.

"Sanchia, you know that Margi and I were not allowed to choose our husbands, either," Eléonore said. "We married not for ourselves, but for our parents, and our children. You will do the same. Family comes first, as Mama always says."

"I don't mean to be selfish. The earl's eyes are always upon me. It frightens me."

"Richard of Cornwall is a passionate man," Eléonore said. "You are fortunate."

"Not as passionate as Jesus," Marguerite said.

<hr />

THE EARL OF Cornwall holds Sanchia's hand. His palm is as soft as if he had never used it. The skin on the back of his hand reminds her of parchment, pale and slightly rough, an old man's hand. Her papa's hand. The Earl Richard is not like her father, though, except that they are both old. Papa is not rich. The earl can afford to feed the entire city of London, it seems, at a feast that fills the Westminster Palace hall and spills onto the lawn. Each dish is delectable: snails in butter sauce on flaky pastry; spicy greens topped with smoked eel; a large pie out of which a dozen snow-white doves fly; pears floating in a saffron-cream sauce. Sanchia has never tasted such food, not even in Provence.

Also, unlike the Count of Provence, the Earl Richard adores fair hair, as he demonstrates by stroking hers at the table, holding it up to the light and letting it shimmer through his fingers. "Liquid gold," he murmurs. He lifts a spoonful of pear to her lips, cooing over the perfection of her mouth and tongue, "as pink as a kitten's," he says, saddening her for a moment, for she never found her kitten after that day in the woods.

"The Gascons will adore you," he says.

Sanchia frowns. Are they going to Gascony?

"Darling, we are going to rule Gascony. As soon as you convince your sister to give it back to me."

"Convince Elli—of anything?" She gives a little laugh. "I was never good at that."

"You will have to learn, then. If you want to be a duchess."

"But I don't." Richard's eyes snap. "I don't want to be a duchess. I just want to be a good wife, and serve God."

"I want to be the Duke of Gascony," he says. His hand tightens around her arm. "And you are going to get the title for me."

"But I can't! I—Elli doesn't listen to me."

"You will have to make her listen. Talk to her tomorrow, before we leave for Cornwall."

"No, Richard. Please don't make me! I—"

"I thought you wanted to be a good wife."

"I do. I can do anything you'd like. Except for this." Eléonore would laugh at her, or get angry. Sanchia couldn't bear either, not from Elli, her protector. She has defended her against Marguerite's tart remarks since they were girls. When their tutor struck her in the mouth for bungling her Latin, Eléonore punched him with her fist, bloodying his nose. Whenever Papa challenged Sanchia at table with a philosophy question, Eléonore defended her answers, no matter if she was wrong. Elli made Papa banish a troubadour from the court for writing a bawdy song about Sanchia. And now she has saved her from that awful Raimond of Toulouse. Eléonore is the last person Sanchia would offend.

"But Sanchia, this is all I require of you, to influence your sister on my behalf. Now you say you will not help me. Have I married you, then, in vain?"

"I—I thought you married me for my beauty."

Why is he staring at her? He looks as surprised as if she had sprouted a tail.

"Darling," he says, "the world teems with beautiful women. But only one has the love of my brother's queen."

"You married me because of my sister?" He offers another spoonful of pear, but she averts her face.

"Not for her, but for what she can give to you. To us both," he says. She shakes her head, confused. He puts down the spoon.

"What is the use of being brother to the king—or sister to the queen—if one cannot profit from the relation?" he says. "The more I know of my brother's plans, the more we stand to gain. Queen Eléonore confides in you." He grins, lifting his eyebrows. "And now you will confide in me."

Sanchia gasps. "You want me to spy on Elli? But she is my sister." She grips the bench to stop herself from fleeing.

"And I am your husband, whom you have pledged to obey. Now"—he lifts the spoon again—"open your pretty mouth. And try to look happy, my pet. All of England watches you today."

⇢ *Beatrice* ⇠

A Pretty Alliance

London, 1243

Twelve years old

*S*HE STABS HER pigeon with her knife, imagining that it is the pregnant belly of the high and mighty Queen Marguerite. "Mind your manners," her mother hisses. "We are dining with the kings of France and England."

She stabs the bird again, so hard it flies off the platter and onto the floor. "You are a naughty child," her mother says. "To the nursery you go." She sends her off with a maid, who stops in the crowded hall to jest with a knight. Beatrice sees her opportunity, and takes it.

She slides around the edge of the room, looking to see if Mama has noticed. But no, she's laughing with the Earl of Cornwall, while Sanchia smiles and blinks as if she might cry. Married not even an hour, and already he has offended her. The earl is not a nice man, in spite of what everyone says, but no one has asked for her opinion. Papa would have listened to her, but he is in Provence, gathering his strength.

Mama has forgotten her, as usual. On her other side, Eléonore and Marguerite chat with their heads together, scheming another match, probably. They had better not try to arrange a marriage for

Beatrice. Who wants a husband telling her what to do? *You are the only man I want, Papa.* He laughed when she said this, and told her his secret. When he dies, she won't need anyone else.

Her sisters will foam at the mouth, especially Marguerite. But why should Beatrice care? Marguerite treats her like a servant, not a sister. When Mama took her to Paris, Marguerite caught her sitting on the queen's throne and made her move to a little stool, saying, "No one may sit on the same level with the queen." Beatrice cried and threatened to tell Papa, but she only laughed. "Do you think he would take your part in a quarrel with me?" He would, in fact, as Beatrice knows. Marguerite will know it, too, someday.

She had thought Eléonore would be kinder—Eléonore, who used to hold Beatrice on her knee and read the stories of Lancelot to her. But she never said a word on Beatrice's behalf today, when Marguerite scolded her and sent her away. This is the sister called "Eléonore the Bold"? Beatrice could tell the "Eléonore" stories in her sleep, she has heard them so many times: Eléonore scaling a cliff on a dare from Marguerite, then being unable to climb down. Eléonore attacking the Count of Toulouse at the Marseille market with a tree branch, surprising him so much he fell over. Eléonore insisting, against Mama's wishes, on marrying King Henry when she was only twelve years old. Mama wanted her to wait a year or two, but she refused. "The English king changes his mind with the seasons, I hear. I'm going to him now, before the winter turns to spring and he finds another queen." She would not be outdone, she said, by Marguerite.

Marguerite and Eléonore. Eléonore and Marguerite. So young was Beatrice when they left Provence, she doesn't remember Marguerite at all, and Eléonore only vaguely. But she has heard about them her entire life, has imagined them in her play, has written them letters that she never sent because, who is she? What does she have to say to the most famous women in the world, even if they are her sisters?

Now Sanchia has joined their ranks, or nearly. In their glittering company, Beatrice wonders again: Who is *she*? What is she, except the baby and her father's favorite?

Romeo once promised to make queens of all the daughters of the Count of Provence. So goes another of the legends that have sprung up around their family. But then Papa engaged Sanchia to Raimond of Toulouse, a nobody. Now Sanchia is married not to a king, but to the brother of a king, which is nearly as good, and the Count of Toulouse is said to have his eye on Beatrice. And Beatrice, judging from the way her sisters treated her today, is the nobody.

The maid approaches, her face bright with relief. "At last, I have found you!" she cries—and Beatrice runs again, through the milling crowd, careful not to jostle the servants with their platters of food, for to cause a spill would alert her mother that she is still in the great hall instead of snoring over psalters and dolls in the nursery. She ducks into the garden and hides behind a tree, catching her breath, when she hears two young men talking and laughing in the strange, harsh French of the north.

"She is the best looking sister, don't you think?"

"And as sweet as a summer breeze. Unlike that bitch Marguerite, whose blood is as cold as a dead man's hands."

Beatrice resists the urge to leap out and defend her sister. She doesn't want to be seen—and besides, how could she argue? Marguerite *is* a bitch.

"Sweet Sanchia of Provence. What a dream! It is too bad that she had to marry that greedy English bastard."

"What is wrong with a bit of greed? Take whatever you can in life, I say."

"Ah. Spoken like a brother of the King of France."

She peers around the tree, beholds the king's brother who hates her sister. He is not tall, but his body is muscular; not handsome, but interesting in appearance, with a prominent nose and snapping dark eyes. "Not just any brother," he says. "I will be the richest and most powerful of the sons of Blanche de Castille—even more powerful than Louis."

His companion laughs. "Charles! Your modesty astounds me. Where will you begin your conquests? With a beautiful heiress? Why didn't you seek the hand of Sanchia of Provence? Or—why not the youngest daughter? I hear she is nearly as lovely."

"Bah. Provence. That little backward county? It might have been worth the taking if Count Ramon Berenger hadn't drained his treasury to entertain simpering minstrels and third-rate poets."

"Careful, man. I come from Toulouse, you know, where the air is fragrant with the troubadours' song."

"Heretics!" Charles spat. "They're all Cathars, you know. The Church would have wiped them out if your Cathar-loving count had not defended them."

"Even as he tried to conquer Provence, do not forget. That 'backward county' must be a more desirable possession than you realize. Their salt mines are more valuable than gold. And the youngest daughter is almost of age to marry, I hear."

"That would be a pretty alliance! Charles, brother of the king, and the daughter of a poor count? If I wanted Provence, I would have no trouble grabbing it by force. That old woman Ramon Berenger would be no match for me."

"Old woman, ha ha! I have met him, and he is as soft as a fawn. It is no wonder that he sired only girls." The youths erupt into laughter—which stops when Beatrice jumps out from behind her tree.

"The Count of Provence is a renowned warrior!" she shouts, waving her fists about. "Even at his age, he could kill you both at the same time."

Charles's friend points his finger at her. "See who defends the mighty Provence? A little girl! Will you challenge me to a duel now, sweetheart, or a game of dolls?"

And then Beatrice is on top of the boy without knowing how she got there, and he is on the ground beneath her, and blood is all over her hands. She hits him again, trying to stop the laughter, and indeed he is cringing and trying to cover his face, but the laughter—coming from behind her—only increases.

"Hit her back, you baby!" Charles shouts. "What is the matter with you, man? Can't you defend yourself against a little girl?"

He raises his arms and Beatrice, thinking that he will strike back at her, slaps him in the face. "Ouch! Hey!" the youth cries, and then hands have grasped her under her arms and yanked her to her feet, and the young man is sitting up, wiping blood from his nose. She struggles to free herself from the prince Charles's grasp but only jabs an elbow into his ribs before he squeezes her so tightly she can barely breathe.

"Hold on, little lion. You can beat my friend here without repercussion, but I am not quite so chivalrous. Hit me again and you'll feel my spank!"

Beatrice kicks him in the shin as hard as she can. He yelps and lets go, and she whirls around to face them. Now the brother of the King of France bends over to massage his leg, and his friend stands beside him, pinching his nostrils shut and laughing.

"Beatrice! Where are you?" Her mother's voice sounds from within. Beatrice darts behind the tree, hoping the youths will not give her away.

"And what is going on here? Charles of Anjou, fighting? Your reputation for trouble appears to be well deserved."

"Not I, madame." He glances toward the tree; Beatrice shrinks back.

"Beatrice!"

She steps out into the open, glaring at Charles, holding her bloody hands behind her.

"He insulted Papa," she says.

"Oh, Beatrice." Her mother's eyes fill with tears. "I have been looking everywhere for you. Your father has taken a turn for the worse, my dear. We must hurry home at once!"

❖ *Marguerite* ❖

My Provence

Paris, 1244

Twenty-three years old

A DIN ARISES from outside: a great noise of crashing and screeching, as if a storm were sweeping through Paris. Inside Marguerite's chambers, barons, wives, clergymen, ladies-in-waiting, servants, uncles, and the healer congratulate one another as if they had borne the king's heir.

"Good work, Margi," Uncle Peter says. She would reply, but she cannot muster the strength for even a smile.

A hand on her brow. Marguerite opens her eyes to see her husband, sporting the hideous woolen cap he has taken to wearing which, he says, demonstrates humility (a quality which Louis is proud to claim). "You have done it, my bride," he says, and for a moment Marguerite's pulse leaps with the promise of love, now that she has given him his prize. Hope, however, is elusive in these times, as is Louis's gaze, and in the next moment both have gone from her as he turns to welcome his mother's embrace.

"You must try to sit up, my lady." Gisele's touch cools her in the overly warm room. Marguerite asks that a window be opened but the physician shakes his head; disease might enter from outside, where a mighty crowd has gathered. "Can you hear them cheering? You have made your subjects happy today."

Blanche, on the other hand, looks anything but pleased as she steps up to the bed.

"He is quite large, while my babies were tiny at birth." Blanche looks at her askance, as if this discrepancy from the Capetian mold were Marguerite's fault. "Your Isabelle and Blanche were small babies, too, *non?*"

All the white makeup in the world cannot hide the disappointment of a displaced dowager queen. Marguerite closes her eyes. Blanche must move out of the castle now, giving Marguerite a reason at last to be thankful. Now the world may recognize her as France's queen. She has awaited this moment for ten years, but now that it is here she only sighs, and wishes she could sleep.

"She looks very pale." She opens her eyes at the sound of his voice. Jean de Joinville rakes a hand through his soft hair. "Are you in pain?"

"Not anymore," she says, smiling into his eyes. He glances around the room, but not even Blanche is watching. Marguerite, queen or not, is the least important person in these chambers. Louis joins in a song of praise to God and Blanche accepts kisses, while the prince gets handed around and admired as though disease struck only from outside the castle walls.

If only everyone would depart these chambers—except Joinville. Were she alone with him, she would answer his question more fully, would tell him that she felt no pain at all during the birth of her son. Why did she ever think giving birth was difficult? Blanche's birth nearly killed her, yes, and the second, Isabelle, took many hours to arrive, knowing, perhaps, that, being a girl, she would be greeted with frowns and sighs by all except her mother. But this third child—nay, second, now, the first is gone—fairly burst forth from her womb, making a boisterous entrance with cries more vociferous than any sound uttered by Marguerite. "My lady was brave," the midwife tells Joinville now. But one must be fearful to be brave, and Marguerite felt no fear today, no anxiety, nothing; the same as she has felt in all the months since sickness took her little Blanchette from her day by day until, one morning, Marguerite awoke to a world without her.

"You look sorrowful." The queen mother assesses her with eyes as pale as a winter sky. "Very unhappy for a queen who has just borne the future King of France."

"I cannot stop thinking about the one who died."

"Tsk! Children die. Accustom yourself to it, or you'll waste many hours shedding fruitless tears." She takes the prince from the midwife. "Be thankful that it was only a girl."

Marguerite lifts her hands—she has to hold the child, she supposes—but Blanche turns away and takes it into the crowd. "Behold the future King of France's marvelous size," she crows. "Behold his magnificence."

There is a stirring at the doorway. A messenger has arrived, asking for the queen. "I am here," Blanche calls out. As she passes the bed, Marguerite lifts her eyes to the babe and thinks she should probably hold it.

The man bows and hands Blanche a piece of folded parchment. She examines the seal and lifts her plucked eyebrows nearly to the place where her hairline should be. Marguerite sits up a bit straighter, expecting the babe to come to her while Blanche opens her message. The queen mother hands it to Louis, instead.

"What a splendid boy," he says, smiling at Marguerite. "Note the alert quality of his gaze. One does not often detect such intelligence in a newborn." Her interest suddenly piqued, Marguerite holds out her hands to Louis.

As he strides toward her, however, the infant begins to cry. Marguerite feels the rush of milk to her breasts as the midwife scoops him out of Louis's arms and, murmuring an apology, hurries from the chambers to find the wet nurse.

"She will be back soon, my lady, and the babe in your arms." Gisele plumps her pillows. Something falls on Marguerite's lap: the parchment that Blanche was holding.

"The fool delivered his message to the wrong queen," she says. "This was meant for you. From Provence."

Marguerite turns the parchment over, her pulse thudding in her ears. This is no message of congratulation, come all the way from Provence so soon after her baby's birth.

We do not know how much time remains to your father, her mother has written. *We have completed his final will and testament, which we hope you will agree is best for all. Hoping to make a good marriage for Beatrice, he has bequeathed Provence to her. She will be anointed as countess in his presence soon, with me as a witness, so that no one can dispute her right to the title.*

Marguerite stares at the parchment. Have her eyes deceived her? She reads the message again, then again, as if missing words might appear if she only stared hard enough. She has lost Provence—to the spoiled, selfish Beatrice? Is there nothing for her, nothing at all? What of the dowry pledged by Papa in her marriage contract? What of Tarascon?

She hands the letter to Louis. "My condolences," he says when he has read it. "I know you loved your father well."

Marguerite tries to speak, but each word turns to salt on her tongue. Her eyes burn. Louis sits beside her and pulls her close. She breathes him in: damp wool, chapel incense, blood.

"My father leaving this world; my Provence, taken from me," she says, sobbing at last. "My dowry, denied. God, how will I bear all this loss?"

Blanche places a hand on her arm and leans over to speak low, so that no one else can hear. "Summon your courage. You are the Queen of France! Your enemies are everywhere, even in this room. Do not reveal your weaknesses to them."

Marguerite looks to her husband; can't a queen mourn her child, or her father? But he is nodding. "One must demonstrate competence. Are you to be brought down by the loss of a castle and a few thousand marks?"

"But I have lost Provence," Marguerite says. "It is lost to France completely. My sister will be its countess, not I." She imagines

Beatrice rustling about the château in her new silks. She had
threatened to go naked rather than wear Sanchia's clothes. *I am
no frumpish nun; nor do I plan to dress like one.* She imagines
Beatrice scheming to squeeze money from her vassals, even as they
kiss her ring in homage.

Blanche stands and plants her hands on her hips. Her rings
glitter, as do her eyes, which look over the crowd, then affix their
gaze across the room—on Charles, sneering down his long nose at
a servant who has splashed wine on his sleeve.

The queen mother's mouth begins to move, as though she were
talking to herself. "Nothing is ever lost to France," she says to
Marguerite. "You would already realize this, were you as clever
with your mind as you are with your tongue."

⇢ *Beatrice* ⇠

A Woman May Rule

Aix-en-Provence, 1245

Fourteen years old

$\mathcal{I}$T IS A splendid sepulcher, beautifully wrought, of rose-colored marble engraved with the dragons Papa loved and a planh by Sordel, with a window for letting in the sun he craved and a bench on which Beatrice shivers and prays for deliverance. Marguerite commissioned this tomb and paid for it, her gift in honor of their father, but surely he cannot rest in it while she conspires with her sisters against Beatrice and threatens war against Provence.

We want only what is rightfully ours, her sister wrote in a letter Mama read aloud in a voice like a hammer, each word striking Beatrice in the heart. *Provence owes ten thousand marks to France or the castle and lands at Tarascon, promised as dowry upon our marriage to the king. We demand full payment or we will take your county by force.*

Eléonore, too, has protested that Papa owes money to England, and Sanchia is making claims, as well. But—why? What is ten thousand marks to the rich and powerful France? Or four thousand to England? And all the money in Provence's treasury would be as an anthill next to Richard of Cornwall's mountain of gold. "Why, Papa?" she cries aloud, here in his tomb, where she can succumb to her grief away from the stern watch of her *maire,* who has not shed a single tear since her father died, and away from the always smiling Romeo, who hovers at her elbow in fear, it seems, that she might have a thought of her own.

Papa could not have known that her sisters would respond with violence. "All my daughters, except you alone, are exalted by marriage in a high degree," he said as he lay dying one month ago. (Has so little time passed since he left her world?)

Romeo smiled even then, she recalls, like a dog with its teeth bared, always smiling, proud of himself, as usual, for arranging her sisters' marriages. "With such a bequest, I should have no difficulty finding a king for her," he told her father. Beatrice's tears flowed in earnest then, for it was her Papa she wanted, the only man she could ever love.

He loved her, too, more than anyone. "My dearest Bibi, more beloved by me than all your sisters," he said that day.

"They're jealous," she says aloud now, and her tears dry up— just in time for her *maire* to find her sitting in perfect composure, a small smile on her face as she contemplates her first official act as Countess of Provence, which will be to write an indignant letter to Blanche de Castille protesting Marguerite's threat. Everyone knows that Blanche is the real Queen of France—and that she has the power to subdue Marguerite.

"Here again, Beatrice?" Mama has never called her "Bibi," even though she still says "Margi" instead of Marguerite and "Elli" instead of Eléonore. Her mother peruses her with folded arms, disapproving, as always, of the time she spends at her father's side.

"You must let your father go. He would want you to do so." Beatrice wonders: what would Mama, who immersed herself in the affairs of France and England, know of Papa's desires? "You must come with me now, at any rate. The Prince of Aragon has arrived, and demands to see you at once."

An hour later, wearing a mourning gown of white, she sits on the dais in her father's chair, Mama beside her, while Prince Alfonso bows low before her to kiss her ring. A ripple courses up her arm as she imagines smashing her hand upward into his nose. Something about the way he bends so far toward the floor—the son of James the Conqueror, kneeling to her!—or the softness of his hands, or the timidity in his eyes, makes her yearn to do so.

"My father has expanded his domain many times during his rule," the prince says, his perfect smile reminding her of Romeo's. "Aragon is now a mighty force, destined to become one of the world's great powers. If God wills, I will become its king someday."

Beatrice rolls her eyes. "Spare me the history lesson and tell me why you've come."

"I- I— Forgive me, my lady. I did not mean to offend you."

"I am not offended. Merely overcome by boredom." She yawns for effect.

He stands in silent contemplation of his feet. His eyes, when he looks up at her again, hold a plea. "I have come to request your hand in marriage. You and I share the same great-grandfather, who ruled both Provence and Aragon—as I am sure you know," he adds hastily.

"Marriage?" His blush causes her to laugh a bit more loudly. "Why would I want to marry, and give up my power to you?"

She watches him struggle with his confusion. "Forgive me, *señorita*. I do not understand."

"In Provence, a woman may rule. My grandmother Garsende—your great-aunt—ruled Provence for seven years after my grandfather died. Why shouldn't I do the same?"

"But you are only a child!" He frowns, and for a moment she thinks he will stomp his foot.

"Old enough to marry, but not to rule? Now I wonder, *monsieur,* what role you would assign to me as your countess. Certainly not a role worthy of my capabilities."

Alfonso's face darkens. His eyes narrow. "If you think you will be able to rule this county alone, then you are mistaken," he says. "The emperor himself is sending ships to fetch you for his son."

"The son of an excommunicate—God save us from that fate!" Mama's voice cracks.

"The situation is worse than you imagined." Alfonso slaps the gloves he holds in one hand against his other palm. "My father aims to reunite Provence with Aragon. If the Lady Beatrice refuses my proposal, he will send an army in my place. And who knows how many others will vie for the cherished prize? Your beautiful daughter and the riches of Provence make an irresistible combination."

He leaves the hall, his armored knights flanking him, Beatrice's eyes hurling imaginary arrows into his back. Her father dead, her sisters opposing her, Marguerite threatening war—and now this? Is the whole world against her? But she is strong. If they think to wear down her resolve, they are mistaken. She will rule Provence.

"Romeo!" Mama cries. "Where is Romeo?"

Her fingers clamp around Beatrice's arm as if she's afraid she might lose her. "What nonsense were you uttering?" she says in a hiss as they climb the winding staircase to her mother's chambers. "Not marry? Who placed that thought into your foolish head?"

"Papa." Hadn't he taught her everything about Provence? Hadn't he said to her many times, "You could administer this county by yourself"?

"He meant for you to marry, and to marry well. Why do you think he left Provence to you, instead of to Margi? *She* was his favorite."

Beatrice bites her lip. Papa did dote on his precious Marguerite, so intelligent and refined, so nimble of tongue. *God has blessed me with four lovely daughters, two of them like me.* But she and Marguerite are not so much alike. She would not have contested Papa's will, even had he bequeathed nothing to her.

Romeo joins them—smiling. "Did you truly rebuke the Prince of Aragon, my lady? I thought you wanted to be a queen."

"Alfonso will never be more than a count," Beatrice snaps. The pope anulled his parents' marriage ten years ago, and King James's new wife has borne him two sons. Romeo knows this. Why must he goad her with talk of queenship?

"Beatrice intends to rule Provence on her own, with no husband," Mama says.

"Indeed?" Romeo arches an eyebrow.

"I want no man acting as lord over me," she says. "Especially a simpering fool such as Alfonso." Who paid Romeo handsomely for his audience with her today, no doubt.

"Count Ramon always admired your independent spirit," he says. His lips and chin, stretched taut by his smile, shine as though smeared with butter.

"And so we may thank the count for the troubles coming our way," Mama says. She tells him of the Aragonian army, poised to attack, and the imperial ships crossing the Mediterranean Sea—and his smile disappears. Beatrice marvels at the transformation: from cunning hyena to worried old man.

"This is grave news," he says. "Frederick would drain our county's wealth and conscript our men for his never-ending war with the pope."

"Perhaps the pope would help us," Beatrice says.

"The pope exacts an even higher price for his aid, my lady," Romeo says. "He would take fees and taxes for the Church, men for his wars against Frederick, and more men for his campaigns in Outremer."

"We must stop the emperor's ships," Mama says. "If he lands in Marseille, we are lost."

"Romeo can find a way," Beatrice says. Now she is the one with the smiling face. "You have friends in Marseille, don't you, Romeo?" A self-governing city, Marseille owes no fealty to Provence—thanks to Romeo, who convinced Papa to allow this freedom. Its people are too independent, and would never support him even if he managed to subdue them, he said. *Befriending them would be more beneficial to you than fighting them.* And more lucrative to Romeo, whom the merchants surely pay for his favors.

"Frederick is powerful, but I do wield some influence at the Marseille ports. I might be able to convince them to block his ships." His smile returns. "The more silver I carry with me, of course, the greater my influence will be."

The Holiest Man in the Kingdom

Paris, 1245

Twenty-four years old

*A*FTER THE LONG carriage ride, Marguerite wants only to walk. By her side, Gisele shivers and remarks on the weather ("It feels like it will snow, don't you think, my lady?") but Marguerite hears only her thoughts jumping about as if her mind were a bed of hot coals with nowhere for thoughts to rest.

"You may stop worrying about your dowry now," Blanche said to her on the ride, as if, having gained the pope of Rome's permission to take what she wants, she can now dictate Marguerite's concerns. And perhaps she can, for no scathing riposte came to Marguerite's lips. Retorts are for clever people and today, having been denied her own petition to the pope, Marguerite feels neither clever nor particularly interested in talking, especially to her mother-in-law.

Even Louis offers no consolation, having testified in Blanche's favor instead of Marguerite's. But when has he ever sided with her on anything his mother opposed?

"Aren't you cold, my lady? Wouldn't you like to go inside and sit by a nice fire?" Gisele's face looks raw and her lips are blue, but Marguerite's answer is no, she does not want to sit. Her blood races far too fast for her to feel a chill. Imagine: Charles of Anjou, with his preening conceit and nasty temper, is to take her father's place as Count of Provence. Marguerite cannot fathom it. Not even Beatrice could prefer him, with his nose like a beak and his skin as pale as a dead man's. Yet Beatrice will not have a choice. Blanche wants Provence for her son and Pope Innocent wants Blanche's allegiance, and no one seems to care what Marguerite—or Beatrice—wants.

If only another man had been chosen for her—anyone but Charles! Marguerite might have convinced her sister to grant her Tarascon, at least. Then she would have a *château* in Provence, on the banks of the beautiful Rhône, a place where she could find peace and solitude. A private place, of her very own.

A gust of wind brings a flurry of snow, stinging her cheeks, blinding her eyes.

"My lady, should we seek shelter in the stables? I see smoke rising from the chimney."

Marguerite follows her handmaid with barely a murmur of assent, too lost in her ruminations to care about cold or fires. What could Mama have been thinking, to petition the pope for aid? The Emperor Frederick is a known rogue, but he would not snatch a woman from her home for a forced marriage, no matter what the rumors say. Poor Beatrice, sold like a slave at auction to the highest bidder! Poor Provence, as well, for, with Charles as count, its people may never see another carefree day.

They walk into the livery stables, where the horses that pulled her carriage today nibble from the heaps of grain under their noses and flick their tails, made nervous by the shrieks coming from a back room.

She follows the noise, indignation rising as she prepares to confront the groomsman again for abusing the king's animals. He has argued that beatings are necessary to make good war-horses, but Marguerite knows about horses. She also knows the excuses people invent to justify cruelty.

"Where are you going, my lady? Wait for me!" Gisele cries, then nearly runs into her when Marguerite stops, her hands on her face, her mouth agape at the sight of her husband hanging naked and bleeding from a rope tied to the rafters, sobbing and begging to be released, as the groomsman lashes him with his whip.

Gisele's cry freezes the man's hand as he lifts the whip again, and now he is the astonished one as Marguerite rushes forward and grabs it from him, then begins beating him with it about the head. "Release the king at once, and prepare yourself for the gallows!" she snarls. The man pulls a long knife from his belt and cuts the rope with one hand while holding Louis with the other, smearing his tunic with the king's blood. He lays the king, facedown, on a pallet.

"Now for the vinegar," Louis murmurs before he faints.

"He does not usually take it so hard," the groomsman says. "You have come on a bad day, my lady."

Marguerite orders Louis's nakedness covered, then demands an accounting from the red-faced groomsman. What, she asks, is going on?

He stares at her. "You didn't know?"

Know what? He averts his eyes, runs a bloody hand through his long hair. "About the king's floggings."

The king's floggings? Marguerite has him repeat the phrase, then again, as if he were speaking in a foreign tongue. To be certain, this is a language she does not understand. Under whose command? she asks, thinking of Blanche.

"Why, the king himself," the groomsman says. Knowing something that she does not restores his composure. He shakes his head, saying he cannot believe that she did not know, that he thought everyone in the court knew that King Louis has himself flogged every day. "Sometimes his confessor wields the whip, and sometimes I do it—with the queen mother's approval. She says it keeps His Grace free of sins."

From under his blanket, Louis calls weakly for the groomsman. "Vinegar," he says. The man pulls a flagon from the pouch on his belt and a sponge, then soaks the sponge with vinegar from the bottle. He steps toward Louis.

"No!" she shouts.

He offers the sponge to her. "Would my lady care to do it?"

"To soak his wounds in vinegar? My God, what anguish! Have you no compassion?"

"The sponge is not for his stripes, but for his mouth, my lady." He smiles as if she were an ignorant child. "The king sucks it when he thirsts, as Christ did on the cross."

Marguerite snatches the sponge and flagon and hurls them to the floor, her vision swimming. Dress him, she commands the groomsman, and bring him to his chambers.

Gisele calls out again, pleading with her to wait as she runs back through the winter-dead garden, frost-frozen grasses crunching underfoot, into the castle and directly to the nursery. There she finds Blanche in a chair with little Louis in her lap, reading to him from a children's psalter although he is barely old enough to speak.

"Unhand my son," Marguerite says. She pulls him out of Blanche's lap and enfolds him in her arms. Lou-Lou smells of honey cakes and milk, and his fat little cheeks are as soft as cushions.

"Mama!" Isabelle cries, such a gay child, and runs up to fling her arms around her mother's legs. Marguerite sits in a chair and lets her climb into her lap, breathes in her children's powders and lotions and innocence.

"What has come over you?" Blanche stands. "Are you mad?"

"Not I!" Marguerite's laugh sounds maniacal even to her own ears. Lou-Lou begins to cry.

Outside the room she hears Louis's moaning, and the groomsman's quiet urging: "Just a few steps more, Your Grace. No, we cannot do the vinegar today. Your wife has forbidden it." Marguerite's stare accuses Blanche, whose eyes glitter when she realizes what has happened.

"Louis is the holiest man in the kingdom," Blanche says. "He will be named a saint someday."

Marguerite calls for the nurse.

"Lou-Lou and I haven't finished our reading," Blanche says as

Denise takes the children from her. When they have gone, Marguerite turns to her mother-in-law.

"Queen Mother, the time has come for you to depart."

Blanche arches a painted eyebrow. "Are you now ordering me about the palace?"

"No, I am ordering you out of it."

"Indeed!" Her laugh spills contempt. "Aren't you the high and mighty one?"

"You have done enough harm in my household. More than enough."

"By teaching my children piety? You could use a dose of it, yourself. I am still waiting for evidence of your 'pretty faith.'"

"And what is pretty about yours, with its sorrow and deprivation and self-inflicted pain?" Marguerite's voice rises.

"Surely even a Cathar sympathizer feels compassion for our Lord's suffering."

"What of compassion for your own son? But then, you had none for his father."

Blanche's hand flies to her throat. Laughter, maniacal and shrill, clangs like an alarm heard only by Marguerite. What has she done? She feels as if she had spent her life saving coins for a special purchase and then lost all in a game of chance. Except that this is not a game of chance. It is a game, yes, but of strategy, like chess, and she has not lost and she will not lose. Blanche will not corrupt her children as she has done her own.

"I don't know what you are talking about," Blanche says when she has found her voice.

"You had your husband killed," Marguerite says. "You and the King of Navarre, so that you could rule France."

"Ridiculous," she says, but the word warbles out on an uncertain note.

"I thought so, too, until I heard it with my own ears."

"Surely you know better than to believe everything you hear. I laid that rumor to rest years ago."

"Tell it to the King of Navarre, for he seems still to think he caused King Louis's death, and all for the love of you."

"You lie!" Her fantasies foretold the fear on Blanche's face, but not the delicious hum in her own veins. This is power. "Thibaut would not confide in you."

"Not in me, but in you—at Alphonse's celebration in Poitou. I overheard his appeals for your love, and your rejection of him." As she recounts the conversation word for word, Blanche's breathing becomes more labored. "He said he had given you the throne, and that you gave only broken promises in return."

"I never promised him anything," she says. "I was dismayed by my husband's failures in England, and by his refusal to return home even after I convinced King Philip Augustus to send ships for him. I complained to my cousin, yes, and said I would give anything to rule, for I knew myself to be more competent. Years later, Thibaut sent an assassin to poison Louis, but without my knowledge or my assent."

"How unfortunate for you." Marguerite smiles. "Not so for me."

"You would not reveal my secret. No one would believe you."

"I have witnesses," she lies. "Two servants heard your conversation. The poor souls came to me wringing their hands, wracked by guilt. They feel duty bound to report to Louis, but I have kept them silent—for now."

"You would not tell my son. It would destroy him."

"No, it would destroy you, which would please me immensely. Only one thing would delight me more: your immediate departure from this court, never to return."

Outside the room there is a shout, and a scuffle, then more shouts. "The king! The king! Help!"

Both women start for the door. Marguerite elbows past her mother-in-law. "You have done enough," she says. In Louis's chambers: a cloud of stink, a stench like death, the ashen king slumped in his groomsman's powerful arms, trembling and dripping sweat.

"Come no closer, my lady, or you will step in it," the man cries, pointing to a dark pool at his feet.

Then servants run about, one with a wash basin, another with cloths, a third sent by Marguerite to fetch the healer, his chamberlains removing Louis's soiled and bloody clothes and replacing them with fresh ones as she holds her husband's hot, limp hand and forces herself to murmur comforts. She is the queen now and must behave as such, no matter the burn behind her eyes, no matter the feeling that the ground under her feet has broken apart and carries her ever farther from the world. Who in this court would hold *her* hand? Only Joinville—but he has gone to Champagne to make heirs with his new wife.

Blanche comes in but Marguerite averts her eyes, unable to bear the sight of that white face and exposed forehead, the very image of death. The healer stands by the bed, feeling Louis's pulse, ordering wet cloths to be placed on his forehead. Louis groans and trembles, bathed in sweat. To lie on his back, on his fresh, inflamed welts, must be excruciating, but Marguerite says nothing, for then she would have to explain what she has seen and she cannot, even to herself.

When he has fallen asleep and Marguerite drifts back toward the nursery, she finds the groomsman waiting, his face ringed with worry. "He never fainted before, my lady," he says.

"He comes to you every day?"

"Every day the priest doesn't do it. Most days." His face is as red as his hair. "I never wanted to, my lady, but the queen—"

"When did this begin? How long ago?"

The groomsman scratches his chin. "It was right before the king married you. The queen said he needed to be whipped. His tutor used to do it when he was a boy but then the tutor died so she had me do it at first. Now the king comes to me himself and demands it. Just ten lashes a day, my lady, not so bad, except lately he has been making me use all my force, which causes the blood to run."

Sickened, Marguerite turns from him. This man will be gone

on the morrow, she vows. Let Blanche take him with her when she leaves.

In the nursery, her children cling to her and fret. "Is Papa ill?" Isabelle asks. Rocking her babies in her arms, she thinks of his ugly cotton cap; of the shirt made of goat's hair he wears under his robes, ignoring—or enjoying—the bloody and weeping rash it raises on his neck and back; of the times he has fallen asleep—at dinner, during meetings, while hearing pleas in the courtroom—after kneeling in the chapel all night to pray for God only knows what. She thinks of daily floggings with a knotted whip, and vinegar-soaked sponges.

"Yes," she says to Isabelle, "your papa is very ill."

"Will you become ill, too?"

"Do I appear ill?" She gives a little laugh, tickles her daughter to make her laugh, too. "Do not worry yourself, Isabelle. Your papa will not infect me."

"Or me? Will I get his sickness?"

"Absolutely not." Marguerite caresses Isabelle's fine, dark hair and contemplates Blanche. She has inflicted her son with her madness, but she will not affect these children.

"Do not worry, my darling." She kisses her daughter's cheeks, holds her sleeping son a bit more closely. "Nothing will harm you. Mama will see to that."

❦

A HAND ON her shoulder awakens her. Gisele hovers like a spirit in her white nightgown, a burning candle in one hand and Marguerite's gown in the other. "You are summoned to the king's chambers, my lady. Hurry!"

And then she is running from her room, her gown thrown on but not tied, her bare feet slapping on the floor, racing death. But the tall shadow of the priest thrown against the wall, the soft hiccuping sobs of the maids, and the cover laid across her husband's face tell her that she is too late, that she has lost the contest. She stands over Louis's bed looking down at his body which can redeem him no more. His soul is on its own.

Thank God I gave him an heir. With a son to rear for the throne, she remains France's queen, and may even rule as Blanche did until young Louis comes of age. Otherwise, she would be sent home with empty hands. Louis never endowed her with a single castle, and her dowry was never awarded. She has nothing except her children to call her own.

Blanche's cry cracks like a limb snapping off a tree as she throws herself into the room and, shoving Marguerite aside, onto Louis's bed. "My love," she shouts. "My darling, do not leave me. Come back to me, Louis. Every man I love, taken from me! Oh, why is the Lord so cruel?"

As she sobs, prostrate over his body, she inadvertently pulls the cover off his face—and his eyes open. Gisele gasps and grabs Marguerite's arm. Blanche continues to sob, her face pressed against his stomach. His lips move. "The cross," he rasps.

"Holy Mary, Mother of God." Tears stream down Gisele's face. "It is a miracle."

"The cross," he says again, more loudly. Blanche sits up, looks at him, and faints to the floor. "Father, give the cross to me."

Marguerite stares, enthralled, at the gentle confessor, Geoffrey of Beaulieu—Louis's other flogger—as he removes the crude wooden cross from the wall and hands it to Louis. Louis brings it to his lips as, beside the bed, Blanche's ladies revive her.

"I am going, Father," Louis says. "To the Holy Land, to fight for Jerusalem. Praise the Lord for calling me back."

Blanche struggles to her feet. Her face is nearly as white as if she were wearing her makeup. She stares down at Louis with eyes so red from weeping that they seem to glow in the candlelight. "You are going nowhere," she says. "You are delirious."

"God has given me a new life this day, Mama." He sits up in bed. His voice rings with an authority Marguerite has never heard. "And I am going to use it for his glory."

"You have a kingdom to rule." Blanche's tone is pleading. "You don't know what you are saying. You cannot go!"

"Summon the barons, Mama. Send for Joinville." Marguerite's gaze careens about like a startled bird, smashing against the windows. "We must notify the pope of Rome, and begin making preparations."

The room is abuzz with chatter. Giselle shushes two bickering chambermaids, each blaming the other for covering the king before he was dead. Louis sends out messengers to announce his decision to take the cross. Blanche pleads with him to reconsider. And all the while, the priest chants, in Latin, a prayer of thanksgiving. Standing in the middle of it all, Marguerite has stopped waiting for Louis to acknowledge her and has started waiting for something—someone—else altogether.

Joinville is coming back.

"Summon the tailor Antoine," she says to Gisele as they walk back to her chambers. "I'm going to the chapel to give thanks for this miracle—and then I wish to celebrate in a new gown."

⸙ *Beatrice* ⸙

The Rules of the Game
Aix-en-Provence, 1245

Fourteen years old

*M*AMA HAS BEEN reading her letter for a long time. She stands beside one of the Tower windows, squinting at the parchment in her hands, her eyes moving over the words from left to right, top to bottom, then returning to the top to start again. Beatrice, huddled in furs against the Tower's chill, watches from her chair as the frown on her mother's face deepens, sees emotions flicker like shadows from a cloud-strewn sky: Confusion. Disbelief. Dismay. Anger. Resignation. She peers out onto the roil and clash of the men at their feet.

"My God," she says. "I have made an enormous mistake."

Beatrice braces herself for more bad news, the only kind she has heard in the months since Papa died—three months and two days, according to her marks on the Tower wall since the day the Aragonese began battering their gates and shooting fire into the palace windows. The knights of Provence have fended off the attackers thus far, being skilled at resisting siege after years of battling Toulouse. But the Emperor Frederick, blocked from landing in Provence, leads one thousand men overland, coming for her. In a panic, Mama appealed to the pope of Rome for aid. For three months and two days they have waited for his army. Judging from Mama's stricken face, Pope Innocent has not responded as they had hoped.

"We must comply, Beatrice." Mama moves over to sit beside her. Her expression is grave; trouble clouds her eyes. "The pope has declared that you will marry."

"No!" She jumps to her feet and walks to the window, sees Alfonso of Aragon with his knights trying to light a fire under the fortress wall, as bumbling as jongleurs—but no one is laughing. "Not a man down there is worthy of me," she says.

Mama's laugh is dry. "Pope Innocent seems to agree."

She turns to her mother. "He has chosen someone else?" Her mother avoids her stare. "Not the emperor's son!"

"Heavens, no. His Grace aims to defeat Frederick, not to enhance him."

"Who, then? Tell me!" She snatches the letter from Mama's hand. *As brother to the French king, Charles of Anjou will be amply equipped to keep Provence out of Frederick's control.*

Charles of Anjou. The beaked nose; the sardonic wit; the braggadocio of the youth in the garden come rushing back to her. Her heart begins to thump.

"That strutting rooster? He crows more loudly than the rest, but can he fly? That's the only way he'll reach me here." Her blanket falls to the floor as she looks out the window again, to the north. To Paris.

"He is the worst possible choice for you, and for Provence." Mama pats the seat beside her and Beatrice settles herself into it. Her mother takes her hand. "My poor darling, please forgive me! Charles is his mother's baby, a spoiled and selfish young man. At your sister's wedding I heard him boast that he will become the King of France someday."

"What treason!" Beatrice cannot help her grin. Charles is so far removed from the throne that a half-dozen men and boys would have to die before he could claim it. "What ambition," she says.

Noting the breathless edge in her voice, her mother slaps her hand. "Arrogance may excite from a distance, but, like the shark, it turns ugly when viewed up close. Charles would exploit you, and our land, to gratify his desires."

Beatrice pulls away from her mother and moves to the window again. Is that dust rising from the northern hills?

"He knows nothing of Provence," Mama says. She could teach him, Beatrice thinks. "He cares nothing about family, not his own and certainly not yours." She could influence him. "He desires only to compete with his brother." She knows that feeling all too well. "He hungers for power." She and Charles of Anjou, it seems, have much in common.

A knock startles them, loud and ringing. Mama's handmaid ushers Romeo, rarely smiling these days, into the room. The emperor's forces have swept through Marseille, he says. They took all the food in the city and one hundred horses, besides. "They have been given orders to kill every man on the field and every servant in our castle, if necessary, to reach our Beatrice."

Beatrice rankles. When did she ever belong to Romeo? But her mother is shouting and pulling at her hair. "Where are the pope's men? My God, why did I turn to him for help? Whose idea was that?"

Romeo glances at Beatrice, who is tempted to stick out her tongue. She doesn't recall any suggestions from *him* that day. "It was Romeo's plan," she lies.

He smiles, but his eyes glint anger. She must look out the window again, or laugh. The day she marries Charles will be Romeo's last day in this castle.

"Mama!" Beatrice grips the stone at the base of her tiny window. "Come quickly. Look!"

In the distance, dust clouds rise. Dark shapes crest the hills, then spill over the top like a dark river. "The emperor's army," her mother says. "God help us."

"No," Beatrice says. "See their flag?" Blue, with the fleur-de-lis: the flag of France.

"Just in time," her mother breathes. "Thank the Lord."

"Thank the pope," Romeo says, eager to claim the idea now that it pleases his mistress. Beatrice laughs, drawing a dark look from him.

She wants to jump about and clap her hands, but it would never do for Charles to hear of it. Instead, she smiles more and more broadly as the army approaches and as, below, the men of Aragon shout and scurry about like ants whose hill has been kicked.

———⋅✦⋅———

*L*ATER, WHEN HE has smashed his axe against their heavy door and sent it crashing to the floor; when he has flung the shrieking Beatrice over his shoulder, men slashing their swords all around them; when he has ridden off with her on his galloping horse, his whoops of laughter making music with her own; when he has dragged her into his tent despite her feigned resistance and overwhelmed her with his passion; as she lies beside him, swirling her fingertips in the hair on his chest, he tells her how he outfoxed the other suitors as well as the castle guards without drawing a drop of blood.

"I would have killed for you, my darling," he says, "but the pope forbade it. And he is the man to please these days. He has the ear of God and the testicles of the emperor, and the keys to our future."

But how did he do it? Beatrice smacks his chest, bringing him back to her. How did he get through all those men?

Charles flares his magnificent nostrils. "I told them that your mother had appealed to the pope, and that he had sent me to organize a series of contests. The winner, I said, would take you home as his prize." As his men filtered among the competitors, explaining the "rules" of the games, Charles called to the Provençal knights inside the castle walls and invited them to compete for Beatrice, as well. "When they came out, I went in."

"All those men, competing for my hand! Why didn't you vie against them? Afraid you might lose, I warrant."

"I don't 'vie' for anything, my queen." He rolls on top of her and pins her wrists to the ground, making her gasp. "When I want something, I take it. And the moment you knocked my pal Guillaume to the ground, I knew that I wanted you."

→ *Sanchia* ←

A Countess to Make Me Proud

Wallingford, 1246

Eighteen years old

*H*AVING A CHILD is such hard work, and so painful. But feel the soft warmth of her babe in her arms! And see the delight on Richard's face. He tickles their little son's chin, but Sanchia is the one who laughs at his crossed eyes and his gurgling baby talk. He is not supposed to be in the birthing chambers during her lying-in period, but neither custom nor the Church can stop him from fulfilling his desires.

"He resembles me more every hour, doesn't he?" He does, with that high forehead and honey-colored hair. Yet Sanchia sees something of herself, too, in his delicate nose, tilting slightly to the left, and his lips like a bow.

The babe opens his mouth and belches.

"Indeed, the resemblance is very strong," Sanchia teases, as Richard's eyes meet hers. She kisses his cheek. He slips his arm around her shoulder, pulling her in more closely. The cat in her lap, a gift from Richard, begins to purr.

"You have made me very happy." He chuckles. "The curse is lifted."

"Richard! There was no curse. The Lord does not work that

way." Justine has told her many times how Isabel Marshall died in childbirth. Four babies, and only one of them lived, which must have made for constant sorrow in this house.

Sorrow has been her dinner, her supper, and her pillow to sleep on since coming to Wallingford, the castle he built for Isabel with the great nursery never filled. Yet she had rejoiced to leave Berkhamsted, where his Jew Abraham's new wife stole Richard's every glance. Sanchia feared his heart might follow. He had already lost interest in her. She couldn't convince Eléonore to allow him to keep Gascony, and she couldn't convince Beatrice to pay him the five thousand marks in dowry that Papa had promised. "My sisters do not listen to me," she had told him, but he didn't listen, either. When he realized the truth, he stopped talking to her, too.

Then the Jewess Floria arrived in her tight gowns and her shining black hair, causing Richard to light up like a sparked tinder whenever she appeared. "Flor-r-r-r-ia," he would say, trilling the "r" in the way of a nightingale, his eyes caressing her as if she were made of gold. In bed with Sanchia, he closed his eyes and murmured the Jewess's name, making her cry, which he hated.

Tension grew and stretched at Berkhamsted, quivering like a cord pulled too tightly before it snaps. Then some small thing would upset him: Sanchia had forgotten, again, to order his brandy. ("Between getting out of bed in the morning and keeping my brandy stocked, you are obviously overwhelmed with duties.") Or he found her cat sleeping on his pillow again. ("At least someone in this household desires to share my bed.") Each insult made a tiny hole in her heart that can never be repaired.

She always tried not to cry, but she always failed, and Richard's sarcasms would turn to mockery and sometimes worse. Then, his temper exhausted, he became contrite. Floria forgotten, he would cater only to Sanchia, giving her jewels and gowns and delicious wines from Toulouse and sitting her in his lap the way he did when they first got married. Soon, however, his eyes would turn to Floria again, and Abraham would glare at Sanchia as if she were the cause of it all.

The baby opens his eyes—destined to be brown, although they are innocent blue now—and roots at her breast. She calls for the wet nurse, but Justine comes in, instead.

"I'll take him to her, my lady," she says, as respectful as can be now that Sanchia has had a child. "You must rest for your big day tomorrow."

The day will be big indeed. At last Sanchia will claim her rightful place by her husband's side. Her churching ceremony will show all of England that she, not Isabel Marshall, is the Countess of Cornwall now. She imagines herself on Richard's arm, moving from guest to guest, welcoming England's barons and best knights to her home. He is proud of her at last. "I had my doubts when first we married," he will say, "but I was wrong. She was only a girl then. But look at her now! She has become a countess to make me proud."

A countess to make him proud. Sanchia dresses the part the next morning, with Justine pulling and tucking and tightening and tying, and laying a net of diamonds over Sanchia's curls. She looks as if she had dipped her head in stars. "You will be the most elegant and refined woman there. Perhaps then the tongues will cease their wagging," Justine says.

"Tongues are wagging? About me?"

"Aren't you one of the famous sisters of Savoy? Aren't you married to the richest man in England? Everyone is talking about you, especially today, for you have given the count a real son."

Sanchia's laugh is uncertain. "A real son? Is there any other kind?"

Justine's pressed lips make a thin line in her fleshy face.

All of England, it seems, comes for the ceremony. She stands at the cathedral door with Marguerite, Eléonore, and Justine, unable to enter for all the onlookers stretching their necks the wrong way for a glimpse of her.

"Is the pope of Rome attending, too?" Marguerite says. "I did not have so large an audience at *my* churching."

"Everyone loves Sanchia," Eléonore says.

She moves through the ceremony as if in a dream. On her knees before the altar of the Virgin Mary, she gives thanks for her splendid life, which she does not deserve, and for the love of her sisters who have traveled from afar to honor her. Richard's gaze warms her like a lover's breath although she thinks he does not love her—not yet. Now that she has borne his son, though, his feelings seem to be changing. For that she gives thanks, too.

After the service, she and her sisters cross to the field where today's tournament will take place—the first tournament Sanchia has ever seen.

"I brought Joinville to fight as my champion," Marguerite says. Her eyes hold a soft glow, like candlelight. "Wait until your English knights test his mettle! They will discover why France's army is the most fearsome in the land."

Sanchia smiles in spite of her dread. She has heard tales of blood and gore at these games, even of death. Their father never allowed jousts in Provence: "War is neither a game nor a spectacle," he said. King Henry has forbidden them, and Richard hates them—but neither could refuse the French challenge to a contest.

She sits on the high dais beside the jousting field with her sisters, not a queen as they are but feeling like one, drinking wine from bejeweled cups and admiring the knights in their hauberks, plate armor, leather helmets, and shields bearing colorful coats of arms. "Beauty!" someone cries. "Beauty, these are for you!" A bouquet of red roses sails through the air but Margi's handsome knight, standing just below, catches it in his gloved hands before presenting it to her.

"There, sister—Joinville has saved you from the thorns' prick," Eléonore cries.

"Now watch him prick the English vassals with his lance," says Marguerite.

On the field, Richard and King Henry vie with the archers to split a tree branch with their arrows. The muscles ripple in Richard's back and arms as he draws the arrow back in the stiff longbow—but he cannot quite make the full draw, and the arrow falls short of the mark. He grins as King Henry slaps him on the back, but his face flushes a dark red. When Henry shoots the arrow true, Richard glances around as if to see who is watching—and frowns at Sanchia as though she had caused him to miss. She hopes she will not be made to pay for his humiliation. She takes a drink from her goblet and the flutters in her stomach subside.

"Any news from the boy king in Edinburgh?" Marguerite asks Eléonore.

"He has accepted our offer." Eléonore clasps her hands together. "Our little Margaret is going to be Queen of Scotland. Soon our entire family will comprise queens and kings."

"Except for me," Sanchia says.

"Why not? Richard is ambitious. I expect to see you on a throne someday."

She winces. "May God protect me from that fate."

"Don't you want to change the world?" Marguerite smirks.

"It is enough for me to change Richard's world."

"Aren't you the devoted wife, all of a sudden? Isn't Jesus jealous?"

"You have improved Richard's life immeasurably with this new child," Eléonore says, giving Marguerite a stern look. "I have not seen my brother-in-law so happy in years."

"Richard has had a hard life, in many ways," Sanchia says.

"King John treated everyone cruelly, including his children," Eléonore says. "Henry has told terrible tales. He inherited his father's temper, alas."

"But he does not abuse you?" Sanchia grips her sister's arm.

"Eléonore, abused? I pity the man who would try," Marguerite says.

A trumpet sounds. On the field, the archers gather their arrows and retire to their tables. The jousting knights converge on the meadow astride their destriers: the English on one side, the French on the other.

"Wait until you see how skillfully Joinville wields a lance," Marguerite says.

"Henry is too gentle a soul to treat me roughly," says Eléonore. "The same is true of Richard, I think."

"He dislikes his mother greatly." Sanchia looks away. Should she tell her sisters the truth? Would they laugh at her, as Marguerite loves to do? "He resents her for leaving him after his father died."

"Henry laments losing her, as well. 'I never had a family of my own,' he always says. And now she has retreated again—to a convent."

Sanchia sighs. "I envy her."

"She said she's doing penance for the lies she told Henry and Richard, to trick them into fighting the French. As well she should! Henry was nearly killed."

"She wanted only to help her children," Sanchia says. "That is what I have heard."

"Instead, she has left them destitute," Marguerite says. "Blanche has taken La Marche for Alphonse, too. When Hugh of Lusignan dies, his heir will receive only Angoulême. His other children will inherit nothing."

"Do not be so certain," Eléonore says. "Henry's half-brothers and sisters arrived in London two weeks ago, six of them! They fell like long-lost lovers into Henry's open arms. At last he has the family he has always wanted. He would give them the entire kingdom if I would allow it."

"Shh!" Marguerite says. "It's Joinville."

He rides his horse far to the west; his English opponent rides far to the east. There they wait, their lances couched underarm, their free hands ready to bring down whips on their horses' flanks. At the trumpet's blast the horses tear forth as fast as each will go, aiming head-on for each other. Is it Sanchia's shriek rending the air or that of the horses when they clash? The French knight's lance strikes the Englishman's shield so forcefully it splits it apart. The English knight falls to the ground with a thud, then lies still for a long moment. Sanchia's pulse races and she says a prayer for him as his fellow knights help him struggle slowly to his feet.

"Not a drop of blood," Eléonore says, frowning.

"Joinville is saving his best efforts for the more skilled English fighters," Marguerite says. "If there are any."

Meanwhile, Marguerite's young knight has removed his helmet and bows to the sisters, then to the cheering crowd. "Give me a flower," Margi tells her. She takes one and tosses it to her knight, her complexion as brilliant as the rose she throws.

And so it goes for hours, it seems, crash after crash, smash after sickening smash, men striking each other down, cracking helmets, crunching bones, shattering teeth, and, often, smiling even as the blood pours from their noses and mouths. Sanchia thinks she will be sick to her stomach. "Stop!" she cries, wanting it to end, but her protest is lost in the crowd's excitement. Even her sisters cheer and boo as if they watched children playing pretend or cocks fighting in the ring instead of flesh-and-blood men endangering their lives for others' pleasure. When Margi and Elli begin placing bets with each new match she would scream at them, too. They are like the Roman soldiers casting lots for Jesus's clothes as he hung on the cross. But she cannot scream; nor can she cry, nor even hide her eyes. As the honored guest, she must hide her disgust behind a smile. The things that men do for pleasure. It is a wonder that they have not destroyed the earth and everyone on it by now.

At last the contests end, and she can breathe. While Marguerite collects her winnings from a pouting Eléonore, the men arrive to escort them to the great hall and the feast that awaits. King Henry looks pale. "He hates tournaments. He has forbidden them in London, to everyone's disappointment." Eléonore pats his hand, smiling. "For all his manly bluster, my Henry has a woman's heart."

"No tournaments! But how will you train your knights to succeed in battle?" asks Joinville. Sanchia leaps to the king's defense.

"If they kill and maim each other in tournaments, then who will remain to fight the battles?" she asks.

"My thoughts precisely," Henry says. "The last tournament held in my court caused the deaths of eighty knights, including my beloved Gilbert Marshal."

"Didn't you like the games?" Richard asks Sanchia. "Your sisters seemed to enjoy themselves immensely."

Have they been married three years? And yet Richard knows so little about her.

Trumpets herald their entrance into the hall, where the nurse, Matilda, waits to present the baby to Sanchia. Richard looks down at the child in her arms, then at her, and she sees at last the pride that she has dreamt of since their wedding day—the pride she wanted her father to feel in her, too, but he never liked her fair hair nor understood why, at dinner, she did not leap into arguments with the rest of them. He thought she had nothing to say, while the truth was that she did speak, but her voice was too quiet to be heard above Marguerite's commanding tone and Eléonore's excited shouts. How pleased he always looked when one of his daughters proved him wrong on some matter! She had dreaded Eléonore's leaving home but she secretly hoped that, with her sister gone, Papa would finally notice her. But then she fell ill and had to stay in bed for a week, and when she emerged Beatrice had caught their Papa's eye and she kept it for the rest of his life.

Now, at last, Sanchia sees not only pride but also love on a man's face. Richard loves her. As she gazes back at him, claiming him before all of England, her smile stretches so broadly it pains her cheeks.

Uncle Boniface, newly appointed archbishop of Canterbury by King Henry—at Eléonore's urging—flashes his smile at her, his famous smile that makes women call him the "handsome archbishop." Such beauty is wasted, they say, on a celibate man. (Richard laughed when he heard this, and said that a man like Boniface would be of no use to women, anyway. Sanchia cannot imagine what he means.)

"Have you decided on a name for the child?" Uncle asks. Richard nods toward Sanchia. They have agreed to name the boy Ramon, after her father. Now, though, enveloped in her husband's love, she changes her mind.

"We will name him Richard." As the room fills with cheers,

he kisses her cheek. A tear forms in the corner of his eye, but he quickly wipes it away.

The nurse takes the baby so Sanchia can dine. "We had hoped to arrive earlier," Eléonore is telling their uncle, "but we have been stomping out fires in Gascony." Already the Gascon rebels have overthrown the man Henry appointed to administer the county. "They want to wrest the duchy away from us, but we will not allow it. Gascony is Edward's."

The question trembles on her lips, like a bird about to fly for the first time. "M-m-might you send R-r-r-ichard? You know he would be a strong ruler."

Eléonore turns a little pale. The corners of her mouth droop. "Gascony is Edward's," she says again.

The feast is exactly as she dreamt it: She and Richard sit with Henry, Eléonore, and Marguerite at the high table, the king and queens on elevated thrones—talking and laughing and drinking wine. Richard's gaze caresses her, and his boasts about her increase as the day continues. "God has blessed me with an angel for a wife," he says. "A beautiful angel, who has performed a miracle and lifted the curse against me."

Sanchia bites back her reply. God doesn't kill babies, not anymore, not since His son died for the sins of all.

After the feast, the wet nurse brings the baby. Sanchia walks with him about the hall, showing him off. "He looks like me, don't you think?" Richard says, his voice vast with pride.

The Countess of Beaulieu, her cap perched percariously on a high, tightly wound spool of gray hair, squints down at the baby. "Yes, he does resemble you," she says. "As do all your children."

"All your children?" Sanchia whispers to her husband as they walk away. "Do you have others besides Henry?"

"The countess is growing old. Her mind is enfeebled."

Eléonore sweeps up and scoops the baby into her arm. "What a darling," she coos, and kisses him all over his face, laughing—until a stranger steps into their circle, and her expression tightens as if pulled by a drawstring.

Richard introduces the new Earl of Pembroke, his half-brother William de Valence, whose sharp features remind Sanchia of a hawk's. He is richly dressed even for this noble gathering, in a green undertunic and silk overtunic of brilliant blue embroidered with gold fleurs de lis, and purple leggings.

"He arrived from France last winter wearing a coat of coarse wool, and now behold his finery," Eléonore murmurs to her. "The Lusignans seem intent on grabbing all the land and titles they can coax from Henry. By the time they finish, nothing will remain for our children."

"Montfort calls me a thief and a foreigner," William de Valence is saying. "He fancied that Pembroke belonged to him."

"Henry did award it to him," Eléonore puts in. "To settle their dispute over Eleanor's dowry."

"Yes, all the world knows about the Montforts and their endless demands on Henry." He speaks as though Eléonore has brought up a most tedious topic.

"Simon de Montfort is an upward-reaching man," Richard says. "He thought to become rich by marrying my sister."

"Our sister," the Earl of Pembroke reminds him. He nudges Richard as though they are long-lost friends.

"The Montforts are very much in love," Eléonore says, her color rising. The baby begins to cry.

"Love, between a husband and wife?" Richard begins to laugh.

"What is funny?" Sanchia frowns. "My parents loved each other."

"They respected each other." Richard pats her cheek. "But love, my sweet, is like a delicate oil. Marriage is like vinegar. The two cannot mix. Do I speak correctly, Lord Pembroke?"

"Marriage is one thing, and love quite another," the count says. "That is why men have mistresses."

Before either sister can retort, the trumpet sounds to announce a late arrival: The Baroness of Tremberton, Joan de Valletort, and her son Philip. The baroness stands like a statue, her dark hair swept smoothly back from her high forehead and gleaming through pearl-studded crespinettes, her skin like alabaster, her long, slender fingers clasped lightly, her full lips in a half smile. Sanchia wonders at her composure, so like Mama's. How does any woman gain such confidence? Then her gaze moves to the young man in priest's robes beside her. He looks familiar, but she cannot imagine why.

Eléonore grasps her hand. "Keep breathing," she says. "Calm is essential."

With eyes like glittering obsidian the woman crosses the room with her slump-shouldered son to where Richard and Sanchia stand. Her steps make dainty tapping sounds on the tiles, sounds elevated by the silence blowing before her like a warning wind.

"Richard. How divine to see you! How many years has it been?" He lowers his lips to her hand; her eyes watch him knowingly, as if they shared a private jest.

"Baroness." Richard's voice sounds as brittle as dried leaves. His mouth puckers in that way he has when he gets annoyed. "I'd like you to meet my wife, the Countess Sanchia."

"Oh, yes, I'd heard that you married one of the sisters of Savoy." Under her cool appraisal, Sanchia feels as if, without this woman's approval, she might be sent back to her mother. "You are famous, my dear, and now I can see why. What a beauty! Richard, she's darling. And the baby! He's nearly as cute as Philip was."

Sanchia blushes. She feels Eléonore watching her, but she cannot meet her gaze. Her eyes are locked to the face of this woman whose smile is one thing when it falls upon her and quite another when it shines on Richard. Her son joins them; the baroness steps aside so that he can stand beside Richard. Sanchia gasps. His wavy, sand-colored hair; his sturdy, square body; his soft, full mouth: He could be Richard's son, he is so like him. Eléonore takes her hand. "Sister, I am weary after today's journey. Will you come and sit with me?"

"Go along, darling." Richard moves his hand from her waist.

"I will join you soon." Sanchia moves as if in a fog, or as if the fog were in her, slowing her steps and obscuring even her thoughts.

"That boy must be at least sixteen years old," her sister says.

"Sixteen years ago, Richard was married to Isabel Marshal," Sanchia says. "The love of his life. Or one of them."

"'Love is the delicate oil, and marriage the vinegar,'" Eléonore quips. "I wonder if Richard invented those lines?"

Marguerite

Against the Winds

Egypt, 1249

Twenty-eight years old

THIS IS NOT what she imagined. The triumphal entry, yes—fifteen hundred ships, sails billowing, covering the sea in canvas. But the zeal in Louis's eyes, his restless pacing across the deck, his constant talk of Jerusalem, Jerusalem, Jerusalem—this Marguerite did not envision, nor the men's screams as the Saracen gallies burn and crumble, sunk by balls of flame launched at Louis's command.

She has been told to remain in her cabin, but she is free to do as she wills now, the Queen of France at last, not in Paris as she had hoped, but queen nonetheless. And she does not wish to huddle in that cramped room while her imagination spins scenes of terror from the sounds coming through the door. Yet the view from the deck is grimmer than anything she imagined.

"Lower two dinghies for rescue," Louis commands. Is he mad? Two dinghies will not hold all the men flailing in the sea and shouting for help. "Save the Saracen captains and nobles, and leave the rest to God," he tells the crewmen clambering into the boats. She wants to argue, to intervene for the lives of the others, but she holds her tongue. If she would prove herself to Louis here in Outremer, she must not begin by publicly challenging his decisions.

Beatrice joins her at the rail but Marguerite says nothing, having asked her for her dowry and been refused—again. "I will not violate our father's will," Beatrice said. "You can ask me as many times as you please, but my answer isn't going to change." Marguerite has now decided to ignore her. Why listen to Beatrice when she will not listen to Marguerite?

Nothing can dissuade Beatrice from speaking, however. "Isn't this an exciting start for our campaign," she drawls. Marguerite turns away from her sister's knowing eyes to watch knights pull silk-wearing Saracens into the boats, then smash their oars against the heads and hands of the rest who cling and claw at the dinghies. Blood sprays. Eyes roll. The knights laugh. Marguerite bends over the rail to heave bile from her empty stomach into the death-dark sea.

Beatrice lays a hand on her back; Marguerite flinches away, spitting and wiping her mouth with her handkerchief.

"I hope you are seasick, and not heartsick, O Queen," Beatrice says. "We came to conquer these people, not to befriend them."

The Frenchmen climb ladders from the dinghies to the deck, prodding their prisoners before them. Marguerite moves closer for a better view of the heathens and savages, half-expecting horns or forked tongues, but they look only like frightened men in dripping garments. Charles and Robert bind their hands with rope, then shove them below deck. One of the men shouts in the melodic Saracen tongue. A sailor replies in the same language. Marguerite asks him to translate.

"He says his boats came to greet us, and not to fight," the sailor says.

"They do not appear armed."

"Trickery, my lady. They conceal scimitars and daggers under their robes," he says. "Or they may have released them in the sea, to keep from drowning. They only wanted to find out why we'd come, he says. Ha ha! I guess they know now."

Robert passes, his mouth a rictus of cruelty. Marguerite touches his arm. He turns to her, his eyes out of focus.

"What will you do with them?" she says.

Robert blinks as if she, too, spoke Saracen. "Louis wants to question them, that is all," he says. "Then we'll chain them up below. If they talk, they will be left in peace there."

"And if they don't?"

"The sting of a barbed whip will make any man talk," Charles says as he walks by.

"Charles," Beatrice says, "did you see that the fourth Saracen ship escaped our fire? They'll return to Damietta."

"Good! Let them tell their neighbors that the mighty French have arrived."

As the Saracens pass, some lift hate-filled eyes to leer at her breasts and body. She stumbles backward, her hands on her chest. Beatrice strides forth and slaps a man's face.

"Show respect for our queen," she says. The man laughs and spits on her shoe.

"Damned heathens—pardon me, my ladies," the sailor says. "The Muslims have no love for women except what's between the legs. Be careful when we get to land. Take a man with you everywhere you go. It's no sin in the Saracens' religion to rape a Christian woman."

Shrieks rise from the hold, following Marguerite to her cabin, where she lies on the bed with her pillow over her head. They are heathens, she reminds herself, but wasn't the same said of the Cathars whom she knew as kind and gentle folk? *O Lord, why have you sent me here to witness these atrocities?* But it was not God who placed her on this ship. For that, she can thank Blanche.

She had thought herself so clever to send Blanche running from the palace with her threats. How blissful were those years at the court without her mother-in-law's gargoyle of a face ever turned her way, and without her sneering remarks. The result, however, wasn't quite what she had hoped. Instead of welcoming her to rule with him, Louis began holding court at Blanche's castle, excluding Marguerite altogether. But her children, at least, were safe from their grandmother's sick influence.

How naïve of Marguerite to think she might prevail over her

mother-in-law. Blanche was not gone, but only biding her time. As Louis prepared for his Outremer campaign, Marguerite prepared to rule France in his stead—only to find, mere weeks before his departure, that Blanche had a different idea.

"Why not take your wives along, and encourage your knights to do the same?" she said to Louis and Charles. "Your men may not be so eager, then, to return home before the task is finished." Now, after eight months away, Marguerite is the one yearning for home.

Sleep is her only escape from the terrible screams of tortured men. And yet it is silence that awakens her and brings her to the deck again. Louis, Robert, Charles and the pope's legate emerge from the hold, their faces grim—except for Robert, who grins as if he had just enjoyed the finest entertainments.

Beatrice hastens to Charles's side while Louis speaks to the ship's captain, who sends a boy scampering up the mainsail to the crow's nest. At the blast of his trumpet the surrounding ships crowd in, nobles and knights filling their decks. Marguerite stands outside her cabin door, staring at her husband's blood-spattered tunic.

"Friends and followers," Louis shouts, "we are unconquerable if we are undivided. The divine will has brought us here. Let us show our thanks by waiting to land after Pentecost, be the enemy's forces what they may."

Cheers and whistles mingle with mutterings. "Pentecost?" Beatrice says. "That's more than a week away. While we linger here, the Saracens will be preparing to fight."

For the love of God! Can she do nothing but criticize? Marguerite feels compelled to defend Louis. "We cannot hope to inspire others to our faith if we don't even keep our holy days."

"I thought we came to kill Muslims, not to convert them," her sister says. She tells Marguerite the secrets spilled by their prisoners: convinced that the French would land at Alexandria, the sultan of Egypt sent his army there, leaving Damietta virtually unguarded. "Charles says we should take the city now, and press on to Grand Cairo before the Saracens return."

"It is not I who am the King of France," Louis cries. "Nor am I the Holy Church. It is you yourselves, united, who are Church and King." As cheers gather and rise, he finishes. "In us shall Christ triumph, giving glory, honor, and blessing not to us, but to his own holy name."

𝒫ENTECOST HAS COME and gone, the Holy Spirit descending this year as a devastating wind that blew more than one thousand of their ships away from the harborless Damietta coast, scattering them to places unknown. Only a fourth of their army will land. There is talk of retreat, but this is the day for which Louis has dreamt, planned, and awaited for many years. "The Lord will lead us and protect us," he keeps saying, as if to convince himself.

Marguerite watches the landing from the ship's deck, her breath a ragged cloth snagged on a branch. Before her spreads an expanse of sea as blue as tears, and beyond that, the rock-jumbled shore of Egypt, where the knights of France have just begun to tumble from their boats and stomp their feet, adjusting to the firmness of solid ground for the first time in weeks. They have not yet seen the flashes of light, the clouds of dust, the horses and men in golden armor pouring forth from the gates of the walled city and racing toward them.

Jean, look up! Shouting would be pointless. He could not hear her from this distance. Yet she can hear the strange-sounding horns and kettledrums and shrill cries spurring the Saracens to action. The Frenchmen wedge their shields into the sand and thrust their lances into the ground, sharp points facing outward, then stand behind their barricade with their swords lifted high overhead. The Saracens thunder on as if the French weapons were made of dreams, easily trampled.

"Charles!" Beatrice, standing beside her, starts to scream for her husband, whose boat has not yet reached the shore. "Come back, Charles! You will be killed!"

"They are sailing to their deaths," she says to Marguerite. "And it is all your crazy husband's fault." Marguerite says nothing, for she cannot argue. If there are too few men on shore to withstand the Saracen attack, Louis will be at least in part to blame. The galley carrying Charles, Louis, their brother Robert, and the others from their ship is far from the shore, having been delayed by the fall of the old knight Plonquet into the sea and by Louis's insistence on halting to pray for his soul.

But Marguerite isn't going to malign her husband, especially to Beatrice, who is so quick to judge others and find them wanting. Besides, she is still trying to discern Joinville among the men on shore bracing themselves for the enemy's approach.

Sweet Mother, spare his life.

The attackers press forward, their cries audible even from this distance. Marguerite hears, also, the pounding of their horses' hooves—but no, that is her own pulse. The Saracens are gaining ground, and quickly, covering the beach in an attack that the French cannot flee, there being only the sea and enormous jagged rocks behind them. Every muscle tenses as if her body would armor itself. She searches for Joinville, but he is lost in the huddle of men standing *en garde* with only a barrier of shields and lance points between them and death.

"What a disaster," Beatrice says. "This mission has been flawed from the beginning. First Louis shames his barons into joining him instead of recruiting men who want to fight. Then we set sail at Aigues-Mortes, when Marseille is so much closer, and tarried eight months on Cyprus, spoiling our chances of a surprise attack, to await more troops that never came. Why he does not heed Charles's advice, I do not know."

To Marguerite's ear, these laments are as the sound of the wind rattling the sails: unremarkable, having been heard so many times before. Beatrice arrived for this journey with a scowl, one which she has nurtured ever since. "I would not have come except for you," she told Marguerite. "Since you are accompanying the king, now every man wants his wife along." As if Marguerite had a choice, as if she desired to leave her home and her babies with

Blanche and live among heathens in the desert. Joinville's joining the expedition has made it more agreeable—but now, watching what is sure to be the slaughter of their men, she would give anything, her life, if he had remained at home.

She grips the rail: now is the moment. The Arabs halt. Their horses, confused by the wall of shields and points, wheel and rear, tossing riders to the sand. French knights run forward, on the attack, and the fallen men leap to their feet. Marguerite presses her hand to her mouth as the next wave of Saracens crosses the bridge over the Nile and crashes onto the scene, cutting down the fighting Frenchmen, until a shower of arrows from behind the barrier sends the Saracens falling to the ground.

"Our men should not land. Why doesn't Louis turn the boat around?" Beatrice says. "His refusal to listen to Charles is going to make martyrs of them all."

"Be quiet, or I will arrest you for treason," Marguerite snaps. "Do you think Louis intended for this to happen?"

He envisioned a quick victory, the Saracens falling to their knees at the sight of the great French force, the innumerable ships. They embarked last August with a giddiness that dissipated when Alphonse failed to appear at Cyprus with the army he had promised. The debate over how to proceed turned nasty, as happens when anyone disagrees with Charles.

"If we go now, we can swoop on the Saracens like hawks," he insisted. "If we winter here, we give them months to prepare. They will never even allow us to land."

Robert, however, had the barons on his side—men who, as Beatrice points out again and again, Louis tricked with his gift of cloaks last Christmas. He laid the garments over their shoulders, then pointed out the red crosses embroidered in their folds. He grinned in childish glee at the sight of their stunned faces. They were now obliged to join his fight for the Holy Land. Why wouldn't they choose to tarry at Cyprus for as long as Louis would allow?

"The added troops will make France an unstoppable force,"

Robert argued. "If the Saracens are not surprised by our arrival, they will be stunned by our numbers."

But of what advantage is the greatest army in the world if the winds are against you? They lost so many ships, and men—of three thousand knights, only seven hundred remain, fewer than half of those on the shore now. Marguerite thinks of King David, how he slew the mighty Goliath with only a stone and a slingshot, and prays now for a similar miracle. The Lord is their only hope.

Again her prayers are answered. The battle dissolves. The Saracens ride away, save for the few on the ground fighting hand-to-hand, who will certainly be killed or captured. The galley carrying the Oriflamme, the red flag of St. Denis, lands ashore. Cries of *"Vive la France!"* sound across the water, along with shouts and cheers as two men plant the flag in the rocky sand. Its flame-like points flicker in the wind, announcing that France has arrived. The victorious knights yank off their helmets and embrace one another, while the foot soldiers gather the bodies of those killed in the skirmish. Marguerite squints into the sun, looking for blue-and-white stripes with a gold border—the coat of arms of Champagne. *Please, O Lord, let him be unharmed.*

Then shouts of a different sort arise from the royal galley, still some distance from the shore. Odo of Châteauroux, the pope's legate, leans over the rail on the top deck and waves his arms, crying out, as Louis clambers down the port side ladder in full armor, his shield around his neck, his head helmeted.

"What is the lunatic doing now?" Beatrice says as Louis leaps from the ladder into the sea. Marguerite cries out, unbelieving. He cannot swim. Worse: the water terrifies him.

And yet the chest-high sea barely slows him as he sloshes to shore, holding his lance and shield high overhead. Robert follows close behind, with several of his knights, and then Charles and the rest are scrambling down ladders and wading after him, for the king must not land alone and unprotected.

"How disappointing for Louis," Beatrice says. "First he misses the fighting. And now he finds himself walking *in* the waves, not on them."

Marguerite is not listening, however, not any more. For, as Louis nears the shore, she sees at last what—whom—she has been seeking. Jean, his helmet removed and his hair lifting in the breeze, has climbed atop the rocks and extends his hand to help the dripping Louis up and out of the water.

→ *Beatrice* ←

Real Sisters

Damietta, 1249

Eighteen years old

*S*HE ANSWERS THE cabin door with held breath, dreading bad news—but the captain is smiling. "Good tidings from the king, my lady. We have taken Damietta." A boat has arrived for her and Marguerite. They are to sail at once, before the afternoon winds blow.

And then she waits to board with her ladies and her belongings, watching Sir Jean de Joinville fold his long body to kiss Marguerite's ring. He lingers just a breath longer than he should; his eyes smile into hers. Marguerite pinkens, and who can blame her? Joinville is a handsome man, and most entertaining, with a quick wit and ready laugh. Louis, on the other hand, is a bore.

"We conquered Damietta in just two days?" she asks Sir Jean as he helps her aboard the galley. "I am astonished."

"Why, my lady?" His voice teases. "Do you expect our mission to fail?"

"Three-quarters of our army is blown off course and our second contingent has yet to arrive. If we succeed, I will consider it a miracle."

"Then we are fortunate to have the Maker of Miracles on our side, *non?*"

She cannot tell whether he is jesting. Marguerite's rapt expression offers no clues—not to Joinville's state of mind, at least. "But the Arabs worship our God, don't they?" she presses. "How do you know he isn't on *their* side?"

"They don't believe in the resurrection," Marguerite says. "They're like the Jews."

"Except the Jews crucified Christ," Joinville says.

Beatrice rolls her eyes. She would remind Joinville that Pontius Pilate, a Roman, ordered Jesus crucified, but Marguerite is saying, "Is that more heinous than occupying Jerusalem? I hear the Muslims have barred Christians from Abraham's tomb," as they walk away from her. What use is arguing, anyway? The French are cruel and unforgiving—as she has learned from Charles.

In this way, he could not be more different from Beatrice. She learned beauty and compassion at her father's knee. Charles swept into Provence like a violent storm. Upon becoming count, he ordered the tongues cut out of the mouths of dissenters, be they poets, merchants, or common vassals. The slightest whiff of revolt incites his crushing response. He destroyed an entire village because six of their men plotted against him. He killed a youth in the market at Aix for hitting him with a stone. He imprisoned Marseille's wealthiest merchants for refusing to pay homage to him, and hangs one of them every year in an effort to subdue the stubborn city.

"Weakness begets failure," he said when Beatrice protested his cruelty. "You want to become an empress, don't you?"

The galley comes to rest a short distance from the beach, where a dozen knights stand ready to retrieve them. Joinville lifts Marguerite into his arms and slowly—quite slowly—carries her across, taking care to bind up her skirts so they do not drag in the waist-high water.

Beatrice bounces in place. Outremer, Charles has said, will be a part of their empire. She cannot wait to begin helping him.

"Your brother the king treats me well," she said to him the night before he sailed to shore. "Let me try to influence him on your behalf." All those years by her father's side haven't gone to waste: Beatrice knows men, and how to coax them. Louis, for all his pious austerity, listens when she speaks—while his gaze flits to her bosom. She'll soon have his ear, which she'll turn away from the shortsighted Robert of Artois's advice and toward the astute suggestions of Charles (who ought to be King of France; his own mother has told him so). Together they will make this campaign the most successful of all, exceeding the pope's wildest expectations. Perhaps he will reward Charles with lands and castles—with Jerusalem, perhaps, the holy city! Or with Gascony, whose turmoil England seems unable to control.

"The cat loves fish, but hates to get its feet wet," she taunts the men still standing on shore. "Who will reach me first? Who will be my champion?" They rush into the water, their eyes on her, the beautiful countess, the wife of the king's brother, one of the famous sisters of Savoy, the prize.

But this is not the day for a mere knight to brag that he held Beatrice of Provence in his arms, for here comes Charles galloping up on his horse, splashing past them all. He slides into the water and swoops her up, making her laugh.

"What took you so long?" she teases. "I nearly had to go with another man."

"For you, there is no other man."

They ride across the sand, over the bridge spanning the broad, lazy Nile, past the high walls of Damietta, into a pastel world of stopped time and discarded dreams. Clothing and other objects litter the broad, stone-paved street—a dropped sandal, a yellow silk scarf, a candlestick, a scrap of white cotton collecting dust as it tumbles, leaf-like, in the skittering breeze. Candy-colored houses stare with empty eyes, their heavy doors agape. A wagon missing a wheel lies crookedly where it fell, its load blackened from a fire set, no doubt, to prevent the French from taking its contents. Atop the pile, a rooster flaps and crows in confusion. The market, too, has been set afire, its tables and shelters and clothing and food now so many piles of ash, making a charred hole in the elegant city like a gleaming smile with a rotted front tooth. Sooty remnants of books, fabrics, rugs, meat, and vegetables dissipate in the hot breeze, sending up puffs of ash.

"They thought to deprive us of sustenance. They might have spared themselves the effort," Charles says. Louis has arranged for merchants from Genoa and Pisa to provide food to the women while the men are at battle.

She takes his arm and steps with him into the sultan's palace, a grand, elegant building of white with minarets, arched doorways, and many windows. Louis, Robert, and the legate recline on red rugs and blue cushions on a floor tiled in yellow, blue, and white. Rich tapestries of blue and gold hang on the walls. This is the only residence that was not stripped bare, perhaps because the sultan is in Grand Cairo, Charles says. Or perhaps the palace guards kept looters at bay before finally fleeing.

"How considerate of the Saracens to evacuate this city and leave it for us," Robert says. "We must have presented a frightening spectacle indeed for the fearsome Turks to turn tail and run."

"And with only one quarter of our army," Louis says. "Praise be to God for increasing our numbers in their eyes."

Beatrice offers her hand to Robert in greeting. He brushes the air over it with a kiss, but Louis presses his mouth to her skin and then, as he smiles up at her, gives her hand a squeeze.

"Welcome, little sister," he says. "We are pleased to see that you have arrived in safety."

"Thanks to the Lord and to the saints," she says with a deep curtsey. "I only hope I can be of use to you here. As you know, I helped my father govern Provence for many years, during which we were constantly under attack."

"She is a brilliant strategist," Charles says as they take seats across from the king.

"Our strategy is simple: terrorize and conquer," Robert says.

"Yes, imagine the terror we will inspire when the rest of our ships return. One thousand of them! And do not forget Alphonse's army." Louis rubs his hands together. "We shall move across this land like a swarm of locusts, all the way to the Promised Land."

"Surely you don't intend to wait for reinforcements, when the men we have here are eager to fight," Charles says.

"The men who fought you on the beach are on their way to Grand Cairo now. Why not chase them down and kill them? That would strike fear into the sultan's heart," Beatrice adds.

Louis's smile is indulgent. "We appreciate your insights, but we would like to hear from our man Joinville. Didn't he escort you and your sister to shore?"

"I am here, Your Grace." Joinville enters with Marguerite on his arm. "I bring your incomparable Queen." He gestures to Marguerite, who blushes for reasons that Beatrice can guess.

"Come and give us your advice." Louis sits on his cushion again. Marguerite steps around to take her seat beside him. Joinville, following behind, slips a cushion beneath her, as skillful and attentive as a servant.

"What is your opinion, Joinville?" Louis says. "Robert suggests we wait for the rest of our army to join us before we proceed to Grand Cairo. Charles recommends we attack now."

"Cairo? I thought we came to take Jerusalem," Marguerite interjects.

Louis furrows his brow. "Military strategy can be difficult for a woman to grasp."

"Didn't the Egyptian sultan offer in the last campaign to surrender Jerusalem in exchange for Damietta?" she says.

"My predecessor Pelagius refused, then lost them both," the pope's man says.

"Then Damietta must be very important to the Egyptians—crucial, I would imagine, as a port of trade with the Italians. Perhaps we might strike a similar bargain now."

"The queen's idea is excellent." Joinville's dark eyes watch her with a bright intensity.

Robert's laugh sounds like a bark. "Yes, but unfortunately she is a step behind."

"The sultan has already made such an offer," Louis says. "We received the message this very day, while Joinville retrieved you from the ship."

"Praise God, then," Marguerite murmurs.

Joinville smiles. "That is good news, especially in light of our losses. With so few men in our camp, we would be hard-pressed to defeat the Turkish army in Cairo."

"You have provided me with my answer." Louis crosses his arms and sits back in satisfaction. "We shall remain here until our ships rejoin us, or until my brother arrives with our second army. Then we shall consider which city to conquer next, and how."

"But—is the sultan allowing us to remain here?" Marguerite asks.

"He has no choice," Robert says. "We own Damietta."

She frowns at Louis. "Didn't you say you had traded for Jerusalem?"

"The sultan offered. The king said 'no.'" Charles's tone drips with disgust.

Beatrice gasps. "Deliberately?" She stares at Louis, unable to believe he would be so stupid.

"Of course we said 'no,'" Robert says. "Why would we give up Damietta? We'll keep it, and take Jerusalem, too."

"That might be possible if we set sail up the Nile today," Charles says. "We might reach the holy city before the sultan's troops can get there from Alexandria."

Robert folds his arms over his chest.

"We shall wait," Louis says. "Alphonse will be here soon. And our lost ships are bound to return to us. Then we will conquer Jerusalem for the Church—not just for today, but for all time."

"Don't wait too long," Beatrice says. "In the last campaign, the army became trapped here for six months. The Nile floods every year, I hear, and it's impossible to cross."

"Excuse me, Your Grace, but do women now rule in France?" Robert says. He turns to her. "We men came to conquer the holy land for our lord Jesus Christ. We brought you women along to cheer for us—and to keep us out of temptation." He grins. "My wife had best hurry before a Saracen beauty seduces me."

"Moving slowly has been the fatal error in all the campaigns of the past," Beatrice says. She leans forward to place a hand on Louis's. "Charles is suggesting a new way. Why not try it?"

"Yes, you must remember the mistakes of the past, so that you don't repeat them," Marguerite says.

Louis's expression sours. "Why does a king bring his queen on a mission such as this? For support, and not to be argued with."

"I am not arguing," Marguerite says. "Merely advising."

"If a woman's advice had been my desire, I would have brought my mother along," Louis says, turning away from her. "She, at least, knows a thing or two about waging war."

Marguerite's gaze drops; her face reddens. Beatrice can well imagine the scathing retorts pressing against her teeth, but she says nothing—and neither, now, does Beatrice. Robert of Artois has always been a fool and the worst kind, Charles says, who regards himself as a genius. Louis is a bigger fool for heeding his advice—and for disregarding Marguerite, who is always the smartest person in any room.

Her gaze lifts, then, to meet Beatrice's. Instead of the humiliation she expects, however, Beatrice sees disdain in her sister's eyes. Louis's disrespect is nothing new, it seems. No wonder she so desperately wants Tarascon! Without her husband's support, she lives precariously, never sure of her fate. Having a castle of her own in Provence would give her a measure of security, at least.

But no. She has asked Charles too many times, causing him to snarl at her. Marguerite wants all of Provence, he said. Giving Tarascon to her would be like inviting a wolf into the poultry house. "She would devour us," he said.

Looking at her sister now, Beatrice is not so certain. Couldn't Marguerite contest Papa's entire will, if she so desired? The Church supports the firstborn's right to inheritance. All she has ever asked for, however, is her dowry. "Otherwise, I bring nothing to my marriage," she says. "It's a matter of respect."

Respect. Beatrice suddenly understands why the Queen of mighty France would care about a castle in little Provence. Gaining Tarascon would enhance her status in her subjects' eyes. No longer would she be seen as the landless daughter of a poor count, but as the heiress to a portion of her father's domain. Tarascon is a fortress that would protect her sister in more ways than one.

For the first time, as she looks into her sister's eyes, Beatrice feels what Marguerite feels. And, for the first time, she feels something else: the desire to help her sister. *Family comes first.* Tomorrow, before the men leave for Cairo, she will speak with Charles again. This time, she'll make him listen—and gain the love of her sister, at last.

⇢ *Eléonore* ⇠

Liars and Traitors

London, 1250

Twenty-seven years old

*I*F SHE WERE dreaming, this would be a nightmare. But alas, the trial is no dream from which she will awaken with a laugh of relief. Simon de Montfort, Henry's man in Gascony these past three years, stands before the barons' council with a sneer and boasts of the cruelties he has inflicted against the people there. And yet, it is not he on trial today, but her cousin Gaston—who saved her life while she gave birth in Bordeaux—charged with opposing Simon and, by extension, the English crown.

Gaston, it must be said, is no innocent. His lust for power—and his unscrupulous pursuit of it—shows in his cocksure swagger, his haughty tone. Although he is here as Simon's prisoner, he never hangs his head. Instead, he winks at her—winks! At her stern expression, he arranges his mouth in a peculiar shape suggesting that it has been somewhere not quite clean but highly enjoyable. His dark mustache only heightens the impression. With no beard on his chin, it resembles a smear of dirt that Eléonore itches to scrub away.

"He is a traitor to England," Simon says. "His attacks on your castles have cost an enormous sum in repairs and fortifications."

"Gaston de Béarn, where does your loyalty lie?" Henry asks.

"With England, or with Castille or Navarre, whose kings conspire to take Gascony from us?"

"I am loyal to Gascony."

Eléonore smiles. With this clever response, he has managed to answer Henry's question without answering it. His evasiveness will allow her to help him out of this predicament. *I will not forget,* she promised him after little Beatrice was safely born, after he saved both their lives in Bordeaux. She owes him a great debt, one which she will now repay, with hopes of gaining his allegiance for England. As Viscount of Béarn and the patron of the Church's popular Order of Faith and Peace, he wields much influence in Gascony.

"Why do you resist English rule?" she asks. "Would you rather be beholden to the White Queen, harsh as she is, than to Henry and me, who have granted you so much freedom?"

"Freedom exists in the minds of men, and in their hearts," he says. "It can neither be given nor taken away."

"Then why fight against us?"

"My lady—my dear cousin—surely you know the answer. The people of Gascony are not unlike the inhabitants of your own home, Provence. See how the Provençales have fought the impositions of the Frenchman Charles of Anjou? We Gascons do not want a foreigner ruling our land, either. Nor do we care for the administrators you send—incompetent men, and corrupt ones, who extort coins from our barons to increase their own purses."

"Simon de Montfort is impeccably honest," she says.

"He may be honest, my lady. But he is also cruel."

She shakes her head. She can believe certain things of Simon— that he is ambitious, that he is persistent, that he has a temper as volatile as Henry's, that he stands with one foot in England and the other in France, where he is reported to love King Louis as a brother. But—cruel? Surely Eleanor would have mentioned it last night, as she and Eléonore supped in her chambers and talked like sisters into the morning.

"We have heard these accusations before," Henry says. "Tell us more."

Now the salacious smirk of Gaston de Béarn is gone. The cock-sure swagger in his voice becomes a sorrowful quaver. Eléonore wants to cover her ears. Simon, he says, tied candles to men's hands so that the fingers might be burned along with the tallow. He injected vinegar into their bodies, then watched as they screamed and writhed. He tied their hands behind their backs and attached heavy bars of iron to their feet, then hanged them from the rafters, pulling their limbs loose from their bodies.

"If these tales are true, then why have you escaped unharmed?" she blurts, interrupting his litany. "You are, after all, a leader in the Gascon rebellion."

He bows his head to her. "I do not know, but I can surmise."

She turns again to Simon. His eyes glint, as cold as flint. "I spared him my torments out of respect for you, my lady."

So he admits the tortures. Eléonore falls back against her throne. What has happened to Simon? Once a noble man and a faithful friend, he has betrayed them both with these terrible—forbidden—punishments. Yet he expects them to hang her cousin for treason. Is this a test? If so, Simon is the one who is failing. And yet—she must keep his friendship. She needs him on her side more now than ever.

"You wanted information," Simon says. "You wanted order. You wanted your taxes collected. Now you have all three, plus the rebel leader in your custody."

"How can we retain him after hearing these tales against you?" Henry cries. "Don't you see? By dealing so harshly with Gascony's most respected men, you have stirred anger against us as never before. As for the taxes you collected, the sum does not begin to compensate for all you have so fruitlessly expended. You have wasted our time, our money, and our good relations with the Gascons."

"The Gascons are liars and traitors." Simon's gaze careens about the room. His eyes, wildly blue like the sky behind a storm cloud, catch Eléonore's for a fleeting moment before he turns to Gaston.

"I gave ample warning. They knew what they stood to lose

if they continued to rob, rape, and burn the houses of England's supporters. And I did nothing without the assent of Parliament." He produces a document, signed by the leaders of the barons' council.

Relief floods her: Simon was authorized. The court will have to acquit him.

"See here!" With a laugh of triumph, he waves another parchment before Henry's nose—the agreement he signed appointing Simon to Gascony for seven years and promising to reimburse him for the costs of fortifying the duchy's castles.

"I have been there fewer than three years, yet already I am in arrears over these repairs." He pauses and then, in a high, commanding voice he adds, "I demand that you repay all the money I have spent in your service."

Henry's face turns red, then purple. His eyes bulge. His lips press together so hard they turn white. Eléonore holds her breath. She, Henry, and their chancellor Sir John Maunsell spent many hours crafting this agreement; later, she spent hours more convincing Simon to accept it. "Henry will never pay," he said to Eléonore then.

If only he would lower his eyes. A show of humility might gain him what he desires. Instead, though, the headstrong Simon glares at the king as though they were equals, or worse, as though he were the stern father and Henry a petulant child.

Henry sees the look. His gaze tightens.

"No," he says, "I will not keep these promises." A gasp sucks through the room. "I never gave permission for cruelty to the people of Gascony—people who serve me, who rely on me, their duke, for justice, not coercion and torture. You have betrayed me, and so now I will betray you. You will get no money from me."

Simon steps forward, pushing aside the king's guards who try to keep him at a distance. "Betray! That word is a lie," he cries. "Were you not my sovereign, this would be an ill hour for you."

Eléonore grasps the arms of her throne, feeling as if she might fall out of it. Henry, too, sits in stunned silence. Mistaking their astonishment for weakness, Simon steps forward again and points a finger at Henry. "With lies such as these, who could believe you to be a Christian?"

Eléonore sits up in her seat. He has gone too far. "That is enough, Sir Simon!"

"Do you ever go to confession?" he says to Henry.

"Don't answer him," Eléonore says. Having laid many a verbal trap, she knows Simon's game. As strained as her marriage has been of late, she does not desire to see Henry played for a fool.

"I do, indeed, go to confession," Henry says, pride tingeing his voice.

"Tell me, O king: What is the purpose of confession"—Simon turns to face the crowd—"without repentance?" He folds his arms, pleased with himself in spite of all he has just lost: his friendship with Eléonore; his favor with the king; his chance to succeed in Gascony.

Henry leaps to his feet. "I have indeed repented!" he cries. "I am sorry that I ever allowed you to enter England, to marry my sister, and to take over lands and honors here. And, by God, I am sorry I ever sent you to Gascony.

"But you will return, and you will cease these cruel measures, and you will keep the peace without a penny from me. And if I hear any more slanders from you, I will hang you from the London Bridge and dangle you there until my duchy is at peace."

<hr />

AND THEN HER dear friend Eleanor Montfort is gone. Simon, in custody in the Tower, managed somehow to send his wife away as if she were in danger of imprisonment, too. Eléonore wonders if she will ever see her friend again. Henry's quick temper will soon subside, but Simon is a nurser of grudges. He may keep Eleanor from them, out of spite.

She paces the floor outside the chancellory, where Henry meets with John Maunsell and her uncle Peter to decide Simon's fate. After the council's verdict in his favor, clearing him of wrongdoing, he tried to resign from his post—but Henry would not allow it. "You cannot extricate yourself from the seven years you promised simply by insulting me," he said.

In the candlelit hall Eléonore walks and worries. What are they doing behind that door? How will Simon fare without her influence on their talks? How will Henry fare without Simon's goodwill? He and the French king have become friends, Marguerite says. *Simon trots behind Louis as if he were a puppy and Louis's pockets were filled with treats.* Indeed, he had planned to join King Louis's crusade before Eléonore, hearing of his intentions, convinced Henry to send him to Gascony, instead.

She can do nothing for him now. She is excluded from the meeting, shut out because of her friendship with Simon. Henry blames her for the Gascony appointment, although, were the truth to be told, Simon's decision to take the cross with France unnerved him, too. Simon knows Henry's secrets. Might danger's sharp edge cut loose his tongue, causing him to spill those secrets before the French king?

In the chancellory, Henry's voice rises, then falls. Eléonore presses her ear to the door again.

"My lady." She jumps, startled, and turns to see Henry's Lusignan half-brother, William de Valence, twitching his lips at her.

"Sir William!" She hates her nervous laughter, the titter of a child caught in some naughty act. "What are you doing here?"

He puts on that infuriating false smile that he reserves, she knows, especially for her. "I am summoned to a meeting."

She does not even try to hide her dismay. Looking pleased with himself, he sweeps past her and into the chancellory. "Lower your voices, if you would keep your words private," she hears him say. "I caught someone listening outside the door."

With a flaming face she runs up the stairs and into her chambers. Fortune, her hawk, turns its head to peer at her through its cage, hanging from a hook on the bedpost. She falls into a chair and stares into the fire, watches its capricious shadow dance on the walls. William de Valence's participation does not bode well for

Simon. The men have hated each other since William married Joan de Munchensi, the heiress to Pembroke. William seized Pembroke Castle for his own, although William Marshal had given it to Eleanor Montfort before he died. The men have been fighting over it ever since, disrupting meetings of the barons' council with their shouting and name-calling. And William's complaints have harmed the friendship Simon and Henry once enjoyed. Simon's "Charles the Simple" insult, for instance, made nearly a decade ago, might be forgotten if William de Valence did not so often repeat it.

A rift with Simon might bring trouble. Eléonore has warned Henry of this many times—but he doesn't listen to her as he once did. He listens to William now, who speaks against her, coveting for his own family every title, every grant of lands, every marriage that Henry has arranged for Eléonore's relatives. Thanks be to God that Uncle Peter has summoned to England three hundred Savoyard cousins, nieces, and nephews. Eléonore will arrange advantageous matches for them all, and they will support her when she needs them.

William's aim is clear: to antagonize Henry toward her and her relations. Henry, so hungry for family, makes the task easy for him. That business involving Uncle Boniface at St. Bartholomew, for instance. Eléonore's cousin Philip witnessed the whole ugly incident and told them what happened, but Henry's mind was already set. He exclaimed in his usual red-faced way, pacing the room, hands flying about. An embarrassment, he said. After all he has done to help her family. If only he had listened to William and appointed their brother Aymer as archbishop of Canterbury. (Aymer, who cannot even read!) But he did Eléonore's bidding, instead. As if she were a hen pecking at him, directing him.

Eléonore sat on his bed with her hands in her ermine muff, clasping them against the cold and reminding herself to remain calm.

"Archbishop of Canterbury is an important post," she said. "I hardly think Aymer would have qualified."

"At least he would not go around murdering monks!" Henry cried.

"Nor would Uncle Boniface."

"Your uncle nearly killed the subprior at St. Bartholomew."

"That report is exaggerated."

"He threw him to the floor!"

"After the subprior attacked him with his cane. The subprior is an old man. He probably fell."

"Your uncle drew his sword, Eléonore. The monks had to restrain him, or he would have run the poor man through."

Eléonore harrumphed. "My sweet uncle would not harm a fly. Having a volatile temper does not always translate into violence—as you know."

"William says—"

"Why should I care what William says?" Eléonore snapped, forgetting to remain calm. "Why do you care? Why you listen to that braggart is beyond my comprehension."

"He is my brother," Henry said. For the first time, his face closed against her like an iron gate. Eléonore knew then that the rules had changed for her and Henry.

If she had not fought Richard's appointment to the Gascony post, perhaps Henry would not have distanced himself from her. Given his reverence for the very idea of family, it must seem heretical, in a way, for her to speak against a brother. For her to oppose two brothers would be akin to blasphemy.

Eléonore understands this: she too reveres family. "God first, family second, country third." These were Mama's last words before sending her off to England. Yet Mama knows that loyalty need not be blind. The more clearly one sees, the more skillfully one may fight.

Eléonore sees Henry quite clearly. She sees Simon, too. She sees how much alike they are, yet how different—like steel and flint, harmless apart but producing sparks when rubbed together. Each is as stubborn as the other, each as temperamental, each as ambitious. She had thought it might do them both good to gain distance from each other. She had thought to save Simon by sending him across the channel. Most of all, she had thought to keep Gascony out of Richard of Cornwall's grasping hands.

She should have suggested Richard for the Gascony post. He might have negotiated peace with the rebels, and at a much lower price than Simon's endless wars have cost. Sending him far away might have helped Sanchia, too.

Her sister's letters have become increasingly disturbing. *He goes very hard against me since our baby died.* Although she soon had another son, Richard had lost too many, it seemed, to develop affection for another child. *He ignores our little Edmund, which breaks my heart, for he is a precious child, although brutally conceived.*

"Brutally conceived." Should Eléonore be alarmed, or amused? The caw of a crow can make the timid Sanchia tremble. Why, though, did she turn as pale as a corpse when Eléonore refused her request to give Gascony back to Richard? Eléonore's "no" made Sanchia recoil as if it were a punch from Richard's fist.

But Richard is not a fighter. He is a negotiator, the best in England. He is a lover, too, as Joan de Valletort made clear last year. Her appearance at Sanchia's feast with Richard's illegitimate son sent scandalized ripples through the hall—which she appeared to relish. Apparently, she intended to ensure that Richard would not forget who bore his first son. Richard, it seemed, had forgotten nothing: the moment the baroness walked into the room, he snapped to attention like a dog on point.

Sanchia could not compete. Golden hair and full lips do not compensate for a lack of sophistication, not with a man like Richard. Mama knew this, which is why she sparkled at Sanchia's wedding feast as though she were the bride. Dazzled by Sanchia's beauty and bedazzled by Mama's wit, Richard failed to notice his new wife's blush and stammer, her twisting of the tablecloth in her lap, her uncertain laughter at the banter she did not quite understand. Had he known, he would certainly have found another to marry, for a loving and pious heart means little to a man who has no heart at all.

Richard married Sanchia not for her heart, but for her influence on the queens of England and France—so he says. Their mother tells another tale, how he visited their château on his way to Outremer and was smitten by Sanchia's perfection. She has the same effect on every man, even Henry—although why should she think "even Henry," as though he were incapable of desiring other women?

Voices rise from the hall. Eléonore springs from her chair and sweeps down the stairs to hear the verdict. John Maunsell bows, hiding his expression. William taps a rolled-up parchment against his thigh, his lips pursed in their usual pucker of condescension. But it is Henry's face she seeks, that long, beloved face with its drooping eyelid that seems, tonight, to sag a bit more than usual. He is tired. Exhaustion dulls his eye when he returns her gaze.

"How have you fared?" she says to Henry, reaching for his hand.

"You mean to ask how Simon has fared," Henry says. "We have drawn up . . . terms."

"Terms?"

"Rules, my lady," William interjects.

"Guidance for his conduct upon his return to Gascony. How we wish for him to deal with the people," Maunsell adds.

"What rules?" she asks. Like Henry, Simon does not prefer the "guidance" of others. "May I see them?" She reaches out but William yanks the parchment away.

"They are reasonable," Henry says. "Given the circumstances." He averts his gaze from her incredulous stare.

"That must be why you are so eager to let me see them."

"My lady, let me say this, if I may: Simon de Montfort will be very surprised at what our Charles the Simple has devised," William says. His laugh—a dry cackle—tells Eléonore everything she needs to know.

⇻ *Marguerite* ⇻
The Time of Sorrow
Egypt, 1250
Twenty-nine years old

*T*HE SILENCE STRETCHES and groans like a man on the rack. Marguerite paces the balcony of the sultan's palace, holding her belly with both hands, the child she carries as heavy as her foreboding. If only the interminable winds would cease—or bring her some news.

The men departed six months ago, horses high-stepping and spirited, off to Grand Cairo once they heard that the sultan Ayyub had died—but not before a lively discussion over which city to conquer next. The barons argued with one another and with Louis, in whom they were already losing confidence. His later decisions had proved as disastrous as his early ones. Camping outside the city walls to guard Damietta had resulted in many deaths, for the Saracens attacked them while they slept. Later, Louis sent home some of their best warriors for succumbing to the Saracen prostitutes who came to their camp. Then they became stranded for months when—*quelle surprise!*—the Nile flooded the land, making a lake too deep to ford. As the waters subsided, Alphonse finally arrived—bringing, in addition to troops, Robert of Artois's plump wife Matilda of Brabant, who jumped into her husband's arms—allowing the party to proceed. But—to where?

Alexandria, Charles urged. Not only is the city near Jerusalem, but the merchant ships at its busy port could keep the army well supplied. The barons agreed, but Robert argued: Grand Cairo must be their target. Conquering Egypt's capital would weaken the sultan's hold on Jerusalem, making it possible to take the holy city.

"If you wish to kill a snake, you must cut off its head," he said.

Louis slapped his brother on the back. "Praise to God, we are of like minds," he said. "Let us take Cairo, then, and claim not only the Holy Land but all of Egypt for our Lord."

The decision was not well received. Everyone grumbled: the barons occupying the Damietta homes, running short of money for food; the foot soldiers camped on the beach, who had eaten most of their provisions, and especially Beatrice and Charles, who never let the presence of either Marguerite or Matilda inhibit them from declaring Louis and Robert to be incompetent fools.

"They would hurl us along the same path to destruction that the King of Navarre's campaign followed," Charles said, pacing in the chambers where Beatrice and Marguerite lay side by side, hands on each other's swollen bellies. "It is as though my brother had no knowledge of the past."

More likely, Louis wants to demonstrate his favor with God by succeeding where Thibaut failed. Marguerite said this to Jean, who agreed with her—smiling, for he loves Louis, and grins over his antics as a parent might indulge a child. Marguerite, meanwhile, wished her husband might camp forever outside Damietta, leaving Jean to guard the palace and keep her company. Every night, after finishing his duties in the camp, Jean would visit her chambers and sit, propped by cushions, on her bed (there being no chairs or sofas in this world) to talk by candlelight. Their discussion ranged freely. Poetry, philosophy, politics, and art. Champagne, Provence, and the *Roman de la Rose*. The papal feud with the Emperor Frederick. The White Queen's love affairs—Marguerite has told him all she knows, of course. The rebellions in Gascony. His children, and her children (but never his wife). Dominicans versus Franciscans. The harmonies of Pérotin, astronomy, the flavor of cardamom. They talked—sharing knowledge, trading witticisms, opening their hearts, feeding Marguerite's long-hungering mind with the sweet fruits of friendship until, depleted of words, they would at last fall asleep with only their hands touching. Mornings she would awaken and trace her fingertips in the indentation left by his head on her pillow, and recall every word, every gesture. Afternoons she would nap in order to remain awake with him that night, for the conversation that she wished never had to end.

Now the absence of his voice is more oppressive than the wind's hum, which amplifies the silence but deafens her, at least, to Matilda's chatter. Robert's wife talks only about her hunger and her babies left at home, and her husband who is, according to her, the most wonderful man on Earth. "He is called 'Robert the Good,' do you know?" she says at least once every day. Marguerite did not know, but she does now.

She had thought Beatrice might keep her company. But pregnancy was hard on her sister, pulling her down to sleep so frequently that Marguerite wondered if she had caught a sickness from the swarming flies. Whenever they talked, the *question* between them, lurking in the shadow of every uttered phrase, would invariably rise and ask itself, and Marguerite would lift her eyebrows, waiting, until Beatrice would snort with irritation and stomp off to her chambers.

The feud ended when Beatrice had her baby. Marguerite remained by her side through the long, difficult birth, holding her hand, mopping her brow, encouraging her sister to be brave, cheering when the infant at last came forth. Afterward, Beatrice's eyes filled with tears as she and Marguerite cooed over the babe, a beautiful child who looks nothing like Charles.

"I did not think you cared for me," she told Marguerite.

"Ridiculous," Marguerite said. "We are sisters."

"I have never felt like one of you."

"Seeing your courage today, I can tell you that you are definitely one of us."

"You strengthened me." She began to cry. "I wanted to give up. If not for you, my baby might have died. How can I ever repay you?"

Marguerite looked away.

"I must be delirious. Of course I know what you want most in all the world. And, of course, I will give it to you."

Marguerite took a breath, willed her excited pulse to slow down. Her sister may, indeed, be delirious. "But you cannot afford to part with ten thousand marks. You said so yesterday."

"I said that we need every penny to defend our castles. But we do not need all our castles. We do not need Tarascon."

"I *do* need it, more than you can know. But, no—you cannot give it to me."

"I can. It is mine, isn't it?"

"You said Charles would not allow it."

"He said you have never given *him* anything but an upset stomach." She grins. "He'll change his mind when he hears how you cared for me today."

Now Marguerite was the one with the eyes full of tears. Tarascon will be hers. At last, she will have her dowry. She will have, at last, something to call her own. Should Louis die before her, she will not be bereft. She will not be forced to enter a convent, the usual recourse for widowed queens whose husbands have failed to provide for them. Louis bequeathed her nothing.

It's only fair a man should find/ His peace with what he's sought so long. Guillem de Peiteus's words ring true: Having finally gained Tarascon, Marguerite feels peace settling, timid and trembling as a rabbit, into her breastbone.

The wind ceases, proving that miracles never do. From within, she hears Beatrice pleading with her infant. "Cry, darling! It may improve your spirits." Fevers and strange rashes have begun to attack the babe after only a few days of life, leaving her too ill even to whimper.

Now, though, Marguerite does hear a cry, and the shouting of the knights of Burgundy and the foot soldiers of Genoa and Pisa outside the city walls. She gazes across the rocky beach to see the Oriflamme flicking like a tail in the wind followed by Louis's knights on horseback and his foot soldiers running, holding up their shields and waving their lances. She lets out a cry. Their approach can mean only one thing: victory for France.

"*Vive la France!*" she shouts, and the entire somnolent city rings with life. The barons' wives pour forth from their dwellings, bare-armed in the sultry April heat, rushing like a snow-fed stream toward the gate. Matilda, on the balcony with Marguerite, cries, "Praise the Lord!" and throws her arms around Marguerite, who throws her arms around Beatrice, whose baby in her arms begins, at long last, to cry.

Their joy is short-lived. "Saracens!" the Duke of Burgundy screams. "Everyone into the palace at once. Hurry to the palace; we are under attack!"

As the men draw nearer, Marguerite can see that, although their armor and shields bear the fleur-de-lis and coats of arms of France and its neighbors, their skin is the color of almonds. Saracens, wearing French armor! Not victory, then, but utter defeat. Her knees wobble. She longs to sit. But she is queen, and must set an example. "Inside, hurry!" she says to Beatrice and Matilda, whose faces droop with disappointment. They make their way inside, to her chambers—where the Lord John of Beaumont awaits, looking at the floor as if searching for something lost there.

He falls to one knee before her. "My lady, I bring tidings most grave."

Had she hoped, only a moment before, for some news to break the silence? Now she wants only to cover her ears with her hands. "Please rise, Sir John. Have you had repast? Let me send for some bread and wine, and then we may talk."

"No, my lady." The growl for which he is known—and feared—returns to his voice. "I must deliver my message. Time is of the essence."

"The king! Is he injured?"

"He is captured, my lady. Taken prisoner by the Turks, and delivered to the Egyptian queen."

Marguerite presses her hands to her chest. If Louis dies, they will all die here. "Who else?"

"His brother the Count of Anjou, my lady. His brother the Count of Poitou. The Count of Brittany. The Lord Geoffrey of Sargines. The Lord Walter of Châtillon."

"The Lord Robert, the king's brother?" Matilda stands in the doorway, clasping her hands as if in prayer. "What of him?"

Lord John drops his gaze again. "Killed, my lady. I am sorry."

Matilda shrieks; her head drops back. Marguerite catches her as she slumps in a faint. Her ladies flutter around. They lay her on the bed, and Marguerite kneels beside her, placing herself lower than Lord Beaumont and not caring. The rules are different—she does not know, anymore, what they are.

"Sir Robert died with honor, my lady," Lord Beaumont says. "He almost took Mansoura. But the Turks came, thousands of them, and there was a most brutal slaughter."

"Thank you, Lord Beaumont," she says, cutting him off lest Matilda hear.

Thinking that he has been dismissed, he steps toward the door. Marguerite's head jerks up.

"Lord Beaumont," she says, more loudly than she intends. He stops and turns to her.

"What of Sir Jean de Joinville? You did not mention him."

At the mournful dip of his head, she thanks God that she is already on the floor. Jean, killed too? But no. "He is imprisoned, my lady," Beaumont says. "With the king."

———◆———

WITH LOUIS CAPTURED, she takes command. Lord Beaumont offers to advise her but she waves him away. She knows what must be done. She sends knights and foot soldiers to delay the Saracens' approach, and learns that the Queen of Egypt, anticipating an easy victory, has sent only a small force. Ha! She will show these Saracens a thing or two about French spirit. She sends galleys to procure more food from the ships offshore. The Genoese and Venetian merchants will brave even a Turkish siege if they stand to profit. She confers with the military leaders on how to defend the city, for if they lose Damietta, they will have nothing with which to ransom the French prisoners. Louis will be lost, and so will they all. She sends Lord Beamont on a ship to Paris, to request money from Blanche for their men's ransom, and she sends the Countess Matilda with him. She sends a messenger to the Templars requesting funds, as well, plus knights to help with the city's defense.

And then, as the few men remaining to them build stone throwers and stockpile arrows, the first dull cramp squeezes her womb. An hour later, there is another.

She writes a letter to the Queen of Egypt. She knows the pains of labor, that sometimes they are false. She prays that this is so now. She cannot cease her duties, for who then would rule? Every man of authority is dead or taken captive, leaving only her. *We pray that you will keep our men in safety while we negotiate their release. We remain securely in possession of Damietta, and offer it in trade for our king Louis and all his nobles, knights, and foot soldiers in your captivity.*

Shouts ring from outside. Marguerite runs to the balcony. The Turks are building a tower and siege engine, and have already begun firing flaming arrows over the city walls. She sees a man fall, and another. From inside, she hears Gisele calling for her.

"Sir John de Voré wishes to speak with you, my lady Queen," she says, breathless.

He bows slowly, as if old age had rusted his hinges. His eyes, draped above and below in folds of skin, look directly into hers. These, Marguerite realizes, are all who remain to fight for France: aged knights and peasant boys.

"The Turks have begun their siege, my lady," he says.

The tide crests, then crashes over her thighs. She cries out in alarm. A dark pool spreads across the front of her gown. She looks back up at the knight, as if he could save her. He holds out a hand to her.

"May I escort you to your birthing chamber, my lady?" he says. "It appears that your time has come."

Day blurs into night fades into day. The clatter of the Turkish engine. Acrid burning pitch. Rowdy laughter and a heathen chant. The old knight's large hand around her own, and the soft scent of Gisele. Beatrice's commanding tone and her palm on Marguerite's brow. Then another squeeze of pain, the Latin prayers of the papal legate, the cloy of incense, the stink of shit. A shriek from outside—a man in Saracen robes waving a scimitar and shouting in Arabic, lunging for her. Marguerite screams.

"Sir John, protect me!" she cries.

Women's arms pulling her up, Beatrice on one side of her and the knight on the other, walking her around the room in circles, in spirals, and then, when she becomes dizzy and nauseated, in a straight line, to and fro.

"Let her rest," the knight says.

"No," Beatrice says. "The baby must come now, or perish."

Men rush into her chamber, armed with crossbows. Marguerite protests: she is in labor, and needs peace. "The Turks are tearing down the walls," the old knight says. "These men are here to protect us."

She clutches his arm. "Promise me, sir knight," she says. "You must not let the Turks take my baby and me alive." They would rape her, then sell her into slavery—and her child, if it lived, would grow up a heathen, destined for hell. Death would be a far kinder fate.

"The moment the Saracens enter this palace, you must kill us both. Please, sir knight, swear that you will!"

"We are of like minds, madame," he says. "I had already determined to do so."

Back in her bed, perspiration and tears soak the coverings. *Hail Mary full of grace blessed are you among women.* A flash of light—a splintering, as if the heavens were splitting in two; the howl of the wind blowing into the room, knocking over an empty drinking gourd and rolling it across the floor. Rain pours from the sky, pelts the roof like stones, sprays across her, quenching her skin. *Push, sister! Push harder! You can do it.* She gulps the sweet air—the breath of God—fills with strength, and pushes the baby out. Her fourth living child, her sixth altogether, Jean Tristan, she has already named him, for the time of sorrow in which he enters this world.

——◆——

*I*N THE MORNING, sun. And, miraculously, quiet. The *squonk* of a gull is the only sound. At the window, Gisele admires the blue day. The Turks, she says, have ceased their attack, and sit in their tents, waiting for God knows what. Everyone is taking credit: the legate, citing his prayers; the crossbowmen, bragging about the thick hail of arrows they fired; Marguerite, privately, crediting the letter she penned to Shajar al-Durr, the Sultaness of Egypt.

The sultaness's messenger waits in the great hall. Marguerite summons him. Before he arrives, though, three soldiers gather at the foot of her bed. "We have come to say good-bye," one of them tells her in broken French.

Marguerite pushes herself to sit straighter, the night's travails forgotten. "Where are you going? You can't leave me now. What will happen to me—to all of us?"

"If we stay, my lady, then we will die," he says. "You would do the same."

"I would not. Not when other lives are at stake."

"Yet you would have us lose our lives to save yours?"

"The life of your queen." Then she remembers: She is not their queen. These men are from Genoa and Pisa, mercenaries hired from the merchant ships off shore. "The life of the King of France," she says.

"The king who promised to pay us, and now is in the Saracen

jail, being tortured to death, or starved," he says. "Forgive me, my lady, but we must eat."

"We have food here," she says. "From your ships."

"Like you, my lady, we must pay for our meals. But the king has not paid us, and our purses are empty. So we must go."

She casts about for a solution. "My purse is not empty. Perhaps I can pay you all now."

He names a sum, and she gasps. "We have been here for nearly six months, my lady. With the sultan dead, King Louis expected immediate victory."

Sweat breaks out on her brow. The silver at her behest could pay only a small portion of the debt to these men. Yet if they abandon Damietta, the city is lost—and she will never be able to ransom Louis, Joinville, and the rest. And with only a handful of knights left to protect them, how will the women, children, and clergymen here survive the Turkish raids?

"Give me a moment, *monsieur*." She closes her eyes to think. It feels good to close her eyes. She has not slept enough; weariness weights her bones, slows her mind. Think. They want to be paid; she cannot pay them. She must save her silver to pay the Egyptian queen. The sultaness will certainly demand a high sum for the men's release, in addition to Damietta—if Marguerite can even hold Damietta.

She opens her eyes. "I do not have enough to pay the salaries for you all."

"Then we will say good-bye, and good luck." He folds his arms. Her head begins to throb.

"If I paid those of you in this room, would that be enough?"

"We could not in good conscience accept such an offer. We have come on behalf of all our men, not just ourselves."

"And so you will leave us to be slaughtered?" Her voice rises. "May God forgive you!"

He unfolds his arms, opening to her. "Look at me, my lady. I was once a rotund man. Now I am only bones covered with skin.

My stomach complains day and night. I have not had a meal in nearly a week. We are all in this same position."

"You are hungry. Gisele! Gisele!" Her handmaid appears; the men eye her, their appetites sharpened for more than just food. "Tell the cooks we will be serving six more at dinner this afternoon."

The spokesman clears his throat. "We could not accept. It would not be fair to the rest of our men. There are a hundred others as hungry as we."

She is thinking aloud, grasping ideas from the air. "Why don't you dine here, in the palace? All of you, at my expense. Every meal." She runs a calculation in her head—one hundred men, and she has several hundred thousand livres still in her coffers.

The men look at one another. Two of them, including the spokesman, are smiling, but the third stands with folded arms. They murmur among themselves, and the spokesman turns to her. "This proposal is unexpected. We would like to discuss it with the others."

Her heart sinks. Once the men have filled their bellies, they are much less likely to agree to her terms.

"I am in negotiation at this very moment with the Queen of Egypt for my husband's release." It may be a lie or, very soon, it might be true. "She expects an immediate response to her terms. I need your answer now."

He bows. "Our men are waiting in the hall to learn the outcome of our talk. I shall return to you within the hour."

As they file out, Marguerite gestures to Gisele. "Tell the cooks I want to dine now," she murmurs. "Tell them not to come the usual way, through the back. Have them come around front and through the hall, with uncovered plates." The sights and smells of the food may entice the mercenaries to remain here, where they have been promised food, instead of returning to their ships, where, without their pay, they may not be able to feed themselves.

Gisele runs out. Marguerite's eyes close. She sees the blade of a knife; hears her baby screaming. She opens her eyes. The wet nurse has brought Jean Tristan to amuse her with his red face and waving fists. She tucks him in the crook of her arm, against her bare skin. "Do not be so sad," she murmurs. He looks up at her and stops crying. "There, there, no need to fret. Mama will take care of you."

In a few moments, the Egyptian messenger arrives and, in perfect French, offers greetings from the sultaness Shajar al-Durr. She has sent her response to Marguerite's missive, written in her own hand—in French.

Louis is safe, she has written, as are his brothers. They are being kept in comfort in the home of a prominent judge. She will release them for a ransom of five hundred thousand livres. Marguerite has one month in which to gather the money, during which time she must also return Damietta to the Egyptians. Meanwhile, the sultaness has commanded her general to halt the siege—for now.

Five hundred thousand livres is more than twice the amount Marguerite has on hand. She must convince the Egyptian queen to reduce the ransom—but how? Before she can begin to fashion a reply, the mercenaries' spokesman returns, his gaze dropping lovingly on her plates of food: roasted lamb, rice with saffron, peas with cardamom, fish from the sea.

"My lady, the aromas of your meal have enticed us to accept your offer," he says. "Unfortunately, we can only remain here for one more month, or miss our ships' departures for home. We trust that we will be paid our wages at that time—in full."

"Of course," Marguerite says, smiling with relief while her mind works, calculating, adding, multiplying. Five hundred thousand livres. And then there is the food she has just purchased, and the mercenaries' salaries to pay. Something must give way, and soon.

When the Genoese spokesman has gone, she calls for Gisele again.

"I need three galleys," she says. "I need horses, and the clothing of a Saracen man. I need enough food and water for several days' journey."

"But where are you going, my lady? Surely you cannot travel—"

"Please summon Sir John, the physician, and the pope's legate, as well." She also needs a sorcerer, but she does not say it.

Gisele frowns at her. "But you cannot get on a boat, or ride a horse. You must heal."

"There is no time for healing," Marguerite says. She pulls herself slowly to standing, wincing at her body's soreness. "We have only one month in which to achieve the impossible. Procure some man's clothes for yourself, too, and for the Countess Beatrice." It will do her sister good to leave her sickly baby for a few days.

"But where are we going, my lady?"

"Up the Nile to Mansoura. To meet the Egyptian queen."

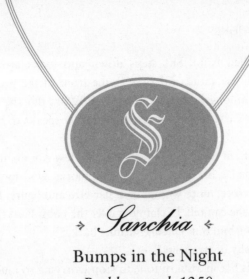

⇥ *Sanchia* ⇤

Bumps in the Night

Berkhamsted, 1250

Twenty-two years old

*S*HE CANNOT HELP comparing this journey to Berkhamsted Castle with her first, seven years ago, after her wedding. Richard rode with her in the carriage. His arm embraced her shoulders. His fingers touched her hair. His gaze never left her face for long. His smile crinkled his eyes, making him appear kind. He called her "my pet" and "pretty doll." When they arrived, he laughed as she exclaimed over the grand château: "It is grand because you are here, my sweet." And then he scooped her into his arms and carried her inside, all the way up the stairs to her gold-and-white chambers, like a fairyland, where he tenderly removed her clothes.

Today hers is a silent ride from Paris with Justine, who sleeps most of the way, and the wet nurse, Emma, who is always quiet, thanks be to God. Sanchia keeps her ever at hand and she cannot bear much chatter. Edmund is quiet, too, which used to worry her, for baby Richard was a subdued infant and he did not live for long. When he died, he took the sparkle from his father's eyes. Sanchia does not like to ponder what Richard might lose if this son died, too.

The carriage stops. A manservant, not Richard, waits for her with outstretched hand. She steps down and looks around for Richard. His horse stands riderless at the front of the procession and he is not among his knights. Ah, well. What did she expect? That he would carry her inside when he hardly speaks to her anymore?

She finds him in the great hall greeting the Jew Abraham, whose beard has turned a bit gray, and his wife Floria, who looks even prettier than before, more womanly in her face and figure. Richard thinks so, too, she can tell. Exclaiming over the baby, Floria reaches her arms out for him but Sanchia shrinks back.

"He's very shy of strangers."

Richard tells her in a sharp tone to stop worrying so much, that he has never seen a women so protective of a child, that she will smother him with love.

"Let Floria hold the child," he says. "It will be good for him."

She gives Edmund to the Jewess and watches her bounce him and kiss his nose, resisting the urge to snatch him back to herself. She hopes he does not catch any germs or illnesses. Abraham, she notices, has little interest in the child. His sharp bird's eyes peer at Sanchia with that look which she had almost forgotten, as though she had sprouted an ear in the middle of her forehead.

"He resembles you, my lord," Floria says to Richard, as indeed he does. He has the same long eyelashes, the flaxen hair, the same eyes with their mixture of colors, the same dimple in his chin. Richard steps around to the Jewess's side and peers at the baby as though he has never seen him before. Floria sings a baby's song, walking her fingers up Edmund's belly to his chin and tickling him there, and he laughs for the very first time. Richard laughs, too, a sound Sanchia has not heard in months.

"Do not excite him overmuch," she says, holding out her arms for the babe. "He will be awake all night."

The baby begins to whimper and clutch at Sanchia's breast. She tries bouncing him in her arms as Floria did, but it only makes him cry.

"The poor little thing wants his wet nurse," Floria says. As if she were an expert on babies, she who has no children after three years of marriage. She reaches out to Edmund again, but Sanchia pulls him close to her chest, saying it is his nap time, too, she must go and find Emma right away.

"Darling dear," she says—Joan de Valletort's endearment. Richard lifts his eyebrows. "Will you come with me? I have matters to discuss with you."

"I will come to your chambers in a little while," he says. "Abraham, I have good news. My brother Henry wants to borrow a huge sum for his adventures across the channel. If he does not repay me in time, he will give me the taxes from all the Jews in England. And I will need someone to collect that tax. It could be very lucrative for you."

"I live to serve you, my lord," Abraham says. He bares his little teeth. Sanchia shudders and hurries up the stairs, her baby's cries hurting her ears.

In her chambers, Emma nurses the baby while Sanchia plucks at her harp. She could hear Richard's breathing as he stood next to Floria. He gave off a fecund aroma, like wet earth and leaves. Could the Jew smell it? Or is she imagining this, too?

"We are friends," Richard said of Joan de Valletort. "Anything more is a product of your foolish, fanciful mind."

She plucks her harp, and sings a song by Peire Vidal:

"People and rivers/ I've sung their praise/ Five hundred ways/ All of my days, To those who treat me/ Worse than they could, /though you'd agree/ They'll hear nothing but good from me."

She wonders if Peire ever heard his wife call him "foolish." If she ever made him cry. If he ever wanted to lash out, to hurt her back.

By the time she finishes, her hands are moist with the tears she has wiped away, and Emma and the baby are asleep on the couch. Richard, however, has not come to her yet. How much business does he have to discuss with Abraham?

Sanchia has not seen Berkhamsted in three years, but Richard has traveled here often. She preferred to visit her sister in London than endure the humiliations these Jews inflict. But Eléonore and King Henry were quarreling, and Richard would not let her stay.

"For you to involve yourself in their disputes serves no one's interests, least of all mine," he said. She felt sorry to leave, for the king shouts at Eléonore with a red face and his new brothers start new rumors about her every week. When they started to whisper that Sanchia and Eléonore were conspiring together as "aliens" to take over the kingdom, Richard forced her to come home.

At least he did not take her back to Wallingford, where the servants give her looks of pity, especially when Joan de Valletort comes to call. And why wouldn't they feel sorry for her? They hear the woman's haughty laugh and her condescending tone, as if Sanchia were a child—and Joan not even a countess! They probably knew that Richard was entertaining her all night whenever she came "to conduct the old man's business," as she said. (Her husband is said to be quite old.)

"Tremberton is neither very large nor very wealthy," Sanchia finally said to Richard. "I wonder what kind of business keeps bringing her here?"

"You would not understand," was Richard's abrupt reply.

But Sanchia understands plenty. Seeing the baroness's son Philip at her churching party made many things clear. While Richard and Joan talked with ease, he stood blushing—Richard's son, nearly her age!—and staring at the embroidered cloth hanging on the wall depicting the Battle of Hastings. Did the young man realize that Richard is his father? Why did Joan bring him to Sanchia's ceremony?

"She is asserting her claim," Eléonore guessed. Until Sanchia bore Richard a son, he had only one heir: Henry, a sweet youth who writes poems to Sanchia and brings her wildflowers. (Where did he learn such romantic behavior? Certainly not from his father.) "If Richard had no other sons, Philip would be next in line to inherit his wealth."

Once she recovered from her surprise at seeing Richard's

features copied onto a younger man's face, Sanchia could shrug off worries about Joan as if they were snowflakes on her shoulders. Gray streaks her black hair. Her eyes crinkle in little lines when she smiles. Her hands look like maple leaves with all their ropy veins. She is old! Richard might have loved her once, a long time ago, but he had Sanchia now, who had given him a legitimate son, and his eyes were ever upon her when his hands could not be. Soon he would grow to love Sanchia, and Joan de Valletort would have to pursue some other wealthy man.

But then the baby died coughing and wheezing a few days after the churching, and Richard blamed her for the death.

"You should have called a physician," he said. "How could you be so careless?" She did not remind him that she had been sick, too, with a fever so high that Justine had plunged her into a cold bath to bring her temperature down, but that Richard refused to call a healer for her.

"Healers are pretenders, more hazardous than helpful," he told her then. "They did nothing to cure my poor wife—and then they wanted their pay."

"I am your wife," Sanchia wanted to say.

Lying on her bed, waiting, she ponders marriage. The women at Wallingford talked endlessly of their marriages, of the business transactions and the children and the households and the travels. Sanchia, who has only one child and whose husband has excluded her from his affairs, spoke tentatively of love, like a child prodding an anthill with a stick. The younger women in the group stared at her, while the older women only shook their heads and clucked their tongues. What was it that Richard said about marriage? That it was the vinegar, and love the oil?

But her parents loved each other. Theirs was a great romance— the beauty from Savoy and the count from Aragon—and a true partnership. Not only did Mama bear Papa's children, and see to their education, but she also administered the household finances, oversaw the servants, handled the correspondence, maintained the castles, and did whatever else he needed. Isabel Marshal had done the same when she was Richard's wife. But he won't let Sanchia do anything for him—except watch the baby, who makes a poor companion for an adult woman.

She at least had Richard's affections for a time, although sometimes after drinking too much German brandy he could be harsh with her. Now he gives her nothing except a pat on the head, as if she were one of his dogs. Oh, if only she were his dog! Then she would at least have his attention, and be given tasks to perform.

In France, he did not even let her try to help her sister. Eléonore had asked her to appeal to Queen Blanche de Castille's piety, "as only you can do," to coax her to give England's lands back to King Henry. Henry has taken the cross but he won't be able to go unless he can get more money—from Normandy, for example.

Richard, in France to negotiate a treaty for England—and to try to get Normandy back—seemed to like the idea at first. "If anyone could touch the White Queen's heart, it is our dear, sweet Sanchia," he said to Eléonore. But she must have said something wrong. When Richard introduced her, she asked if the queen would accompany her to La Sainte-Chapelle, the cathedral that King Louis had built to house the piece of the True Cross and the Crown of Thorns, "that I might venerate the relics of the Christ with your guidance." The queen smiled and said of course, she would be delighted.

"How encouraging to find such devotion to Our Lord in one so young. Of course, it was common when I was your age, but the universities are teaching Aristotle to our young men now, if you can imagine that," she said.

"Our mother taught Aristotle to us," she said, eager to impress the White Queen. "I liked his ideas."

"Really?" The queen lifted one drawn eyebrow. "But his God comprises a divine intelligence, devoid of morality."

"Yes, my lady . . ." She struggled to find an intelligent response, having daydreamed through most of her philosophy lessons and never liking to read, especially in Greek. "But—didn't he write before Jesus was born? We must consider him in context," she said, quoting Mama.

The queen's blue eyes turned to ice. "Yes," she said, "you certainly are Marguerite's sister."

Sanchia felt a glow to be compared to Marguerite, the smartest woman she has ever known, and so quick of tongue. "I think she likes me," she said to Richard when they sat at the meal prepared for them—fresh fish with a tart lemon sauce, baby green beans in butter, a veal roast, a salad of violets, rose petals, and rue. Richard said nothing, and he only grunted whenever, during the next several days, she asked when she might speak with Queen Blanche. When she pressed him, he patted her head and said to be patient, that these were delicate negotiations, that the queen barely had time for him, and that she would need to wait her turn.

Finally, as he ushered her into her carriage for the journey home—scowling over his failure to regain Henry's lands, for his purse would have benefited, too—Sanchia asked one more time: What happened to her meeting with the French queen?

"I promised my sister that I would not disappoint her," she said.

"You will disappoint no one as long as you stay away from Blanche," he said.

He has always treated her as if she were a child. When they first married, she was very childlike, that is true. She was not the confident woman that he wanted her to be. She could not talk her sisters into giving him what he wanted. But she has changed. She is stronger now, and more mature. She could help Richard, if he would let her. She could make him proud of her again, the way he was the night of her churching.

She had looked forward to seeing his eyes glow again, at the celebration for Edmund. But six months have passed since he was born, and Richard has not given a feast. Perhaps it is time to do so. She could arrange it; he would not need to do anything except be proud of her, for she would take great care to make him proud.

This time, there would be no Joan de Valletort to spoil her day—Tremberton being far from Berkhamsted—nor would Floria be a concern, since Jews, of course, would not be invited and she would not dare to make an entrance as Joan did.

She sits up in bed, thoughts whirling. The most prominent English barons and their wives will come, and Uncle Peter and Uncle Boniface, and Eléonore and Henry again. And then, when Richard sees how capable she has become, he might allow her to work more closely with him in managing his affairs. She might become as valuable to him as Abraham, or as much a partner as Isabel Marshal had been—who, if she did not have Richard's fidelity, at least had his respect.

But—where is Richard? The day's light is nearly gone. He must have forgotten his promise to come and visit her soon, or maybe he thinks she must be sleeping. In fact, though, she is wide awake, and too excited to sleep.

She rises and pulls on her slippers, then walks through the castle. He is not in the chancellory, which is empty, lit by a slant of pale light illuminating the dust on the rolls of parchment stacked on high shelves. The Jew is in the treasury, alone, sitting at the large table and jotting notes, squinting by the light of a candelabra. Servants, petitioners, and merchants mill about in the great hall, but Richard is not there. His chambers are empty, too.

She steps out into the garden, where the sky bleeds a breathtaking shade of red, like the blush on a ripe peach—and she hears his voice, only a faint murmur. Following the sound, she steps around a flowering wisteria and sees him holding the Jewess Floria around her waist, grasping her to him, and gazing into her eyes with a smolder he once reserved for Sanchia. Her heart begins to bang against her chest; pressing her hands to it, she steps back, out of sight.

"Where is Abraham?" Floria says, a bit breathlessly, she thinks.

Richard chuckles. "Do not concern yourself with him. He will be occupied for many months collecting the tax, far too busy to disturb us."

"It would be no disturbance, my lord. I enjoy my husband's company."

"If you get lonely, my pet, you know where to find me."

"But what about your wife? She's beautiful. Why would you want anyone else?"

His snort brings tears to Sanchia's eyes. "She's a doll. All beauty, no brains. But you, my sweet—you have both. You excite me, Floria. I can tell that I excite you, too."

"Abraham would kill us both," Floria says.

"He'll never know. This is our secret, Floria. If anyone finds out, I would be ruined. A Christian and a Jew! Even my brother would not forgive it. And if I fall, Abraham falls, and all the Berkhamsted Jews."

"That's a very good reason to release me now, my lord."

"Do not say that!" She can hear him breathing. "Floria, I want you as I've never wanted anyone."

"I doubt if that is true, my lord." A long silence follows. Sanchia peeks around the shrubbery and sees them kissing, sees Floria's throat as her head tilts back. Sanchia wishes she had a knife or a sword; she would hack off the Jewess's head.

"Flor-r-r-ia. Come with me to my chambers. Sanchia is asleep and Abraham will be working until the morning. Neither of them need ever know."

Sanchia turns and flees into the castle, afraid to be discovered, blinking back tears, stifling her sobs. In her chambers, where her innocent babe sleeps in his wet nurse's arms, the dark has overcome the day and settled on her bed like a growling dog. She curls up beside it and lies awake, listening for bumps in the night.

⇥ *Beatrice* ⇤

The Magnificent Queen

Grand Cairo, 1250

Nineteen years old

THE SULTANESS OF Egypt frowns down at them from her high throne, her fleshy face a dark moon in folds of white linen. One of her hands rests on her golden throne; one holds a scepter, also of gold. On her left, a man in a white turban listens to Marguerite's petition and murmurs in the sultaness's ear. Not that he needs to whisper for their sake: Neither she nor Marguerite understands a word of Arabic.

Marguerite, in her men's robes and long headdress, holds up a jar made of animal hide. "This vessel is filled with livres, hundreds of them. We have more coming; many more, all that you have asked for. I pray you, take this money and set my husband free."

"Hundreds?" The sultaness's laugh tinkles like a fountain of water. "Would we release a king for such a paltry sum?"

Marguerite makes her case: The king's health is sensitive. She has heard that he is very ill. He is beloved by his subjects and barons as well as the lords of surrounding lands. If he dies in the Mansoura jail, many kingdoms will send troops to fight against Egypt, seeking revenge.

"And if we free him, he will return to wage war against our people again," the sultaness says.

"We only wish to return home."

Shajar al-Durr smiles thinly. "Do you know how your husband spends his time in our prison? Trying to convert his guards to the Christian religion."

Beatrice imagines him in his hair shirt and coarse tunic, rashes oozing and bleeding, telling the Saracens in their soft gowns that his is the path to salvation.

"He loves God, as you do," Marguerite says.

Her remark has hit its mark: The sultaness's eyes soften as they meet Marguerite's. Her sister stands with a straight back and a bold thrust of her chin, as defiant as a shield. Beatrice marvels at the change: Have her man's clothes brought it about, or is it her success at saving Damietta? So reserved before, so contained, she now moves with vigor, commanding men as though she were a king, even laughing at the bawdy songs the Genoan sailors sang as they rowed the boats up the broad, flat Nile. Nothing could subdue her, not the bump of crocodiles against the galleys; not the swarms of mosquitoes about their heads and faces; not even the white-hot blast of the midday sun.

"Love of God is not why you have come," Shajar al-Durr says. "If it were so, you would heed his commandment not to kill. You are here because you want what we have."

"We want the holy city. It is where our Lord was crucified. Where he was raised from the dead and ascended into heaven."

"Also our ports of trade. Our fine cloth. Our beautiful rugs. Our spices. Our poetry and philosophy. Our music. Our gold. Especially our gold."

Marguerite says, "I know nothing about gold. My husband came to claim Jerusalem for Christians."

"Then why isn't he in Jerusalem?"

Marguerite says nothing, and Beatrice knows why: They heard Robert of Artois and the other barons urging Louis to swoop down like a hawk on Mansoura and seize the sultan's palace now that Shajar al-Durr's husband is dead. "A treasure trove of riches," Robert said, "ours for the taking!" The barons' greed knew no end; nor did Robert's arrogance. They had, indeed, come to Outremer for the gold.

"No matter why we came, we have lost to you," Beatrice says. "We are at your mercy, for now. But the people of France will soon hear that King Louis and his brothers are captive. They will eagerly fight for him."

The man beside her laughs. Shajar al-Durr lifts her hand and he is silent, but his eyes shimmer with mirth.

"Have you come to threaten me," the sultaness says, "or to negotiate your husbands' release?"

"We wish to free all our men—today," Marguerite says.

"Have you brought five hundred thousand livres? No? Then I cannot let even a single man go with you. If I did, I might lose my neck." A shadow crosses her face. "I may lose it, anyway."

"And I may lose my husband." Marguerite's voice rises. "We have four children."

"I am sorry." The sultaness's eyes fill with tears. "My husband died recently. I loved him as only a woman can love. And now my son Turan Shah is slain. I loved him as only a mother can love."

Beatrice's throat tightens. How would it be to lose Charles? Life would lose its luster. Even to lose her babies would strike her senseless. Yet the sultaness Shajar al-Durr sits on her throne and conducts business even while her heart breaks, even while the men who killed her son may be conspiring against her.

"My people are watching me closely," she says. "To have a woman as their ruler has not been permitted before. We hope the caliph will allow it now. But even if he does, the Turks may not. So I must proceed with care."

"And if something happens to you before I can collect the ransom? What will become of my husband and his men?"

Shajar al-Durr's thick eyelashes fall over her cheeks like fans. When she lifts her Nile-green gaze, Beatrice thinks she might burst into tears. "Whether we live or die is for Allah to decide."

"Then, by God, lower your ransom!" Beatrice cries. Marguerite reaches over and grips her hand.

"I have nearly half of what you require at Damietta," she says to the Egyptian queen.

"That is not enough."

How can Marguerite sit so calmly and bargain for their husbands' lives as though she were negotiating the price of corn? Maybe she doesn't care about Louis—and Beatrice wouldn't blame her—but Charles is somewhere in this city, living in filth and disease, enduring terrible tortures, starving to death.

"Did you hear my sister? It's all we have!" Beatrice cries. "You've got to let them go. My husband—I've had a baby, and she is very sick. Charles has never seen her."

Shajar al-Durr is silent.

"If you do indeed fear for your life, then I beg for your leniency, O Queen." Marguerite's voice rings out. Dear God, what has happened to her? It is as if she became a man when she donned a man's attire. "If you die, who will stop the Mamluks from brutally punishing our men?"

"Your men came to kill us. Why should I concern myself with them?"

"And our women? How will the Turks deal with us, sultaness?"

Shajar al-Durr frowns. She speaks in her musical tongue to the man beside her, and he responds.

"My general will ensure safe passage home for you. He has given me his pledge."

Beatrice's heart begins to run around in her chest, causing her breath to come in pants. "Marguerite," she says, "they want to send us home without our men. I won't go!" She glares at the sultaness. "I will not leave without Charles."

"There are many more besides the two of us," Marguerite says. "One hundred women, at least."

Shajar al-Durr lifts a penciled eyebrow. "Your men brought their wives? They must have envisioned an easy victory."

"They trusted in God."

"Foolish women, to come to this place! If the Turks knew you were here, they would invade Damietta at once. You would all be enslaved."

"And children. We have babies. Are they not innocent?"

No one speaks. Beatrice thinks of her baby, crying. There stands Marguerite, implacable. Beatrice shivers.

"Bring our men to Damietta, and I will pay you two hundred thousand livres," Marguerite says. "We will surrender Damietta at once, and sail for home. I will send the rest to you in one year."

The sultaness confers with her general. His voice rises, but she silences him with a single word: *Leh,* with an emphatic shake of her head.

"You must go to Acre, the Christian city, and gather the rest of your funds. When you have paid us, you may return home."

They kiss the sultaness's ring. She rises, large and magnificent, and glides as gracefully as a cat to the palace door. Her companion draws his sword as she leads them out to the street; several other men join them, wielding long, curved scimitars and glaring at passersby.

"My guards prefer that I ride. They fear that I will be attacked," she tells Marguerite and Beatrice. "But how can I rule my people if I cannot walk among them?"

They stop not far from the palace before a sand-colored house, plain and simply built in the Egyptian fashion—hiding a richly ornamented interior, Beatrice guesses—but with a perplexing, five-sided hole in the heavy wooden door.

"That entry was made for your husband, to humble him," the sultaness tells Marguerite. "To pass through it, he had to kneel."

They walk down a hallway hung with softly lit lamps and lined with Turkish guards who glare at them from under their red hats, their hands clutching the scimitars in their belts. They pass two doors, then climb a set of stairs to enter a modest, clean room overlooking a tree-shaded courtyard and, through a window, the sea. Louis sits on the floor, cross-legged, rocking and muttering with closed eyes. He is clean and shaven, but his tunic is ragged and dank.

The sultaness speaks to one of the guards in her language. "Your husband was provided with suitable clothing, but he refused it," she tells Marguerite. "He would have refused the daily walks by the sea we offered to him, but our guards forced him to go. We would compel him to eat, also, if we could."

Louis continues to rock.

"I have brought your wife to you, O King," Shajar al-Durr says. "She has traveled from Damietta to beg for your release."

His eyes open but he does not stand. Nor does he look at Marguerite. "Praise God, I am rescued," he intones.

"My lord, a king's ransom is very high," Marguerite says. "You must remain here for a time, until I can gather the funds the Egyptians demand."

He closes his eyes again. "I should have brought the queen," he says. "She would not have failed me."

Marguerite turns away, blushing a bright red. "His mind is afflicted," she says to Shajar al-Durr once they have left the room.

"Who is the queen of whom he speaks? Aren't you the Queen of France?"

"In name only."

"You do not rule?"

"King Louis privileges his mother. I have no real power."

The sultaness narrows her eyes. "You are mistaken," she says. "I see formidable power."

Marguerite gives a little laugh. "Tell that to my husband. He sees only weakness—when he sees me at all."

"He is a fool," Beatrice says. "A blind fool."

"It matters not what the French king sees, or anyone else," the sultaness says. "True power does not rely on others' perceptions."

"It comes from God, is what you mean."

"No," Shajar al-Durr says.

They follow her down the stairs. "Your husband is in this room," the Egyptian queen says to Beatrice. A guard opens one of the closed doors to reveal a small, windowless room, dimly lit. As her eyes adjust, she sees men lying on the dirt floor. A fecal smell stings her nostrils.

"They have caught the sickness," the sultaness says. "From drinking bad water."

"Thank you, Jesus," Charles says, struggling to his feet. She stares at him as he steps toward her, smiling broadly, for the beard sprouting on his face and the fatigue lining his eyes make him look like an old man. A guard lifts his sword to stop him before he reaches her; the sultaness speaks sharply; and then Charles's arms are around her and she is holding him tight.

"What took you so long?" he says. "I almost had to leave with another man." He steps back to take in her Saracen trousers and turban, his eyes dancing.

"For you, there is no other man."

"You, my love, have spoken the truth." He lowers his head to kiss her, but his breath is so foul that she turns her head, making him laugh. "Thank God you have come to my rescue," he murmurs. "Louis has gone mad, and so will the rest of us if we have to listen to him much longer."

Beside them, Marguerite catches her breath. "Jean," she says.

Sir Jean de Joinville, looking even worse than Charles, has stepped forward and manages a shaky bow. "My lady," he says. "You are the vision I have been praying for."

Marguerite has turned pale at the sight of him, so thin his filthy clothes droop from his shoulders, so emaciated that his face resembles a skull—but her gaze is a lover's gaze. Worried lest Charles take note, Beatrice holds her breath and kisses her husband's mouth.

"My sister has reached an agreement with the Egyptian queen," she tells Charles. Perhaps he will be more kindly disposed toward Marguerite now, and not oppose her claiming Tarascon. "We return to Damietta today for your ransom money."

"Make haste," he murmurs. "I am surrounded by incompetence, and fear it may rub off on me."

TWO WEEKS LATER, Beatrice and Marguerite board the galley that will carry them all to Palestine. An entire fleet waits to escort them, ships that Marguerite summoned from Acre among those blown off course last year. With them are Charles, Louis, and Alphonse, as well as Sir Joinville, Count Pierre of Brittany, and the remainder of the barons from the Mansoura prison. Louis, stricken again in his bowels, needs the help of two men to walk from the Egyptian galley to his own.

The mood on the ship is as solemn as if they were going to a funeral—not at all as celebratory as she and Charles feel to be rid of Egypt. He takes the baby into his arms and she waves her fists, "a fighter," he says, grinning, "like her father."

A melting feeling spreads through her as she watches them. Surely this is how love began between her and Papa. She has heard many times how he carried her everywhere, slung over one shoulder as if she were a sack of grain: into the great hall to hear petitions, up the stairs to his chambers for naps, on hunts—evoking exclamations from Madeleine, who was sure he would drop her, and giggles from his companions to see him carrying a baby.

"Does something amuse you?" Charles says.

"I was thinking that fortune has smiled on our girl, to have a papa so smitten with her."

He looks at her with eyes made bluer by the love they hold, and with his free arm pulls her close for a kiss. Fortune has smiled on Mama, too, she thinks as he calls for the nurse, but she does not say it, for then his arms are free and her mouth is not, and she forgets everything else but Charles.

Later, as they lie in bed, legs wrapped around legs and arms slung across torsos, he tells her about their battles, about the errors that led to their defeat. "Louis heeded Robert's advice on every occasion," he says. "Robert was a brave warrior, and skilled with the sword. But mere courage does not a strategist make."

"As Louis undoubtedly knows now."

"Who knows what my brother knows? He does not speak about Robert except to praise him for his goodness—as if goodness were all one needed to prevail against the Turks. He moans constantly about how he has failed God, as if these crusades had anything to do with God." Beatrice remembers Shajar al-Durr's assessment: *because you want what we have.* "Of course, he is already planning his return."

Beatrice laughs. "Louis cannot get enough of Outremer? It must be the water."

"You laugh, but you do not know the half of it. He does not want to leave."

"Now you are the mad one."

"He says he would finish the task."

"Taking Jerusalem? But the Turks will have it soon enough." As soon as she has said it, she realizes that it is true. Shajar al-Durr's days as sultaness of Egypt are numbered. Beatrice shudders, thinking of that beautiful long neck.

❧

*B*EATRICE'S VOICE IS a frog's voice, all percussion and no melody, which is why others only rarely hear her sing. She sings today, though, as Amelie dresses her for the journey—including a stop at the island of Cyprus to collect her baby boy, whom she left one year ago vigorously suckling at a wet nurse's breast.

They are going home, and just in time to avoid another scorching summer in this godforsaken place. *When spring's grass perfume floateth by, then 'tis sweet song and birdlet's cry/ Do make mine old joy come anew.* Why anyone would want to fight over this barren, dusty desert is beyond her. Jesus would have preferred Provence.

She kisses Blanche's fat cheeks—the baby asleep with an innocence her namesake never possessed—and dances about the cool, mud-brick room with its high, narrow windows until Marguerite enters with a face like winter to dampen her spirits. Or to try.

"You sound happy," her sister says, her arms folded as tightly as her expression. "Betrayal suits you well."

Beatrice stops singing. "I am pleased to be going home," she says, choosing her words as she goes. "I miss my baby boy."

"I miss my babies, too." Her face crumples for a moment, then hardens. "But I am not going home."

"I wish you were." She steps over to her sister's side, touches her arm—and is rebuffed. "Marguerite, why don't you come with us? Leave Louis to his delusions."

"Delusions?"

"You know as well as I: Those men are gone. Louis will never get them back. He does not even know where they are." Although the Egyptian queen released twelve thousand prisoners to them—many from previous campaigns—thousands more are missing still. Shajar al-Durr, whose ship led the grand flotilla, seemed surprised when Marguerite asked about them. *More prisoners?* she'd asked. Her son must have transferred them elsewhere because of crowding in Mansoura. She would find them, and order their release.

That was more than one month ago. Now the rest of the ransom has been paid, thanks to Marguerite's harassing of the Knights Templar, the Order of Hospitallers, the pope of Rome, the Holy Roman Emperor, and the White Queen. In fact, so much money has poured in that they could remain here for years—a prospect the very thought of which makes Beatrice cringe. She has had her fill of chickpeas. The smell of cardamom, once a pleasant fragrance, nauseates her. The Saracen tongue, like music to her at first, now sounds guttural and cruel. She would like to stick a dagger into the next Turk who ogles her body as if she were a camel for sale. What was Louis thinking when he decided to bring Marguerite along? Hadn't he consulted with his cousin Thibaut, or the Count Pierre of Brittany, both of whom fought here ten years ago?

"If I were to leave," Marguerite says, "Louis would never return. He would die fighting for Jerusalem, even if he were the only knight on the field." She glares at Beatrice. "Which he may well be after today."

Guilt tries to settle on Beatrice's shoulders but she shrugs it off. "What do you expect of us?" she snaps. "Would you have us remain here in a futile battle over foreign lands while revolt brews in Provence? Should we abandon our infant son in Cyprus for the sake of the king's tormented soul?"

"You are leaving us to die!" Marguerite's hands drop to her sides. "We are sisters. I thought that meant something to you."

"It means more than you could imagine," Beatrice says. "But it does not mean everything."

"Charles is the reason." Beatrice looks away. In fact, she would have remained here a little while in hopes of convincing her sister to depart with them, but Charles refused.

"Jerusalem is lost," he said. "Now we must return home, or risk losing Provence, as well. And I will not lose Provence."

"God damn his selfishness!" Beatrice flinches, surprised, at Marguerite's sudden shout. "Charles cares about no one else, not about you, and certainly not about me. I feel sorry for you, being married to that monster."

"How dare you speak of my husband in that way?" Beatrice turns on her. "The faults you find in Charles are the faults you possess in yourself."

"Such as?" Having goaded her into a fight, Marguerite now becomes the calm one, the rational one. Beatrice wants to strike her.

"When have you ever thought of me?" Beatrice cries. "You and Eléonore—like two pearls in an oyster! You talk about family, then turn on me because Papa loved me the most."

"He did not love you the most. You were his amusement after Eléonore and I left home."

"That is not what he said." Beatrice blinks back tears. "He told me many times that I was his favorite daughter. He said God had saved the best for last. That is why he left Provence to me."

"He left Provence to you because he knew no man would want to marry you otherwise."

"What do you mean?"

Marguerite shrugs. "God gave so much beauty to Sanchia that he had little remaining for you."

"Oh, were you once prettier than I?" Beatrice laughs. "All those bitter years in the French court have certainly taken their toll."

"You, on the other hand, know nothing of hardship, having been spoiled all your life."

"Spoiled, me? Who is the most powerful queen in the world, throwing tantrums because she didn't get all she wanted in her papa's will?" Charles, she suddenly realizes, will never agree to give Tarascon to Marguerite. Oh, God, how could she have made such a pledge? "How spoiled are you, to demand Tarascon from me when Provence is all I have?"

Fear splashes like cold water on Marguerite's face. Beatrice wants to laugh again. That will teach her to attack Beatrice of Provence.

"That has been resolved," her sister says. "We do not need to discuss Tarascon further."

"Resolved? Have you decided to let the matter drop?"

Marguerite stares at her. "Of course, now that you have awarded Tarascon to me."

"What?" Beatrice affects a puzzled frown. "I am sorry. I don't know what you are talking about."

"When you gave birth to Blanche, you said that I could have Tarascon."

"Did I? I must have been delirious. Of course I cannot give Tarascon to you without consulting Charles."

"You made a pledge!" Marguerite's eyes are wild and tearful. "You cannot go back on your word!"

Beatrice shrugs. After all her sister has said to her today, she cares not a whit what she thinks of her. "You cannot expect me to honor promises made under duress."

"You bitch!" Marguerite snatches up the nearest object—a miniature stone statue of the Virgin Mary—and hurls it at her. It hits the far wall and thuds to the floor. "I knew you would renege on your promise. Did I say that you would be unhappy with Charles? I take back those words. You two are just alike, and perfect for each other. You'll suffer in hell together, too."

"Who is going to hell? You just threw the Virgin Mary against the wall."

"And how I regret missing my mark." Marguerite speaks in a menacing undertone. "But I wasn't speaking of the afterlife. I mean to make you suffer in this one."

"I would like to see you try." Beatrice tries to keep her voice light.

"I will do more than try, sister. You will see. I haven't lived with Blanche de Castille for all these years without learning a few things."

"You can't hurt me," Beatrice says, but she doesn't sound sure.

"We shall soon find out," Marguerite says. She starts to go, but then stops and turns around. "There is another thing you said while you were in labor, gripping my hand because you were afraid you might die. Remember? You told me that you've never felt like one of us, like a true sister of Savoy. Now I'll tell you the truth: You are not one of us. And you never will be."

⇥ *Marguerite* ⇤

A Slow Breeze

Acre, 1252

Thirty-one years old

$\mathscr{S}$HE MUST NOT smile. Marguerite lowers her head and closes her eyes. Beside her on his throne, Louis cries out.

"*Ma mère!* Oh, Lord, take me, too."

If only God were a *djinni* in a lamp, as in the Saracen tale, granting any uttered wish. Immediately she banishes the thought: in France, one cannot be queen if there is no king.

Marguerite turns to regard him, the father of her five living children and one yet unborn, he for whose sake she has remained in this godforsaken land. As he sobs and crumples to the floor in a most unkingly fashion, something seems to snap inside her. Her time of waiting has ended.

"Help the king to the chapel," she instructs the guards who have rushed forth to peel Louis from the floor. When they have gone, she remains in place, summoning grief. She will be expected to cry.

Blanche de Castille is dead, her heart frozen by disuse, no doubt. France has no ruler: She and Louis must return to Paris. Home. She thinks of Lou-Lou, ten years old now, four when she left him. Reared by the queen mother, a fate she would not have wished for any child, especially her own. She thinks of Isabelle, her only daughter, thirteen now, become a young woman without her mother's influence. *Keep them safe, Holy Mother, until I return.* A knight watches her, certainly wondering why she sits so placidly while grief prostrates her husband. She rises and walks to the chapel.

Louis lies on the floor, as expected, crouched over as if to protect himself from injury, banging his head against the tile like a heathen Saracen in prayer. Surely such a show of emotion is unwarranted; already the servants snigger over Louis's floggings and the scabs on his back and chest caused by his hair shirt. Since his defeat at Mansoura and the loss of sixty thousand men, no punishment is too severe for him, no penance too exacting.

"Darling," she says, "my condolences over your mother's death." She kneels beside him and places a hand on his arm, but he seems not to notice. "I know how much you loved her. She was a fine woman."

"You never thought so," he says. He sits up and glares at her, eyes bleary with tears and a want of sleep, for he now prays in his chapel all night, every night. "You hated my mother. Admit it."

"Blanche de Castille was a shrewd and capable queen. She made France the force in the world that it is today."

"She despised you. She said that you were not good enough for me."

Marguerite withdraws her hand. "I came to comfort you. But I seem to be doing the opposite."

"She wanted me to marry a girl of distinction, someone who would elevate our status. You were the heiress to Provence—or so your uncles led us to believe."

"You were happy enough to marry me, as I recall." Her voice rises.

"I was taken by your beauty, as Adam was captivated by Eve. Mother warned me. She told me that beauty does not endure, that women grow fat from bearing children."

Marguerite stands, her hands pressed against her belly, heavy again with his offspring. "I will be in my chambers, packing."

"Packing? Are you taking a journey?"

"I assumed we would return to Paris. No one is ruling the kingdom now."

"Alphonse can take the throne. God's work remains to be done here."

Marguerite's eyes fill with tears. "We are not going home?" She wants to pounce on him and beat him with her fists, pummel away his notions of saving foot soldiers who cannot be found; of conquering Jerusalem without the troops Charles and Alphonse promised to bring; of punishing himself for the foolish behavior of his brother Robert, who has already paid the price with his life.

He scowls. "I am sick of hearing you beg to go home. You know the Lord has called me to this place, for this purpose. I must not forsake him as others have done."

"God didn't call you here, but the pope of Rome," she says. "God loves the Muslims as much as the Christians, or as little, from what I see. He does not seem to care much who commands the holy city."

"Blasphemy!" Louis cries. "Rarely have I known a woman so bold and yet so feebleminded. I should have left you in France."

"Perhaps I shall go there now," she says. "The kingdom needs at least one of us to rule."

"That is the last thing my mother would have wanted. Not that you care about her wishes." He starts to sob again, his arms folded across his stomach, and he bends down anew to bang his forehead on the floor.

Tears burn Marguerite's eyes as she hurries to her room, conscious of the sideways glances of servants who must have heard Louis's outburst. In her chambers, she sends out Gisele and her other ladies and sits in silence, contemplating her babies, trying to conjure their faces, their smells, the feeling of them snuggled next to her, but their names are only words in her mouth and their memories nothing more than the taste of salt on her tongue.

"My lady." Joinville has come into the room; he sits beside her on the bed and places his arm around her shoulders. Marguerite at last begins to cry, glad to press her face against his chest. He rubs her back; she breathes him in, remembers that returning to Paris means losing him to his wife and children in Champagne. Her tears subside.

"Why do you cry, Margi?" he says. "Surely not for the queen mother, whom you hated."

To tell the truth would be to confess that she never wanted to remain here, that, if asked for her advice, she would have urged Louis to return home with Charles and Alphonse and the rest of their men. She imagines how Jean, who urged Louis to stay, would withdraw his arm from her if he knew her true feelings.

"I am crying not for Blanche, but for Louis," she says. "The poor man is heartbroken. And my children: what will happen to them now, without their grandmother to protect them?"

The lie succeeds. Joinville's gaze softens. "I have never known a woman so pure of heart," he says. "When I think of how the king neglects you—"

"I don't mind," she says. "As long as I have you."

His kiss is soft, barely a brush of her lips. His breath is warm on her face. He smells of the sun and strong tea. Marguerite sighs, and he drops his arm from her shoulders. When she opens her eyes, he has moved away from her on the bed. She sees fear in his eyes. She suppresses a smile for the second time that day.

"Please forgive me," he says.

"Forgive you, Jean? For comforting me?"

"It will not happen again. I promise."

"Do not make that promise. I don't want it."

"Because you fear I won't keep it?"

"No," she says. She lifts her face, lets him see her happiness. "Because I fear that you will."

❦

SHE SLEEPS, AND dreams of Beatrice in plate armor, a sword in one hand and a shield bearing the Provençal coat of arms in the other. Her sister stands atop the wall surrounding the castle at Tarascon, impervious to the arrows hurtling upward from the ground below. Marguerite takes aim and, with a *twang* of the bowstring, aims for her sister's heart. The arrow sticks—but Beatrice does not fall. Marguerite hits her again, but she remains upright. A third arrow hits its mark, yet still she stands. Marguerite, puzzled, lifts off the ground in flight and sees, behind her sister, Charles of Anjou propping her up. She fires another arrow, this time at him—but he moves her sister, using her as a shield, and the arrow pierces Beatrice's forehead. Her eyes roll back and blood gushes from the wound. Charles looks at her and laughs.

And then she is awakened by soft kisses on her eyes and cheeks, and hands stroking her breasts and stomach. She opens her eyes to see Jean, soft hair falling across his face, his brown eyes smiling at her.

"You were having a nightmare," he says. "I thought it might be time to wake up." She opens her arms to him and Beatrice dissolves from her mind like fog overwhelmed by the sun.

Gisele's secret knock on their door interrupts them. She stands at the foot of the bed, blushing, and informs Marguerite that Louis is coming to take them all back to France. "He arrives this afternoon, and wants to set sail at first light tomorrow. When shall we begin to pack your belongings?"

Marguerite sends her out, wanting just a few minutes more with Jean. "This is the happiest day of my life, and the saddest," she says to him.

"Sad because of our sin?" His eyes turn down at the corners.

"Is it a sin to love each other? To believe that would sadden me. But, no, I will be sorry to say good-bye to you, Jean. To lose you so soon after consummating our love—"

He hushes her with a kiss. "We are not parted yet."

"But it may be difficult on the ship."

"Our journey will be long."

"The longer, the better."

He kisses her again. "One month, or one week, we will be together again. I promise it to you. Love will find a way."

When Louis arrives at the castle in Jaffa that afternoon in bare feet and the rags he has worn these last four years, Marguerite feels compelled to admonish him. "I hope you plan to don your furs and silks before we land in France. You look like a beggar, not at all befitting a ruler."

Louis narrows his eyes. "Who is this brash wife, telling me how I should dress? Has the desert heat affected your mind?"

"Your subjects will accuse you of the same if you go into France in those clothes."

His smile does not reach his eyes. "I will gladly let you dress me, my queen, on one condition: that you allow me to choose your attire, as well. Paring down your extravagant clothing budget would no doubt save the kingdom a fortune."

This from a man who has spent one million livres fortifying castles in Outremer—nearly all the money in the French treasury. Marguerite presses her lips together and he turns away, but she remembers her night with Jean and the precautions they did not take.

"My lord," she says, unfastening her gown. He turns toward her, and she lets it drop to the floor. Louis's eyes flicker. For all his inattention, she can still evoke his desire.

"Is this the apparel you had in mind?" she says.

When their ship sets sail the next afternoon, tears sting Marguerite's eyes as she watches the shoreline fade. She remembers the queen Shajar al-Durr, her strange beauty, her determination in the face of danger. She is married now to her Turkish general, her only recourse, Marguerite supposes, after the Muslim caliph refused to allow a woman to rule. She thinks of Joinville's struggle to his feet in the Mansoura prison, how his eyes shone as he crossed the room to her—in contrast to Louis, who sat in the corner and pretended she did not exist. She thinks of her babies born, Jean Tristan in Damietta, Pierre in Acre, and now, Blanche, born in Jaffa only a few months ago. She would have named the baby Eléonore, but Louis forbade it. The White Queen's death has left France vulnerable to an English invasion because the truce between the kingdoms has not been renewed. The queen mother is to blame, her sister has written, but Louis points the finger at Eléonore and Henry and their hunger for French lands.

Louis stands beside her at the rail, waving good-bye to the Christians amassed on the beach, who toss flowers to him. "Our most pious king," they call him. "A true saint."

He sees her tears, and arches his brows.

"How touching that you have found affection for the land where our Lord once walked," he says. "It is a pity that you did not experience it while we lived here. I would have enjoyed even one day without complaints from you."

She thinks of the laughter she and Joinville shared in her chambers while Louis camped on the Damietta beach with his men, those long nights of talk when she found a friend so like her that they might have been brother and sister—but, thank God, are not. She remembers their first kiss, six months ago when she was heavy with child and sorrow over Louis's decision to remain in Acre even after his mother's death. She prayed to the Virgin Mother all night after that, begging her to change Louis's mind. In the miraculous way of the Lord, his mind did change. The citizens of Acre, when they heard that Louis intended to remain, sent their most prominent men to urge him to go. They said they were thinking of France, but Marguerite knew better: After she and Louis arrived, the Saracens increased their attacks on the city. It is why he sent her—with Jean—to Jaffa.

The daylight hours stretch and yawn like a cat in the sun. Marguerite has nothing to do except try to help her children amuse themselves and nothing to read but the same worn psalter that she brought with her six years ago. She longs to pass the time with Jean, but Louis must have him ever at hand, "my most faithful knight," he calls him, which makes Joinville blush with guilt and shame—but not Marguerite. If she loves another, Louis has only himself to blame.

As in Damietta, they steal time together when everyone else

sleeps—but not, now, to talk. Marguerite counts the nights. When they have seventeen to go, she closes her eyes and inhales him, moving her nostrils over his hair (sea spray), his back (sweat), his flanks (thyme). On the thirteenth night before they land, she tastes him, committing to memory the softness of his earlobes, the sweetness at the backs of his knees. When seven nights remain, he whips off her gown and presses her body to his, inch to inch, until they are practically one, and they whisper their love until they doze, warmed by the heat from the stove. Until there is an acrid smell and Marguerite cries out, and he sees a flame pass by the bed and the cabin door open and he leaps up and sees her run naked out onto the ship's deck and throw overboard her burning nightgown.

She slams the door behind her, laughing, her body whirring with life, and fastens the latch and pushes him onto the bed. "I see fear on your face," she breathes.

"We nearly set the ship on fire."

"What do you expect from a love such as ours?" She laughs again. Someone knocks on the door.

"My lady?" They hear the quavering voice of Bartolomeu, Louis's chamberlain. "The king sent me. We heard there was an incident? Are you well?"

"All is well, thank you," she calls. "I left my nightgown too close to the stove is all. I cast it into the sea."

"And the Lord Joinville? I have just called at his cabin and he does not answer. His Grace is unable to sleep and is summoning him."

"He was here a few moments ago, making sure I was not hurt," she says. "He went to see the king, I believe."

"Very well, my lady. Most likely we have only just missed each other." Even as Bartolomeu speaks, Joinville is pulling on his leggings. Marguerite shakes her head no, but he dons his tunic. He has his slippers on and is fastening his mantle when the old chamberlain steps away.

"Bartolomeu is so slow he won't shuffle back to Louis until tomorrow morning," she says, unfastening his mantle. "Louis sends him out to be rid of him. He talks in streaks, which Louis cannot abide."

"Marguerite. I must go to the king." His kiss is perfunctory. "I will see you tomorrow night."

He opens the door, and is gone. Marguerite stands naked without even a nightgown to keep her warm. She throws open the door and sees the deck empty except for him.

"Jean!" she hisses. "Come back! When you are finished with Louis, come back! No matter what the time."

She cannot even see the sun when she awakens, so high is it overhead. Her head throbs as she peers out the little window. She hears a knocking at her door, and Gisele's call.

"My lady, are you awake and ready to be dressed? Jean Tristan is crying for you."

Marguerite opens the door to her maid, whose cheeks the ocean breeze has kissed to pinkness. Gisele must have a sea captain in her ancestry, sailing invigorates her so—or else, her queen's love affair quickens her blood.

"Did Sir Lancelot come last night?" she asks as she rolls a pair of leggings over Marguerite's feet and calves.

"Don't call him that!" She forces a laugh. "Yes, he was here. But only for a short time. The king summoned him."

"In the dark hours?"

"I asked him to return, but he never did."

"Perhaps you fell asleep and did not hear him."

Marguerite says nothing. She lay awake until sunrise. Jean did not return.

She passes by his cabin on her way to her children, but the door is closed and she dares not peer into his window with men milling about. She finds Jean Tristan in his nurse's lap, crying. His ear hurts, and, fearing an infection, she sends for the healer, who prescribes garlic oil. There is no garlic on the ship, so she makes do with warm compresses and a mother's love, holding him for an hour, rocking him, and singing softly until at last he falls asleep. The nurse takes him from her and she slips out in search of Joinville.

She wanders the ship, Gisele beside her and sheltering her from the sun with a parasol, the best discovery she made in Outremer. As they stroll, Marguerite looks to her left and to her right, seeking Jean among the men clustered on the deck, but he is nowhere. She steps into the dining room, where members of the crew are erecting tables, and then into the chapel. The young priest approaches with a shining face, as if she were the Holy Virgin. Of course he thinks she has come here to pray, or to confess.

"I am seeking my husband."

She is not far from the mark, for His Grace spent the better part of the morning here, he tells her. He departed for the captain's quarters. Marguerite arrives there as men are filing onto the deck: the Lord Beaumont and his Saracen serving boy; Odo, the pope's legate; and then, at last, Jean.

"My lady," he says, glancing around as he bows to her. Seeing no one nearby, he murmurs, "The king suspects us."

Marguerite feels an ache in her chest as if he had struck her there. "How do you know?"

"He has said so."

Louis emerges, then, with the captain behind, his red-rimmed eyes staring at Marguerite as though he knew her thoughts and found them disgusting. She returns his gaze. For once, she does not blush, although her pulse flutters. She will not give up Jean.

"My queen," Louis says. "Have you business with me, or with my loyal knight Joinville?"

"My lord, your son Jean Tristan is ill. His ear has become infected."

"Not again?" Louis's frown hardens. "You have borne me a sickly child. Have you considered whether it is your own doing?"

"I am sorry, my lord. I do not understand."

"Is your conscience clear? Might God be punishing you for something?" He glances up at Joinville, whose face has turned a furious red.

"I gave birth to him in extreme heat, in a pagan palace, with terror running through my veins as the Turks besieged Damietta," she says. "I was there at your command." He rolls his eyes, having heard these complaints before.

"But I'm not here to point the finger of blame. Our son is ill. Shall we land at Cyprus on the way home to obtain medicine for him? The healer prescribes garlic oil."

"Delay our arrival in France? I thought you were anxious to see our children."

"To stop would be a necessary evil, of course. But—"

"Evil," Louis says, "is never necessary." He links arms with Joinville. "My dear knight, tell me your conclusions after that meeting. Ought we to heed the captain's warning of a storm amid this calm weather, and take shelter in the nearest harbor? Or should we press on, confident in the Lord's protection?"

<hr />

*I*T BEGINS AS a slow breeze, a sweet relief from the summer sun's reflected heat, which shimmers as if the sea were a mirror and the ship a pile of kindling to be lighted. Marguerite sits on the deck in the shade, feeling air kiss her cheeks, not as pleasurable as Joinville's kiss but the only kind she is getting these days.

He has ceased his visits to her cabin. On the first night without him, she paced the floor, anticipating his knock, ready to hear all that Louis had said to him and rebuff each accusation as if her words were fingers massaging away knots of guilt. Of what do they deprive their spouses by giving love to each other? Certainly the seven children she has borne, including the dead (and for what did God punish her with those sorrows?), prove well enough that she has not denied Louis her body. How have they been unfaithful, when Jean's spouse is far away in body and Marguerite's in spirit? What is the meaning of loyalty? Was Jean's wife unfaithful when she refused to accompany him to Outremer? Is Louis faithful when he ignores her as if she were a statue without a head?

She awakens the next morning with an ache all over from sleeping on the floor by the stove, trying to ease the chill in her bones. She does not seek Joinville that day, but waits for him to come to her. She has some of the ship's men move her chair and footstool into a shady spot, under a place where the upper deck overhangs the lower. There she reads de Troyes's *Erec and Enide,* which Joinville had loaned to her, and dozes and dreams of him. In her dream, he comes to her in a panic, having lost his penis. She awakens herself laughing and feels a hand touch hers.

"I am glad to see that your nightmares have ceased." Jean stands beside her, glancing about.

"What makes you think so?"

"Your laughter, my lady." So—she is "my lady" again.

"Laughter can be helpful when one wishes to avoid crying."

He looks at her. Something broken shows itself, like a piece of bone splintering through skin.

"Come to me tonight?" she whispers.

"I cannot." A sound enters her ears like the roar in a conch shell. He moves his mouth. She looks down at the book. When she looks up again, he is gone.

That night, the sea pours forth from her eyes and carries her far away. Floating on her bed, she watches her life swim by and ponders happiness. She swore not to give up Joinville, but that was foolish; they have always known that their love must end. But what of the happiness she feels with him? Must she give that up, as well?

Once upon a time, she'd fancied that to be France's queen would bring happiness enough. Ruling the kingdom certainly seemed to fulfill Blanche; she gave up love for it, and became the most powerful woman alive. Now that she is gone, what is to stop Marguerite from taking her place—at last—as the true Queen of France? Louis will need her if he is to continue the monk's life of constant prayer that he began in Acre.

Perhaps she does not need Joinville to be happy. With him, she feels confident and quick, like a dancer. If she is those things when he is with her, isn't she still those things when he is not? Can she find her happiness in spite of him? She sees herself in the court, deciding cases. She sees herself sitting in the great hall on Louis's right-hand side, interceding for petitioners, accepting obeisance, claiming her power.

Outside, thunder cracks. The wind bangs at her door, rattling the hinges. She gets up to check the latch—and the ship lurches, throwing her to her knees. *Mon Dieu!* She pushes herself off the floor in time to be tossed onto her bed. The ship bucks like an unbroken horse, jumbling her insides. Rain gushes from the sky as if their ships sailed under a waterfall. She clings to her bed, keeping her eyes open, battling nausea, waiting to gain her bearings—and then, as always, it comes to her, her equilibrium is restored, and she can rise and open the door to see who is knocking.

Jean looks as if he had just arisen from the grave. Marguerite pulls him indoors and holds him close against her, bending her knees to move with the ship's surge upward, then plunge downward, breathe and relax, as if they were dancing on a magic carpet, nothing solid underfoot but stardust all around. It is the last time she will ever hold him. She does not want to let him go.

"Why did you come?"

"To make sure you are safe. This is a treacherous storm."

"It takes more than a little thunder and rain to frighten me."

A flash of light fills the room, illuminating him. The hair on her arms and neck stands on end. From outside, a scream pierces the howling wind. Marguerite runs to the door and throws it open. Their ship's mast is struck, burning under the sheeting rain.

The ship lists, hurling her forward. If not for her hand on the door, she would be flung against the rails, perhaps tossed overboard. Joinville yanks her back—"Close that damned door"—and slams it shut. It rocks backward, sending them both stumbling across the floor, crashing a ewer against the wall, which, as they tilt, becomes the floor for a moment. They tumble down together. Joinville leaps up and pulls her onto the bed. She clings to him, staring into the dark.

"The ship is burning. We are going to die," she says.

"Not you," he says. "Not if I can help it." He leaps from the bed and staggers to the door, then out. Marguerite cries his name, heedless of who might hear. She grabs her cloak and pulls it over her head and runs out to find him. She must die in his arms.

She finds him clustered with other men at the front of the ship, where the captain wrestles with the rudder. The sailors are dropping their fifth anchor in attempt to ground the vessel before it hits the enormous rock looming like a sea monster before them. Marguerite crosses herself but she does not pray for forgiveness of her sins, for Jean has certainly not done so, and she would rather spend eternity in purgatory with him than a day in heaven without him.

Joinville has not seen her. He is looking down at the floor of the deck and shouting over the wind. She hears him say, "the queen." She hears, "safety." She moves closer and sees Louis lying prone on the boards, his arms stretched overhead, wearing nothing but a robe. He is shouting, too, but not to Joinville: *Pater noster qui es en caelis sanctificetur nomen tuum*. A prayer.

Gisele tugs at her sleeve with one hand and holds her cloak fast with the other. "Should we awaken the babes, my lady?"

Marguerite pangs: Fortunate babes. Children can sleep through anything. Any moment now, this ship is going to dash itself against that rock and break apart like an egg on a bowl, but the children will know none of the terror that she has been feeling this last hour. No, she tells Gisele, let them sleep and pass to the Lord in peace.

She feels a shudder, as though the vessel trembled in fear. She staggers forward to grasp Joinville's hand. He turns to her with sorrowful eyes. "*Au revoir,*" she says to him, and grasps the rail just before the ship bucks, airborne on the crest of a wave as high as the wall at Tarascon. She will never see Provence again, or her mother, or her sisters. But, God willing, she will see her father very soon. When the ship comes down, it will crash against the rocks, killing instantly a fortunate few and leaving the others to drown.

"Go inside!" Joinville pulls her into his cabin and closes the door just as the wave crests and rolls over the ship, nearly snatching Louis away but for the courage of a sailor who remains on deck to hold him fast. The crashing waters wash the poor man overboard without a sound heard by anyone—not even by Louis, who hears only his own shouted prayers. Then the ship does a most unexpected thing: It rocks and shudders some more, but it does not fly through the air. The anchors have held it fast. After a final spasm, the tantrum is ended.

Not that Marguerite notices. The moment that door closed, she and Joinville commenced to drink each other up and they are still imbibing as Louis is nearly washed overboard, as water fills the sailor's lungs, as the storm rolls over the island of Cyprus and away from the ship, ripping branches from trees, tearing houses apart. In its wake, the sea laps at the splintered ship as innocently as a kitten's tongue. A wheeling gull pierces the air with its cry. Louis lies still, praying his thanks to God for delivering him from evil. But by the time the thought of "evil" has sent him staggering to Joinville's door, the lovers have parted.

Jean opens the door to Louis, and Marguerite helps him inside. "What are you doing?" Louis gasps.

She dries him tenderly with a towel, as if he were her little child. "Sir Joinville saved my life this day, by taking me in from the storm," she says.

"No, my queen, not Joinville," Louis says, gasping as if he were a fish flung forth by the waves. "It is I who saved you both—and all the ship—with my prayers."

Marguerite kisses his brow, and helps her husband to stand. "Joinville," he says. "Let us go."

"Where are we going, my lord?" Marguerite asks. "You, Sir Jean, and I?"

Louis scowls at her. "To put me to bed," he says.

Her laugh is as light as if she were thirteen again. "For that formidable and demanding task," she says, "you need your queen. And no one else." She helps her husband out the door and, hooking her arm through his, walks with him to his cabin with a glance back at her knight.

"Louis," she says, "let us disembark at Marseille. We can visit my sister in Aix, and your brother. I think that, if you and I work together, we can take Provence for our own. For France."

"Together?"

"Yes," she says. "As king and queen. Imagine what we could accomplish, Louis. Together."

"I am thinking," he says as he pulls her into his cabin and takes off her clothes.

→ *Eléonore* ←

The Heart of the Lion
London, 1252

Twenty-nine years old

$\mathscr{S}$HE MOUNTS HER palfrey with Henry's rebuke still ringing in her ears. Arrogance, indeed! She is only exercising her rights. He is the arrogant one, running to the courts with their every dispute and then lashing out when she wins.

This week the judges have ruled twice in her favor. First they exonerated her clerk, Robert del Ho, of wrongdoing after Henry accused him of fraud—his attempt to blame another for his own reckless spending. And today, they agreed with Robert Grosseteste, the bishop of Lincoln, that Eléonore might appoint the living from her church at Flamstead to her chaplain, without Henry's approval. "Arrogance," Henry muttered when the verdict was read, his drooping eyelid ticcing with rage.

Ignoring him, she stepped over to the bishop to thank him for his testimony. "I had hoped only for a letter of support, but you took the time to come and testify in person," she said.

Henry was close behind her. "How much of my money did she pay you?" he demanded. Eléonore wished for a great hole in the floor through which to drop: Robert Grosseteste is one of the world's most learned and respected men.

"Why, Henry," she said, "I give of my own money for the Lord's work, not only to Lincoln but to parishes throughout the kingdom. Would you view my financial records? I shall send them to you immediately, by way of my clerk—I believe you are familiar with Robert del Ho?" It is a good thing that angry looks cannot kill a person.

"Arrogance," he said. "I never thought you would turn against me, Eléonore."

The insult is almost more than she can bear. Turn against Henry? She would sooner have her heart cut out. *He* is challenging *her*, goaded on by those greedy Lusignans, who would take all for themselves were it not for her.

She has tried everything, it seems, to bring her husband back to her. She has given him gifts: most recently, a sumptuous robe of purple-brown velvet with a bejeweled clasp in the shape of a lion's head which she has never seen him wear. She spends hours upon hours reading official documents, the better to advise him, as well as the romances he loves—including the awful *Roman de Renart*—so that they may discuss them together. She arranges dinners twice weekly at Windsor Palace for visits with the children undistracted by the kingdom's demands. She has even given up her best friends for his sake, declining to testify for Simon and Eleanor in their disputes with Henry over money. The only court battles in which she would testify against her husband are the ones he initiates.

He is not a gracious loser. What else should one expect from a man who was given everything as a child? Knowing this, however, does not incline her to defer to him in any contest. She is too competitive for that—a trait that, once upon a time, he admired in her.

She expected his petulance today. So why does her chest feel so heavy, as though she carried a great stone around her neck? Going to Windsor—home, where her children live—will lift her spirits, beginning with the ride. The day is fine, although a bit chilly, and her horse steps lively, proud, she imagines, of its new saddle elaborately embroidered with the white roses she loves—her emblem—and studded all around with gold.

"Let's show you off," she says, stroking its soft mane. Riding through the neighborhoods of London will also give Eléonore the chance to show off her splendid new gown of blue silk from Paris.

Flanked by knights and seven of her ladies, Eléonore's horse trots along the broad, tree-lined avenues near the palace where London's merchants have built elegant mansions in recent years—prompting complaints from the Earl of Gloucester. "Soon they will be wearing silk and calling themselves 'Sir,' and the distinctions of nobility will be obscured," he pouted. A man steps out of his home and bows to her; his tunic, she notes, is not only silk but purple, as well—a color usually worn only by royalty. If only Gloucester were here to see.

The knight Sir Thomas turns to her. "We're approaching Charing, my lady." The district of London reserved for brothels. "It is no place for a queen."

To pass around it would delay their arrival at Windsor by an hour. After Henry's outburst, she yearns for her children's hugs and kisses; she hungers to hold them in her lap, to hear them say, "I love you."

"As I am surrounded by knights, I hardly feel endangered by prostitutes and petty thieves," she says, and quickens her horse's pace to lead the way down the center of the Charing Road. Perhaps she will spy a baron here, or, better yet, William de Valence, arm in arm with scandal.

The knights crowd around her as the houses change from spacious and light to narrow and dark, houses whose second stories jut so far over the road that they nearly blot out the sky. Behind them, along meager and muddy alleys, ramshackle homes rot into the ground along with piles of food scraps, offal, and excrement wafting an inglorious stench. Eléonore blinks her eyes against the burn. Inside these squalid homes live presumably squalid lives, judging by the children squishing their feet in the dirty muck and the smiling, dirt-matted dogs. A man with hair like cobwebs scrounges for food in the trash heaps, eliciting a tossed coin from Eléonore that he fails to notice. As the procession moves into an area of shops, the street writhes with activity: Children chase dogs. A young woman sells fruit from a basket. Horses and donkeys pull carts. A boy with Eléonore's silver coin in his fist jumps over puddles, dodging the grasping hands of the trash heap scavenger. A woman with loose red hair wears the prostitute's yellow-striped hood, yet looks out of place in a silk-and-ermine robe like the one Eléonore gave to Henry—

"Stop!" She slides off her horse and strides over to the red-haired woman, ignoring the calls of her knights. Her shoes scatter gravel and English mud as she walks, *her* mud, for she and Henry own every inch of ground in the kingdom as well as the mantle on this woman's back.

"You have something that belongs to me," she says to the woman. She eyes the clasp: a golden lion with bejeweled eyes, specially made for Henry.

The woman plants her hands on her hips. "Do you think so?"

Eléonore touches the soft fur around the mantle's edge. "I gave this to my husband. As a gift."

The woman throws back her head and laughs. Eléonore glances around to see two of her knights approaching as well as a gathering group of onlookers.

"I doubt that, pet," the prostitute says. "I got this from the King of England."

"From one of his servants, you mean. I'm very sorry. It was not his to give."

"I got it from the king himself." She straightens her back. "He said the eyes remind him of me, and the golden mane."

"Now you are the one making dubious claims." Although she can imagine Henry's saying such a thing. He once oozed with sentiment.

"'But Henry,' I said, 'you are the lion.' And do you know what he said?" A smile tugs at her lips. "He said, 'Maisey, you are the *coeur de lion*.'"

"That is impossible!" Eléonore's voice rises. She tugs at the mantle. "As your queen, I demand this mantle from you."

"Not *my* queen." The prostitute sneers. "Only an Englishwoman could claim that title." She jerks out of Eléonore's grasp and begins to walk away—but Eléonore seizes the mantle and jerks hard, yanking her backward.

"Give it to me now," she grunts. The woman slaps at her with flapping hands, more like the attack of an injured bird than a lion, knocking Eléonore's headdress to the dirt. Cheers arise from the crowd: "Give it to her, Maisey! Show her what we think of foreigners!" A ripping sound; the woman falls as the cloth tears free from the clasp. The crowd presses close; someone tries to seize the mantle from Eléonore's hands but the knights are upon them, swords drawn, pushing everyone back and asking Eléonore if she wants the prostitute taken into custody. On the contrary, Eléonore says; this woman is to be banished from the royal court.

"Aren't you going to pay me for that?" the prostitute says, struggling to her feet—but Sir Thomas knocks her down again.

"Show respect to the Queen of England," he says.

"That robe was given to me for services rendered," the woman says. "My lady."

Eléonore opens her purse and pours its contents onto the street, a stream of silver, then turns and walks away, ignoring the shouts of the crowd.

"A few coins?" the woman cries after her. "Is this all you have to give?"

———◦———

$\mathscr{S}$HE CRADLES EDMUND in her lap, arms around him as if he were a doll, rocking and singing. Waiting for Henry to arrive. "The heart of the lion," he called her—the endearment he uses—once used—for Eléonore. All that garish red hair, her bad teeth. That roll of flesh about her middle, the creases in her neck. The shouts from the people: *Better an English whore than Eléonore!* This is the doing of England's barons. Angered by Henry's awarding of lands, castles, and advantageous marriages to his "foreign" Lusignan brothers, the barons have taken their resentment to the streets, stirring discontent among those with the least reason to care about lands, castles, or aristocratic daughters. She fans her face with her hand, dabs at the perspiration on her upper lip.

Better a whore than Eléonore?

Really, Henry?

"What's the matter, Mama?" Edmund, sick again, half asleep in her arms, pats her face. "Don't cry, Mama. I will get better soon."

She rocks him and remembers their wedding night, the poetry Henry murmured as he covered her young body with his hands and lips:

Lady, I'm yours, today, every day,/ In your service my self I'll keep,/ Sworn, and pledged to you complete,/ As I have been always in everything.

"*And as you are first of joys to me, so the last joy too you will be/ As long as I'm still living,*" she whispers, finishing the song, heedless of the tears dropping now onto her sleeping son's hair.

She remembers Richard's words on the night of Sanchia's churching, that love is the delicate oil and marriage the vinegar. He was wrong, she told her sister. Love can go hand in hand with marriage. Passion can be sustained for as long as both husband and wife desire. She was confident, then, in her power to hold Henry's interest. But quarrels have taken a toll. Henry's tendency to blame others for his errors has fallen hard on her: Simon's troubles in Gascony and his dispute with Henry over Eleanor's dowry are, according to him, partly her fault. She agrees that Henry should pay them what he has promised, and so he accuses her of fueling the argument. But when she declined to testify for the Montforts, did he appreciate her support? He seemed not even to notice. If anything, his esteem for her has diminished.

And yet, she is the same as she has ever been—and, in some areas, much improved. Her figure is more voluptuous, her face more beautiful, her dress more fashionable than when she first came to him. She excels in the hunt, which once brought him delight. She continues to write poems for him, which used to please him, but now he shows little interest in hearing them. He complains that she meddles too much in the affairs of the kingdom, while formerly he included her in every decision. Of course, that was before the Lusignans came to London.

A red-haired whore is the least of her concerns. At least Henry is not going to replace her with such a woman—although she wishes he would be more discreet. Yet to discuss the matter with him will do her no good. He will neither accept blame nor apologize. Instead, she will work harder to attract him, starting tonight. She will fill her chamber with candlelight, bathe and perfume her body and hair, perhaps sing for him as he used to enjoy. She will see the fires burning in his eyes tonight, perhaps to stoke the passion in his heart again.

When he enters the nursery that afternoon, she stands to greet him with a kiss—but he turns aside. "Your uncle Boniface has just arrived," he says. "With a complaint, of course."

Eléonore doesn't know what this means. Her uncle has not complained to them before. She rises to don her crown and follow Henry into the great hall. They take their seats, and Boniface steps in, red-faced and sullen, looking much less handsome than usual, with Uncle Peter at his side.

"A most distressing incident has occurred," he says. "A direct challenge to my authority as archbishop of Canterbury, and a serious breach of our laws."

"You have authority in this matter," Henry says. "Why must you come to me?" He does not like to be disturbed at Windsor.

"Because, Your Grace"—Uncle Boniface sends a warning look to Eléonore—"the offender is your brother, Aymer de Lusignan."

While Boniface was in Rome last month, meeting with the pope, Aymer—still awaiting confirmation of his appointment as bishop of Winchester—appointed a new prior to the hospital of St. Thomas at Southwark.

"He exceeded his authority, as my official, Eustace, informed him, but he would not listen. So Eustace excommunicated your brother's appointee and took him into custody until my return."

Henry's face flushes. "A dire action," he says. "An overreaction, I should say."

"How else to stop him from taking the hospital over?" Eléonore says. "Aymer should be grateful that *he* was not excommunicated."

"As he would have been," Boniface says, "if not for his relation to the king."

Henry's sister Alice and his brothers Guy and William compounded the offense by sending armed knights to Aymer's aid. "One week after the prior's arrest, these men beat the guards at Maidstone with clubs and axe handles and set the prisoner free."

Henry chuckles. "My brothers and I all seem to have a bit of our mother in us."

"They then rode to the chapel at Lambeth and seized poor Eustace and some of my servants. They treated them very badly, beat them until they were nearly unconscious and left them in the road."

"In the road!" Eléonore says with a gasp. "At Lambeth!"

"Without horses or weapons."

"They might have been killed!" The road at Lambeth teems with robbers and murderers.

"But they weren't killed, were they?" Henry asks.

"No, Your Grace."

"So, no serious harm was done."

"No serious harm?" Eléonore cries.

"Your Grace," Peter says, "your brothers snubbed not only the archbishop's authority but yours, as well, since you nominated Boniface to his position. If you do not censure them, you will lose respect from your barons as well as your lesser subjects."

"So I am to sacrifice my own kin for the sake of the barons' esteem?" Henry's laugh is incredulous.

Is she hearing him correctly? "Henry, respectability is essential if you are to govern."

"I don't recall asking for your advice," Henry says through gritted teeth. He stands and, to everyone's surprise, turns his back on the Savoyard uncles as well as his wife and walks across the floor to his chambers.

Eléonore rushes after him. She finds him brooding at a window, silhouetted in the evening light.

"How dare you speak to me that way, Henry," she says quietly.

"How dare you speak to *me* that way, Eléonore?"

"Henry, you know I'm in the right. Your brothers—"

"I know nothing of the sort! My brothers are tired of being treated like vassals to your uncles. They, the sons of a queen!"

"The bishop of Winchester is subservient to the archbishop of Canterbury," Eléonore says. "No matter their parentage."

"Boniface of Savoy thinks everyone subservient to him."

"Among the English clergy, everyone is."

"And he comes to me complaining of violence—after nearly killing that old man over his right to inspect a monastery! Do you remember that?"

"Your brothers were wrong to challenge him, and wrong to harm his men."

"And you? Weren't you wrong to challenge me over the Flamstead appointment?"

"Apparently not, since I prevailed in court today."

His eyes veer as if, having lost the point, he is searching for it somewhere in the room.

"You hate my brothers."

"No, I—"

"Yes!" His laugh is triumphant. "You have hated them since the day they arrived in London. Don't bother protesting. I saw it in your eyes then, and I still see your hatred whenever William or Aymer comes around. But why, Eléonore? Why?"

"You might ask that question of your brothers. It is they who treat me as a competitor for your love."

"There is no competition," he growls.

"You have made that abundantly clear." Tears spring to her eyes. She turns away so that he cannot see.

"At least they do not continually challenge me on every decision, humiliating me before my subjects."

"What do you know about humiliation?" she snarls, turning on him. "You, who have debased me before all of England with your red-haired whore!"

His eyes bulge. His mouth opens and shuts, as if he were a fish yanked from the sea.

"I saw her walking the streets of Charing today in the mantle I gave to you. I thought one of the servants had stolen it! But when I approached her—"

"You approached her? By God, Eléonore!"

"Yes, and why not? I never imagined that you would betray me, let alone with that sad and tawdry tramp."

His face whitens like a fish's underbelly. "You are mistaken. The mantle was someone else's. I hope you did not make a public scene."

"Do not insult me." She turns and runs from his room to her own, snatches up the torn mantle, runs back to him. He stares at her as if someone—or something—were dying. Or already dead.

"See for yourself." She thrusts the mantle to him. He examines it as if looking for clues to exonerate him.

"How did this become torn?"

"I ripped it off her neck."

"You did not."

"I did. I would have started on her face next, the insolent *chienne*. She actually mocked me, Henry! I would have ripped her into shreds but for the knights you sent with me."

"I cannot believe this of you. Is this any way for a queen to behave?"

"And what of a king's behavior? Is it acceptable for you to roll in the gutter with the filth of this kingdom? By God's head, if you're going to be unfaithful, choose a noblewoman, or even one of our servants!"

"Any of them would be preferable to the man I'm married to now."

"Someone must be the man."

A vein in his neck begins to pulse. His eyes hold a crazed look. Eléonore knows she has gone too far. She waits for the explosion.

"How high does the arrogance of woman rise if it is not restrained!" he screams. "I want you out of London. Now!"

"Why, so you can see *her*?"

"Get out. Tonight."

"You want me to leave? Truly?" She presses a hand to her fluttering chest. "Where am I to go?"

"As far away from me as possible."

"I-I'll stay here with the children, then. You can go back to Westminster."

"You are banished. Get out tonight, out of London, and do not return until I say you may. If ever."

She sits on the bed, gripping the coverings, reminding herself to breathe but not doing it. If he divorces her, she will lose the children. She will not be able to help them—for Henry will remarry, and his new queen will advance her own offspring. Edmund will lose the chance to become King of Sicily, for Henry will certainly squander it with his temperamental outbursts and impulsive decisions. Edward will lose Gascony to Richard of Cornwall. Her daughter Beatrice will marry a much lesser man than she would with Eléonore's influence.

"Henry, do not do this." She lifts pleading eyes to him. "The children need me. And I need you."

"You should have thought of that before insulting me. Before usurping me. And do not think of absconding, by the way. I am confiscating your gold and your lands."

"But where am I to go?"

"What do I care where you go? Go to Winchester."

"There is nothing for me in Winchester, Henry." She sounds far away, like a plaintive child, even to her own ears.

"Yes, yes. Winchester is where I'll send you." His grin looks eerie. "And while you're there, do pay a visit to the bishop-elect. My brother Aymer will be exceedingly glad to welcome you."

⪢ *Beatrice* ⪡

Pearls in the Same Oyster

Paris, 1254

Twenty-three years old

$\mathscr{S}$HE AND CHARLES are the last to arrive at court, for Charles refused to leave Provence until every last Cathar had been burned and their ashes shipped to Rome, "to assure the pope that we are on his side." Killing them wasn't enough, however; Charles insisted she watch them burn with him so that no one could ever accuse them of heresy. The screams of those poor people and the gag-sweet smell of their burning flesh will never leave her—and neither, Charles promised, will the pope's gratitude.

"He will repay us in full measure, my love," Charles said.

How he can be so sanguine about taking lives is a mystery to Beatrice, whose father was a noted warrior but who was also kind and gentle with his people. Yes, he sent troops for the pope's Albigensian campaign, but reluctantly, and he anguished the rest of his life over the brutal tortures and killings of the Cathars. Had they come to Ramon Berenger for help as they did to her and Charles, her parents would have fed them, listened to their plight, suggested they abandon their heretical beliefs and adopt the religion of the Church, and sent them home again. When she pointed this out to Charles, he laughed.

"Your father struggled in poverty until he died," he said. "Do you desire a similar fate?"

If one is to achieve greatness, Charles says, one must embrace cruelty. One must be willing to kill, or be killed. One must be willing to betray others—even sisters or brothers, as she and Charles are doing now in their secret negotiations for the crown of Sicily. It has already been promised to her sister Eléonore's son Edmund, "but he is a little boy, and the Church needs a man on the throne," Charles pointed out.

Family comes first, Mama says. Beatrice has never questioned this fact, but she wonders: Which family? She has sisters on two thrones, cousins and aunts and uncles on others.

"I am your family," Charles says. "I and our three children, and the many others you will bear to me." This is his reply whenever she asks to give Tarascon to Margi.

But she does not ask him for that anymore. He made sure of it the day Louis's chamberlain Bartolomeu le Roie came to him aquiver, tormented, he said, by a terrible sight on the journey home from Outremer: the queen Marguerite running naked from her chambers with a burning nightgown, and, lying in her bed, the seneschal of Champagne, Sir Jean de Joinville. To tell King Louis would break his heart, for he loves Sir Joinville as a brother, but keeping this secret to himself is surely treason.

"I told him he had done right in coming to me," Charles said to Beatrice as he picked his teeth after supper that night. "It will be easier on Louis to hear it from a brother."

"You're not going to tell him!" But of course he would. Charles was a little boy when Marguerite came to court, his mother's baby. He hated Marguerite because Blanche hated her, and he goaded and tormented her until she hated him, too.

"I can well imagine the Most Pious King's shock upon learning that his wife is a whore." He chuckled. "I hope he turns her out without delay. I used to fantasize about seeing Miss High and Mighty on her knees, begging."

"He wouldn't turn her out. She is the mother of his children."

"An evil influence that ought to be eradicated. Did you know? She sent my mother out of the palace for reading a psalter to them. Why the glum expression, darling? Do you love her so much? She cares nothing for you."

Beatrice thought of Marguerite's cool hand on her hot brow, the moist cloths she placed on her cheeks and neck as she struggled to give birth in the sweltering Egyptian heat. The concern and—yes, love!—in her eyes. She thought of Marguerite bleeding on the boat that carried them to meet the Egyptian queen, pulling the blood-soaked linen from between her legs and rinsing it in the Nile, then stuffing the wet cloth into her trousers again. She thought of Marguerite standing proud before the queen Shajar al-Durr, bearing herself most regally even as the blood drained from her face and into her cloths again. She saved baby Blanche's life and she saved Louis's life, and she does not deserve to be dispossessed no matter what Charles thinks.

"Don't tell King Louis about Marguerite and Sir Jean. Please, Charles."

He bent down to peer under the chair, lifted up a cushion. "I am looking for my wife, the beautiful and ruthless Beatrice of Provence," he said. "Have you seen her?"

"Charles, please. She is my sister."

"She would have to stop harassing you about Tarascon then, wouldn't she? Without a kingdom, she would have no power. Pope Innocent would toss her petitions against us into the fire. That alone would be worth the breaking of my brother's heart." He smacked his lips as if enjoying a flavorful dish.

"You don't have to break your brother's heart to hold on to Tarascon." From her desk she pulled a parchment, newly folded, its wax sealed with her signet ring.

"I wrote this letter to Pope Innocent, supporting my sister's appeal for Tarascon," she said. "I have not sent it because I feared your reaction."

"A wise choice."

"As heir to Provence, I may instruct the pope to award Marguerite her dowry. I testify that Papa made his bequest in the throes of death, when his thinking was unclear. He most likely intended to leave Tarascon to her, for he did honor his contracts, but in his confused state he forgot that he had promised it."

"How inconvenient." Charles snatched the letter and tossed it into the fire.

"I have a copy. Several copies. One of which is right here." She tapped her forehead. "I can write another and another, as many as you can destroy."

Charles glowered. She took a deep breath. She had anguished over Marguerite's dowry since leaving her in Acre four years ago. The look of betrayal in her sister's eyes haunts Beatrice still, and her parting words—*You are not one of us. And you never will be*. She spoke them in anger, but they convey a certain truth. It is as if her sisters spoke in a tongue all their own which she cannot comprehend: the language of love. *Family comes first*. To join her sisters, she must speak their language. Her letter would have been her first attempt.

But now she was undone. Unless she gained Tarascon for Marguerite, her yearnings for true sisterhood would never be fulfilled. Her sisters would ever stand against her, for they know, as does she, that Papa honored his pledges. Yet if she would silence Charles about Marguerite and her knight, she must offer him some reward. In order to save her sister's honor—and protect her from imprisonment—she had to forswear Marguerite's love.

"I will withhold my letter for as long as you remain silent about Joinville and my sister," she said. "And you must command Barolomeu to hold still his ever-flapping tongue, as well. If I even hear rumors—"

"I can keep a secret well enough. Can you?"

"I would never spread tales about my sister."

"And about your husband? I would not wish it to be known that my wife had coerced me to submit to her. If you swear never to tell a living soul—not even Marguerite—about our pact, then I will not reveal your sister's infidelity."

And so it is with dread that she approaches the royal palace in Paris for their first ever family Christmas celebration. She had hoped to give Marguerite a copy of her letter to the pope as a Christmas gift. How many times has she imagined the pleasure on her sister's face, on the faces of all her sisters, as she revealed her love to them. Now they will never know. They will always think of her as spoiled, selfish Beatrice, the Cleopatra of Provence.

Family comes first. Having lost her sisters, she must consider her children, instead. She must think of her baby Charles's future, and help her husband Charles to build an empire for themselves and their future generations—starting with Sicily.

"That sickly little crouchback Edward would only squander the opportunity that Sicily offers," Charles says. "Whereas we, my darling, will employ it as a gateway to the East."

He wants Jersualem; he wants Constantinople; he wants an empire greater than the pope of Rome has even thought to fear. And he wants Beatrice by his side, he said, "fighting with me and ruling with me, the greatest empress in the world." He need only speak these words for her to fling herself on top of him, arms and legs flailing, a swimmer on a cresting wave of passion. She does love a man of ambition.

Now, as they wheel up in their mud-splattered carriage—a fresh rain having drenched the roads—she sees from her window the ornate carriages of her sisters parked in the courtyard: the red carriage with the English flag, carved with white roses and gilded with gold, the interior covered in brilliant blue cloth; and Sanchia's carriage, even more opulent, gold within and without, and studded with precious jewels. Her own little carriage, of gleaming wood in five different colors with ornate gold pieces and hinges, appears almost tawdry in comparison. *It is not a contest,* she can almost hear her mother saying. But what would Mama, who had only seven brothers, know of the rivalry between sisters—especially queens?

The competition is fiercer than anyone knows—anyone except Beatrice, and, of course, Charles, who grew up as she did in the shadow of a royal sibling. Marguerite fancies that she knows the game, but she does not comprehend the rules. She should have sent an army to seize Provence before Papa's blood had cooled. Of course, Marguerite was not the real Queen of France then. The woman she showed herself to be in Damietta makes Beatrice glad of that now. She will never forget Marguerite's comportment during that terrifying time—indeed, her most fervent wish is to be like her, strong and wise and loyal to her family.

When last Beatrice saw her sister—only a few months ago, when the French ships landed at Marseille on their return from Outremer—the weather was pleasant but for the chill blowing off Marguerite's every word. She warmed up well enough when she led Jean de Joinville out to walk the Mediterranean beaches, but at Beatrice's curious look she shut fast like a bolted gate. Beatrice could almost hear the clang. Her letter to the pope would have opened that gate, would have won her sister's love—but not now. Not ever.

"Hold your head high, my dear," Charles murmurs as they step into the royal palace. "Remember whom we are, and whom we are destined to become."

Louis and Marguerite await them on their thrones at the far end of the great hall. Off to one side, musicians play a pretty tune on lutes and pipes. Candles and lamps illuminate the room. Marguerite looks resplendent, softened by the blurred lines of age, her skin glowing, her eyes alight. Or maybe her proximity to Louis improves her. Even a dead man would seem vital next to his pale, stern self, clad like a pauper in dull rags, liver-colored circles giving his eyes a bleak, bleary look. Beatrice bends her knee to kiss his ring, forbidding herself to recoil from the touch of his hand with its long, scaly nails.

"Welcome, brother, sister," the king says—his voice booms, surprisingly strong. "Merry Christmas."

"My favorite time of the year," Charles says.

"Really?" Louis brightens. "I did not know that about you, Charles."

Beatrice grins. Charles detests everything to do with Christmas, but he knows his brother well. "Will there be a midnight mass?" he says. "How wonderful."

Marguerite steps down from her throne to embrace her. "What need is there for formalities between sisters?" she says. Her voice is calm; her face, smooth and radiant. She has known love, Beatrice thinks.

Marguerite turns to Louis. "Charles, welcome. We shall see you at the feast this evening. Our cooks are preparing the roast duck you always enjoyed."

Beatrice and Charles exchange glances. Where is Marguerite's pinched tone, as if she were holding her nose? Where is her sour frown? She tucks Beatrice's hand into the crook of her arm and leads her up the stairs, her head erect, her shoulders back. Regal.

In Marguerite's bedchamber, Eléonore rises from her chair, laughing at Beatrice's expression. "I am horribly fat," she says. "Katharine was born more than a year ago, yet I still appear pregnant."

"Losing baby fat becomes more difficult as one ages," Marguerite says. "I am sure I will never see my waist again."

Marguerite leads Beatrice to her bed, where Sanchia is lying down. "Sit up, dear. Don't let a little headache spoil your enjoyment."

"You don't know," Sanchia says. "Being married to Richard is making me ill."

"Marriage is difficult," Eléonore says.

"You don't appear to be suffering."

"Henry and I have had our trials."

"He banished her from London last year," Marguerite says.

"He said I was too domineering." Eléonore grins. "Can you imagine that?"

"Richard has the opposite complaint," Sanchia says. "He calls me a dormouse."

"You've always been timid," Beatrice says. "Didn't he know it when he married you?"

"Mama kept him from noticing," Eléonore says. "While his eyes were on Sanchia—constantly, as I recall—Mama amused him with her wit."

"Later, he thought I had said all those clever things," Sanchia says. "He keeps asking where that other Sanchia has gone, the one with the quick tongue."

"I wonder at the whereabouts of the man I married, as well." Marguerite grimaces. "Louis has gone from majesty to martyr. He spends all his time devising tortures for blasphemers and heretics—as if eternal hell weren't punishment enough—and punishing himself for failing in Outremer."

"That sounds like a merry time," Beatrice says. "Do you ever regret saving his life?"

"You saved the king's life?" Sanchia says to Marguerite.

"She saved Damietta from collapse even while giving birth," Beatrice says. "Two days later, she sailed up the Nile and negotiated Louis's release with the Egyptian queen. You should have seen her!" She smiles at Marguerite. "Louis must have been impressed. You rule by his side now, don't you?"

"Louis is too absorbed in himself to notice my achievements. He has never said a word of thanks or praise to me. I rule in spite of him, not because of him."

"Eléonore is now a powerful queen, also," Sanchia says. "She ruled England while King Henry was in Gascony."

"Was that before or after he banished you, Elli?" Beatrice says.

"He ended my banishment after one month." Eléonore gives a little smile. "He needed me."

"You should have refused," Beatrice says. "That might have taught him a lesson."

"Holding on to Gascony was more important than teaching Henry lessons. Besides, he learned well enough when he went and left me the keys to the treasury."

"England's finances were never so well managed as when Eléonore was in charge," Sanchia says. "Richard told me so."

"What of you, Beatrice?" Marguerite says. "Is Charles letting you have a say in Provence?"

"We're like two pearls in the same oyster. We rub against each other at times, but it polishes us."

"Truly?" Marguerite frowns. "So you agreed with his decision to burn those poor Cathars?"

"The pope of Rome commanded it." Beatrice feels her blood rise. "As you well know."

"It was good for them to burn at the stake before they could gain any more converts," Sanchia says. "Think of all the souls you saved."

"'Let he who is without sin cast the first stone,'" Marguerite says. "Or do the Lord's words not apply to Cathars?"

"We came to celebrate the birth of Christ, remember?" Eléonore says. "And to unite our husbands. If we fight amongst ourselves, they may follow our example—and our plans will be ruined."

Sanchia nods. Marguerite smiles and takes Eléonore's hand. Beatrice looks at the three of them—Eléonore embracing Sanchia, Marguerite holding Eléonore's hand—and wonders, what plans?

"I seem to have missed something," she says.

"Things seem to be going well so far," Marguerite says. "Louis adores King Henry."

"And Henry has the highest admiration for King Louis. He thinks he ought to be made a saint."

Marguerite snorts. "Please tell him not to mention it to Louis! He is zealous enough without that sort of encouragement."

"But wouldn't Henry's praise make him more amenable?" Sanchia says.

"Amenable to what?" Beatrice says.

"Peace between England and France," Marguerite says. "We have been writing a treaty with Eléonore's man John Maunsell."

Beatrice snorts.

"Why do you laugh?" Sanchia says. "Don't you think peace is possible?"

"Possible, but not likely. Men live to conquer and kill."

"We are bankrupting our treasuries with these endless wars," Eléonore says. "Nothing will remain for our children, at this rate."

"Do you think your funds are better spent on Sicily?" She snorts again.

"For Edmund? I do," Eléonore says. "But the barons refuse to fund a campaign there. Their shortsightedness is appalling." This will be good news for Charles.

"Will you lose Sicily, then?" Beatrice asks.

"Come, sister, you know me better." Eléonore laughs. "The greater the obstacles, the harder I fight, especially for my children's sake." She lifts her chin as proudly as if she had already won. "I expect to see Edmund crowned Holy Roman Emperor someday." Beatrice wants to laugh, too: The sickly little Edmund, taking the Stupor Mundi's throne? He might hold it for an hour—if the fickle pope doesn't turn against him as Pope Gregory did to Frederick.

A bell rings: the feast is about to begin. Marguerite escorts Beatrice to her chambers to freshen up. "I hope I didn't embarrass you," she says. "I have a soft spot in my heart for the Cathars."

"As do I. You could not be our Papa's child without sympathy for them."

"Some of the troubadours in Papa's court were Cathars, and as god-fearing as you or I. Their beliefs are not very different from ours. Almost the same, really."

"Their beliefs *weren't* very different, you mean to say. Charles has wiped Catharism off the face of the earth, or so he tells the pope. But I doubt that the Church cared about their beliefs overly much. Pope Innocent wanted their wealth, and their lands, to fund his campaigns in Sicily and Germany."

"And Charles was eager to help him."

"They could have saved themselves by renouncing their religion. Why wouldn't they, if their beliefs were similar? And their zeal to gain converts only threatened the Church's income more. Stubbornness and stupidity killed the Cathars, not Charles."

They are standing outside the chamber doors. Marguerite tilts her head and studies Beatrice. "Is there nothing that you would die for, then? No belief you cherish so strongly that you would give your life protecting it?"

Beatrice's mind roams over the featureless terrain of her passions, thinks of her children, her mother, her God. "Nothing and no one is worth dying for," she says. Then she remembers, and laughs. "Of course—Charles!"

A light in Marguerite's eyes flickers off, then on again. "Your precious Charles. I should have known, watching him grow up, how suited the two of you would be for each other. You were much alike as children."

"We do have much in common."

"Such as ambition."

"We hope to accomplish great things."

"So do we all. But your sisters keep the family's interests foremost in our hearts. Can you say the same?"

How she would love to boast about all she has done for the family. But she cannot say a word, or Charles would destroy Marguerite. So she focuses instead on the request that she must make.

"Charles and I do care about family, in spite of what you might think. Take the matter of Sicily, for instance."

"Sicily?" Margaret looks at her askance. "What of Sicily?"

"The pope offered it to Charles when Frederick died."

"Louis forbade him to accept. It was offered to Richard, too, and he also refused. The pope's price is too high, as Eléonore and Henry are now discovering."

"Yes. But Charles wanted Sicily. He thought he should have been consulted. He was very upset over losing it."

"I can imagine." Marguerite's smile is thin.

"When King Henry and Eléonore pursued it for Edmund, though, he turned his eye elsewhere."

"He turned his temper on the people of Marseille. The Sicilians are fortunate to have escaped that fate."

"He quashed a rebellion, which our mother incited. The Marseille rebels tried to assassinate him."

"They hate the French, and with good reason," Marguerite says. "Poised as we are now to swallow them up along with Provence."

"Peace has returned to Provence. And the pope of Rome has approached Charles again."

"Out of thanks for his Cathar-roasting fête? I hope the prize is worth all that innocent blood."

"He has offered Sicily."

Marguerite sneers. "And of course you will accept. Even knowing that it has been given to your nephew."

"We are discussing it."

"Agonizing, I'm sure."

"Do not patronize me." Beatrice's hiss echoes through the room. "We do not want to harm Eléonore or Edmund. But you heard her today: Taking Sicily will be impossible without money and troops. The English barons will commit neither. They will lose Sicily, and who better to step in than Charles and me? At least it will remain in the family."

"Your sudden concern for family is touching. What do you desire from me?"

"We need France's support."

"We have neither money nor knights for you. Our escapades over the sea all but drained the treasury."

"Your money would be helpful, but it's not what we need. We want yours and Louis's endorsement. We would raise the funds ourselves."

"By squeezing the people of Provence? They will love you more than ever for it."

"And by soliciting the aid of our neighbors. With France's endorsement, Toulouse might contribute, and Normandy, and Castille."

"Sicily is a quagmire. Why would Louis and I involve ourselves?" She turns to leave, but Beatrice clutches her arm.

"Please, sister! We're not asking for your involvement. We only need a letter supporting Charles as Sicily's king. It would mean so much. It would mean everything."

In the long pause that ensues, Beatrice studies the emotions passing like clouds across her sister's face—but she cannot read them. How little they know of each other, even after two years in captivity together.

"I might help you," she says at last. "If you would do something for me."

"I would do anything, Marguerite. Not only to gain your help, but simply because we are sisters." She cannot help the smile on her face. She tries to chase it away, but it persists. Sicily will be theirs!

"Give me Tarascon."

And then she feels like a butterfly whose wings have just been pinned to a board. "You know I cannot," she says.

"Mama has signed all her claims over to you. I received a letter from the archbishop. He says she was paid a sum. Where is mine?"

"Papa willed Tarascon to me, Margi. He did not want Provence divided."

"He promised it to me, or ten thousand marks. Where is my sum?"

"You know the revenues of Provence. You know we do not have it."

"But you do have Tarascon."

Beatrice sighs. How different this conversation would be if not for Marguerite's indiscretion. Marguerite might be laughing with her now, happy to know that Tarascon is hers, rather than scowling.

"Tarascon is not mine to give, Margi. It belongs to Charles now."

"Papa would not have wanted Charles to have it. He aimed to keep Provence out of the hands of the French."

"Perhaps that is why he did not will it to you!" Beatrice clenches her hands. "You seem to forget that *you* are the French."

"You are not going to help me."

"Tarascon is a great fortress. With rebellions always brewing against us, we may need it."

Marguerite's eyes harden as if she had turned to stone. "Then I will not help you. Ever. With anything."

"Don't say that, Margi! We are sisters—"

"You are not my sister."

"I am." She crosses her arms over her chest, holding her heart in one piece. "You cannot take away what we have. What we are."

"We shall see about that," Marguerite says, and walks away.

⋯•⋯

*T*HE AROMA OF spiced duck fills the hall. Charles feigns indifference—no doubt, the kitchen, too, has declined since his mother's death—but the flaring of his nostrils gives him away. Beatrice cannot imagine eating; her stomach feels full of the tears she refuses to cry.

The hall is bedecked with the green of the season: holly dripping with red berries, and mistletoe with its white ones; evergreen branches wafting the fragrance of pine. Her sisters sit on a high dais in the front of the room. Marguerite is in the center, with Louis. Eléonore is on her right, with King Henry. Richard sits beside Henry and, beside him, their mother, her once-luxuriant chestnut hair gone gray, her skin puckering around her mouth like a piece of wet leather. Once a renowned beauty, she reminds Beatrice now of a flower on the verge of dropping its petals. She ascends the platform and wraps her arms around Mama's neck. Her fragrances, lilac and dust, the scents of old age, make Beatrice pang.

Where, she asks, is Sanchia? "Lying down," Mama says. "The poor dear has a headache." She pats Beatrice's arm; the skin on her hand seems thin and brittle, like dried leaves. "She is still as delicate as ever. And your sister Margi is as stubborn as ever."

Beatrice glances at Marguerite, who glares at her. The seats at this table are all filled, she notes. "Do not blame Margi too much," Mama says. "Her life has not been easy compared with yours."

Charles, who has stepped over to speak with his brother, comes frowning to her side. "Apparently, we have been assigned to a lesser table."

"There must be a mistake," Beatrice says. "My mother and sisters are here."

"Lower your voice, my dear," Charles says. "Do not give the *chienne* the satisfaction of your anger."

Beatrice sees triumph in Marguerite's eyes. She jerks her arm away from Charles's guiding touch and turns to confront her sister.

"What is the meaning of this?" she demands, not caring who hears, hoping the entire world will take note of Marguerite's pettiness. "I thought we were to dine together, all four of us and Mama."

"Eléonore and I are queens," Marguerite says. "It would not be appropriate for you to sit on our level."

"Mama is not a queen."

"Yes, I suppose you are right. Would you have me move her to a lower table, then?" Marguerite's lips curl in the tight smile of minor victories. Charles steps over to take Beatrice's arm.

"Behold, my brother Alphonse and his pretty wife are at our table, and all the major counts," Charles says as he leads her away. "In any other circumstance, we would feel honored to be seated with them."

"This is an insult, and you know it," Beatrice fumes. "Marguerite has humiliated me before all the barons of France."

"Have patience, my love," he murmurs as she takes her seat. "You are made of better cloth than she."

"She will not help us gain Sicily, Charles," Beatrice says. "Not unless we give her Tarascon."

"We do not need her help, or Louis's, either," Charles says. "We are unstoppable, Beatrice! Do not doubt it. Someday, I will make you an empress. You will be a greater queen than any of your sisters—greater than any woman in the world."

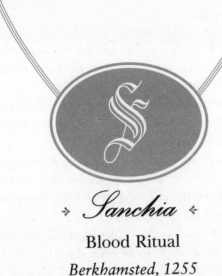

Sanchia ✦

Blood Ritual

Berkhamsted, 1255

Twenty-seven years old

*M*URDER AND SUPPER make a bad combination. Sanchia pushes her plate away as the messenger makes his report: A Christian boy's body has been found in a well in Lincoln, at the home of a Jewish man. For his murder, King Henry has arrested the Jew and eighty-nine others.

"Ninety Jews!" Richard leaps up from his seat, nearly knocking his supper off the table. "For the death of one child?" The startled messenger stumbles backward, hiding behind his hands as any man from King Henry's court might do.

But Richard is not one to lash out, except at Sanchia sometimes. He has treated her kindly, though, since last Christmas in Paris when he came to her chambers and held her until her headache went away. He kissed her and coaxed her, then, into the great hall for the feast. Elated by his show of love, she even accepted a goblet of wine. As she drank, she began to feel even happier. She shone—yes! Why not say it?—as never before, alight with Richard's love. The French barons drooled over her as if she were the main course, their eyes moving like hands on her arms and bosom. For she and Richard sat not at the queens' table, but with Beatrice, to console her after Marguerite so cruelly shunned her. How vicious sisters can be, in spite of their love for one another, or maybe because of it.

"You made me proud," Richard said to her later, as he escorted her to her chambers. "The French nobles will not forget you—or me. Can Gascony be far from our grasp?"

Forget Gascony! She wanted to beg him. Eléonore would not forgive them if Richard took Gascony for his own. And besides, the rebellions there have stopped now, after King Henry married his son Edward to the King of Castille's daughter. But Richard will not stop talking about Gascony. He is like Margi in that way, clinging to his notion of what ought to be even when it isn't. Marguerite will always think of Provence as hers, and Richard will never forswear Gascony, for it was given to him once, never mind its being taken away again.

So pleased was he with Sanchia that night, he took her to her chambers and made love as tenderly as if she were one of his mistresses. He has not spoken a harsh word to her in the month since their return to Berkhamsted. Only now does he erupt—but not, thank the Lord, against her. This time, his anger explodes against his brother.

"Ninety Jews! And some of them the wealthiest merchants in Lincoln," he says. "Henry will confiscate their lands and their goods for himself if the judges rule against them. What are the charges?"

"Ritual murder, my lord," the youth says. "They are said to crucify a Christian boy every year and drink his blood."

"Nonsense," Richard grumbles. "Henry awarded the Jews' taxes to me as repayment for a loan, but now he misses the revenue and wants it back. I wonder who invented the crucifixion tale?"

"It sounds plausible to me," Sanchia says. She has noticed how Abraham stares at her when she emerges from the chapel after prayers, wearing her cross and holding her rosary. She can imagine him coaxing some poor little boy into his clutches and doing terrible things to him just because he is a Christian.

"Even more incredible is that people believe these stories."

Richard scowls at the messenger, who blushes. "Are you acquainted with any Jews? They are an erudite race. Thinkers and talkers, for the most part. Certainly not killers."

"I know a Jew or two," Sanchia says. "They do like to talk. But they killed Jesus, don't forget."

"Even so, the story seems unlikely. Concocted, no doubt, by greedy men for whom the Jews are lucrative targets." He sits down in his chair again. "Please ask the king to postpone any hearings or judgments until I arrive. I will leave for London on the morrow."

The messenger bows and takes his leave, and another—an older man, richly attired—steps into the hall.

"My lord, I am the bearer of bad news. The pope of Rome's nominee for the German throne, William of Holland, has fallen gravely ill."

"Is he a friend of yours, Richard?" Sanchia asks. He rubs his hands together; his eyes are bright.

"My best friend in the world, should he die." He hands the messenger a purse of coins and sends him to the baths, then leaps up to dance Sanchia down the steps of the dais and around the floor. "Bad news, bah! Germany is a heartbeat away from being mine, my dear. And you shall be my queen."

"I, a queen?" She laughs. "In paradise, I hope."

"You will not have to wait that long, my pet." He grips her hands. "Sanchia, I know of what you are capable. I saw you in Paris, stunning the nobles."

A flirtation, she wants to say. They were, after all, French. He twirls her away, pulls her close. He smells of wood smoke and lime. His eyes shimmer. "We are going to be king and queen of the Germans," he says. "Or the Romans, as some say. I prefer Romans."

"But the Roman empire is gone, while Germany thrives."

He grins. "This is what I have been talking about."

"The fall of the Roman empire?"

"No, you!" He pulls her in, touches her waist. "You're an intelligent woman, Sanchia. You're conversant on many topics. But you need confidence to shine."

"I like talking with you, Richard."

"The Germans are going to love you. My charming queen."

Sanchia takes him by the hand and smiles. She likes the excitement on his face, like the flames in a fireplace. He leads her up the stairs to the second level, where her gown trails across the blue and gold floor, inspired by the sultan's palace in Outremer, Richard says, paved with ornate tiles in many, vivid colors. This is something else she loves about him: his eagerness to try every new thing.

He leads her into her chambers and lays her down and strokes her skin and kisses her cheek, her throat, her arms. She gazes at the canopy over her bed and imagines herself a queen: always in demand, her every move scrutinized, her every word recorded, her every hour filled with obligations. She has observed Eléonore and Marguerite in their courts. And she has thanked the Lord many times for her quiet life, more comfortable than theirs—for Richard is wealthier even than kings—and unburdened by a crown on her head. The only kind of queen she ever wanted to be was the Lord's.

"Sit up, love. I want to undress you," Richard says. Sanchia's head is beginning to ache. He pulls off her surcoat, her gown, her chemise. She shivers. The maids have forgotten to stoke the fire. His beard tickles her breast. "My queen," he says. Her temple throbs.

He rolls over her, a ship on her sea. Pain swells and crests, rocking her on its red tide then unfurling, velvet beneath her feet, plush, climbing an endless stair to a far-off throne. Her legs tire and the heavy crown squeezes her skull; the velvet is soft. She spreads her fingers and kneels, presses her palm against the carpet, feels it sink in like a cheek on a down pillow, settles on her knees in the pile, feels it envelop her like a blanket.

When she awakens, the room is dark except for the flicker of the fire, revived by a servant, for which she is glad because her clothing is nearly all removed and she lies on top of her bed in only her stockings. Someone might have laid a blanket on her, except that no one does more than necessary in this household. Richard likes to be left alone. To oblige him, the servants keep a distance from her, as well. As though she were an extension of him rather than her own person.

A pulse of pain in her right temple brings her back to herself. Richard had been making love to her. *My queen*. He wants to make a queen of her. She hears a gasp. She sits up, listening. Nothing. It was only her imagination. Perhaps it was she who gasped. The very idea of being a queen makes her want to suck in her breath and hold it until she faints away again.

A long cry streams like a moonbeam into her room. She feels in the dim light for her robe—where are her ladies?—and grasps it on its wall hook, slides it around her then steps barefoot through the music room where her harp glints like stars and where, at the other end, her ladies stand in a whispering clot outside Richard's chambers.

Sanchia slides across the floor until she hears the sound again— a shout this time, and Richard's uttered name. She touches the backs of her ladies and they give way; like parting waters they spread. She moves through them to see Richard in the moonlight making love to Floria, her back arched, her hair a dark pool on the linen sheet, her eyes open and staring into Sanchia's.

She steps backward, her heart pounding, into the cushion of her ladies, who swarm about her like drones about their queen, shielding her across the floor, murmuring condolences—"Men are good for making babies and breaking women's hearts." "Do not fret, my lady: His interest in her will pass. It always passes." No wonder he so eagerly brought her to Berkhamsted. She'd known he wanted Floria, of course—hadn't she seen them kissing once? But that was years ago. She'd never thought he would go so far. Richard has such affection for Abraham—but even more, it seems, for Abraham's wife. Sanchia lets her ladies flutter her to the bed, their sighs drying her tears, their murmurs singing her to sleep. In her mind she sees what she has just seen. And she envisions what will be seen tomorrow: Richard's lying smile. *You were dreaming, my pet*. Floria's tears: *Don't tell my husband, I promise you, I will never come near him again*.

That is how she will rid herself of the Jewess—by telling Abraham what she saw tonight. Richard will be angry. He may lash out at her. But she will endure. She must, for that temptress Floria is endangering his mortal soul. *Forgive him, Lord*. She is his wife. *Give me strength*. What is her duty if not to save him?

— ◆ —

*S*HE VISITS RICHARD's chambers in the morning, gives him a kiss as he eats his fruit, ignores the smell of Floria drifting about like smoke from a spent fire. He yawns; is he tired, poor thing? Was he up late last night? "I am sorry I became ill, darling. What did you do after I went to sleep?"

"I tended to business. We depart for London today." And that will be the last he ever sees of Floria. "What, no protests?" he says. "I thought you might be upset."

"I truly do not understand it," she says. "Why must we go to London? For the sake of a few worthless Jews?"

"If they were indeed worthless, we would not trouble ourselves. Nor would Henry, I dare say." He pushes himself out of his chair, on his way to the stables to arrange horses and a carriage for the journey.

"Justine is ill. Might I ask Floria for help packing my things?"

She watches his eyes, but they give nothing away. "I expect she would enjoy your company," he says. "I have Abraham occupied in the treasury room, figuring our losses should Henry execute his new prisoners."

"So," Sanchia says, "your concern is money."

"I am also concerned about the deaths of innocent people."

"If they are innocent."

As soon as he has gone, she pokes through his bed and under it, not even knowing what she seeks—love letters or tokens of affection from the Jewess, a lock of her hair, perhaps. The only clue she finds is the unfinished chess game on the table between two of his chairs. Does Floria play, then? Marguerite and Eléonore used to, competing as fervently as jousters at tournament, shouting and goading each other while Sanchia tried to paint or play her harp. She has always avoided contests. If she won, then someone else would lose, and she doesn't want to make anyone feel bad.

Yet she knows enough about chess to see that this game is evenly matched. Of course Floria would play, being married to Abraham, who gave this ivory set to Richard last Christmas. Such funny pieces, and quite large. She picks up the queen, cool and solid and smooth, its chin propped on the heel of one hand, its face scrunched in a painful wince. This is how she will look if Richard makes a queen of her. But if his affair with Floria becomes known, he will be no one's king. Sanchia must stop it now, for his sake as well as hers.

She slips outdoors, through the gardens and across the broad meadow behind the château, hurrying lest she be spied by Justine or some other servant who would try to accompany her. Her words, forming in her mind, are for the Jewess's ears only. When she reaches the door of the long, low stone house she pauses, her heart pounding. (*Stay away from my husband, or else!*) She is glad for the large shrub which hides her as she gathers courage. A movement on the other side of the window catches her eye: Floria sprinkling flour on a table, then plunging her hands into a ball of dough. (*I want you out of Berkhamsted. I don't care where you go. Just leave!*) As she kneads, the muscles bulge on her bare arms, the arms of a vulgar working woman.

(*You seduced my husband, you whore.*) No, she could never use such language, not even to the devil, not even to this woman who has placed Richard in peril. He seemed so loving toward Sanchia last night. She thought she had won his heart at last. Now Floria has ruined everything. But if she can make the Jewess go away, she might gain his love again, in time—and lead him back to the Lord.

She knocks. Floria's eyes pop open when she sees Sanchia, as if she were a murderer or a ghost.

"My lady," she says with a curtsey. "Forgive me for greeting you in my apron. You have surprised me." She brushes back a curl, smudging flour on her cheek.

"Will you invite me in? I must talk with you privately."

She steps aside, allowing Sanchia in. For a wealthy man, Abraham lives in quite a modest house, just one large room with a dirt floor. The silk coverlet on the bed in the far corner is the only sign of prosperity—and the copper pans hanging on hooks near the cook fire in the center of the room. Floria moves to the wooden table and lays a cloth over the loaves she has formed, then removes her apron and smoothes her hair. Although her face glistens with perspiration and her skin is ruddy with the heat of the cook fire, she is so lovely that Sanchia has to look away.

When she rejoins Sanchia, Floria stretches her mouth across her teeth as if doing so were painful. Would the countess enjoy a drink of wine or ale? Would she care to sit? Sanchia declines. She does not intend to remain here long.

"Richard and I depart for London today," she says. "When we return, you will be gone from Berkhamsted."

Is that worry in her eyes? Good. "But Berkhamsted is my home. I do not desire to leave it."

"I am aware of your desires. And I could not be less concerned about them." Thanks be to God for making her tall. She has always envied her petite sisters, but suddenly she understands the advantage of height. Surely she intimidates the Jewess, towering over her so.

But Floria does not appear intimidated. She looks Sanchia in the eyes, bold wanton that she is. "Because of last night? My lady, all is not as you think."

"I know what I saw." My God, is she going to deny it? "And I am determined not to see it again."

"Then—forgive my saying so—you will need to blind yourself."

"No, I need only to rid our household of you."

"If you think that, my lady, then you are already blind."

Her laugh is incredulous. "If only I were! Then I would not have had to watch you flaunting yourself like a Jezebel, tempting my husband into sin."

"If not for me, the lord Richard would be free of sin? If you think so, then you are the only one at Berkhamsted. His appetites are widely known."

"I caught you in bed together!" Sanchia shouts. "Where is your shame?" Her clenching fist closes around something; she looks down to see the chess piece still in her hand. She wants to hit Floria in the mouth with it, to stop her ugly words. She would bash it into her teeth, feel them crunch against the ivory, hear her beg for mercy. She opens her hand, lets the piece fall. "You are a married woman."

"My husband is an old man, with no appetite."

"And so he does not mind if you indulge yours? Or—does he know about you and my husband?" Perhaps Abraham is using his wife to ingratiate himself with Richard. That would make her a whore, indeed. "I wonder what he would say if I told him?"

Fear, at last, crosses Floria's face. Sanchia wants to laugh. "The consequences would be dire."

"I will gladly tell him if I see or hear of you in Berkhamsted—or anywhere in Cornwall—when Richard and I return."

A tear glistens in the corner of her eye. "The blood will be on your hands, then."

"Do you dare to threaten me?"

"Abraham becomes mad with rage if another man looks at me."

"All the more reason for you to depart." She turns to go, but Floria stops her with a hand on her arm. Sanchia jerks free from her touch.

"I cannot leave, my lady! My parents are dead. Please, I have nowhere to go. Especially in my condition."

Sanchia gasps and turns, her mouth open, to stare at Floria. The Jewess's face is slick with tears, just as she had imagined—but the satisfaction she had hoped for does not come.

"I am pregnant," Floria says in a low voice. "With the lord Richard's child."

"My God!" Sanchia cries. "Pregnant?"

"Shhh! I beg you, lower your voice."

"Why should I, when all the world will soon know?" Dear Lord, and with a Jew! The scandal will destroy him. "You must leave this place as soon as possible—and without a word to Richard, do you hear?"

"But how will I provide for the child, my lady? Surely you wouldn't want to cause an innocent babe to suffer."

"You should have thought of that before you seduced my husband."

"No, my lady. It wasn't like that. Richard takes what he wants, you know." Floria clings to her arm as Sanchia starts for the door.

"Don't touch me, you filth!" she cries, and flings the Jewess to the floor, where she belongs.

And then she runs. She runs as she has not done since her childhood, when she and Margi and Elli would race to the sea, her long legs carrying her past them, at last, the year she turned eight. Now those long legs take her out the door so fast she forgets the blond head as soon as she's seen it, over the grasses and the flowering heath and into the chapel, where she falls on her knees before the Virgin Mother. Never has she felt so alone. *Please guide me, Dear Mother.* What is she going to do? How can she win Richard back without causing harm to the babe, which would be a greater sin than his?

And yet the Jewess cannot remain here. Richard is fair-haired and has blue eyes. Were the child to resemble him, not only Abraham but all of Cornwall would guess the truth. All of England would know—the whole world! He would never be able to bear the disgrace.

She must save him. But how? *Our Father, who art in heaven, hallowed be thy name. Please help me!* Floria's child must not be seen. Her pregnant belly must not be seen—for who would believe that old Abraham is the father? Yet how can she send Floria away and be the cause of the child's misery or death? Then blood would taint not only her hands, but also her soul. Her stomach twists and she moans, begging God to relieve her of this burden—for why should she bear it when she has done nothing wrong? Abraham married Floria. He, not she, bears responsibility for the child—and for its mother. He, not Sanchia, should decide Floria's fate.

Time is running out. Richard will return at any moment, ready to go. She runs up the stairs to the counting room, jumping in her skin, her teeth clacking together, but Abraham is not there. His chair is empty at the table stacked with coins. The door to the treasury, always locked, hangs open for anyone to loot. She touches his still-warm seat. Sweat breaks out on her brow. Foreboding fills her mouth with a metal taste.

She calls his name tentatively, half-expecting him to pop out from behind a door, or from inside the treasury, laughing at her stupidity. But he is gone, and strangely so, for any servant could walk in and take whatever he wanted. She steps into the treasury, her eyes roaming over the sacks of silver, years of riches gleaned from Richard's tin mines, from his brother the king, from the taxes paid by his Jews. One of these sacks alone would take care of Floria's needs for years.

The blood will be on your hands. But Abraham need never know. Floria could disappear and her husband would not know where she had gone, or why. There would be no scandal. Sanchia would take the secret to her grave.

She picks up a sack of coins so heavy that she must hold it with both hands. To hide it, she tucks it under one arm, under her surcoat, and draws her mantle about her shoulders. Then she heads across the meadow again to present Floria with her gift. She imagines the shine of gratitude in her eyes. *Thank you, Mother Mary, for showing me the way.*

She hears the groaning before she reaches the house. The sight of the open door brings her running—but she stops at the threshold. Within, Abraham kneels, weeping, on the floor beside Floria, in the very spot where Sanchia left her. "Wake up, darling," he begs. "Come back to me, my love." He gathers her head in his arms, pulls her to his chest for an embrace, but she does not move. Her head lolls. Her face is as pale as water. Her lips are faintly blue. A pool of blood spreads behind her head.

"Help," Sanchia squeaks, but no one hears her except Abraham, who jerks his head around. His pupils are so large they engulf his eyes in blackness, making them look like fathomless holes, like sunken wells of hatred. Suddenly, she understands why Floria feared him. Poor Floria.

"You killed her," she says, holding onto the doorjamb as her legs begin to shake.

He picks something up from the floor, then raises it for her to see: the frowning queen from the chess set that she had brought from Richard's chambers, matted with blood and hair.

"No, Countess," he says. "I didn't kill her. You did."

✣ *Eléonore* ✣

Family Comes First

Edinburgh, 1255

Thirty-two years old

THERE IS NO carriage for Eléonore, not on this journey, only the fastest horses in the royal stable racing her and Henry with John Maunsell and one hundred fifty knights through the northern forests and across the blooming heath to Edinburgh, where their daughter Margaret may or may not be alive.

This ride requires all her skill, all her concentration. The terrain is unfamiliar and she has not ridden a galloping horse in many years, not since her days became too filled with children for the hunt. Unable to find a tutor to engage Margaret's keen mind— *She is a girl, and does not need to know Latin,* her last teacher sniffed—Eléonore began teaching her children. Her efforts have borne rich fruit: Edward is a bold and daring knight—too bold, at times—with the confidence of a king. Beatrice is a formidable opponent in the art of debate who, like her mother, can ride and hunt as well as any man. Gentle Edmund is a philosopher, wise beyond his years, and a comfort to his mother. The baby Katharine, born deaf and mute and with a peculiar wizened appearance, is sweeter than any person on this Earth, bestowing kisses and sitting in laps with her arms around the necks of her nurses, her brothers and sisters, her mother and father. Looking at books, however, is her chief joy.

But Margaret, with her keen wit, holds the place nearest the center of Eléonore's heart. Her ready laugh always bubbles near the surface of her calm strength, making her every bit like her namesake. There were years, yes, when Marguerite's laughter went unheard. *That harpy Blanche de Castille has strangled our Margi's mirth with her iron hand,* their mother said once, but Eléonore never believed it. She knew her sister could not be repressed for long. And she was right: Returned from Outremer, with Blanche in the grave and Louis descending into madness, Marguerite, now ruling France, laughs more loudly than ever, not caring who thinks such behavior unseemly for a woman. How gay and confident she appeared at the Christmas gathering last year! Yet she seems, also, to have absorbed some of the White Queen's less desirable qualities.

The shock and hurt on their sister Beatrice's face during the Christmas feast, when Marguerite denied her a seat at the royal table, haunts Eléonore still. Should she have intervened more forcefully?

She did try. "Beatrice is our sister, Margi. Family comes first, remember? Family is more important than anything, more important than land or castles, more important than pride," she said.

"She may be your sister, but she is mine no longer," was Margi's response, shocking Eléonore into silence. By saying nothing, did she betray Beatrice? Should she have done as Sanchia did, and moved to Beatrice's table? But of course she could not have done so, not when she and Margi had just begun the work of establishing peace between their countries for the first time in nearly two hundred years.

Each of them has her reasons for wanting peace. Marguerite fears Henry might try again to re-take the lands his father lost. France would fare badly in a battle now. The Outremer campaign cost everything the kingdom owned, and more—including King Louis's interest in this world. Eléonore, on the other hand, wants France's help against the rebellion Simon is plotting.

Simon has reached the limits of his tolerance, and Eléonore cannot blame him. Henry has refused to pay the money that by right should be his and Eleanor's. Yet she cannot criticize Henry's obstinacy, either. Simon's acerbic tongue has estranged Henry from him. When Eléonore declined to argue for him any more, he turned his vitriol on her. He now mutters against her, calling her a "foreigner," which is laughable considering his own French ties, and blaming her for the fiasco in Gascony. She supported the rebel leader, her foreign cousin, he has been saying. She will do anything to further her family's interests, even if it means harming England's.

But of course she cannot argue with Henry, not even to help Simon. As much as Henry loves her, he is proud. He insists on loyalty. *If you are to be my queen, then you must work with me and not against me.* She had to agree, or be banished permanently from court. Now when she disagrees with him, she does so privately, and is careful to hide her displeasure when he ignores her counsel—which is rare.

Meanwhile, Simon is guilty of the very crime—selfishness—of which he accuses her. Ejected from Gascony, then recalled to help save it from the rebels, Simon struts like a rooster before the barons' council, boasting of his worth to the kingdom while maligning its king. He blames Henry for the loss of Eleanor's dower, although William Marshal's relations have divided among themselves the lands and money he promised to her. He demands that Henry return Pembroke to him, although William de Valence holds legitimate claims to the castle. He insists that Henry pay him a higher sum for his expenditures in Gascony than the court required.

Eléonore has become increasingly alarmed as the barons, one by one, shift their allegiance to Simon. He tells them what they want to hear: That "foreigners" have taken the wealth that should belong to them, that their king's "foreign" queen and "alien" brothers are enriching their relatives at the expense of the English. What is more, he leads the resistance to every new tax Henry tries to levy, saying that England should reserve its funds for England, not spend money on "foreign" lands such as Gascony and Sicily.

Then, having turned the barons' attention inward, he sails to France to praise King Louis and make unflattering remarks about Henry. So far, his tactics have failed, Marguerite says. Louis and Henry are like brothers, with a shared love for God, art, and architecture. Bringing them together for Christmas is the best idea the sisters ever had. A peace treaty will certainly follow.

France's treasury is finally recovering, thanks to Marguerite's capable management. With peace between their kingdoms, France can help England should Simon stage a coup. And if Henry, under the treaty's terms, gives up his claims to Normandy, Poitou, and Aquitaine, the barons may be satisfied at last. Battling across the channel has depleted their purses, too, causing much grumbling, especially since they also must defend their castles in the Marches, on England's border, against the Welsh noble Llywelyn—and against the rebellious Scots.

Dusk falls as they arrive, horses lathering from the long ride, at the timbered gates to the massive Edinburgh Castle. The fortress sits high on a rock bluff, its towers and turrets and buildings seemingly impenetrable. They expect to be turned away, they and England's finest knights—including Edward and his cousin Henry, Richard's son. If they cannot enter the castle, they will lay siege to it.

Behind her, she hears Edward and Henry discussing strategies: Edward has learned the formula for Greek fire, and is eager to try it.

But Margaret may be in danger. They have heard nothing since the physician Reginald of Bath sent word that their daughter was indeed ill. *The melancholic humours have overwhelmed her.* She refused to leave her bed, he wrote, and would take only a small portion of food. *I shall demand a change in her circumstance.* Two days later, Reginald of Bath was dead. Poison, some whisper. Will the Scottish lords kill Margaret next?

To her relief, they are admitted at once, Eléonore and Henry and John Maunsell as well as Edward, Henry, and several of Edward's Lusignan cousins. Soon they are in the great hall, a vast but narrow room with a steeply angling timber ceiling. The regent Walter Comyn sits on the throne as if he were born to it. His clothing—a hood on his head!—was fashionable in England a century ago. His eyes glint like steel in the sunlight as he nods to Henry, but soften at the sight of Eléonore. During Margaret's wedding Walter sent sly, winsome looks her way, and danced her until she was footsore. Eléonore, not Henry, will make their case to him.

For the occasion, she has removed her fillet and crespinettes and allowed her hair to hang loose, in the Scottish fashion. Walter of Comyn licks his lips as she speaks. They wish for an audience with their daughter and with King Alexander, she says. Reginald of Bath's sudden death has alarmed them, and they need to know that Margaret is well.

The regent claps his hands, and a young man comes running from across the room. "Send for the young queen," he says—but Eléonore interrupts.

"We wish to visit her chambers. We would observe her living conditions."

With a snap of his fingers, he dismisses the youth, then turns to Henry. Margaret's misfortunes, he says, are Henry's fault. He should not have demanded King Alexander's allegiance to England. The Scottish barons are determined to prevent the young king's making such a pledge.

"He would do anything your daughter asks. For that reason, we have kept them apart. Scotland will never submit to English rule."

Henry blinks, clearly not remembering his "demand" from the boy-king, made at the wedding. It was not, after all, his idea. The barons of the Scottish Marches urged it upon him, wishing to expand their domain.

A guard leads Eléonore up the narrow, winding steps to the castle's tower. Margaret, still in bed, is pinching her cheeks to color them as her maids brush her long, tangled hair. Seeing her, Eléonore feels as if a hand were squeezing her heart. Her beautiful daughter looks like a skeleton, her cheeks sunken, the contours under her eyes darkened, her arms like twigs. Eléonore cries out. Margaret drops her mirror, and then they are embracing, the girl as light as a bird, as if her bones were hollow. Eléonore holds her carefully, afraid she will break, but Margaret crushes her mother to her.

"Take me with you," she whispers. "Don't leave me here to die."

"Command your ladies to leave us," Eléonore murmurs. Margaret stares in wonder, as if she has never considered doing so. When she announces in a quavering voice that she wishes to be alone with her mother, none of them moves. They stand in place, giving each other confused looks. Clearly, they have been instructed to spy.

Eléonore stands and points to the door. "Refusing to obey your queen's command amounts to treason."

When they have gone, Eléonore sits on the bed and enfolds Margaret in her arms again. "Mama," she says, and begins to cry. "I knew you would come."

❦

*T*HE LORD ROGER de Clifford is shouting, his fur hat fallen off (a good thing, Eléonore thinks, for in it he resembles a mole), his lips glistening with spittle, his face predictably red. Shouting has become *de rigueur* in the barons' council of late. Even Simon de Montfort has taken to it, not red-faced but with eyes that shine and look outward through the walls, as though he surveyed a far horizon.

"I see blood—England's lifeblood, draining away," he shouts. "Gascony. Poitou. And now, Sicily. Why should we pay one hundred thousand pounds for the pope's war against Manfred of Hohenstaufen? If the queen's uncles want a Savoyard on the throne in the Regno, let them pay the price. We cannot give any more! These foreign ventures are sucking us dry."

Eléonore rolls her eyes, but the barons are enrapt. The young Earl of Gloucester leers at her. "Sucked dry, yes," he says into the Earl of Chester's ear, but she can hear him. "By foreigners." He lifts his face to join in the shouting. "Sucked dry by foreigners!"

"Oh, for goodness' sake," she mutters, and walks over to Henry, to whom Richard is saying, "Surely you do not expect me to lend you the money, after you have robbed me of the taxes of eighteen wealthy Jews."

"They were accused of heinous crimes. Crucifying that poor child! And they refused to be tried in a Christian court," Henry says.

"And now they are dead, and their property is yours."

"But I released the others at your request. Including your personal Jew."

"I am not going to lend you money for Sicily. I have already contributed one thousand pounds to ransom Thomas of Savoy." Uncle Thomas's rule being unpopular with his subjects in Turin, they have imprisoned him and now demand an exorbitant ransom.

"My uncle will repay you," Eléonore says. Thomas promised to pay the pope's new fee—with a new pope come new demands—for an attack on Frederick II's son Manfred, who has crowned himself King of Sicily. "Until we pay the pope, we cannot claim the throne for Edmund."

"If I were going to conquer Sicily, I would take it for myself," Richard says.

"Are you interested in being King of Sicily now?" Eléonore asks. "After you refused it before?"

"My lady." Her niece, Agnes de Saluzzo, curtseys before her. Sanchia has awakened at last, she says. Eléonore sweeps out the door, her ladies behind, lifting her skirts.

In her chambers, Sanchia lies on the bed and stares dully with eyes swollen from last night's tears.

"I did not kill her."

"I know, dear." She sits on the bed and holds her sister's trembling hand.

"You must believe me."

"Of course I do."

"Richard doesn't."

"Richard believes whatever is expedient."

"He convinced Henry to free that murderer Abraham, and now he'll bring him to Berkhamsted to live with us again." She grips Eléonore's hand. "Abraham will kill me next."

"Sweet Sanchia! Why would anyone want to kill you?"

"He killed her to save his honor. He'll kill me to keep it quiet."

When did her sister develop such a vivid imagination? When they were girls, Eléonore and Marguerite were the ones who wrote songs and sang them, pretending to be troubadours, or invented tales about Lancelot and King Arthur and acted the parts, while Sanchia sat in the corner and drew pictures, content in her own, presumably dull, world.

"Abraham's confession is more sordid than anything you might reveal." According to the document, penned by Richard, he smothered his wife to death for cleaning a Madonna and Child painting he had hung over the toilet in an act of desecration.

"Richard doesn't know that I saw him fornicating with Floria," she says. She grips Eléonore's hand. "He hates scandal! He would want me dead, too. Like his last wife."

"Isabel Marshal? She died in childbirth."

"After confronting Richard's mistress. Joan de Valletort doesn't let anyone stand in her way."

Eléonore musters her patience. "No one is going to die. If your Jew killed his wife, it was in a fit of passion."

"*If* he killed her? You don't believe me, either."

Eléonore stands. "What I cannot believe is the way you are talking. I find it quite alarming. You must gather yourself and cease these wild accusations. Otherwise, you are going to find yourself subject to an exorcism ritual, or worse." In Paris, a scholar has proposed boring holes in the skulls of madmen to allow the release of evil spirits.

"Why are you being unkind?" Sanchia begins to cry again.

Eléonore bites back her own complaints: To hold Sicily for Edmund—to pay the pope—Eléonore and Henry must ask Marguerite and Louis for a loan. The barons will not relent, not as long as Simon leads them. Simon has begun brandishing a "Charter of

Liberties," an outrageous set of restraints on hers and Henry's ability to rule, drawn up by men who care only about their own wealth. She and Henry will refuse to sign it, of course, despite Simon's menacing talk of "consequences." And then there is her sorrow, limning her every thought with darkness, over her daughter Katharine's illness. First the poor child was born without hearing, and now she has gone blind. Sanchia's bit of messiness seems inconsequential, especially since Richard has already cleaned it up for her.

"I have much to do," Eléonore says. "I don't have time to dry your tears."

"We're sisters. We're supposed to help each other."

"By God, Sanchia! When will you grow up?" Her sister's face contorts as if slapped. "We are capable women. We are supposed to help ourselves. And now, you must help yourself out of bed and into a gown for Edmund's coronation."

The pope's legate will arrive within the hour. She hurries out of the chamber and down the stairs, through the great hall where servants are setting up tables, into the kitchen to inspect the dishes being prepared for the feast: roast guinea hen, venison with wine sauce, trout from the pond, spring greens and asparagus from the gardens, boiled potatoes tossed in butter, apple tarts and lemon cake. Back in the hall, a servant carries vases filled with daisies to set on the tables but she intervenes. She wants roses, no matter if her white roses aren't blooming. Edmund prefers red, anyway. Everything must be perfect today.

She finds Henry in his chambers, already dressed in his white-and-gold robes, standing before the mirror as his chamberlain, William de St. Ermain, fastens his crown to his head.

"My hair is turning gray, Eléonore," he says with a rueful grin. "You will soon be married to an old man."

"An experienced man." She steps up to give him a kiss. "And more handsome than ever. The silver in your hair goes wonderfully with the gold in your crown."

"I'm afraid Simon is having the same thoughts about the silver in *his* hair."

"Let him think whatever he likes."

He sighs and slips his arms around her waist. His drooping eyelid twitches. "He certainly seems intent on creating difficulties for us. His outrage over Sicily is quite surprising."

"It's only an excuse to stir up the nobles. Simon wants company in his misery. When they see Rostand place the royal ring on Edmund's finger today, their hearts will change." She and Henry have spared no expense for the occasion.

"John Maunsell and I have made an addition to the ceremony." His smile crinkles his eyes. "Wait until you see. Only a heart made of stone could be unmoved."

Edmund's nurse brings him to the hall, his hair still damp from its washing, his eyes large, his expression solemn even as they kiss his cheeks and call him their Little King.

"I became King of England when I was nine," Henry tells him as they walk to the cathedral, each of them holding one of his hands. "Only one year younger than you."

"Did you command sweets for all the children in the land, and many special holidays when there would be no schooling?" Edmund grins. "That is what I will do in Sicily."

"Your subjects, particularly the young ones, will adore you for it," Eléonore says.

"Unfortunately, you cannot rule until you come of age," Henry says. "Until you become a man, I will be in charge of Sicily."

"And then I can do anything I want!"

"If only that were true. You will find, Little King, that your barons are eager to direct you. You will have to listen to them, and you will sometimes have to do their bidding even when you do not want to."

He frowns. "What is the point of being a king, then?"

Henry and Eléonore laugh. "That is a good question," Eléonore says. "Your father has been asking it a lot lately."

At the door of the cathedral, they wait to make their grand entrance, Edward's damp hand in her cool one. When the trumpets sound, the three of them begin the long walk through the crowd, their attendants behind them. The barons have all come—and there is Eleanor Montfort. Eléonore's pulse leaps, but she cannot capture her sister-in-law's gaze. Gloucester, on the other hand, watches her with an appreciative eye. She must speak with him later: his support for the Sicilian campaign will be crucial to its success. She nods to her uncles Peter, Philip, and Boniface, their faces heavy with their brother's absence. Boniface heard the news of Uncle Thomas's capture shortly before leading a mass, and wept so profusely that one of his bishops had to finish the ceremony. Weeks later, he still looks as if his world had come to an end.

The pope's legate stands before the altar, his ringed fingers clasped in front of his chest, his weathered face wearing the expression of a kindly grandfather rather than the right arm of power who has come to collect his employer's fee. He smiles at Edmund, who steps forward with bowed head to accept the blessing. The Latin liturgy, the waving of the incense, the monks' haunting song, her boy's sweet face uplifted for his anointment oil: Eléonore feels as if her heart might burst. She looks at Henry; his eyes, like hers, are moist.

After the prayers have ended and the pope's large ring has been slipped onto Edmund's small finger, Henry steps forward and kneels before the altar. He removes his crown and bends his head. His shoulders shake as he weeps. The crowd murmurs.

"Dear Lord, we thank you for these blessings," he says. "We thank you for the opportunity to battle evil in this world—including Manfred of Hohenstaufen, who has defied your Church.

"I vow, O Lord, before all these witnesses: We will defeat Manfred. We will send a mighty army to crush him! For we know that you depend on your faithful servants to accomplish your work on this Earth. Soften our hearts, I pray, so that we may come to the task as guilelessly as the child you have chosen to rule, our own Edmund, who loves you as no other."

When he stands again and faces the room, the choir begins to chant anew. His face wet, he offers his arm to Eléonore. Together they walk behind the boy-king of Sicily, who cups the fingers of his right hand to keep the ring from falling off, back through the crowd and toward the cathedral doors. The Earl of Gloucester nods to her. Sanchia's face shines. Doubt softens Simon de Montfort's scowl. Her uncles whisper to one another, their expressions bright. How can the barons refuse the pope's fee now?

"A stroke of brilliance," the legate murmurs from behind them. "A miracle." Eléonore hopes he is right. Today, Edmund is a king without a kingdom. For Sicily to become truly his, a miracle is what they will need.

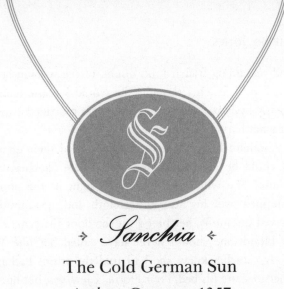

Sanchia

The Cold German Sun

Aachen, Germany, 1257

Twenty-nine years old

*S*ANCHIA SNIFFS THE air. "Do you smell smoke?" At the opposite end of the long table, Richard gestures toward the crackling and popping fire without lifting his eyes. She looks down; an ember has landed in her lap and is burning a hole in her new gown. She leaps up, exclaiming, brushing the fire from her skirt, knocking over her goblet of wine.

"Oh! How clumsy." She laughs as servants rush forward to clean the mess she has made. Richard takes a bite from the joint on his plate. She could have burned up, and he would not have noticed. She lifts her goblet. "More wine, please," she says, looking around. One good thing about Abraham: he keeps her goblet filled. But they are at Wallingford, and Abraham is nowhere near. Thank goodness.

They have spent only a little time at Berkhamsted since Floria's death, one miserable month, in fact, in which Richard's indifference toward her soured into sullenness. Abraham's fawning presence only made things worse: He followed Richard everywhere, adding fuel to the fireplace, tucking pillows behind their backs, serving their meals, filling their goblets, reminding Sanchia of her terrible guilt—and reminding Richard, no doubt, of the woman he loved. He hovered until Sanchia thought she would scream, haunted as she is already by Floria's ghost, for she is too mortified even to tell the priest what happened that day.

Only Abraham knows. He must have heard their quarrel, or else how could he have killed his wife before Sanchia returned to the house? She will never forget the sight of the poor dead woman flopped over his arm like a cloth doll, her mouth open with unasked questions, her blood on the floor the same color as Sanchia's blood. She should never have called her *filth*. Staring at her body, Sanchia knew she had told the truth: Richard had coerced her to share his bed. Poor Floria, a Jew, yes, but not filth, a woman like Sanchia, with as little heed paid to her desires.

Her killer shadowed Sanchia relentlessly, mocking her with his eyes as his lips called her "my lady." Even after Abraham accused her of Floria's murder, Richard allowed him to serve them, a worse haunting than if she dreamt of Floria three times every night.

"Why don't you send him away?" she said one day. "Then we can have some time alone."

"Time alone? For what?"

She placed her hand on his arm; he jerked it out of her reach. "I could comfort you."

"Can you go back and undo her murder?" he says. "Can you remove the blemish it has placed on my name? Because of you, I may never become King of Germany, or any other land." She did not respond, for how many times must she plead her innocence?

It is better to be at Wallingford, far from the reminders, even if the servants here are slow to refill her goblet. Richard, who never drinks wine, frowns as she lifts her cup again. If he were nicer to her, she would not need help relaxing.

He has been tenser than ever of late. William of Holland, who recovered from his illness to become the German king, is dead. He fell through the ice on his horse, then dragged himself to shore only to be hacked to death by his enemies. Richard has asked Henry to nominate him as the next German king. But the succession is not so simple. A growing number of men are claiming the throne—including Manfred Hohenstaufen, still ruling Sicily, and Alphonso, the King of Castille, who is also a Hohenstaufen and in favor with the new pope.

Only a few days ago, a council of German barons met to decide who would be the new king. Richard's temper is worse than ever as he awaits the results of the vote.

"I've paid every elector on the council who would take my money," he grumbles. He has paid the pope, as well, which is why he is a contender—his wealth, and the lack of opposition from King Louis of France. If he is crowned, England would claim both Sicily and Germany. King Louis might have fought for a Frenchman to take the German crown, but he didn't. He likes King Henry is why, Marguerite says.

"Go easy on the wine," Richard says to her. "I cannot afford a new tablecloth, and a new dress for you, every night."

A servant enters with news. A delegation from Bohemia has arrived. Now Richard topples his glass as he stands to greet his guests. He straightens his clothing. Sanchia rushes over to help, smoothing his hair through which he rakes his hands so often now, as if he were always frustrated.

Three bearded men walk into the hall, their boots squeaking on the tile floor, their woolen layers steaming with snowmelt. Their steps thud in unison, like a hammer pounding nails in a coffin. Their smiles agitate her quelling heart. *Please, Lord, no.* But, yes: they have come to make her a queen.

"Our lord, Ottokar, Duke of Bohemia, has given his support to you as the new King of Germany," says a man whose gray brows creep like caterpillars over his forehead. Sanchia drops her goblet, which clangs on the tile—and which is, fortunately, empty.

"My God, this is the best news I have ever heard," Richard says, wringing the Bohemians' hands. "I am filled with gratitude, not for my own sake but for the sake of Germany. My God!" (She wishes he would not take the Lord's name in vain!) "I hope to rule wisely and well, and to bring stability and prosperity to your troubled kingdom at last."

And then he does what Sanchia longs to do: he bursts into tears.

<hr/>

SHIVERING IN HER too-thin gown, she stands near the fire and wishes for wine to warm her blood.

"Not all of us welcome the pope's involvement," the man says, or so she guesses, for his accent is as thick as his beard. "William of Holland discovered what may happen when a man tries to impose his will."

"The pope imposes God's will," Sanchia says. The man yelps, having caught a popping ember in one hand, saving the gold leaves, saving the delicate pearls, saving the fabric of pale green silk swirling like water about Sanchia's slippered feet.

"Of course it burns, but only a bit, not to worry," he says, flicking the coal back into the fireplace. The flames' reflection flickers in his eyes. "I only wish that I had not moved so quickly, or I might have had the pleasure of brushing it from your exquisite person."

She lowers her gaze away from his florid face—she will not think of his fat hands touching her—and turns toward the white-clothed table glittering with candlelight and silver and strewn with flowers. Behind it, Richard waits for two German nobles to seat him. Although it is May, they wear woolen cloaks and tunics, clothing as heavy as their stern expressions. This is a cold kingdom indeed. Sanchia, who brought silks from England instead of wool, rubs her arms with her palms as she abandons the fire to join her husband, crowned today the King of Germany.

"Here is the real reason we supported your election," one of the men says. His long teeth and furry face remind her of a wolf. "Germany will be the envy of the world, having the most beautiful of queens."

"I thought it was *my* good looks that impressed you," Richard says, but only Sanchia laughs. "Obviously, my debilitating sense of humor isn't why we are here," he mutters as she takes her seat.

"I wonder if they ever laugh in Germany," she says. "They look as if it pains them to smile." The servant refilling her glass hears her, and pinches his lips together. She sips from her goblet. "When is the wine coming? This sour ale unsettles my stomach."

Under the table, Richard's fingers grip her knee. "Lower your voice, my love." He sounds anything but loving. She is acutely aware of his hand on her leg. He has barely touched her since Floria died. She places her hand on his, and he pulls it away. One step at a time, she reminds herself. At least Richard has broken his silence toward her. Every day that he did not speak, Sanchia felt herself fade a bit more until she became nearly invisible. Until she felt as if she were the one who had died. But now he has turned to her again. Now he needs her.

Winning the crown is only the first step toward ruling Germany. Next, he has told her, they must win the hearts of the German people. "I have seen how you can shine, how your light can dazzle." He said that to her the first time after the Christmas feast in Paris, where she surprised even herself with her brilliance. She would shine more brightly tonight if the Germans would give her some wine.

What they have given her instead is so foul that the Germans gulp it down, dreading its taste, no doubt. She follows the lead of those around her and pours it down her throat. At last, that sweet, familiar warmth spreads through her. Men and women enfolded in colorfully stitched garments sit around them, speaking in their harsh, guttural language, heedless of the fact that, although Richard speaks English and can understand them somewhat, Sanchia does not.

"Richard, what are they saying?" she whispers. "How can I shine for you when I cannot understand a word?"

"Smile, darling," he says. "Try to look like you are enjoying yourself."

She wants to kick him under the table for speaking to her as if she were a child. But he must be as tired as she. Their week began with a journey by sea to Holland, whence William of Holland's prothonotary, a man named Arnold, escorted them up the Rhine to Aachen. Sanchia found the town charming and quaint, its houses reminding her of gingerbread, and the Aachen Cathedral more beautiful than most churches in England—with its painted arches, and intricate stained-glass windows, and ceilings painted with majestic falcons and characters from scriptural tales in flowing robes. Perhaps the German people are not as crude and brutal as she has been told. "They break wind right there at the table," the Countess of Brabant told her. "Their hair grows as wild as weeds, unchecked, all over their bodies—on the women, too."

The servants set down heaping platters of food and refill their goblets, and soon everyone is pink-cheeked and smiling, including Sanchia, who devours the meats and boiled barley as though they were the delicate sauced partridges and sweet peaches of Provence. The flavors do blend well with the beer, which is tasting quite nice now.

The barons rise and begin giving speeches that, to Sanchia's ear, sounds like throat clearing and gargling. Richard's grin widens with each tribute. "The more money I spend here, the more they like me," he murmurs.

And why shouldn't they? she wants to say. Richard has spent thousands to improve castles and towns throughout his new kingdom. God knows it needs improving. Its choice of drink is not its only shortcoming. Germany is cold—not only its weather, but also its people. The wild, inscrutable landscape makes her shiver, as well. Could all the money in the world lend warmth to this awful place? It is a wonder that she, who craves the sun, should be sent ever more deeply into shadow and chill. What does the Lord mean by all these trials? What does He want her to learn?

Trumpets blast; the crowd rustles. The doors to the cathedral open. The herald announces Ottokar of Bohemia, who swoops like a falcon down the steps and through the hall, as tall as a tree in brown and green wool and an ermine-lined mantle the color of plum, his heavy beard blanketing his face in flaxen curls. People sway toward him as he passes. Here is the man so powerful that his vote decided, at last, who would be King of Germany. Here is the man who caused the crown to be offered first to Alfonso of Castille, then rescinded, then placed on Richard's head. An indecisive man, one might say, except that he carries about him the air of one who knows exactly what he wants. When he looks at Sanchia with those gray eyes, what he wants is very clear.

"May I have this dance?" he says.

As if on cue, the music begins. Sanchia takes a drink of her beer. Ottokar offers her his arm. She feels delicate beside him, he is so big and tall. He leads her into the circle of dancers. She follows, laughing, for she does not know the step and the music is fast. She twirls with him, faster and faster, growing dizzy, closing her eyes. She should have known German dancing would be bold and rough—and the music raucous, just like everything here, in her new kingdom. Slow down, she wants to say, but he would not hear her and besides, everyone is twirling and laughing and shouting and looking at her, happy to share their music and their life with her, their new queen.

Then Ottokar releases her to join the circle which is forming around them. She steps back as he does, looking left and right for outstretched hands, but whose hand should she take? Blushing, for they are all watching her now, waiting for her to join the dance, she lurches toward Ottokar whose palm touches her bosom, making her cry out in surprise and stumble backward. As she falls to the floor, the room whirls and people look down at her and she gasps, right into the scowling face of Richard, on whose head sits the crown of the kingdom and on whose arm hangs a young woman with rosy cheeks and laughing mouth and hair as pale as the cold German sun.

⊰ *Eléonore* ⊱

A Parliament Gone Mad

Oxford, 1258

Thirty-five years old

*S*HE TRIES NOT to stare as Uncle Thomas picks at his meal of songbirds that are admittedly scrawny but, to a hungry queen, mouthwatering.

"I am a broken man, Eléonore," he says, pushing his cold meat around in its congealed brown sauce. "My captors tortured me most cruelly. The brutality of humans! It has left me little appetite for ruling them."

"Or for food," she says. She wonders what the servants will do with his leftovers. In the past, they would have given them to the dogs, but the dogs are not as fortunate these days. These days, they get only the bones, and the servants are the ones licking their masters' plates.

"I have tasted little meat these past weeks." She hears the note of accusation in her voice, but cannot help it.

"One grows accustomed to hunger." He passes his trencher to her and she falls upon his leavings as if she were that poor, deprived dog. "This famine has been hard on you," he says when she has finished.

She laughs self-consciously as she savors the last bite of sauce-soaked trencher. "At least I have finally taken off the weight I gained with Katharine." Three years on this Earth and not a trace of her left, now.

"My dear, when did she die? Six months ago? Yet you continue to mourn."

"She was the joy of our lives." Eléonore accepts his handkerchief and wipes away her tears. "You would have loved her. Everyone did."

"The servants who settled me into these chambers remarked that the palace has been cheerless since she died. They sounded disapproving."

"Should I fret over the opinions of servants? Really, uncle."

"Your subjects' opinions do matter."

"When they've walked in my shoes, I will gladly listen to their opinions."

"Only a few ever wear such privileged shoes. Are the rest unimportant?"

"What do they know about administering a kingdom?" She stands, knocking her chair aside. "I am besieged by critics, all of them ignorant."

Simon de Montfort has turned his personal grudge against her and Henry into a public vendetta. He criticizes their "excesses" at every meeting of the barons' council, and rails against the favors given to "foreigners"—not only the Lusignans, but the house of Savoy, as well. Never mind that her uncles have benefited England in countless ways. Uncle Peter raised funds to quell the Gascony uprisings and negotiated Edward's marriage to Eleanor of Castille. And now Uncle Thomas, rescued from his imprisonment, can at last pay the sum needed to place Edmund on the Sicilian throne. If Richard becomes the next Holy Roman Emperor, England will be the world's most powerful kingdom—far greater than France. And all because of her "alien" uncles.

Simon, however, cares only about his lands, his castles, and his legacy to his sons. Henry will never have a day's peace, he swears, until he gives to the Montforts the money and lands they claim. Never mind that others claim them, too.

"Now he complains because Henry gave to the pope the tax he collected for his campaign in Outremer," she says. "We thought the idea most excellent. We won't need to tax the barons, now, for the Sicilian campaign."

"But the barons are unappreciative?"

"We do not know what they think," Henry says as he sweeps in, followed by his usual entourage: William de Valence, Uncle Peter, John Maunsell, and Edward, bleary-eyed again. "But, after today, we do know what Simon thinks."

Eléonore stands to embrace her son, whom she has not seen in weeks. He has been in Wales, showing off his castles to his bride.

"Simon thinks the world revolves around him," Eléonore says. And then, whispering, "Are you getting enough sleep, Edward?" He winces and turns his bleary eyes away. How she would love to separate him from those wild youths he carouses with these days: the reckless Henry of Almain; Simon de Montfort's cruel sons; his lazy Lusignan cousins; the violent sons of the Marcher barons.

"Montfort wishes the world revolved around him." John Maunsell paces the floor while Henry sits on the bed and the others, including Eléonore, take chairs.

"He is working diligently to ensure that others think it does," Henry snaps.

"He is arranging secret meetings with the barons, I hear," Peter says. "They are drawing up a charter."

William snorts. "A charter? That was tried with King John, wasn't it? I don't know why they think it would succeed with us."

Uncle Peter leans to murmur in her ear: *We must talk.*

"King John had to ask the barons' permission before levying new taxes or fees," he says aloud. "Simon would require the same of King Henry."

"How can anyone rule a kingdom if they must continually beg for funding?" Eléonore says. "What if an emergency occurred?"

"Such as in Wales," Edward says. "Mother, the Welsh have overrun my castles in Gwynedd. Deganwy is stripped to the walls, everything gone—the paintings, the tapestries, even the candlesticks."

"Savages," Eléonore says. "If not for you, dear, I would have urged your father to divest England of Wales. After all our attempts to civilize them, the people are still heathens." They are like small and bony fish: too troublesome to bother with, they are best thrown back into the sea.

"Llywelyn calls himself Prince of Wales," Edward says. "He struts about like a cock with full reign of the coop—and asserts himself on our lands."

"A prince! Was his father a king, then? Of what—London Tower?" She rolls her eyes. Gruffydd ap Llywelyn was never king of anything; his brother ruled a small portion of Wales while Gruffydd languished in the Tower until he fell to his death from a window.

"Llywelyn would appreciate your notion to abandon Wales," William says, sending Edward a pointed glance.

"Of course I spoke in haste," Eléonore says. "Those lands belong to Edward. Think of the example it would set if we let them go."

"The Gascons would take note," John Maunsell says.

"God forbid it," Henry says. "I have never known a people so resistant to rule."

"The solution is simple. We must crush Llywelyn," Eléonore says.

A stunned silence follows. "The king had thought to negotiate, my lady," Maunsell says.

"Negotiate? Destroy him, I say. Llywelyn is too ambitious to be trusted."

Edward springs up in his chair as if he has just awakened. "I have made the same argument, Mother." Mother. How cold the word sounds. "Mama" is more affectionate, but speaking English is the fashion—in spite of its harshness to the ear. "I've been begging Father to let me fight. I'll show Llywelyn who is prince."

"Yes, yes, we must invade Wales," Henry grumbles, hating as he does to be challenged or corrected—especially by Edward. And by Eléonore.

"Invade Wales! What a brilliant idea, Henry," she says. The others nod. But how, Maunsell asks, will they pay for an invasion?

A discussion ensues: What remains in the treasury? (Almost nothing.) Can they levy scutages from men who pledged to take the cross, then did not go? (Richard has already collected from all who pledged, and from many, Eléonore suspects, who did not.) When did Henry last raid the Jews? (Too recently to profit from another raid.) Can the clergy be forced to pay? (They have already given fifty-two thousand pounds for the war in Sicily.)

Henry covers his face with his hands. "Wales is lost."

"Thousands spent to gain Sicily for Edmund, and nothing left for Edward?" William says, frowning at Eléonore. "I thought a mother loved her eldest child the most."

"That may have been true of your mother," Eléonore retorts, "but I love all my children with all my heart."

She goes to the bed and places her hands on Henry's shoulders, blocking his view of his smirking brother and his glowering son.

"Not everyone in this kingdom feels as Simon does. The barons of the Marches will support a war in Wales once they realize their holdings are in danger. The Earl of Gloucester will insist that we invade."

"But the barons of the Marches are not here." Henry drops his hands; his face droops.

"Why not summon them? And the other barons, too."

"Call a council of the Marcher lords?"

"Call the full Parliament into session. Henry, we must eradicate this so-called 'prince.' If not, he will return to threaten us again. But we will need money, for knights and weapons and armor and food—"

"I'm sure we all know the price of war," William says.

"Here's what you do," she says to Henry. "Call a grand meeting, not just of the barons but of your friends, too. Invite King Louis. Invite Alexander from Scotland. We'll talk about the Welsh problem, and what to do about it. Before it ends, the barons will declare war against Llywelyn—and they will think doing so was their idea."

---

*H*ENRY'S HANDS TREMBLE. His beard quivers. His voice, however, rings like a great bell across the tiled floor and through the
high arches of Oxford, up through the ceiling to the Lord God
and his angels.

"This is an insult," he roars. "How dare you humiliate us with
your petty complaints and your foolish demands, when the future
of England hangs in the balance? Wales is on the brink, and all you
can do is push your ludicrous charter at me."

"We are squeezed dry by your follies," Simon cries. "You have
drained our lifeblood to pour it over Gascony, Scotland, Sicily, and
now Wales!" The hall fills with shouts.

Eléonore leaps to her feet. "Do you think we preferred to wage
a seven year war in Gascony? Lord Leicester, you of all people
know what a formidable challenge we faced there. And we have
made peace with Scotland after years of strife."

"You have thrown pound after pound down the bottomless
hole that is Sicily, and for what?"

"For England," Eléonore says. "The more territory we command, the greater our position in the world. We all gain."

"The pope gains," Simon says. He turns to the barons. "And
gains, and gains, and gains. At our expense!" They begin to shout
again.

"Sicily has cost you nothing," Henry roars.

"Our parishes paid, and paid dearly," Gloucester says. "And
we all contributed to the fund for your so-called expedition to
Outremer—which is, apparently, not going to occur."

"We are grateful that Pope Alexander agreed to use that money
for the Sicilian fight."

"Our money!" Simon shouts. "Wrested from us by corrupt
bailiffs and cruel sheriffs—under royal authority. Funds we gave to
fight the heathens and Turks—but now used for what task? To kill
Christian men in Sicily."

"It is an outrage!" the Earl of Norfolk bellows. "We demand a change. We demand that you sign these provisions."

"For God's sake, we are administering a kingdom!" Eléonore cries out. "How will we ever accomplish anything under these terms?" A council of twenty-four barons to tell them what they may do, and when, and how? A committee to appoint Henry's most important staff—chancellor, treasurer, steward? What tasks, Eléonore wonders, will remain for her and Henry?

Has the Parliament gone mad? She was not prepared for these restrictions. She and Uncle Peter, working late at night, fashioned language for the charter that would eject the Lusignans from England. The necessity of this is clear to her: Although Henry cannot—or will not—admit it, William de Valence and his brothers have caused nothing but harm. William has alienated Simon, whom, as she suspected, is proving to be a formidable foe. Although still waiting to be appointed archbishop of Westminster, Aymer acts as though he were king of the world, attacking anyone who challenges him. But Henry shrugs off every complaint.

He is blind where his brothers are concerned. He denies they are influencing Edward against her. *I thought a mother loved her eldest child the most,* William said in his sneering tone. And in front of Edward, in front of everyone! As if, with Isabella of Angoulême for a mother, he knew anything about a mother's love. Yet his tactics are succeeding. Edward has become sullen toward her, and he argues more and more vehemently with Henry. The Lusignans must go, and soon.

With these new demands attached to the charter, however, Eléonore wonders if she and Peter have betrayed the Crown. Henry is so angry at Peter for joining the opposition that he will not speak to him. Eléonore dare not inform him of her uncle's true motive, which is to rid her of the Lusignan problem. She feigns outrage, too, and keeps her distance from Uncle Peter—in public.

William de Valence's empurpled face is her reward.

"We are the king's brethren," he bellows. "You, on the other hand, are nothing."

"You and your brothers are tyrants who take what you want with no regard for others," Simon retorts. "You care nothing for England! You think only of your own interests."

"Whose interests do you consider during your meetings with Llywelyn ap Gruffydd?" William snarls.

Eléonore catches her breath. Simon, meeting secretly with Llywelyn? It cannot be—but why, then, is he turning pale?

"You are not the only man with informants." William puffs out his chest. "I know about your treasonous talks, with the Earl of Gloucester's involvement. Conspiring with the enemy! Were I king, you would be in the Tower and your lands confiscated."

"You have already confiscated my lands, and with no legitimate reason," Simon snarls. "And I hold properties in the Welsh Marches, as does Gloucester. Why wouldn't we talk with Llywelyn?"

"Because he has attacked our castles in Wales." Henry leaps to his feet. "He has declared war on England."

"And I cannot imagine what your interest in the Marches might be," William says. "Unless you are referring to Pembroke, which is mine by right, and which Llywelyn besieged—at your instigation."

"Grievous slander!" Simon cries. "Had I hired Llywelyn to attack Pembroke, you would not be here today to accuse me."

Shouts clatter about the room, hurting Eléonore's ears, compelling her to rise and leave the noise, but she would not miss the outcome of the debate. The Lusignans must go.

Peter de Montfort, officiating at this mad Parliamentary meeting, pounds the gavel. Lord Norfolk is recognized.

"Your Grace, these provisions did not spring up independently, but from increasing unrest. We have watched helplessly as you and the queen award the sweetest fruits of the kingdom to foreigners, passing by your own lords. We have seen aliens flood our lands and take what should be ours as you tax the rest of us to enrich their holdings.

"Now you want to extort even more from us to benefit your foreign ventures, even as the people of England suffer the deprivations of a terrible famine. Have you seen the emaciated bodies lying in the streets, as I have? Have you seen the mass graves of victims? The price of corn has risen so high that even I can scarcely afford to feed my family and my tenants. Hang Sicily! Let Wales be Wales. The people of England need our aid."

"Had we Sicily, England would receive all the aid she needs. Famine has not struck there," Eléonore says. "We cannot isolate ourselves on this island and expect to thrive."

"Yours is just the sort of thinking we reject," Simon says. "We have had enough of foreign ventures. You want to be a great power? Look to France, where the good King Louis is eradicating injustice in his kingdom."

"And without asking permission from his barons," Eléonore points out. "His hands aren't bound by a charter that robs him of his sovereignty."

"Your sovereignty depends on the goodwill of your barons," Norfolk says to Henry. "The majority here support this charter, and now you must sign it. Let the wretched and intolerable Poitevins—and all aliens—flee from your face!"

"Enact what you will, you cannot be rid of us," William says. "I am Earl of Pembroke, and my brother is archbishop-elect of Westminster, supported by the papacy."

Simon turns on him. "Are you so concerned about the loss of lands and titles? Were I you, Lord Pembroke, I would flee this island with my brothers today. Because, if you remain, you will lose far more than your possessions. You will lose your heads."

❖ *Marguerite* ❖

A Woman's Grasp

Paris, 1259

Thirty-eight years old

This Christmas, there will be a grand procession, led by Marguerite and Louis. She wears the most opulent gown imaginable, blue velvet covered in peacock feathers, each fastened to the skirt with an emerald or sapphire and sewn with thread of real gold. Her cap is of gold cloth, also, and her slippers, and her crown sparkles with jewels and glimmering gold—reminding the Parisians, she hopes, that their king was once a young and vibrant man with a zeal for life befitting his suit of gold chain mail. If she glitters enough, might they not see him as he was instead of the wraith he has become, grim and haunted and filled with self-loathing? Might they overlook the slump of his back, as though he carried a great weight, and his suspicious eyes, like those of a bird of prey scouting for blasphemers and heretics to attack? (He has now, famously, had a man's lips cut off for blasphemy.) She would comb his hair if she could, and shave his grizzled beard, and put him in a bejeweled tunic, boots of soft leather, and a mantle of fur instead of the rags and hair shirt. She would put his crown upon his head, for God's sake.

"Whether you like it or not, you are still a king. You ought to dress like one," she says when she enters his chambers and sees him attired as usual on the morning of the big day. He used to don shiny red cloth and holly for Christmas. He used to wear rings. He used to dance under the mistletoe with her, and stand on his throne to lead the Yule Log carols as the city's peasants streamed through. But nothing, with Louis, is as it used to be.

He used to rise from his chair when she entered a room, and kiss her in greeting. No longer: He has not done so since Egypt. Is it because she saved his life?

"My lord, your valiant queen rescued us even as she recovered from a difficult birth," Jean said, noticing Louis's indifference to her when the men returned to Damietta at last. He knelt before her and kissed her ring. "I offer my most humble thanks." Louis harrumphed, and said one needn't be thanked for doing one's duty. And yet if she were Blanche, he would have kissed her feet.

Marguerite refuses to take offense. Louis has not been himself since Egypt. She rarely sees him smile except in the Saint-Chappelle, the breathtaking chapel he built, as he prays over the relics of Christ displayed there. In the throes of passion, he forgets his guilt over losing the holy city, thousands of men, Damietta, and his favorite brother. At all other times, self-pity seems to ooze from his pores. "The Lord called me to glory, and I failed," he moans, until Marguerite thinks she will scream.

Has his mind left him? He seems to relish the stares and whispers his bedragglement attracts. Wonderment or derision, the reactions are the same to him—so long as he can draw attention to himself. "Not to me," he says, "but to our suffering Lord." That is fine. Do what he will, he cannot detract from her accomplishment. Peace with England is at hand, and the replenishment of France's bankrupt treasury. Such is her achievement today, hers and Eléonore's: the signing, at last, of the treaty between the two great powers.

"You may display humility and yet be well-groomed," she says. "Allow your men to prepare your hair and beard for the procession, at least, my lord. Rise to the grand occasion! We will enjoy peace with England for the first time in two hundred years." He scowls until she adds, "And the scholar from the university, Thomas of Aquino, will join us at the feast."

"Yes!" He lights up. "Albertus Magnus's young philosopher. He has just written a new treatise, I hear. I hope he will read to us." Yet when Louis arrives for the ceremony, he looks the same as always, unkempt and clad in sackcloth.

She, on the other hand, glitters like the queen she is on her jennet, a smart, sure-footed mare, a high-stepper in ceremonies who has also served her well on many a hunt. The sounding of the trumpets brings the citizens running to the roadside to cheer and toss flowers, shouting Louis's name, but rarely hers. That adulation was reserved for Blanche: Marguerite is no White Queen. If she were, Louis would look like the King of France today instead of an abused slave.

Behind them, Eléonore looks stunning, although her gown is simpler. She needs no glitter to outshine Marguerite, as always. Gray has only just begun to appear in her hair, like silver threads woven in the dark curls springing daringly from her hat—and, having borne only five children to Marguerite's ten, she is as trim of figure as ever in red taffeta studded with diamonds, red silk stockings and silver slippers. She blooms like a flower in all that red, in spite of the paleness of cheek that Marguerite has noticed in her lately. Simon de Montfort's intrigues are exacting a toll from her and King Henry, who looks peaked even in his cheerful green and gold.

Marguerite knows Simon. She has heard him groan to Louis about his sad lot as the King of England's brother-in-law. Poor man! The landless third son destined for a dreary clergy post, he became, thanks to King Henry's magnanimity, Earl of Leicester, a leader on the barons' council—and the king's loudest detractor. He is like a pampered pet who begs for food, then bites the hand that offers it. She will be surprised if he has any new thing to say during his arbitration hearing with her tomorrow—but she also knows better than to treat his allegations lightly. Simon de Montfort has befriended many powerful people in England, while Henry has made formidable enemies. Richard of Cornwall's return from Germany couldn't be more timely.

Richard has never appeared happier; his opulent crown suits him well, as do the royal robes he wears about his broad shoulders. Sanchia, on the other hand, looks as if her heavy German garments weigh too much for her delicate frame. Her face is thin; dark circles rise like bruises under her eyes—and yet her remarkable beauty is only enhanced. How is it that Richard never looks at her, while the rest of the world cannot tear its gaze away? What is the song by Bernard de Ventadour? *Endless talk about love may breed boredom, and set deception weaving.*

Poor Sanchia has the beauty, but not the intellect, to hold her husband's attention—as Mama knew when she pressed her into marrying him. Raimond of Toulouse would have been worse, but Sanchia would be with him now if she and Elli had not conspired to save her. If Sanchia's happiness were Mama's concern, she would have sent her to an abbey or convent as she desired. In truth, she sacrificed her daughters for her own interests. (Even Eléonore, who craved queenship, had to lie with an old man.) When she told them "family comes first," she appears to have meant the house of Savoy, not the sisters from Provence.

And yet, Mama has made one daughter happy—the least deserving one. Beatrice, bathed in sable and mink, her green-and-gold eyes slanting like those of a tigress, looks as if she had a mouth full of juicy secrets. Her latest triumph is no secret, however—Provence is indisputably hers at last! Or so she thinks. Nor is her newest venture a secret: she and Charles have cast their eye on Sicily now that the pope has withdrawn it from Edmund's grasp.

Never mind that Eléonore and Henry are still begging for funds for the battle against Manfred. No one grieved more than her sister when Uncle Thomas died earlier this year, leaving unfulfilled his promise to pay Pope Alexander the rest of the sum he demanded. Beatrice and Charles pounced on the opportunity—not for Edmund, but for themselves.

But when was Beatrice ever moved to help her sisters? She might have been forced to marry Charles, but now she openly supports his schemes. How can she bear to look at him? Always preening that long hair of his, displaying himself like a peacock, as though he didn't know that his nose is beaked and his eyes set too closely together. And his cruelty! The stories make her shudder: A boy of twelve whipped to unconsciousness for making a jest about the size of Charles's nose. Villeins turned out of their homes with nowhere to go, punished for a poor harvest after a season of drought. Merchants executed in Marseille for protesting his enormous tax increases. The troubadours banished from court, Charles having declared music and poetry—more dear than food in her father's court—to be a frivolous expense.

Disloyal though it may be, she hopes Charles loses Sicily, for no tyrant should rule over those pleasant folk. She would give Eléonore and Henry all she owns to thwart his ambitions. The French treasury is only now recovered from the campaign in Outremer, however, and Louis insists on hoarding every coin. "We will need a great deal of money soon," he says mysteriously.

If saving money is Louis's concern, then he should be grateful to her for the treaty he and King Henry are about to sign. After decades of squabbling over the lands King John lost to France and years of pleading from their wives, the two have at last agreed to stop fighting. Neither will gain everything he wants: Henry will not give up all the disputed lands, but he will be content with Gascony, Saintonge, and a few other territories. In exchange, France has promised to help England during this time when it teems with troubles. Louis would rather see Henry and Eléonore abandon all claims on this side of the channel, but he also wants an end to the costly battles between them.

"Now our children will be as brothers and sisters, all as one family," he says to Henry.

All as one family. Marguerite and Eléonore link arms as they and their husbands lead the way into the great hall, their sisters and brothers-in-law behind. No more will they be parted from each other because their kingdoms are at war. Henry and Louis beam at each other like sweethearts.

Mama awaits them in the hall, her bearing so regal that one might think she were a queen, as well. A queen, however, does not sell her people to a tyrant as Mama has done. Marguerite stiffens her body against her mother's embrace and wishes she could conjure lightning in her kiss, or a snowstorm.

"This is a great moment, and you girls are to be thanked for it," Mama says to her and Eléonore. "After two hundred years of fighting, peace comes to France and England at last. The men may claim the credit, but I know who did most of the work."

"We learned from the best, Mama." Mama widens her smile, apparently missing the dryness in Marguerite's tone. "You've signed a pact in Provence, too, I hear."

Mama wrinkles her forehead. "Don't blame me, darling."

"Whom should I blame?"

"I had no choice. I could not keep up my castles without an income."

"So you sold them over to Charles."

"And Beatrice. Your father wanted—"

"He wanted Provence to remain independent!" She lowers her voice. "Not sold to France for five thousand marks."

"Per year. And I have sold my share to Beatrice and Charles. Not to France."

"But the money has come from the King of France. You wouldn't accept Charles's coin."

"I don't trust him. Surely you can see why."

"And I don't trust you!" Her words come out in a hiss. "Not any more. Not after this." Is that a smirk on Charles's lips? And is he escorting Beatrice to the royal table? She sweeps across the hall to them.

"Your table is here." She gestures to the front table on the floor, at the foot of the dais where she, Eléonore, Sanchia, and their husbands will sit. Beatrice narrows those green cat's eyes. Marguerite shrugs. "I am sorry, but you are still not a queen."

No matter that a man who is not a king has been
their table. Thomas of Aquino, the famous regent of theology at
the University of Paris, sits on Louis's left, with Henry on his other
side. He is a dour-looking man, his frown deepening the prominent
cleft in his chin. He appears older than his years by virtue of the
tonsure on his head, fringed by tight curls. Albertus Magnus, now
in Cologne, sends fond greetings to the king, he is saying.

"Albertus has spent many hours in this court discussing the
compatibility of science with religion," Louis says. He gives a rare
chuckle. "He vexed my mother sorely, God rest her soul."

"Women are not easily able to grasp such matters," the scholar
says. "As The Philosopher said, 'the female is a misbegotten male.'"

"Misbegotten?" Marguerite says. "Did God err in the creation
of woman, then?" Louis cuts his eyes at her in annoyance.

"Heavens, no!" The little man's eyebrows shoot up. "Nothing
created by God is imperfect. We might also translate Aristotle's
words to mean 'unfinished.' God chose to omit certain . . .
attributes . . . from woman's body for the sake of procreation. It is
the sacrifice of woman for the sake of man, one might say."

"And the lack of these 'attributes' prevents a woman's mind
from functioning properly?" Eléonore puts in. "And yet God
created woman, and her mind. Are you accusing him of shoddy
work?"

Louis titters. "As you said, my good Thomas, women cannot
always comprehend these intellectual matters. Rigorous thoughts
are best reserved for men, while women focus on the less taxing
work of bearing and rearing children." Marguerite wonders how
he knows about rearing children, since he pays little mind to theirs.

"My lady, it is not the work of God but the influence of external
forces that taints woman's being. Her essence—her soul, if you
will—was indeed created as perfect as that of man."

"External forces?" Eléonore frowns. "What do you mean?"

"Sexual temptation, no doubt," Louis says, giving her a pointed
look. "See how easily Eve was tempted in the garden. By a serpent."

"Yes, and we all know that men have no such temptations,"

Sanchia says from her seat at the end of the table. Marguerite and Eléonore exchange surprised looks. Hearing this harsh note from Sanchia's lips is like hearing a nightingale utter a raven's cry. She has removed her gloves for dinner and washed her hands in the bowl before her. Her fingernails have been chewed to the quick. "More wine, please," she says, lifting her goblet.

The talk turns to virtues, and which are the most important. Louis suggests humility and justice. Loyalty, says Eléonore, to which Marguerite agrees, glancing at Mama and Beatrice who are sharing their meal in silence, having brought their unhappiness on themselves. Honesty is Sanchia's offering, to which Richard adds temperance. Kindness, she retorts. Temperance, he says again.

"We must not forget patience," Henry says, "which has produced today's treaty after five years of negotiations."

Marguerite hides her amusement. Henry's intransigence over Normandy, Anjou, and Maine is to blame for the treaty's slow progress. Only the threat of revolt from his barons convinced him to give up his stubborn claims. Louis had resistance from the French barons, as well, who thought he gave up too much. But as he pointed out, Henry will have to pledge fealty to him, since the treaty establishes Gascony as a fief of France. "He was not my man before; now he will be. So I have gained a man—a king, in fact, and a most excellent man," he said. Now he will do as he pleases, which is his tendency. Daily floggings and contempt toward Marguerite are not the only legacies he inherited from his mother.

At Louis's signal, the trumpets sound. Marguerite walks with him to their thrones, at the opposite end of the hall, followed by Henry and Eléonore. The crowd rises as they make their way. She returns the smile of Jean—who has brought his wife, a nice enough woman, if you like the bland sort; then of St. Pol, the celebrated knight, twirling his great mustache. She smiles at Thibaut, the King of Navarre, seated beside her mother and looking as delighted as if the countess were his beloved Blanche returned from the dead.

Beatrice glowers, which satisfies Marguerite. She recalls how, years ago, Blanche humiliated Isabella of Angoulême by refusing to honor her as a queen. Isabella started a revolt because of it; might the hot-tempered Beatrice do the same? Marguerite would then have the perfect excuse to invade Provence.

Mama, however, gives her a smile. Seeing the pride on her face softens Marguerite's heart toward her. That conniver Charles must have deceived her, or threatened her, to make her abandon her fight and sign over her Provençal castles to him.

Noise arises from the doorway, where commoners jostle to watch the ceremony—and to greet King Henry. "Welcome back to France, good king!" a woman shouts, and more cheers erupt. They remember his generosity—his extravagance—on his previous visit, when he sprinkled coins like falling rain into their open palms. Now, with so many demands on his dwindling treasury, he has come with his palm out, too, in hopes that she and Louis can supply him with money and men to quell the uprising in Wales. They have not yet told him that their answer is "no."

If he knew, would he bend his knee to Louis, his crown removed, humbling himself? Would he place his right hand between Louis's hands, signifying his submission?

The pledge made, Henry rises. The two men embrace. The shouts and chants of the onlookers fill the hall with happy cacophony. She and Eléonore kiss. Mama rushes up, her face rosy, her eyes bright.

"I thank God that I lived to see this day, when my eldest daughters have joined two kingdoms in peace," she says. "If only all my children could get along."

"Convince your youngest to give to me what is mine, and your wish may come true," Marguerite says.

Odo, the Abbott of St. Denis and the only man who makes Marguerite laugh in this cheerless court, bows to her and kisses her hand. "Your beauty is exceeding on this day, my lady. I will have to trust my horse to lead me to Rome until I can clear the bedazzlement from my eyes."

"Not too dazzled, I trust, to remember my petition," she says.

He pats the bag slung around his shoulder. "I have it here, and shall present it as soon as I arrive." He winks. "I shall use all my influence with His Grace. He may grant you Provence in spite of it."

When he has gone, Mama turns to her. "Provence? But Margi, I have signed it to Beatrice and Charles."

"You have sold what is not yours to bestow," she says, sorry for her curt tone but, really, Mama should know. "Tarascon is mine, Mama. I have the documents to prove it."

"Oh, Margi." Her mother sighs. "What do you hope to gain by continuing this battle?"

"Only what has been promised to me."

"Forget it, dear! You have other castles. You have an entire kingdom. What do you want with Tarascon?"

"I want a place of my own, in Provence." Marguerite blinks away her tears. "I thought you, of all people, would understand. Since you have been so recently forced to leave."

"Yes, a lot of benefit I gained from years of fighting," Mama says. "Beatrice is your sister, Marguerite. I thought I had taught you girls to help one another. She admires you so."

"She has a strange way of showing admiration."

"She has a very strong-willed husband."

"I am just as strong."

"This struggle will weaken you, Margi. Fighting against your family amounts to fighting against yourself."

"Charles of Anjou is not my family," Marguerite says.

"Do you hear yourself? Stubborn—just like me. Or as I used to be. Do you remember, O Sheba, how you once wished for wisdom? Let me pass some of mine to you: a bit of land and a castle are not worth the loss of a sister."

Sanchia approaches, listing a bit. "Have you injured yourself?" Marguerite asks.

"Have I?" she says. The fragrance of wine blooms from her mouth. "I don't feel any pain."

"Sanchia, help me," Mama says. "Don't you agree that Margi should stop fighting over Provence?"

"Yes, I do. Beatrice loves you. When are you going to give up, and accept things as they are?"

In her incredulous head, Marguerite's laugh echoes as if she stood alone in this hall. "Excuse me," she says.

"Where are you going?" Mama asks.

"To congratulate Thomas of Aquino," she says. "We argued earlier, but I find myself agreeing with him." And off she goes to concede his point: some ideas are, apparently, too complex for woman's grasp.

⇒ *Sanchia* ⇐

The Opposite of Love

Berkhamsted Castle, Cornwall, 1261

Thirty-three years old

THE LIGHT. SHE opens her eyes. Light billows in, rolls like fog over the chairs, the tables, the bed, pours over her like water, fills her nose and mouth. She opens her mouth, sucks it in, seeking air but getting only light, strangling on the light, oh where is the blessed darkness now? Her lungs wheeze and cough, light flies from her lips and then hands are slipping under her back, arms lifting her up, *Papa*, she smiles but he turns away, the light falls away and there is breath again, ah.

I knew you would come back. He lowers her and pulls his arms away, she reaches out but he is gone and her confessor, John of Trent, presses a piece of wood to her lips, would he suffocate her, too? But then it is gone and he is singing a strange tune. *Miserére mei, Deus: secúndum magnam misericordiam tuam. Glora Patri, et Filii, et Spiritui Sancti.* God knows she is innocent. But does Richard?

Her chest rises and falls as he chants, the air so thick the candle flames lick it away before it reaches her, she labors for every drop, like sucking the juice from an apple. She breathes in with pursed lips, filtering out the light so the air can seep in, cooling her tired lungs, ah. They have come to pray for her, to beg God to save her. *Stop,* she tries to say but candle smoke burns her lungs and she wracks, choking, her hands flail until the candles are knocked over and the priest and Papa are stomping out the flames at last and she can breathe. *Take me now, O Lord.* Her beloved Jesus awaits.

Exaudi nos, Domine sancte. Fingertips etch the sign of the cross on her forehead, her hands, her chest, crosses she will wear like proud badges when she greets her Lord at the mansion he has prepared for her. He will put his arms around her and hold her close. Love, at long last, and for all eternity. *Take me now.*

But not like this, scrambling for breath. She gasps. "My lady, it is time to confess your sins."

She thinks of Richard's face, excited, like a child's, he was to be Holy Roman Emperor, Stupor Mundi, and her tart response, that he is no Frederick II, no Astonishment of the World, only a man, although—after his expression changed, his eyes glaring at her—he is a great man, one of the best.

"No thanks to you," he said, hoping to offend her, but she took another sip of wine and felt only warmth in her blood. Is it a sin to tell the truth, even when it hurts? She should have started long ago. She should have confronted him instead of going to Floria, he might have respected her more instead of snorting with contempt when she speaks. His hand over her mouth while he pushed himself inside her. *Your beauty is most perfect when you are silent.*

How beautiful she must have been, then, as they rode into Germany. She never uttered a word, her dread of that awful place bunched up in her.

"I have no intention of taking you back so you can offend our subjects again," Richard had promised but he did not keep his word. When she reminded him, he only laughed. "Don't you want to be empress? We shall rule Germany, Italy, Burgundy, and Sicily." But she had not wanted to be a queen, let alone an empress. The people are so rude, never smiling until she fell—and then they laughed, red-faced and loud, embarrassing Richard. He removed her to her chambers and said she would have no more German beer on this visit. But neither was she offered wine. *The only thing I asked was that you charm the people. Where is your tongue, Sanchia?*

Her tongue is in the goblet, but there was no goblet in Germany, only stern faces and a language of clearing throats and throats in need of clearing. Even "I love you" sounds coarse: *Ich liebe dich.*

Papa lifts her again and carries her to the bed, back to the light, but she wants darkness and quiet so she can breathe. She squeezes his arm, *don't place me in the sun, I will die,* but he lays her in the beam and her head fills up and begins to crack apart. *No,* she tries to say, but Richard has closed his eyes and is crossing himself as if she were dead. But where is Papa? Dead, for how long? She was barely a bride and now she is thirty-three. And yet, he was here. Or was it he? While he lived, Papa never held her in his arms.

The light has wrapped itself around her throat but gently. Her headache is gone for the first time in weeks.

"I thought she might like a little wine, she enjoys it so much." The nasal voice of Abraham wriggles like a worm into her ear. The way he looks at her, as if they shared a secret and not a pleasant one. As if she were the shameful one. As if Richard brought her home without an empress's crown because of something she did and not because the man tasting Richard's food fell over in a heap.

After the taster died, a note was delivered to Richard, signed by Manfred. *You are next, unless you leave my kingdom today.* She saw his fear. His red eyes, his haggard face. Mr. Arnold marched into her chambers and ordered the maids about: pack this, roll that up.

Manfred is coming, and the German knights have refused to fight him. The bastard son of Frederick II is as a god to them. Richard cannot compete, spend what he will. And he has spent so much, thousands and thousands of marks on backward little villages, on crumbling castles. They never appreciated his efforts even though their revered Frederick lived in splendor in Italy on the taxes his German subjects paid, and never spent a cent of it on them. Frederick was a Hohenstaufen, and Richard is an

Englishman, and their little minds cannot forget this. Yet they overlook Manfred's birth to a concubine, one of Frederick's harem, a Muslim woman, not even a Christian. She was probably a belly dancer, too.

"Thank you, Abraham. That is very kind." Sanchia's mouth begins to water for the taste of the wine. It would ease her pain, although she is feeling better now. The Father's prayers have worked like magical spells. Perhaps she should confess her over-enjoyment of wine to him, but Richard might hear and then he would never allow her to have more.

"I think Sanchia is resting now, but she may welcome a bit of refreshment later." Don't leave! she would cry if her voice were not lost. If Abraham did not hold her tongue in the goblet on his tray.

She dreams of a unicorn sleeping with its head in her lap. Light streams from its horn and across her thighs, her belly, her womb. The light purifies her. She is innocent again, happy as she has been only once in her life, as a young girl playing with her sisters. Who cared if Margi and Elli always gave her the worst roles in their play, and made her carry the arrows to their archery lessons, and invented foolish lyrics to sing in falsetto as she played her harp? Who cared if Beatrice clung to her as a babe to its mother's breast, slowing her down as she tried to keep up with Elli? She had her sisters to love, and she felt loved. Then Margi and Elli went away and Beatrice caught Papa's fancy, and she was left all alone in that big château with only the servants, who ignored her, and the poets, who paid too much attention. She hid in the nursery from their staring eyes, their whistles, their songs in praise of her beauty; while the gaze for which she yearned almost never turned her way. *I have never cared for fair hair.*

The unicorn awakens and lifts its head, wraps its golden horn in her golden hair. Jesus loves her hair. He came to her in wedding clothes, holding out his hands to her. She betrothed herself to him, but Mama didn't care. *The Earl Richard is the richest man in England, the king's brother, and he wants you. Think of how you may help your sisters, your uncles, your mother.*

She has been of no help to anyone, not even to Richard. She lies in the dark, thinking of the light, the blessed light from the unicorn's horn. She has lived all her life in the dark, hiding herself away, wishing she were ugly so that only her Lord would want her. He who sees our souls and not our bodies. He whose love is the fruit of fruits, in rare abundance.

That would be like throwing the keys to the treasury down a deep well, Mama said. *You can serve the Lord better by serving your family.* But she has done neither. She is a failure as Richard's wife, a disappointment as his queen. She has tried—for seventeen years—to be all that he wants her to be, to be all that her mother hoped. To deny herself.

She sits up in bed. It is not too late. In England, the citizens have joined the barons in revolt. Henry and Eléonore have locked themselves in the Tower of London, fearing for their lives, and have begged for Richard's help. But he has refused to become involved. He doesn't want to anger the barons, he says. *He is the only one who can help us now,* Eléonore wrote. *You must use all your charms to convince him.* Then she will have done her duty. And she can join the abbey at Hailes with a clear conscience, and Richard can find a new, more queenly, wife.

"Thank you, Jesus," she whispers. Her heart's beating is steady and strong, more sure than it has been in months. She first fell ill upon returning to Berkhamsted one year ago, after their flight from Germany. First there were headaches, mild at first and then piercing, filling her head with screams, perplexing all the physicians. She sat at dinner with Richard unable to form a sentence, unable, after a time, to remember what day it was, what year, talking one night about becoming the Holy Roman Empress, forgetting that they had made the journey and been threatened, that they had fled their kingdom in a most unkingly manner.

"I have had a new gown made for our coronation, would you like to see it?"

His scowl. He did not appreciate her humor, he said. Abraham came to refill her goblet—he has become so solicitous. Richard sent him away that night, saying that she had apparently drunk more than enough.

"No, I have had only one glass. Please, Richard, it makes me feel better." Her face burns at the memory, how she begged him. Was that a grimace on his face as he denied her? Or was it a satisfied smile? He did not approve of overindulgence in strong drink, saying it made fools of men and women of fools.

She used to appreciate his taking care of her. He pampered her, then scolded her and then, after Floria's death, ignored her. Abraham blamed her, holding up that chess piece as if it proved her guilt, although he was the one who killed her. Had he heard their quarrel? Did he know about the baby his wife carried? He took two lives, and although Sanchia felt relief mixed with her sorrow, she would not have done it. *Thou shalt not kill.* She keeps the commandments faithfully, except for *Thou shalt not commit adultery,* because, even though she has already married Jesus, she lives as wife to Richard.

She has done her duty to him. She has given him two sons, Edmund, so intelligent, his mind inherited from his father, and Richard, a thoughtful boy of ten who shares his father's interest in money. How they love their mother! But they spend their days and nights at Windsor Castle with Eléonore's children, and will not miss her when she joins the convent. Her spirits soaring, she calls for Elise, her handmaid now that poor Justine has died, who approaches her bed with wide eyes. Why does she cover her chest with her arms? Is she wearing a new gown? But it looks familiar.

Richard is awake, as she knew he would be. He likes to stay up late with his money and his books and his men—Mr. Arnold; his son Henry, when he is not off competing in tournaments with Edward; and Abraham. She thought he might smile at the sight of her sitting up in bed, but instead he frowns as though she has disappointed him yet again.

"Should you lie down? Do not over exert yourself," he says.

"I am much improved," she says when he has sat on the bed beside her, "and I have some matters to discuss with you." He must intervene with the barons on behalf of Henry and Eléonore. "Their lives are in danger. Only you can help them."

He pats her hand. "I will take care of my business as it befits me," he says. "As I always do."

"Don't speak as though I were a child," she says. He lifts his eyebrows in surprise. "Your first 'business' ought to be to your brother and my sister. Family comes first. And if not for them, you would have nothing."

"Henry might say the same of me. If not for my loans, he would have forfeited Gascony."

"And that is as it should be. Each of you depends on the other. I have a letter from Eléonore. Richard, you must assuage the barons. You must convince them to placate the people. Simon de Montfort is not our friend. Henry and Eléonore are."

Abraham arrives with a tray bearing her goblet and a flagon. "My lady is much improved, I hear," he says. "Strong enough for a bit of wine, perhaps?"

Richard's frown deepens. "Or strong enough to say 'no.'" Abraham takes a step back and begins to turn toward the door.

"No!" She looks at Richard and laughs. "I mean, no, I would love a glass. I feel so much better; it is time to celebrate, don't you think?" Abraham sets the tray on the bed and fills her goblet. "Richard, join me! Just this once." Perhaps the feeling of the wine in his blood will warm him to her.

"I will fetch your goblet, my lord," Abraham says, lifting the tray. Will he take it all away again?

"Nonsense! He can drink from mine. Set down the tray, Abraham." He stands in place with his mouth open, waiting for Richard's instructions. His face is strangely pale.

"I will gladly bring you a goblet of your own, Master Richard," he says. "It will be more celebratory to drink a toast together. And my lady's illness might be contagious."

He would have become ill by now if she were contagious. She would say so but Richard is shaking his head and saying, no, he does not care for wine no matter how it's watered, and that he needs nothing to drink at the present.

"Since you are recovering, I will leave tomorrow for England," he says. "You are right, my dear, I must intervene for my brother, who, as usual, cannot manage his own affairs."

Sanchia lifts the goblet to her lips and drinks deeply, relishing the deep fruit, the heat in her veins. Abraham fills her goblet again, although it is only half-empty. "Do not dull my senses before I have fully regained them," she says, laughing again.

"You do not need it, Sanchia," Richard says. "You are enough without it."

She takes another gulp, and thinks of how she will leave him soon, how she will go to Hailes Abbey and live there, and never have another drop of wine to drink. It will be her sacrifice.

"You may go," she says to Abraham, "and take the flagon with you. This will be my last drink." She lifts the goblet in a toast to Richard. "Out of honor to my husband." Richard clasps her hand. He thinks, of course, that she is speaking of him.

———◆———

OH, THE BURNING, the burning, there is a fire in her belly, she cries aloud and then she is vomiting pure red liquid, *this is my blood which was shed for you* and Elise is crying out as her gown is splattered—Sanchia's gown, one of her favorites, a gift from Elli. Elli always loved fashion. "Richard!" she cries, there is something she needs to tell him, about Abraham, but he is gone, gone to England, and her bowels spill in the bed and she is cold as they clean her, shivering.

"Richard!" Here is Melody, another of her ladies, wearing Sanchia's dress of green with roses of red cloth, and Abraham then, when all have gone, grinning and pouring wine down her throat.

"You called my name. I knew what you wanted."

"You are poisoning me," she says, and he nods. *Killed my wife, you murdered her.* Sanchia's body seizes and twists, a rustle in the bushes as she fled from Floria's house, a glimpse of flaxen hair, Richard's hair. Not Abraham, not Abraham. Richard's coldness to her not love for Floria, not love but the opposite of love.

Pain shoots up her arm; her heart begins to clang like a struck bell. *My God, my God, why have you forsaken me? Where are you? Dear God! My Lord!*

I am here. You are She.

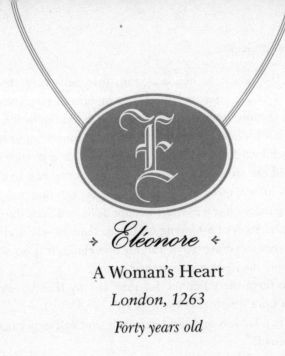

→ Eléonore ←

A Woman's Heart

London, 1263

Forty years old

$\mathcal{T}$HE ANGER IS what stuns her, the twisted and violent faces of the crowd pressing up against the walls surrounding the Tower of London. These are not the usual villeins and beggars (for the poor always have grievances). From her window she sees merchants, too, in their colorful linens and silks, and the cone-shaped hats of Jews, and old women, and young women with babies in their arms, snarling and brandishing fists and shouting insults and demands that occasionally organize themselves into chants.

"Send the foreigners home!"

"England is for the English!"

"No more for Eléonore!"

Stupidity. They have no idea what they're talking about. They only repeat, like parrots, what they have been told by Simon's followers—or, to be more precise, by Roger Leybourne, Roger de Clifford, and Hamo Lestrange. Savage youths, rapists and murderers. Now they've turned their anger on her and on Henry, who divested them of the castles Edward had given to them and sent them back to the Welsh Marches, as far away from their son as possible.

When they came to her last year, their faces held the same expressions as she is seeing below, their mouths like wounds, their eyes bulging with thunder. Leybourne's weak chin quivered under the weight of his outrage, but he should have known better than to try to turn Edward against her. Lestrange glared as if he were a bull. She gripped the arms of her throne, fully expecting him to charge. Roger de Clifford, meanwhile, stood in the background picking his teeth and grinning like a hyena, the same as he had done during his hearing on charges of molesting his female tenants—three children born last year to young women in his household. It is no wonder that Eléonore insisted on seizing their castles.

"I gave them these honors, for they are my friends," Edward said. "You can't simply take them away."

"They're a lawless and reckless bunch, and will only cause you harm," she said.

"'What you scorn may be worth much more than you think.'"

"If you have read de Troyes, then you know that your friends' behavior hardly conforms to the chivalric code."

"My friends are loyal and courageous knights. And they would give their lives for me in battle."

"Off the battlefield, they will destroy your life. A man is judged by the company he keeps—and you are no ordinary man."

"I would proudly be judged according to my friends."

"Roger Leybourne used a sharpened lance in a jousting tournament to exact vengeance on one of our knights. He spilled the defenseless man's entrails all over the field. Chrétien de Troyes would most certainly not approve."

"And he has paid the price. Papa sent him to Outremer to atone for the deed." Indeed, Eléonore and Henry hoped he would not return.

"Hamo Lestrange tied up the Lincoln bailiff and whipped him until he fainted."

"We caught him beating his horse with a cat-o'-nine-tails." His eyes sparkle. "He should thank God that Hamo didn't use it on him."

"Your laughter is the reason why I am sending these boys away," Eléonore said. "The farther they go, the better you will fare."

His drooping eyelid twitched as Henry's does when he becomes angry. "We are not boys, Mother, but grown men, and hardly in need of your discipline."

"There is more to being a man than exacting murderous revenge and self-styled justice."

"What do you know of manhood? But I forget that you are more man than woman."

She bristled, recalling a time when Henry said the same to her. "Strength of character does not make me a man."

"Where, then, is your woman's heart?"

"My mother's heart would protect you from the errant knights whom Simon de Montfort has assigned to you."

"Henry of Almain and Roger Leybourne are my closest companions, and I would trust Hamo and Roger de Clifford with my life." Tears filled his eyes—a grown man, indeed! "You may deprive them of my gifts, but you cannot—will not—deprive them of my love."

Instead, Eléonore seems the one so deprived. After leaving her that day, Edward and his friends joined Simon's army of rebels, opposing her and Henry. What did he hope to gain from this mutiny? Didn't he realize that Simon craves the throne for himself? When he ran out of money, he discovered who are his true friends—and he came back to Henry. But not to her. He still has not spoken to her.

Losing Edward must have been a great blow to Simon's cause—the latest of several setbacks. The pope has nullified the provisions forced upon her and Henry at Oxford, and the French and Castillian courts have sent knights, including the famous Count of St. Pol, to defend their God-given rights as king and queen. The influx of foreign mercenaries, however, is partly to blame for today's protest. As the Londoners rail against "aliens," they seem to have forgotten that Simon, too, is a foreigner.

"Simon de Montfort is coming to London," their chancellor,

Robert Walerand, says. "Stories have spread about all the blood he has spilled. The people are terrified."

"And so they chant his name?" Eléonore says.

"Simon and the Marchers have attacked castles held by your kin, my lady," Richard says. The Lusignans are gone, but Simon wants revenge against her, as well. Already she has lost family members, incuding Uncle Boniface, who fled to France with a number of her cousins. "The Londoners fear he'll punish them for supporting the Crown."

"Simon has no authority for punishing," Henry says. "I am still the king."

"He sent a letter," Walerand says. "He demands the city's aldermen honor their vows to support the Oxford provisions."

"They took those vows under duress, virtually at sword point," Eléonore says. "Yet Simon accuses us of being the oppressors. And now, Richard, I hear that your son Henry has been sent to Boulogne, to capture our John." Although not an "alien," John Maunsell fled across the channel, as well, under attack for his service to them and narrowly escaping with his life.

Richard's face reddens. "My boy is still young. And he believes Simon's talk about the people's right to govern themselves."

"It is a very good talk, I hear," Henry says. "Simon has always possessed a gifted tongue."

"Yes, and that is why young Henry will benefit from his time in the French prison," Eléonore says. Richard's mouth drops open. "It will do him good to spend some time away from Simon's influence."

"Prison!" Richard's voice is gruff. "My boy? Oh, this is too much to bear." He sits down, suddenly looking as old as his fifty-four years. Good: Let him suffer, as Sanchia suffered when he left her to die alone.

"We must end this battle." Richard rakes his hands through his thinning hair. "You must negotiate, Henry. Not long ago the barons tried to overthrow our father, and we were almost vanquished by the French. England cannot withstand yet another war with itself."

"Negotiate?" Eléonore snorts. "Because Simon marches about with a band of ruffians, smashing up castles? Edmund has secured Dover, and Edward holds Windsor." She grins every time she thinks of Edward's ride to the New Temple with his knights, pretending that he had come for the queen's jewels. Once inside, he smashed and looted the barons' boxes—Simon's money and that of his supporters, thousands of marks in coin and treasure.

"Simon and his men are furious. They blame the queen."

Eléonore laughs. She wishes she had suggested the Temple raid, but that act of genius and bravado was all Edward's. Without his hotheaded friends—including Henry of Almain—to distract him, he is becoming quite the remarkable prince, bold and courageous and smart. He will make a fine king someday. Perhaps someday he will look into the mirror and recognize his mother's influence.

"Simon's talk against 'aliens' excites people," Eléonore says. "Now the common man has someone to despise—besides the Jews."

"Do not be so quick to laugh, my dear," Henry says. "Have you heard their new demands? They want all English castles returned to native Englishmen." He pulls a parchment from his robe and opens it, squinting to read Simon's scribbled hand.

"And what of Leicester? Will Simon abandon it?"

"All aliens must be expelled from the kingdom forever, except those they permit to remain."

"Oh, how absurd!" Eléonore paces the room, glances out the window at the sea of anguish below, at the poor Londoners who think the hypocrite Simon de Montfort will help them. "Henry, we have St. Pol and his men here, and they are exceedingly loyal to us." St. Pol is a little in love with Eléonore, and would do anything to win her favor. At forty, she has not lost her allure.

"You favor an attack, I presume." Henry's eyes are wary.

"We silenced Simon before, but he returned. Now we must silence him again—permanently."

Richard's skin pales. He is thinking, she knows, of his son, locked in French prison. A supporter of Simon's, he will not be released should war break out.

"Killing Simon would make a martyr of him," Richard says. "He would become larger in death than he is in life."

Henry sighs and rolls the parchment, then tucks it back into his robe. "Richard is right. We cannot kill Simon, and we cannot ignore him." Noise surges from the crowd as if the people had heard him. "We have no choice but to talk with him."

"Talk?" The fling of her hands sends a vase crashing to the floor. "Our sons are under attack, and you want to talk?"

"For their safety, yes." Henry walks to the window, looks out at the roiling crowd.

"For God's sake, Henry! We've had talks and arbitrations and rulings at the highest level, all in our favor. Simon is like a cur with its teeth in our throat, refusing to let go, afraid we might bite him back. I say: bite back!"

"He is my sister's husband," Henry says. "He was once our friend."

"He is a traitor and our enemy. He must be stopped."

"But he is a friend to King Louis," Richard says. "If we harm him, we may harm our relations with France."

"Always the conciliator, aren't you, Richard? Especially when your son is in the enemy's camp."

His eyes cloud. "You, with your woman's heart, should understand my desire to protect him." That term again! As if women had only hearts, and no minds.

"When I have two sons under siege at this moment, fighting for their lives and for the future of England? My 'woman's heart' tells me to fight for my sons, with my sons. And that is what I am going to do." She snatches up the gown she has been embroidering—useless, stupid waste of time, sheer vanity—and glares in defiance at the man she has loved for nearly thirty years. His drooping eyelid twitches. His face has begun, in its old age, to sag. Where is she going? he asks.

"I am going to join Edward at Windsor. He needs support, Henry, not these endless vacillations. This is his kingdom, too. Come with me!" She holds out her hand to him. He does not take it.

"I am sending messengers to our sons today, instructing them to surrender their castles."

"No, Henry!"

"This kingdom is sick. Dying, perhaps."

"All because of Simon. Eliminate him, and you have eliminated the disease."

"He is like the Medusa," Richard says. "Cut off his head and two more will appear."

"Utter nonsense, and I am sick of it!" She turns to Richard with an exasperated sigh. "You sound like a braying donkey with your predictions of doom. Simon de Montfort is no Medusa, but only an arrogant mortal, as easily killed as any other man."

Richard gives Henry a wan smile. "Did I say she had a woman's heart?"

"Yes, and I thank God for it," Eléonore says. Their glances of commiseration tell her that Henry and Richard will not fight, that they are committed to conciliation. "Seeing, as I do now, the weak, trembling vessel that is the heart of man."

"You do not have my permission to leave," Henry growls.

"I do not recall asking for it," she says, stepping toward the door.

"Are you defying my authority?"

"Apparently so, if you insist on capitulating to the rebels."

"I insist that you respect my rule. I am your king, and I command you to remain here."

"As your queen, I refuse. Simon wants the kingdom, Henry. He will not stop until he gains it. By God's head, he will not do so under my rule."

"I can stop you, if I so desire."

She narrows her eyes at him, ready with a challenge—but then Richard steps in, ready to smooth over their quarrel with his usual flow of words.

"My lady, you would be ill advised to venture forth in this melee. You will not venture far should you be discovered. You might be captured or even killed."

"I am aware of the risks." She turns pleading eyes to Henry. "Relent, I beg you. Do not force me to this."

"What will you do if you cannot reach Edward?"

"I shall return here. But I must try, Henry. As father to our sons, surely you must see that."

"You will not be allowed back."

"What do you mean?"

"If you leave against my wishes, I shall not allow you to return."

Her steps clip briskly on the floor. She calls to Agnes, instructs her to pack their belongings and to call for her uncle Peter's protégé Ebulo di Montibus. She needs a boat, she tells him. She needs a crew and additional knights, for protection. They will slip out a back door and into the boat, then row upstream to Windsor in hopes of reaching her son before Henry's messengers do.

One hour later they are on the Thames, slipping silently behind the backs of the crowd beating at the Tower walls with clubs and irons and trying to set fire to it, as though the castle were under siege, as though Henry were not at this moment conceding to all their demands. She would never have believed it of him—but Richard has always been a coward, too timid to fight even in Outremer, a flaw he hides under conciliatory words like hands trying to smooth a puckered garment's wrinkles. He talked those French knights out of the Saracens' grip and made himself a hero without shedding a drop of blood. His aversion to battle is why he urges Henry to negotiate with the rebels. Not that he is incapable of passion; she knows, from Sanchia, that he reserves his attacks for those weaker than he.

He tried to diminish her, with his talk of a "woman's heart." But she has never considered herself weaker or less capable than men— and why should she, given the examples of manhood around her? Sanchia was worth one thousand Richards of Cornwall, yet he left her to die bereft of love or comfort. He never even mourned her death; according to rumor, he began giving away her belongings before she died. And then he did not attend her funeral service at

Hailes Abbey. Therein lies weakness. And he is the one to whom Henry listens.

Edward, on the other hand, is strong. Now that she and Henry have rid him of the Marchers, he has ceased his carousing and jousting and has turned, at last, to the task of defending the kingdom. He possesses none of Henry's impulsivity, none of his petulance—but all of his determination and will, as well as the self-confidence that Eléonore has instilled. If she were a man, she would be Edward. Does that mean that she has the heart of a man? It draws her to her son now, to stand beside him and fight—whether he would want her with him or not.

Their little boat slices the water without a sound as they slide past the Londoners whose shouts bounce off the castle walls and box Eléonore's ears.

"Send your Provençal trollop home!" a man shouts, then turns and sees the boat. "The Queen!" he screams. "She is trying to escape!" The hatred in his eyes—why? A flash of his hand and then she is struck, the stone smashed into her forehead.

Her hand flies up to touch the wound; blood covers her fingers and runs into her left eye. "Oh!" she says faintly as another stone flies past her head. Ebulo lunges for her, his mouth open as if to shout, then falls, struck. The protesters have abandoned the castle and now face the river, hurling insults as well as rocks, sticks, and mud. The captain cries a command to pull away from the shore and the ship moves into the center of the stream, out of range of the objects hurtling toward them.

But they will not avoid the onslaught once they reach London Bridge, where the crowd waits for the boat to pass under. A boy of no more than four years, held aloft by his father, hefts a stone the size of a dinner plate. Four women wearing prostitutes' hoods shake their fists. Henry's red-haired whore is among them, packing a ball of mud and narrowing her eyes at Eléonore.

"Sorceress!" she screams. "You have bewitched our good King Henry."

"Down with foreigners," others shout. "Aliens out of England. Save England for the English!"

Eléonore looks about for shelter—a blanket or a mantle, at least, with which to cover her head. Hamo Lestrange sneers from the bridge. He holds a boulder, large enough to sink a great hole in her boat, poised above the spot where they will soon pass.

"Guard the queen!" another knight cries. "Please, my lady, if you will lie down, we will cover you and prevent more harm to you."

"Stop," she says. "Turn the boat around."

"I beg your pardon, my lady? Do you wish to return to the Tower?"

She recalls Henry's warning, that she would not be allowed back. Send a messenger, she says. Tell Henry we are in danger and must return.

Ebulo, his head bandaged, insists on going. Eléonore balks. He will be discovered and killed. But he knows a hidden path, he says, and can swim to shore undetected. In a moment he is gone and, as he promised, the crowd does not notice the tiny ripple he makes, or his stealthy reemergence in the brush.

Waiting, Eléonore sits in the boat in the middle of the river and ponders the angry faces. The hatred in their eyes. The attacks, the cries against her, accusing her of seducing the king with her "woman's tricks," whatever those are. Are these the people whose kingdom she has worked so diligently to increase?

Ebulo pops up from the water and pulls himself into the boat. His bandage is brown from the dirty water, and red with his blood.

"The king," he gasps, "said, 'no.'"

No? Eléonore frowns.

"You may not return to the Tower. He has sealed off the entrances to you."

She presses her lips together, holding in her cry of dismay. Would he leave her to die, then, at the hands of this mob? But, no. Henry loves her. He is in a fit of temper, that is all.

"We will wait," she says, "and appeal to him again."

The shouting subsides. The crowd on the bridge parts. A man in a brown tunic waves red-sleeved arms. "My lady, you may come to shore," he calls. "I guarantee your safety."

She recognizes Thomas FitzThomas, the newly elected mayor of London, whom she and Henry fêted only weeks ago.

Knights amass on the bank, forming a fence with their armor beyond which the citizens cannot pass. The anchor hoisted, the boat floats to the bank. Ebulo lifts her out of the vessel and carries her across the mud to the grassy hillock where the rosy-cheeked mayor stands wringing his hands.

"I deeply apologize," he says. "This is no way to treat our queen."

He has brought a carriage for her. She folds herself inside. He follows, to her dismay, for she would not be seen trembling with fear.

"I would offer you sanctity in my home, except that it is too modest for your comfort. I have but four rooms and five children."

Eléonore closes her eyes, hiding her tears. Is this what she is reduced to—begging for lodging in the home of a town dweller? Outside, more shouts arise. There is a banging on the carriage door, then a scream. Eléonore pulls aside the curtain to see Ebulo running his sword through a man's body. This, she thinks, is the only language these people understand.

⟶ *Marguerite* ⟵
The Same Tune
Provence, 1265
Forty-four years old

*H*ERE'S WHAT DEATH DOES: it mortifies us. Marguerite can barely look at her mother's red-rimmed eyes, her blue and gasping mouth, her flesh sagging so heavily that it seems it might slide off her face. Beatrice of Savoy, the Countess of Provence, was celebrated for her elegance and beauty. She would not choose to be seen like this, not even by her daughters.

But here she lies with her final breath in her teeth and life seeping from her edges, too weak to sit but not too feeble to grip Marguerite's hand as if she feared she might fall. Beside her, Beatrice weeps—remorseful, Marguerite imagines, for all the pain she and Charles have caused—while Eléonore fusses, fluffing pillows, mopping Mama's sweating brow, ordering fresh flowers to replace the ones wilting on the bedside stand. Marguerite can only hold her mother's hand and breathe the stagnant air through parted lips, and force herself to return her mother's desperate gaze with a comforting smile that, she hopes, holds none of the disgust that she is feeling.

Mama's lively dark eyes are dimmed. Death's slow strangle has reduced her fire to a smolder. Marguerite remembers her laugh—as hearty as a man's—and the sight of her striding, her skirts lifted, across the hills in Provence with her hawk on her arm, her falconer trotting to keep pace with her. She closes her eyes.

Breathe in—rattle, cough—breathe out. "My boys." Her endearment for them when they were children. "But where is Sanchia?" A long rattle in her chest, a fit of coughing. Then, a long exhale. "Oh, yes. I shall see her soon."

"Don't give up, Mama," Marguerite urges. She feels limp, as if her spine were dissolving. She sits on the bed, still holding her mother's hand.

"*You* give up," Mama says. "Cease this struggle. Beatrice is your sister."

Marguerite closes her eyes again. She should have known that Mama would do this. She is relentless about anything that she wants.

"This doesn't seem like the time—" Eléonore begins.

"This is the only time!" Mama snaps, then begins to cough again. The healer rushes in, his thin hair frowsing.

"I told you not to excite her, my ladies."

"They are not exciting me," Mama barks. "They are boring me to death." He ducks out again.

"You have always loved excitement," Eléonore says. It is true. When they were girls, it was Mama who planned the hunt and who led the chase—tearing after the hounds, jumping over fallen trees and splashing through streams, shouting all the while. She married her daughters to the richest, most powerful men she could find, then spent her life traveling from court to court to challenge and encourage her daughters to greater feats. It was she who stirred the people of Marseille to rebel against Charles's oppression, and she who continued to fight for her rights in Provence until age sapped her of strength and of health.

"It is not worth the struggle, Margi," she says. "You are sisters." Marguerite will not argue with a dying woman. But Mama will not let the matter go. "You must join together," she says. "You must help one another. As men do. Think what you might have done for Sanchia. Poor Sanchia."

Eléonore colors and nibbles at her lower lip. She would say that she was locked in the Tower of London and could not go to Sanchia. She would say that Richard didn't tell her that her sister was dying. Marguerite has her own excuses: grief over her son's death; a kingdom to govern now that Louis has lost interest in this world; her fight, by Eléonore's side, for the Crown of England; Charles's attempts to turn her son Philip, now heir to the throne, against her.

Beatrice, on the other hand, is all justification and no remorse. "I am sure I had no part in Sanchia's death," she says. "I have been quashing a rebellion in Marseille, as you should know. And"—a fleeting smile—"preparing for Sicily."

"Sicily?" Eléonore says.

"Charles has been offered the Crown," Beatrice says.

"And you are going to take it? After all my years of work on Edmund's behalf?"

Beatrice lifts her chin. "Edmund's name has been withdrawn. The pope grew tired of waiting for the funds you promised. We, on the other hand, are prepared to send money and troops. Should we forgo the opportunity because you squandered it?"

Marguerite's laugh is raucous, like the squawk of a crow.

"Squandered?" Eléonore cries. "How dare you? Is it our fault that we have a civil war on our hands?"

"If your husband cannot control his own kingdom, how does he expect to subdue Sicily? Charles has an excellent record in this regard."

"Yes, subduing is Charles's specialty," Marguerite says. "He imposed taxes on the people of Marseille, then used rats to torture those who didn't pay."

"At least we have ended the troubles in Provence."

"At what price? You and Charles have beaten the people down, and now you are reviled."

Beatrice shrugs. "If popularity were our aim, we would have become minstrels."

"What is your aim?" Eléonore asks.

"Power. The same as yours."

"My aim is to help my family, including my sisters," Eléonore says.

"Yes, you have been such a great help to me," Beatrice says with a snort. "And to Sanchia, too. She died alone, but I'm sure her heart was warmed by your love and concern."

"You, on the other hand, will not suffer that fate," Marguerite retorts. "No one is sending love your way." She glances at her mother, forgotten now that she has stopped gripping Marguerite's hand. Mama stares at the ceiling as if she were listening to music far away. Marguerite wants to shake her, to say, See, Mama? Beatrice is the one you need to correct, not me.

But it would do no good, for Mama is beyond seeing and beyond correcting. Her eyes do not blink. Her breath has stopped. Always agitated by her daughters' disputes, she apparently has decided to leave them behind, once and for all.

———◆———

A͟T THE FUNERAL mass in the Hautecombe Abbey, the sisters do not speak, not to one another and not to the mourners who fill the cathedral and spill onto the lawn. They have not spoken to one another in days, their tongues bound with the mortification of having bickered over their mother's deathbed. *Forgive us,* Marguerite prays as Philip, Charles, St. Pol, and a number of other young knights lower Mama's coffin into its tomb close by where Uncle William lies. Peace was all their mother asked for in the end, yet they could not give it to her for even five minutes.

It is all Beatrice's fault. She announced Charles's intentions for Sicily at the worst possible time, as Mama lay dying—and in the presence of Eléonore, whom she knew would be distraught. Of course, she is never happy unless she commands all the attention. Look at her now, sobbing as though Mama's death were the end of her world, as though she hadn't made their mother's final years miserable by forcing her to leave Provence.

Even Charles looks uncomfortable, squeezing his hands into fists as he holds Beatrice up—wishing he could stuff one of those fists into her wailing mouth, Marguerite supposes. But no, he doesn't hit Beatrice. She doesn't duck her head when he comes near, or soften her voice to a tremble, as Sanchia did with Richard. A meek and submissive wife would never satisfy him, for he enjoys the battle even more than the victory. Perhaps that is why he continues to sneer at Marguerite even after he has won the fight for Provence (or so he thinks). Perhaps that is why he has enlisted her son against her, even when she has, for the time being, laid down her arms.

Cease this struggle. Mama's admonition still burns her ears, although Marguerite knows she has no reason for shame. She is doing what she must. With her son Louis dead and her husband Louis always ill, Philip may find himself King of France very soon—and Marguerite may find herself without a home or an adequate income.

Louis has left her almost nothing in his will. "What need will you have for worldly goods in the nunnery?" he said. It is the nunnery for which she has no need. A life in the cloister is his desire, not hers. But she cannot say this to Louis, or, if she did, he would not comprehend. He cannot imagine that anyone would shun a life of complete devotion to God. Marguerite prefers to honor him in the world which he so gloriously made. Hers will be a bleak existence when Louis dies, unless she can claim her portion of Provence—which she fully intends to do.

"I thought I agreed with Mama, there at her bedside," Eléonore says on the carriage ride to Paris—a rare and delicious occasion, just the two of them in complete privacy. "I saw your jaw clench when she admonished you to abandon the fight for Provence. I thought, we are sisters. We ought to pull together, not apart. Women should do this generally."

Marguerite laughs. "Blanche de Castille would agree, don't you think?"

"But she provides a perfect example. How much better for France—and for you both—if she had taught you instead of fighting you. You have only now regained the strength and confidence you possessed at thirteen—which you lost because of her."

"And now you want me to cuddle with Cleopatra?"

Eléonore gives her a dark look. "I thought so, yes. Until she revealed Charles's intention to take Sicily for himself. Henry and I had planned to travel to Rome and petition the new pope in person. But the barons' revolt has lasted longer than we thought."

"Popes keep dying," Marguerite says. "Six in the last fifteen years. Each time, we are cast into uncertainty." To each new pope she sends a request for her share of Provence. She has spent most of her life since Papa's death waiting, it seems, for men to decide her fate.

"Pope Clement has barely had time to warm his seat. How has he already withdrawn Edmund's name from Sicily and named Charles in his place?"

"Charles and Beatrice attended his confirmation ceremony. They must have been granted an audience." Having exiled Mama to Paris, then killed all the rebels in Marseille, Charles and Beatrice had ample time to travel to Rome and more time in which to linger there. Time is a luxury which neither Eléonore nor Marguerite has enjoyed lately.

"I feel as though I'd been stabbed in the heart." A sob catches in Eléonore's throat. She dabs her tears with a lace handkerchief. "I worked for years to obtain Sicily for Edmund. I've coaxed and wheedled and placated every lord and earl and clergyman in England. We were so close to the prize. So close. Now my boy will have only Lancaster when Henry dies, not nearly enough for his own sons. Beatrice be damned, and her ambitions, too!"

"One word from Charles and she leaps to his side, no matter how heinous his crimes. She is not one of us, Elli."

"I suppose not," Eléonore says. She looks out the window, watches her dreams of a Sicilian kingdom slide past. "Margi," she says, "do you think he beats her?"

"I think *she* beats *him*."

Later, the carriage driver will tell how the sisters mourned their mother, their shrieks and wails ringing so volubly from within that he almost thought it was laughter he heard.

———◆———

HENRY OF ALMAIN has grown. How long has it been since Marguerite saw him last? Richard and Sanchia brought him to the first Christmas feast eleven years ago. He was a skinny youth with a reckless edge, a swagger belied by the roses in his cheeks. Now he is a man of thirty with broad shoulders and a somber mouth who stands with his legs planted just so, at ease in his body. As much as he has changed, no one needs to announce him to Marguerite. He is the very image of his father at his age, except that he wears a scrap of a beard and his sand-colored hair falls to his shoulders.

He bows deeply to her and Eléonore upon entering the great hall. The pope's legate, Guy, accompanies him, wearing a brown tunic and broad-brimmed hat that captures Eléonore's eye.

"We have come from England. The situation is very bad," the legate says. "King Henry and the Prince Edward are prisoners, captured in battle against the rebels at Lewes. The Earl of Leicester has placed himself in Westminster Palace and called the Parliament into session. I hear that he sits on the throne."

"On the throne!" Louis's voice rings through the palace as he strides into the hall. "On the seat where generations of God's anointed have reigned? Simon de Montfort has gone too far."

"His Grace Pope Clement agrees with you," Guy says as, kneeling, he kisses Louis's ring.

"Simon has presumed upon the king's position."

"Yes, Your Grace."

"This is mutiny! And blasphemy."

"Yes."

"Good. Then Pope Clement will censure him?"

"He has issued a writ of excommunication."

"A wise decision. But—you have not announced it in England?"

The legate pauses. He lowers his eyes. "England is in a shambles. I lifted my voice, but it was not heeded. And now there are other crimes. More serious—"

"My Henry?" Eléonore presses her hand to her chest. Richard's son bows to her.

"Safe, my lady," he says.

"Edward?"

"Safe, thank God."

Eléonore narrows her eyes. "Yet you are Simon's man now."

"I am his hostage." His glance, Marguerite notices, brushes her sister's cheek. Eléonore, the queen of captivation, even at forty. "Had you not heard? I, too, was captured at Lewes—fighting alongside Edward." Richard's pleas to King Louis, accompanied by the clink of coins, resulted in his son's release from prison in France.

"The prince has come to present the Earl Simon's terms," the legate says.

"I will not negotiate with Simon de Montfort," Eléonore says. "I am Queen of England. He is barely an earl, and a traitorous one."

"He holds the king and Prince Edward hostage," Henry says.

"I have an army of men from Flanders, Poitiers, Ireland, and France preparing to sail for England," Eléonore says. "If Simon desires a fight, we will give him one."

"The king begs you to refrain." Guy hands Eléonore a letter. She reads it quickly, then passes it to Marguerite.

"By God's head, we will rescue them," she says as Marguerite reads. *They will kill us if you send foreign troops.* "Simon will not intimidate me."

"I have a plan." Henry's expression is eager. "I think we can free Edward without a fight—and he can liberate the king."

"Simon de Montfort is your friend," Eléonore says. "Why would I listen to you?"

"He *was* my friend," Henry of Almain says. "But Uncle Henry and Edward are family. As are you, my aunt." He blushes sweetly. Eléonore's mouth twitches upward. How long has it been since a man looked at Marguerite with desire? But she has turned gray and grown to plumpness, an old woman. Unable to watch their tête-à-tête any longer, she slips out to her chambers, needing rest.

On the way, she mutters to herself, a habit of late. Now that she finally has a voice, she doesn't seem to be able to stop using it. "Envy of a young man's attention, at your age? Of what use is beauty to a woman, anyway?" Her good looks only incited jealousy from Blanche de Castille, causing Marguerite much misery. Sanchia's perfection gained her a husband more than twenty years her senior who quickly grew bored with her. Eléonore's charms have won her many admirers, but where are her supporters now? Scurried like vermin to their dark corners, too afraid of Simon de Montfort to defend her against stones, mud, or charges of adultery.

Their hostility is misplaced. Eléonore brought her relations to England, yes, as any queen consort from another land would do. A woman, having so little power on her own, must rely on the support of powerful men. Uncle Boniface, Pierre d'Aigueblanche, and Uncle Peter are not why England suffers. The barons of England and Wales are to blame—their ruthless squeezing of money and work from their tenants and serfs. They point the finger at Eléonore because she is a woman, an easy target made more contemptible, perhaps, because of her beauty.

You are sisters. You must help one another. In this struggle to navigate a world made by men, for men, are not all women sisters? But they do not all help one another. Women—Blanche and Beatrice—have presented the greatest obstacles to Marguerite's success. And now, she is doing the same to Beatrice, but that cannot be helped. Beatrice has brought her troubles on herself.

And it is Beatrice who waits in her room, who slumps for one unguarded moment in Marguerite's purple chair, looking as if she might cry. When she sees her sister enter, she stands and smiles, but melancholy clouds her eyes.

"Sister," she says. "I know you said once that we are not sisters, but we are."

"In name. Not in spirit."

"I hope that's not true!" She takes a deep breath. "Margi, I need your help."

Marguerite laughs. "What, a jester now, too? Good, then—I have been craving amusement." She steps to her chair, edging Beatrice aside, and seats herself with slow regality, her maids spreading her gown and mantles about her. She gestures to a lower chair and Beatrice sits with her hands in her lap.

"Charles needs troops to fight with us in Sicily. Louis has given his assent—"

"*Quelle surprise!*" Marguerite gives an indelicate snort.

"But only with your approval." Her voice softens. "I did not realize that you had attained such power."

"Only because Louis has ceased to pay attention. He would rather persecute blasphemers than count his coins, so I administer the treasury. I hold the key in a very tight fist."

"We hope you will loosen it for us. For me."

"What, I wonder, inspires this hope?"

"Your empathetic heart."

"Your sarcasm is touching. As always."

"Surely you can understand my desire to be a queen. It is a prize that all my sisters have gained, except for me."

"I never wanted to be a queen. I wanted to be Countess of Provence."

"I would trade places with you, if I could."

Marguerite scrutinizes her sister for signs of disingenuousness, sees a face as open as a book. "Perhaps you can."

She sighs. "That would require Charles's cooperation. And I do not think he would loosen his hold on even a single Provençal castle."

"Then I will not loosen my hold on the treasury key. Eléonore is more in need of France's help, at any rate."

"You would waste your men and money on that futile cause? Henry has lost the kingdom. Simon de Montfort has won the battle and made himself king. And he has promised aid to Charles."

"Has Charles pledged fealty to Simon? My God, Beatrice! Have you no sense of loyalty?"

"I spoke against it, but he wouldn't listen. Charles and Simon are longtime friends." Of course. Simon spent many months in the French court, following Louis around as if he were a toddler who lives only for his papa's pat on the head. Although he enjoyed the attention, Louis was often occupied with his prayers and self-immolations, leaving Simon to exercise his charms on others in the court. Marguerite was not deceived despite his ardent flatteries. Charles, however, succumbed instantly to his charm.

"If Simon is such a close ally, let him supply your troops."

"You know he cannot. He has given money, but he needs all his men at present."

"To overthrow our sister."

Beatrice colors. "Yes."

Marguerite's raucous laugh—the laugh of an old woman, ha!—grows even louder at the sight of her sister's worried frown. "I might coax troops from my cousin Alfonso of Castille for you, in exchange for my fourth of Provence. Including Tarascon."

"You know I cannot promise that."

"Then why are you wasting my time?" She leaps up from her chair. Beatrice cringes as if afraid she might attack. "You dare to come to me for help, yet you can offer nothing in return."

"When Charles and I are King and Queen of Sicily, we will be valuable allies."

She laughs again. "You have shown already how valuable you are to me." She turns toward her bed. "Leave me. I need to rest."

"Sister, please! Do not be so cold. I would help you if I could." Beatrice's voice snags.

"False tears and false tales. I have had more than my share of them from you."

"They are not false!" She clutches Marguerite's sleeve, tearing the silk. "Sister."

"Stop calling me that."

"Sister. Sister, sister, sister! You cannot deny it. You cannot deny me."

"Please, Beatrice! These histrionics are unbearable."

"I have spoken for you many times to Charles. You have no idea how many quarrels we have had over your rights to Provence."

"That is correct. I have no idea, because you have told me many times that you support his wishes over mine."

"I have never said that! But he is my husband, Margi."

"You would bend to a man's will even when it conflicts with your own—and even when it harms your sister?" She slaps Beatrice's insistent hand from her arm. "You were not reared by our mother, then."

"No, our mother was occupied with the queens in the family." Her voice quavers. "It was Papa who raised me."

"How unfortunate for you." She intends sarcasm, but Beatrice is nodding.

"I learned from Papa that men control everything. All the power that women have, men have given to us."

"Except for the White Queen."

Now Beatrice is the one who laughs. "Do you think that Blanche controlled France? Do you imagine that she was powerful? She had a council of barons to appease. Had she not done so, they would have forced her from her throne and appointed a man to rule until Louis came of age. As the barons did in England for King Henry."

"But she had her way. She did as she pleased."

"Do you think she wanted her son to marry the daughter of a poor Southern count?" *You remind me of one of those vulgar flowers that grow in the South.* Marguerite has wondered many times why Blanche approved Louis's marriage to a "country bumpkin."

"The Count of Toulouse was her cousin. He wanted Provence."

"But he never gained it, did he? Blanche could not even help him with that task. The French barons wanted our salt mines and they wanted the port of Marseille. They thought to have them once Papa died—once Provence went to you. But Papa outsmarted them, and left it to me, instead."

"How do you know this?"

"Papa's meetings, remember? Meetings with Romeo, with the White Queen, with the French barons. I sat in them all."

Marguerite sits on her bed, feeling as if someone had punched her in the stomach. The high-and-mighty Blanche was not as powerful as she seemed. If Marguerite had known, she would have defied her more, would have asserted her own authority.

"As Mama said, we women need to help one another," Beatrice says. "Won't you help me, Margi?"

Marguerite's eyes fill with tears. She stands and opens her arms to Beatrice, and the two of them embrace. She notes the thickening of Beatrice's waist, the result of an inordinate fondness for honey, as Marguerite knows all too well. Mama was right: Beatrice and she are very much alike.

"I cannot help you." To help Beatrice is to help her enemy. "I would rather cut off all of my fingers than to lift one for Charles's sake."

Beatrice stiffens. "Then you spoke correctly before. We may be born of the same parents, but we are most definitely not sisters."

"Don't leave on this note."

"Will there be another note on which to leave? Because I am hearing only the same tune playing over and over again." She pulls on her gloves. "When next you see me, I shall be a queen."

"And I shall bow before you, honoring you as you have honored me."

Beatrice sweeps out of the room blinking back tears, her head high.

"But I shall never bend my knee to Charles," Marguerite says softly. She sits at her desk to write a letter, in her own hand, to the new pope of Rome, requesting the dowry that is rightfully hers.

→ Eléonore ←

A Lost Cause

Paris, 1265

Forty-two years old

$\mathcal{S}$HE PEERS INTO the dark, searching, her fingers knotted, her insides gnarled. In the melee of horses and armored men, shouts and grunts, the clashing of swords, Edward sits tall in his saddle. *Constrict yourself,* like her heart, *make yourself small, my son, become a target a man might miss.* He slashes and thrusts, cutting down greed, cutting through lies, cutting away the treason spreading like a tumor across the land. A knight's horse plunges into the roil, stirring dust, scattering blood, skidding around her son. His lifted shield flashes a roaring lion with a forked tail, the Montfort coat of arms. His lance is aimed for Edward's back. He charges. Eléonore cries out, but it is too late. Edward has been pierced through, and lies in a boody slump over his horse's neck.

"My lady, are you well?" Eléonore turns, her heart racing, to see her handmaid Agnes watching her with frightened eyes.

"Yes, I am fine." She presses a hand to her breast. *Breathe.*

"You gave a shout."

She glances out the window, sees only moonlight gilding the pear trees, gives a little laugh. "I must have fallen asleep on my feet," she says. She has not slept since yesterday, when messengers brought news of a battle brewing at Evesham. The rebels have vowed to kill Henry, but it is Edward they want. Simon aims to place his own son on the throne.

She turns away from the window and sits at her table, peering into her hand mirror as if it could show the future. If only she could conjure the battle, and forgo the agony of waiting. *We will prevail.* For all its bravado, Henry's last message gives her little confidence.

Simon's force has thinned, yes. He has lost many of the nobles who backed him at first, most notably Gilbert de Clare, the powerful red-haired Earl of Gloucester. *Montfort speaks of sharing power, then hoards lands and castles for himself and his sons,* he wrote to Eléonore. At last, the barons realize his true ambitions.

The bishops, however, support Simon still, as do the common people, whom he has won by blaming Eléonore and her "alien" relations for poverty and abuse. Greedy lords and corrupt sheriffs are apparently her fault, as well as famine, pestilence, leprosy, adultery, and anything else adding to the people's misery.

This battle is Simon's last resort. It is Edward's, too, who, angered over her injuries and humiliation at London Bridge, has relentlessly—and cleverly—plotted revenge. Gloucester is Edward's man now, as are Roger Leybourne, Roger de Clifford, and Henry of Almain. Eléonore can resist his friends no longer, not even that dangerous Hamo Lestrange, for they have protected Edward since he escaped from Simon's clutches.

She conceived the escape plan, she is proud to say. Working in Gascony, where she could command her own men and ships using France's funds, she welcomed, of all people, William de Valence. How astonished she was to receive him! Despite his banishment from England, his loyalty to Henry has not wavered. He strutted about, as always, bragging about his valor in battle, magnanimously "forgiving" Eléonore for "conspiring" against him—but none of it mattered in light of his outrage over Edward's imprisonment.

"Our Prince of England held captive by that preening little Frenchman?" he fumed, forgetting his own Poitou origins. He returned home to recruit an army, then sailed to Wales with one hundred twenty knights and her letter to Gilbert de Clare.

Soon the earl had delivered her letter, with its plan for escape, to his brother Thomas de Clare, one of Edward's guards. Her strategy made full use of Edward's competitive nature: one day, as he and his guards sat idly about, he boasted that he was the best rider in England. Thomas scoffed, as planned. Others joined in the argument, and soon wagers were involved.

To raise the stakes, Edward proposed to switch horses frequently as proof of his skill. "I can best any man, no matter what horse I ride," he bragged. Being men, they took his bait. One after another they raced, and Edward won each time. Then, when he was down to his last competitor—Thomas de Clare—he changed horses once more, making sure to choose the fastest and strongest. Off they went on their fresh horses, tearing at top speed into the woods, never to reappear. The captors gave chase on their tired horses and could not catch up.

"He is my son," Eléonore said when she heard. "Ever eager to test himself against others, ever certain of winning." He is more like her than anyone alive.

Dinnertime. The morning has passed with excruciating slowness. She heads to the great hall, where she and Margi will dine with Uncle Boniface, Edmund, King Louis, Prince Philip, and, sure to make the meal most interesting, Sir Jean de Joinville, visiting for the first time since Eléonore's arrival in Paris. Rising to kiss her, Margi positively glows in her new gown of purple with its draping gold silk sleeves, as though she were made for purple, or it for her. Never mind that her figure has grown stout or that the tendrils of hair springing from her headdress are a dull gray: Her eyes are as bright as a bird's. Her complexion is smooth and, today, blushingly pink, and her wit is as sharp as a rapier.

And as sly.

"Tell me, my lord, how it is that Sir Thomas of Aquino has now declared the flesh of birds to be fit for monks to eat?" she asks Louis as Eléonore takes her seat.

"He has classified poultry as having aqueous origins, like fish," Louis says in that I-am-trying-to-be-patient voice he uses with Margi.

"I declare that I never saw a chicken in, or near, the water," she says. "Or a peacock, neither, nor a *becfigue*." She lifts a morsel from the songbird on her plate, observing it. *Becfigue* was a rare treat when they were girls in Provence, served on special occasions roasted and stuffed with flower petals. "I have never seen a fish flying in the air, either. Nor does poultry taste of the sea."

"God created fish and fowl at the same time," Louis says, giving Margi a stern frown. "Read your scriptures."

"He created man and woman at the same time, too. I wonder if that makes us the same, after all?"

"Many birds eat fish," Edmund says.

"As do monks. Except for Thomas of Aquino. I have never seen him take a bite of fish at this table."

"I have noticed the same. It seems that he does not prefer food from the rivers or the sea." Jean de Joinville is grinning at her. Margi blushes even more profusely. "He does enjoy chicken greatly."

"Sir Thomas is no longer a monk, but an esteemed philosopher," Louis grumps. "He may eat what he wishes, yet he chooses to observe the monk's diet. I dare say you would not utter these statements were he at table today. You border on blasphemy."

"Questioning philosophers is blasphemy? Uncle Boniface, what is your opinion?"

Uncle Boniface, who has also added weight—to the detriment of his former good looks—shrugs and places a morsel of songbird in his mouth.

"I am certain Sir Thomas is glad to be absent from this meal," Eléonore says, "for my sister's arguments have always sharpened with her hunger, and grown more refined with satiety. He might find himself at a loss."

"He would, no doubt," Joinville says, smiling at Margi.

"Especially against a woman," Margi says. "Thinking the female inferior to the male, as he does."

But who cares, really, about the hypocrisies of the Church? Eléonore looks down at the little skinned delicate birds lying on the trencher, and sees their broken necks and glazed eyes—the eyes of her husband and son lying on the battlefield at Evesham, broken and bleeding, England's future lost, and that of her children. But who cares about the future, either? Without her family, there is no future for Eléonore. Thank God Edmund is here with her, out of harm's way although he has fumed and scowled many times these months as she has refused, again and again, to allow him to return to England and fight. She pushes the plate of birds away.

"Do you not enjoy the *becfigue*? I thought it was your favorite," Margi says in a low voice. "We sent to the Aix market for them, hoping they would revive your appetite."

"I am sorry." Eléonore can barely speak. Her throat, like the rest of her body, feels tight with the effort of holding herself all in one piece. "Today, everything reminds me of death."

One week has passed since Edward captured Simon's son and his men at Kenilworth. *The Earl of Leicester hastens to confront the Prince Edward, but the king's age makes him a slow companion,* Henry of Almain wrote. Eléonore smiled to think of her spry husband feigning tiredness, an aching back, an upset stomach, all to delay Simon's progress. But she has not smiled since. She will never do so again, she warrants, until Henry and Edward are safe.

Margi orders peas for her, and carrots roasted with honey, and a salad of fresh greens. This she can stomach. She tucks in, but as Louis begins to talk of Outremer, Margi is the one pushing away her plate.

"The Sultan Baybars has taken Nazareth, the city of Our Lord," he is saying. "The Turks will not stop until they have claimed every city we Christians have built, including Jerusalem."

"Will there be another pilgrimage to Outremer?" Edmund asks, too hopefully for Eléonore's liking.

"Should the pope of Rome issue the call," Margi's eldest son Philip says gravely. "And I shall be the first to take the cross."

"You will be the second," Louis says, beaming.

"Nonsense," Marguerite huffs. "What is the use of dying a miserable death for a lost cause?"

Eléonore's head begins to throb.

"A lost cause, the holy city? What cause could be more worthy?" Louis rises from his seat but, weakened from a recent attack of dysentery, he collapses before he can even unfold his legs.

"I agree with the queen," Joinville says. "Christians have sent troops for nearly one hundred years, wave after wave, and we are repulsed each time. Perhaps God does not smile on the endeavor, since he has not seen fit to make us victorious."

"God judges us in this world, as in the next, according to our sins," Louis says. "The righteous he awards with victory, and the sinner with defeat."

The words hit Eléonore like a slap. Is God judging her, then, by casting her family into danger? What sin has she committed to deserve this sorrow?

"Ruling any people far from home is too costly and too difficult to sustain for long," Joinville says. "Just ask the good King Henry of England—or his queen."

All eyes turn to her, but she brims with tears and dares not open her mouth to reply. She mumbles an excuse and rises from the table, bringing her ladies running over to carry her skirts. Voices float after, calling to her, but she can hear only her own questions as she hurries over the floor and up the stairs.

What is her sin? Ambition? Gaining Sicily, while expensive— God knows she paid enough to popes over the years for their battles against Manfred—would have reaped many rewards for England's treasury. England's power would have eclipsed that of France. Eléonore would have been the most powerful queen in the world, more powerful than any of her sisters.

But—who cares which kingdom has more power, which kings and queens have more lands? We fight and scheme for our children's sakes and then we die, and they may lose all that we built up for them. There is nothing we can give to anyone that lasts—except love.

Is greed her sin? She has been accused of it. She has been greedy, yes, but for her children's sakes, not her own. She wanted the best for them that life can offer. She wanted to ensure that they would never suffer hunger or fear as she did in Provence—and what did it avail her? Edward imprisoned, nearly killed more than once, his life in the hands of enemies. Edmund hiding here with her, not King of Sicily, never to be king of anything—and who cares? None of it matters to Eléonore now, not when her husband and son might lie dead on the ground, or in the gallows.

She should not have waited to make amends with Edward. She has neither seen nor heard from him since their quarrel at Windsor—years ago, before her attack at London Bridge. She pulls her arms to her chest. *Holy Mother, save my son so that I might hold him close to me again.*

Marguerite finds her lying on her bed. "Can you believe Louis's talk of returning to Outremer?" she says, pacing the floor. "Apparently, our last campaign wasn't enough of a failure."

"Why are men driven to fight? They kill one another over castles, over a patch of land in the desert, over ideas." She wonders if they realize how meaningless are their pursuits, if any man ever wishes he had given himself over to love rather than to killing. Love is the only thing that matters. Does any man ever know this?

Family comes first. Suddenly, Eléonore understands her mother's words in a new way. Family is all. She has spent her life lifting uncles and cousins, nieces and nephews to greater wealth and status, and competing with her sisters for the same. Now, though, these goals seem as foolish as the games they played as children—although far more dangerous. Her efforts to gain Sicily for one son turned all of England against her, and may end in death for Edward and Henry.

Now Beatrice wants Sicily, but does she know the price? Her pursuit has cost her much of Eléonore's love—and more of

Marguerite's, if there was any left to lose. Oh, it will be awful. Manfred is a fearsome warrior, and will fight to the death. Charles may be killed—and Beatrice may discover what Eléonore, facing the loss of her husband and son, has now realized. She threw all her weight behind the "Sicilian business" as though nothing else mattered—when, in fact, ruling Sicily mattered not at all.

Not even being a queen matters to her now, or Henry's being king, or Edward's being prince. *Take it all, O Lord. Just let my son and husband live.*

"Egypt is a brutal place. They will die if they go," Margi is saying. "I don't want my children to die."

From outside the door, a flurry of female voices, the handmaids' tittering. Margi's maid steps in and, with a curtsey, announces Henry of Almain. Eléonore dries her tears but her hand is damp when Henry drops to one knee and kisses it.

"My lady, the battle at Evesham is ended." He remains on the floor with his head bowed. A sharp ache twists under Eléonore's breastbone.

"So soon! I only heard late last night that the fighting was at hand."

"It began and ended in two hours' time." Why doesn't he lift his face to her? "The Prince Edward fought most valiantly."

"By God's head!" Her pulse bounces about as if her heart had untethered itself. Tears gush forth from her eyes. "Have you come to deliver his epitaph?"

He glances sharply up at her. A smile tugs at his mouth. "Not an epitaph, my lady, but sad news for many. Our army trampled over the rebel forces like a thundering stampede. We are victorious."

"Praise be to God!" She wipes her tears with the back of her hand. "Your downcast eyes told a different tale. Or"—she presses a hand to her chest—"do you bear bad news of Henry?"

"He is safe, my lady," and no thanks to Simon, he tells her when he has stood. Maliciously, Simon placed his own helmet on Henry's head and stood him amid a small group, weaponless, in the battle. "His Grace would not have been recognized save for his constant calling out of his name, and his crying, 'Do not strike me! I am too old to fight.'"

"My Henry, too old to fight?" Eléonore smiles. "Were his tongue as sharp as a blade, he would have cut Simon down long ago."

Henry of Almain lowers his gaze again. "Simon is dead now, my lady, and his eldest son."

How strange that she feels no remorse, not even a shimmer of sorrow for a man whom, once, she called friend. But that was many years ago, before he tried to destroy her and the people she loved. "You are certain? You have seen his body?"

"I have seen his head, my lady, with his testicles wrapped around his nose." He blushes, but Eléonore bursts into laughter. Roger, the Earl of Mortimer and Simon's most impassioned enemy, killed him and sent his head thusly adorned to his wife, Dame Maud Mortimer, at Wigmore Castle.

"May he rest in peace, and his sons, and all the good Englishmen who died for his lost cause," he says.

"Lost, indeed! Good riddance. England is better off without Simon, and will not even notice that he is gone." Henry of Almain may feign grief all he likes—gloating over the deaths of one's enemies is not considered chivalrous behavior—but she will not conceal her delight. "Have you come to fetch me home, I hope?"

"I have, my lady." He pulls a parchment from his surcoat. "Here is a letter from Prince Edward, summoning you."

Eléonore tears it open, her eyes filling with tears before she has read the first word.

O brave Queen Eléonore, you have saved us. Now come home and reap your rewards. All of London wants to kneel before you, to pay homage to you and beg your forgiveness—I, most of all.

⇒ *Beatrice* ⇐

A Queen at Last

Sicily, 1266

Thirty-five years old

*T*HE WHOLE WORLD is white, the sky blankly ablaze, a page on which anything might be written, queenship or death, the snow like quicksand sucking at her feet and tugging at the furs swaddling her body, fur wet and heavy with the cold, white breath of God. Strange how she never thought of God as cold. Disturbing that she never knew.

The snow she expected. No one crosses the Alps in November without the sting of blowing ice, the numb of cold. Fingers are lost, the tips of noses. But her own tired desire surprises her, the yearning to float like a feather down to the pillowy white, to succumb, to enfold herself as though the snow were filled with sun instead of the lack of it, as if all that pale light could save her from the teeth of the biting wind as she slogs up the mountainside through the billowing snow. These could be clouds, the world is so far below. The crown that awaits her is a lifetime away.

Her head feels light. Oh, she is tired, so tired. Her eyes close, weighted with ice. She stumbles. "Hold on to my hand, my dear!" Uncle Philip is with her, his horse on the rein behind, stepping surely up the narrow path as though a single slip would not send him plummeting to his death. These are Savoy lands. He has traveled this route many times. He grips her hand and pulls her close, away from the falling edge. From behind, someone cries out. She lifts her head to look around but sees only white. Hears only the wind's high moan. Has someone fallen? Dead for her sake. Her eyes so heavy. Uncle Philip's arm tightens around her waist, lifting her. Almost there. Rome, near? She had not known it was so cold.

"Charles?" she cries. In the blowing snow, a dark shape. He will warm her. "I see him," she says to Uncle Philip. He leads her onward, revealing a rock. This is not Rome. They are in the Alps. Rome is far away. Charles. If not for Uncle, she would be dead. Philip appeared while she was feasting her army, bringing with him one hundred men including St. Pol, just returned from England and whetted for a fight. Simon de Montfort made an easy conquest in the end. Had Charles known, he would have not bent his knee to him.

"We have reached the summit." Uncle Philip's shout whirls in the wind and blows to the back, prompting cheers. Six thousand knights, six hundred crossbowmen, twenty thousand foot soldiers. Beatrice's conquests. She lured them with gifts, flirtation, cajoling, promises. Her cheeks became stiff from all that smiling.

But she could not convince King Louis. Not a cent from France. "I will be in need of my men and my money," he said. But France is at peace. Margi's doing. She holds the keys to the treasury. If not for Beatrice, she would have been revealed as an adulteress. She would hold nothing today except her rosary.

Now for the descent, turn after turn after turn. Philip grips her in an icy dance. She rests against his arm, lets her eyes fall shut, sees Margi with her long hair streaming in the Egyptian sun, bludgeoning a crocodile with an oar. Oh, to be like that. Something presses against her mouth, forcing her lips apart: Bread, stale and hard. *You must eat.* She gags and swallows. Her eyelids turn red. The sun's white light splinters the clouds, exposing the sky's blue underbelly. She breathes it in, filling herself with light. A ray touches her cheek. Warmth. Her uncle relaxes his hold. "Queen

Courage," he calls her. "Like your sisters. Were you men, you four would rule the world."

This she knows. Charles could not muster an army for this campaign. Beatrice recruited the men of Provence, men who hate Charles but love money, and men from Flanders and Anjou. Her father's daughter, she lured them with promises. To the Provençal nobles she offered lands in Sicily; to the Marseille merchants, commerce; to the rest, booty by the trunkfuls. "We will all be rich," she said. If they can conquer Manfred. If they can recapture Rome for the pope. They will be rich and she will be queen, with as much power as a woman can wield.

Next Christmas, she will sit at the head table with Eléonore and Margi. The year after that, who knows? They might bow to her. "I will make you a greater queen than they," Charles said. He dreams of an empire, stretching across the Mediterranean into Outremer. She will be empress of all, omnipotent. Then Charles may agree, at last, to award Tarascon to Margi. Provence will be as nothing to them, while, to Margi, it is the only home there is. Giving it up would be a small price for the esteem of the sister she loves best.

WHEN YOU ARE being queened in a strange land, you peer into your audience as if seeking your reflection in a pool but find only dazed and curious stares, as if they were fish looking back at you. Their shouts of acclaim, rendered in their foreign tongue, swirl like snowflakes to land on your head and shoulders and then disappear. You walk into St. Peter's Basilica with all the majesty you can muster, uncertain of each next step, as if you were an actor playing a spontaneous part, although you have rehearsed this moment in your mind many times. A chorus of monks pours music over the opulents—the cardinals, now gilded with song; the bishops and archbishops, tunefully illuminated; the velvets of the nobles, alight with melody—singing up majesty, singing up reverence, singing up gold in the shape of a crown ornamented with a lifetime of dreams.

"Smile, my queen," Charles murmurs to Beatrice as they sit

beside each other in their fur-lined robes, their cloth of gold, their unadorned arms and throats—for Beatrice has sold her jewels to pay their army—their conspicuous, soon-to-be-crowned heads rained upon with Roman love. These people are not even their subjects, no more than ten of them Sicilian if the truth be told, yet they exult as if Charles were the Christ and she were the Virgin Mother, and this were the second coming. They lay flowers at Beatrice's feet, shout accolades, blow kisses, embrace one another. "Your bewilderment is showing. People seek confidence in their leaders, not confusion."

"But why are they cheering so? We are not going to be King and Queen of Rome."

"They enjoy the fête, these Romans. Decadent to the bone. Our celebration will last three days, so of course they love us. Plus, they hate Manfred."

And no wonder, for the Stupor Mundi's bastard son has proved shockingly ruthless, first trying to poison his young nephew Conradin, the rightful heir to Frederick's throne, and then, after failing at that murder, declaring the boy dead anyway and crowning himself King of Germany and Sicily. When the pope excommunicated him, he invaded Rome.

Now Pope Clement hides from Manfred in Viterbo. Five cardinals have come in his stead to lead today's ceremony. Beatrice cannot help feeling cheated. The pope of Rome is supposed to set the crown on her head. Will the hands of mere cardinals tarnish the gold? Without a papal blessing, will hers and Charles's authority be challenged?

Last night, Charles laughed at her furrowed brow, her pursed lips. Has she forgotten how they stomped out the fires of mutiny in Marseille, how they rid Provence of heresy, how they defeated the Queen of France's attempts to annul their father's will and wrest their lands from them? "Together, we can do anything," he said, then took her to bed and showed her what he meant.

As she sits with him now, throne to throne, his hand cups hers and she feels a current from his touch, as if rivers of power flowed from his fingertips to hers and back again. They are unstoppable. When the goose meat stuffing the roasted, silver-dipped swans has been devoured, when the minstrels have piped and drummed and sung themselves dry of notes, when the dancers have churned themselves into a froth and floated away, when the men have told tales until their tongues are knotted with lies and everyone except Beatrice's twenty-six thousand warriors has gone home, then will the real feast begin. Charles will fling their troops headlong into Sicily, aiming like a well-shot arrow for Manfred's heart, for he and Beatrice will not be king and queen of anything until the last of Frederick's heirs is dead. While Charles fights, Beatrice will be his general in Rome, launching ships, mobilizing troops, planning strategies, raising and spending money. Commanding men. A queen at last.

"Looking for your hero St. Pol?" Charles asks, jealous as ever, as she watches the crowd stream into the cathedral. Every seat is filled and yet they continue to arrive, merchants, clergy, nobles, common folk.

"I am thinking of my sisters," she says. "I wish they were here."

He shrugs. "You have done well for yourself thus far, without their approval. Or their help."

It is their love she desires. But Charles would think her weak. "I want only their acknowledgment."

"You think a crown will make a difference? Will they at last place you among their ranks?"

"Why not? I will be one of them. A queen."

"Cast them from your mind, my dear. You do not need them now. In fact, they will soon need you. You are going to be an empress. Your sisters will bend their knees to you. And Louis will bow to me."

So many conflicting thoughts bounce in her head that she cannot speak: She will always need her sisters; she belongs to them, and they to her, even if they do not acknowledge this fact; the only way to gain their acceptance is to give them the lands and money they have claimed; if Charles loves her, he must increase her happiness by doing so.

But love takes as many forms as there are faces in this room, each of them strange, most of them unseeing. Charles's love begins with himself. "Why would I give even a fistful of Provençal soil to that harpy Marguerite? Or to my brother, who would not spare a single mark for my battle after I fought so valiantly for him in Egypt?" he says.

He loves Beatrice, but not her affection for her sisters. Sanchia was sweet enough, he used to say, but she lacked confidence except what she found in the bottom of her goblet. "She will never be of use to us, or to anyone."

Eléonore is too bold, he says. A wife should enhance her husband's authority, not diminish it. She makes King Henry appear weak, and the people resent her for it. Never mind all the good she has done for England, if she has dispirited her subjects by outshining their king. See how the White Queen reigned with Louis in her lap, puppeting him so that he appeared to rule?

"The people will bend to man's authority, but not to woman's," Charles says. "The woman is head of the household, but man is head of the woman. That is the natural order, established by God."

Marguerite he calls conniving and weak, relying too much on her mind and too little on might. Had Beatrice's inheritance been snatched away, she would have fought for it with an army, he points out, while Marguerite flails like a poor swimmer in too-deep waters with her endless petitions to the pope and her little intrigues. What's more, she now has tried to usurp the power of Louis's heir, Philip, by coercing from him a promise to give her "supreme authority" over all his kingly decisions.

"She would rule France—and her son—as Mama did, but she is no Blanche of Castille," Charles said with a sneer. In Beatrice's mind, this is reason to love her sister more, not less.

The cardinals step forward, their rings flashing in the splintered light. The spectators stand. One cardinal waves incense; another lights candles; another prays. They flit like birds all around her and Charles. She remembers a scene: Marguerite playing at her own coronation, giggling and jesting, making grotesque faces—until Eléonore placed a crown of daisies on her head. Her grin became a serene smile. Her shoulders squared themselves. Beatrice, just a tiny girl then, never forgot the transformation. And when she later saw Margi as a real queen, in the palace at Paris, the change proved to be real. The mirth had faded from her eyes, replaced by gravitas. "Our Margi has grown up," Mama said, but Beatrice thought she had merely grown sad. She had not wanted to be queen; she wanted to be Countess of Provence. But, being a woman, she was not allowed to choose.

Beatrice had no choice, either, in spite of Papa's efforts. "In Provence, a woman may rule," he said to her the day before he died. "You are more than capable. Hold on to your power at all costs." But there was no holding on, not in this world. By the time Charles strode into her chambers and scooped her up, her fate had already been decided and her power usurped. Not even Mama could protest.

Protest Mama did, however, as Charles took her castles away. Papa would not have wanted it, but Charles waved away Beatrice's complaints as though they were gnats. Papa administered the county poorly, he said, pointing to the blooming Cathar communities, the self-governing Marseille, the money spent on troubadours and minstrels "sucking our blood like leeches and flouting their desire for my wife with their shameless verse."

As much as Beatrice adores the troubadours—only Sordel remains, and a few others—she does not complain. Charles shares power with her in every way but one: he will not allow her to negotiate with Marguerite. This bothers her until he lays her down and removes her clothes with his slow hands. At those times, she thinks not at all of her sisters. Instead, she begs God, in her heart, to let her keep Charles always.

"What if you die?" she has taken to asking, lying in his arms. "What will happen to me?"

His grin skewers her. The gap between his front teeth. His ruffled hair.

"You would soon find a strapping Sicilian bull to take my spot in your bed."

"At least two would be needed to replace you. Perhaps three."

She jests, even with a lump in her throat the size of a broken heart. She has no illusions about her future should Charles be killed in this campaign. Manfred would take her as a hostage, perhaps lock her in a tower or donjon and leave her to die. Would her sisters help her then? Would anyone?

She has no desire to find out. As she kneels before the cardinals and takes the Holy Communion, she touches the vial around her neck, filled with a sweet and deadly poison. Death before dishonor. Marguerite's courage in Damietta still reverberates, like a battle cry. Beatrice will be every bit as brave.

⇥ *Marguerite* ⇤

Never the Enemy

Paris, 1267

Forty-six years old

Were Beatrice still alive, she would mock Marguerite.

Are those tears of sorrow or of joy? You wished for this, did you not?

"Yes," she says into her handkerchief—only she and Eléonore are in the carriage—"yes, I did wish her dead. But only once, when she reneged on her promise to give Tarascon to me and then left us in Outremer to rot, I thought, or lose our heads to the Saracens. I watched their ship sail away and hoped it might sink to the bottom of the sea."

And now Beatrice is in the vault, dead of dysentery contracted in the rank Sicilian heat, an ignoble end to a reign begun on a velvet couch in a grand procession just two years ago.

"I entertained murderous fantasies when I heard that she and Charles were pursuing Sicily," Eléonore says. "Remember how excited she was? Thinking, as always, of herself. She could be quite maddening."

"She was obsessed with queenship," Marguerite says, dabbing at her cheeks. "That, and her precious Charles."

"She seemed not to need anyone's help. Not as Sanchia did."

Eléonore presses her face into her hands. "I wonder, still, if I should have known Sanchia was dying. If I could have saved her."

"Perhaps, if you had not been hiding in the Tower in fear for your own life." Marguerite cannot help the edge in her voice; she and Eléonore have explored this terrain many times, and they never find anything new in it. "And Sanchia seemed always to complain of one malady or another."

"Beatrice said we neglected her. That we should have done more."

"Are we physicians? Seers? Beatrice thought queenship conferred magical powers. She discovered the truth before she died, I suppose."

"I hear she was admired in Sicily. The poets praised her there. Charles, on the other hand, is despised." So hated that he could not hold a proper funeral for her in Sicily, for fear he might be attacked.

Marguerite scowls. "I am sure he is just as cruel to the Sicilians as he has been to the Marseillais. Our sister's death will be a cause for rejoicing in Provence. Now Charles will have to abdicate, and name Charles the Younger as count."

"But he is still a child!"

"No matter. Papa's will is clear: when Beatrice dies, her eldest son inherits the county—not her husband."

"Charles cannot rule until the boy comes of age?"

"No. That task falls to Sanchia—or, now, one of us."

"Which one, do you suppose?" Eléonore smiles through her tears.

"I thought—since Paris is nearer—"

"Please take it. I am fully engaged," Eléonore says. She and Henry have not completely quashed the rebellion in England. Simon's death only agitated his supporters, including Llywelyn ap Gruffydd, the self-styled Prince of Wales.

"Llywelyn is like a child with a stick, prodding a hornet's nest just to watch the confusion. Every skirmish that flares up, we find he instigated." She and Henry have given castles to Edmund in Wales, and have sent him there to fight.

"And Edward?" Her spirits lift at the very thought of him, the brave knight, the bold prince beloved by his people. He is the son Marguerite might have had if not for Louis's indifference to their children and Blanche's influence upon them.

"He is as restless as ever," she says, sighing, "roaming about with his Marcher friends in search of jousting tournaments."

"Jousting? That's a foolish risk."

"Yes, but what son listens to a mother's counsel anymore?"

"Especially when the mother is so like the son." Marguerite smiles. "Remember when Mama likened you to Artemisia?"

"The warrior queen." Eléonore smiles. "I remember. I was foolish, too, always eager to prove myself for no good reason, always willing to fight for things that didn't matter—just like Edward and his tournaments. And yet"—she lowers her voice—"I hate to see him risk his life, and England's future. His wife is particularly anxious, being so eager to take my place."

"That won't happen for many years," Marguerite says, putting her arm around her sister.

"I hope you are right, but I fear that you are not." Elli's voice quavers. It occurs to Marguerite: she has not seen her sister cry since she fell off her horse at the age of nine. "Henry is getting old. He has become sickly."

"Louis, as well. But I expect he will live long. A lifetime of mortifications have made him immune to death." And sent his mind staggering from his body, too drunk with pain, apparently, to find its way back. She wonders how he has fared in her absence. Will she find him, again, lying on the chapel floor in his own mess, too sick and exhausted to take his bowels to the toilet?

But, no, here he comes riding up in full hunting regalia and surrounded by a crowd of fifty men: counts, dukes, bishops, priests, knights. She sees his sallow cheeks, his too-thin body curling like a whip, his mouth open as if he were laughing, which he is not, for he has not laughed since their son died—indeed, not since they returned from Outremer thirteen years ago.

When they have passed through the palace gates, Eléonore

exclaims. "What is this?" Horses, carriages, chariots, nobles and servants fill the courtyard.

"Jean," Marguerite breathes.

"Oh, my," Eléonore says.

When the carriage stops and the door opens, Jean bows and kisses Marguerite's ring—something he would never do for Louis, not being "his man." He was Marguerite's man. He still is, judging from the look he gives her.

"What a pleasant surprise," he says as he helps her from the carriage, leaving Eléonore to the servants. "I had not expected to see you until the king's announcement this evening."

"Announcement?"

The clop of horses' hooves; the clatter of wheels. She turns to see two more carriages and a chariot, with their attendant knights and servants and horses, entering through the gates. "What is happening?" she says.

"I hoped you could tell me." He pulls a handkerchief from inside his sleeve and mops his brow. His eyes closed, he takes a deep breath. When he opens them, they appear almost milky.

"Jean! You are ill. You should be at home."

"So I told the king. But he insisted that, even were I on my deathbed, I should come to hear his news."

After sending a servant to escort Jean to his chambers, Marguerite steps into the castle, across the floor of the great hall where the hunting party has gathered for the afternoon meal, and up the stairs to Louis's rooms. She finds him within, embracing Charles, whose arms hang limply by his sides.

"My condolences over the death of your queen," Louis says.

"I am bereft," Charles says. "I scarcely know what to do without her." The catch in his voice sounds forced. She meets his hard gaze with her haughty one.

"You will feel better when you have heard my announcement tonight," Louis says.

"Louis," she says, "my lord. What is this announcement?"

His smile is as sly as if he has caught her in some deception.

"You must wait to hear it, the same as everyone else. Now, if you will excuse me, I must go and pray for God's guidance." And then Louis has gone, leaving the two of them.

"Are you mourning the loss of my sister, or that of Provence?" she says to Charles.

He frowns. "I am yet the Count of Provence."

"Not according to my father's will."

"No," he says, "but according to the agreement Beatrice signed with me."

"What sort of agreement?"

"It made me Count of Provence in my own right. Our son will inherit, but after I die."

Marguerite's heart begins a slow pumping, as though she were climbing a hill. "Beatrice would not have signed that. She loved our father, and would have respected his wishes."

"The only man she loved more was me," he says. "And that is why I have come to you." Her hasty burial at Viterbo was necessary for the time being, he says, but it was not what she wanted. "She begged to be laid to rest beside her father."

"In the mausoleum I had built for him? That is impossible." She turns away, twisting her hands. She is too late! Beatrice has already signed away her share of Provence. Her heart feels shrunken, like a shriveled walnut in its shell.

"Impossible? Why is that? The tomb is certainly large enough. Hadn't you intended to bury your mother there? Yet she preferred the company of her brothers to that of her husband." His tone is accusing, as if Marguerite were to blame.

"Your point escapes me."

"Your sister's final wish was to lie between her father and me."

"She never considered my wishes. Why should I care about hers?"

"She adored you. But you couldn't see it, blinded as you were by greed."

"You accuse me of greed?" Her laugh is loud, like Eléonore's, raucous as a raven's. "It is time to end this discussion." She tries again to step around him, but he grabs her by the arms.

"It would be a pleasure to send you to the jail," she says. "A single shout from me would do it."

"I advise against it." His eyes are red at their rims, as though he has not slept for days. "You do not want anyone to hear what I am about to say."

Then, in a voice raspy and low, he tells Marguerite her secrets. She was seen that night on the voyage home from Outremer, running onto the ship's deck unclothed with her burning gown. Joinville, too, was seen, through her cabin's open door. Marguerite begins to perspire.

"Do not worry. Bartolomeu told no one. When he returned to France, however, he came to me, tormented by guilt and his love for Louis."

Marguerite feels suddenly weak, as though she might faint. Yet she cannot sit down, for Charles grips her arms, bruising her. "But you never told Louis," she says.

"No. I intended to, for I have never cared for the noble Joinville and I care even less for you. How I would have enjoyed causing your destruction!" He is so near that she can feel his spittle spraying her face. "But I kept your secret. You may thank Beatrice for that. She begged me not to tell."

"You agreed out of the goodness of your heart, I suppose."

He laughs. "You know me better. She had to give me something in return: a promise. Which she kept until she died, even though she sacrificed your love."

The urge to flee rises up; she pushes hard against him, freeing herself from him. She does not want to hear the rest of his sordid story—and yet, she does.

"Why should I believe you?"

"Why would I lie? Everything I want is mine, thanks in part to your indiscretion."

"I don't see what my private life has to do with your ambition."

"Beatrice paid a price for your privacy. At the time I told her my informant's tale, she was preparing to petition the pope, asking him to grant Tarascon to you."

She reaches out and finds the edge of her bed, then slowly sits. Beatrice had intended to keep her promise, after all. She was never the enemy.

"I forbade her to send the letter, of course. But Beatrice was not a submissive woman. She agreed, in exchange for my silence, and Bartolomeu's."

"Why didn't she tell me?" Marguerite begins to cry again.

"That was our agreement—that she never tell anyone, especially you. I would not wish to be known as a man who must utter threats and make bargains to control his wife."

"And now—what? Do you think you can threaten me? Go! Tell Louis what you think you know. I will deny it, and so will Joinville." Already, a lie has begun to shape itself. Joinville, on the deck, heard her screams. He rushed inside as she was running out with the burning gown. When she ran back into the cabin, he stood by the bed with his eyes shut, offering her a blanket with which to cover herself.

His smile is ghastly. "Why would I threaten you? You have nothing that I want."

"Provence is no longer yours. According to my father's will, it goes to Beatrice's son. I'm going fight your attempt to rule the county. And I will win."

His laughter sends her leaping to her feet, her fists balled. "You will not win," he says. "Your father's will has been changed. The pope of Rome amended it—at Beatrice's request."

Marguerite stifles a cry. How can anyone amend a man's will after he is dead? But Charles, she sees, has found a way.

"Your sister Eléonore paid a high price for her ambition. She promised the very stars to the pope of Rome in exchange for the Sicilian crown. But revolutions are expensive."

"That's why you helped Simon—because you wanted Sicily!"

"My tactic succeeded. After spending every coin in the treasury fighting rebels, Queen Eléonore could not deliver the sum she had pledged to the pope. He threatened to excommunicate King Henry. Had he done so, his reign—and your sister's—would have ended. Beatrice pleaded with me to help. So of course I offered to pay their debt—for a price."

If she must endure his smug smile for even one more moment, Marguerite will be ill. "I am going now," she says. She turns away—but his words stop her.

"Beatrice would have given anything for your love. To be one of you—one of the sisters of Savoy—was all she ever wanted. Yet she gave up that desire for your sake. Now you can repay her by allowing her body to be buried next to her father's."

Marguerite sighs. How did she misjudge her sister so completely? "I shall agree to it," she says. "It is the very least I can do for her, given all she has done for Eléonore and me."

He bows. "And you agree to my burial there, as well?"

Marguerite bursts into laughter. She would sooner see him eaten alive by wild boars.

A knock on the door. Gisele enters. "My lady, King Louis summons you and Sir Charles to the great hall."

"I am a king now," Charles tells her. "'Your Grace' is the appropriate title."

"If you call him 'Your Grace,' I will dismiss you," Marguerite murmurs to her on the way down to the main floor, where a crowd of hundreds surrounds the dais.

Charles is forgotten at the sight of Louis on his throne in full royal regalia—furs, silks, gold cloth, even his crown—for the first time since their return from Outremer. As she wends her way through the crowd, Jean approaches, his expression bleak.

"The king intends to take the cross again," he murmurs. "And he will ask us to accompany him."

Marguerite's step falters; his hand reaches out and she takes it, steadying herself. "Sir Jean," she hears, and turns to see Charles standing beside her, eyeing their linked hands.

"Charles," she says, letting go of Jean, "Louis is going to take the cross."

Charles's eyes narrow. Marguerite can almost hear his plot hatching: *how can I benefit?*

As she steps up onto the platform, Louis begins to bounce in his seat. Excitement dances in his eyes. As soon as Marguerite has sat beside him, he leaps to his feet. The crowd's murmurs fade to silence. Louis makes his announcement.

Marguerite, thinking of the heat and dust, the bloodthirsty Saracens, the scorpions, the stinking camels, wonders—why? Why does he want to return? An eternity in hell would be preferable to another year in Outremer.

The Lord has called him, he says, to a "most noble and sacred purpose." The holy city, he says, is like a damsel in distress, awaiting a chivalric rescue. "We must save her from the heathens," he cries. "If not us, then who? If not now, then when?"

It is a rousing speech, but the response is mild. Only a few young knights—boys too young to join the previous campaign—step forward to pledge their assistance. And then—a dagger in Marguerite's throat, stopping her cry of *No!*—Jean Tristan, born in Egypt amid fear and sorrow, now a winsome young man of seventeen, as fragile as his father and too sweet-natured for battle, steps forward and declares that he will join his father. She forces a smile, wills her gaze to admire and shine for her courageous son while on the inside she shrieks at Louis and scratches his face. *Are you insane?* Of course he is. *I won't let you do this!* Yet—how will she stop him?

Their son Peter, just sixteen, and daughter Isabelle, the Countess of Champagne—said to be the very likeness of Marguerite—step forward. They, too, will go. And then Philip steps up to the dais. He bows his dark head before Louis. Gasps arise. The heir to the crown! Will the king allow it?

"This is my son," Louis says, "in whom I am well pleased." In an obviously rehearsed scene, Philip climbs the steps to the dais and kneels before him. Louis pulls his sword from the scabbard on his hip and touches the blade to each of his shoulders and then to the top of his head, knighting him. Marguerite wipes the tears from her face, still forcing a smile.

And then he turns to her. "My queen," he says, "your valor and ingenuity saved our life on our last campaign in Outremer. I trust that we can count on you to join us again?"

The eyes of the nobles and knights, their wives, the servants, her sons and daughters turn to her as she stands silent, perspiration drenching her gown, her pulse hammering in her ears. *Beatrice, I am sorry.* Jean's dark gaze soothes her. His head is moving almost imperceptibly from side to side, telling her the answer she already knows.

"No, my lord," she says. The room is a held breath. "God has not called me to this journey. He would have me remain in Paris to rule our kingdom.

"And besides"—she finds Charles in the crowd and smiles warmly at him—"I know you will be in the best of hands. Your brother Charles, the King of Sicily, plans to accompany you." She is already basking in Charles's cold glare. "He promised me today that he will remain by your side until the end of your campaign."

❦ *Eléonore* ❦

Family Comes First
London, 1271
Forty-eight years old

$\mathcal{G}$RIEF HANGS AS thick as a shroud over the funeral of Henry of Almain. Remorse bitters Eléonore's tongue. She'd hoped to bring her nephew into the court as her steward, to reward him for helping to free Edward from captivity. But with Henry weakened by illness and Edward seeking his own glory in Outremer with King Louis, Eléonore has been occupied putting down minor rebellions by hotheads and glory seekers. Six years after Simon's defeat at Evesham, England still surges and plummets like a storm-tossed ship—with Eléonore its only anchor.

The monks lay the coffin in the grave, next to where Sanchia is buried. Across from Eléonore, Richard begins to sob, clinging to the arm of his new, beautiful, sixteen-year-old wife, Beatrice of Falkenburg, whose distaste for marriage to a sixty-two-year-old man shows on her face like a bad smell. Eléonore watches Richard closely. When he lifts his eyes to hers, she sees hatred. As she knew she would.

She approaches him when the service is finished, as they walk past the lovely old chapel and majestic spires of the abbey he and Sanchia founded. His tears have stopped, but he looks as if he might explode.

"I know what you are thinking, and I beseech you to think again," she says. "This fighting must stop, for England's sake."

"Simon de Montfort's sons are the ones who need stopping. For England's sake."

"We will find them, Richard, and we will hang them high."

"Using a garotte, I hope." His mouth twists. "I want to see them suffer."

He wants revenge. Eléonore would feel the same, no doubt, if the Montforts had killed Edward in such a cowardly manner. Poor Henry of Almain: he had never the chance to defend himself, for the Montfort brothers stabbed him in the back while he prayed, on his knees in the chapel of Viterbo.

"Richard, their mortal souls will suffer in hell. Isn't that enough?" The pope of Rome has already excommunicated them for the shocking murder.

"Will it bring back my son?"

A shout arises, and the rumble of running horses, six of them, stampeding through the cemetery, kicking up clods of grass and heath, headed their way as if to trample them down. Edward lifts his sword but Hamo Lestrange, Roger Leybourne, and his Lusignan cousins cut him off, begging him to take refuge in the chapel. Eléonore takes Henry by the arm and runs as fast as she can drag him on his arthritic legs—which is not quite fast enough.

"Death to the monarchy!" the riders shout. "Death to the killers of Simon de Montfort!" An egg hits Eléonore's gown, streaming yellow yolk on dark blue; Henry cries out as another splats against the side of his head.

"Come on, let's get them," she hears Hamo say.

Eléonore turns abruptly. "No!"

Why don't these men see that fighting begets fighting, that killing only causes more killing? "I forbid you to attack," she says. Edward sends her a dark look but his men hold their swords by their sides as the horses speed past, the youths laughing and taunting as they disappear into the woods.

"Why did you stop them?" her daughter-in-law Eleanor of

Castille asks. "Don't you care that we are mocked and ridiculed?"

"By youths such as those? No." Edward's wife purses her lips in obvious disagreement—an expression she wears often in Eléonore's presence. "Idle young men spend most of their time plotting and committing mischief. I'm sure Edward has told you about his own marauding years."

"That was a long time ago. England has changed. Our subjects need stability."

Our subjects? "Stability is what I am trying to give them."

"By shrugging your shoulders when these incidents occur? You make us appear weak."

"Refusing to fight requires more strength than attacking every downy-cheeked lad who waves his sword at us."

"The people want a strong ruler. That's why they supported Simon de Montfort."

"Oh, is that why?" Eleanor of Castille wears the look of a hound on the scent of a hare these days. She has begun to hunger for queenship.

At Berkhamsted Castle, men are running across the lawn toward them, waving their hands. Richard leans over his horse, exchanges words with one of them, then spurs his horse to a gallop. Edward follows close behind, with his knights. Eléonore, too, races across the lawn, around the château, dodging shadows, determined to stop the fighting, ignoring Henry's attempts to call her back to him. She follows the men to a stone house behind the castle and dismounts in a hurry to run after them.

"Mother! By God's head, leave this place," Edward says, but it is too late. Eléonore has seen the hanged man swaying from the rafters, his open and bulging eyes, his blue face. Bile rises to her throat, but she cannot look away. Edward's face is pale as he and his friends hold the body while Hamo, who has climbed up to the ceiling, cuts the rope with his knife.

"Why, O Lord?" Richard sits on the floor, tearing at his hair. "Why take my man from me today, of all days? Haven't you punished me enough with the death of my son?"

Eléonore bends over, touches his elbow, helps him gently to stand. She leads him to a chair and sits near him, hand on his arm, trying to comfort. Who was he? she asks.

"Abraham," he says, weeping. His Jew, who murdered his wife all those years ago. "My most loyal servant. My most trusted friend." His sobs increase. "Dear God, why didn't you just take me, instead?"

Edward hands him a parchment, sealed with Richard's wax seal, bearing his name in ink. Richard opens it with trembling hands. As he reads, emotions sweep across his face: Sorrow. Disbelief. Anger.

"Damn him to hell," he mutters, dropping the letter. Eléonore scoops it up. "Damn his Jewish bastard soul to the hottest hell forevermore."

"Let me have that, Mother." Edward holds out his hand but she will not take orders from her son, not until he is a king and perhaps not even then. She unfolds the parchment and reads.

> *You will never forgive me. Nor can I forgive myself, which is why I must leave this world. I have killed an innocent woman. Not my beautiful wife Floria—beloved by you, also, my lord, yes, I knew. Although I was accused of her death, I was not her killer. Yet I am a murderer, and so I must die.*

As she reads, she discovers the circumstances, at last, of the Jewess Floria's death sixteen years ago. She reads how Abraham's young servant Samuel came to him as he worked in the treasury, his eyes filled with a horror that sent Abraham racing across the meadow to his house. He found his wife on the floor, blood pooled under her head, a large chess piece—*the queen, my lord, from the set that I gave to you*—matted with blood and hair on the floor beside her. *Samuel told me of a quarrel that he had heard only moments earlier between Floria and the Lady Sanchia.* Abraham sent him to find his father, Joseph, but Sanchia soon appeared and began to call out for Richard.

How cruel of her, I thought, to blame me for her crime, to kill my Floria and then allow me to be locked in the London Tower, where I signed a false confession that slandered my entire race. I might have been hanged if not for you, my lord. You saved my life, which makes my crime against you all the more egregious.

I killed your wife, the Lady Sanchia, by means of a poison mixed into her wine.

"Sanchia!" The words begin to swim. A teardrop falls on the letter, smudging the fresh ink.

I killed her in an act of revenge that any man would take, and I never thought about her again. An eye for an eye, a tooth for a tooth. But today Samuel came to me. His father is dying, and Samuel blames himself. "There is a blot on my soul," he told me. "I must atone, or God will kill my father."

Samuel murdered Floria, he confessed, in a fit of passion. He had professed his love to her (Alas, who did not love Floria?) and she rebuffed him, saying she was a married woman and an honorable one. So he contented himself with spying on her. One day he spied her embracing the Lord Richard, in the gardens; running from the horrid scene, he collided with the Lady Sanchia's sister, Beatrice, who had also seen them. Floria was a wanton, she told him, who had broken many hearts at Berkhamsted.

Seeing Samuel's anguish, she tucked her arm into his. Floria had mocked him, she said, telling everyone in the court how he cried for love of her. Having stirred his wrath, she then encouraged him to kill Floria.

The lad protested, saying that he would suffer guilt and shame all his life for committing such a deed. "Perhaps this will ease your pain," she said, and gave him a pouch filled with silver coins—more money than he had ever seen.

Still he hesitated. He spent many days and nights watching his beloved from behind the hedge by her front window, agonizing. Then one day, he heard Sanchia and Floria within, shouting. He heard Floria say she carried Richard's child. His mind went blank with rage. When Sanchia tried to leave, Floria clung to her. Sanchia flung her to the floor and ran out, and Samuel saw his chance for revenge. He threw himself upon Floria and hit her with the object nearest at hand—the chess piece, which lay on the floor beside her.

Abraham forgave the lad, he said, knowing that he was the victim of womanly wiles. He forgave Richard, too, long ago. *Being an old man, and unable to please my wife, I looked away when I saw you together. But women are jealous creatures, and cunning. Would that I had killed the Lady Beatrice instead of your innocent Sanchia! I hope that you will find it in your heart someday to forgive me, as well.*

When she has finished, Eléonore throws the parchment into the fire, before anyone else can discover the scandalous truth about Richard (An affair with a Jewess! His name would never recover.) or Beatrice's awful crime. Edward scowls—his usual expression with her these days—and reaches toward the fireplace.

"Let it burn," she says.

"I would know its contents," he says, reaching for the document.

"I am yet queen, and still your mother, and I say, 'Let it burn.'"

His jaw thrust forward, he touches the edge of the parchment, as if to pull it from the flames. Eléonore would knock his hand away and box his ears—how dare he defy her, and before all these people!—but Richard interrupts.

"Your mother is right, Edward. Let it burn. Abraham's confession was meant for me alone."

"But Mother read it."

"Yes, I did," she says.

"As heir to the throne—"

"Which currently belongs to me, and to your father. I am yet the queen. And I am telling you now to let it burn."

His friends, having laid Abraham's body on a table, gather

around him. Hamo folds his arms across his chest, his expression hooded. Roger Leybourne smirks and the Lusignan cousins eye her warily, as if afraid she might attack her own son.

"It is time we returned to London," she says. Her voice is firm and clear, her gaze steady into Edward's sullen eyes.

Abruptly he bows to her. "Yes, my lady," he says, then turns and strides out the door with his entourage.

"Thank you, Eléonore," Richard says. "I would not want Edward to know of my indiscretions."

"I imagine that you are paying the price for them at this very moment."

"Yes." Tears slide down his face.

"Richard, I had no idea that Beatrice was so evil."

"I am the evil one. I, too, thought Sanchia guilty of Floria's murder. I punished her for it all the rest of her days. Beatrice was only protecting her sister from dishonor—and possibly from divorce."

"Many men keep mistresses. They do not generally divorce their wives to marry them."

"No, but my affair with a Jewess would have caused a devastating scandal if it had been discovered. What would your uncles have said?"

Uncle Thomas, in particular, would have insisted that Richard and Sanchia's marriage be annulled. Sanchia confessed every week her sin of marrying Richard after promising herself to Jesus. How would an annulment—and the disinheritance of her children—have affected her? Shame would have tainted the entire family.

And yet—to plan a murder, and to hire a poor simpleton to commit the act. "I wonder why I was shocked," she tells Henry that night, lying in his bed. "Beatrice was never like the rest of us. She lived by her own rules."

"It sounds to me as if she embodied the most important rule of all."

"Which one is that, dear?" She kisses his cheek, glad that he was not excommunicated, grateful to be here by his side, loving him, being loved.

"'Family comes first,'" he says. His smile is gentle. "Had you forgotten? Or is there another, more important, rule now?"

Later, as Henry's snores jostle one another softly in the dark, Eléonore lies in bed and ponders her sister. *We never knew you, Beatrice.* So much younger than they, and so caught up in her own ambitions—or so they thought—she never seemed like one of them. But while they forgot her, she never forgot them, or the fact that they were sisters. Marguerite has told her how Beatrice saved her from ruin and Eléonore from mutiny. Now, it seems, she saved Sanchia from humiliation, as well. Yet none of them ever helped her at all.

❖ *Marguerite* ❖

The Flavor of Peaches

Paris, 1271

Fifty years old

*S*HE TURNS SLOWLY around. All around her they lie in their bejeweled coffins: Louis; Isabelle and her husband, Thibaut; Jean Tristan. Before her stands Philip, suddenly a man in royal robes, a fashionable point of hair beneath his lower lip, like a smudge. She wants to spit on her finger and rub it away.

"They died nobly," he says in his new, man's voice. He sounds like pain. She rounds on him, but slowly.

"Nobly? Drowning in a pool of vomit and shit? I've seen your father with this sickness many times. He is more helpless than an infant." She glares at his coffin. She begged him not to take their children. "Was."

They landed in Tunisia, far from the holy land, in the stifling July heat. Louis's paltry force could not take the capital city alone, so they waited for Charles and the Sicilian troops he promised. And they waited. For more than a month they camped at the city of Carthage, outside the walls, enduring the sun, the flies, the thirst. Soon they were forced to drink from a brackish pond, the only water they could find. Almost immediately, they fell ill.

"He died in the service of God," Philip says.

"Then God must be cringing in shame."

Philip's spine stiffens. "Mama, you blaspheme!"

"Do you think God would have wanted this?" She gestures toward the caskets. "And not only this, but hundreds, thousands of dead. Trust me, son, the Lord would not have conceived this campaign so poorly, nor executed it so disastrously." Her gaze drops to her daughter's casket. Isabelle, her father's favorite, so pious that she would not choose a gown to wear without praying about it. "But your father did not consult God. He was too vain for that."

Philip flinches. "Do not speak ill of my father."

She laughs. "Another Capet who fears the truth? Do not live in illusion, as Louis did, or you will die as futilely."

"You forget that we are now the King of France. You are forbidden to speak to us with such disrespect."

She closes her eyes so that her son cannot see them roll. How did she bear such a tedious child? "Why Tunisia, Philip? I thought they had sailed for Acre."

"Uncle Charles suggested it. He told Papa the Tunisian emir was friendly to Christianity. Papa hoped to convert him, then join forces with his troops and the Mongols for an attack on Egypt."

Marguerite narrows her eyes. "How did Charles know the Tunisian emir's religious views?"

"The emir owes money to Uncle Charles. A great deal of money." He shrugs. "Uncle Charles has met with him many times in an effort to collect it."

So—Charles manipulated Louis's campaign to enrich himself. Where, she asks, is Charles now?

"He marched on Tunis after Papa's death. But the emir begged for peace, so we did not attack." He frowned. "Uncle Charles said that enough men had already died."

"An unpopular decision, I'm sure." Marguerite remembers the eager faces of the foot soldiers—peasants—who accompanied them on the first Outremer campaign. When they talked of their hopes and dreams, few ever mentioned Jerusalem, or God. These men fought for the loot. They had heard tales of unlimited gold in Outremer. They braved death and disease hoping to enrich themselves. On this campaign, they never got a glimpse of Saracen gold. Charles got his share, of that she is certain, and much more. And Louis and her children are dead.

"Uncle Charles signed an agreement with the emir and sent me home to you. Aren't you glad, Mama?"

"Of course I am glad to see you alive. But—" She looks down at the casket of Jean Tristan. A more pure and tender heart the world will never see. Jean of Sorrow, born and dead in Outremer, a desolate land watered only by tears. Her tears fall like raindrops about her feet and she follows them, sinking to the floor until she is surrounded by death.

If only she had a dagger at hand, or a vial of arsenic. What is the use of living? All her dreams, all her efforts to make a difference in this world have led only to this, to loss and sorrow and regret and death. What was the point of queenship? What was the point of anything?

Women have only the power that men allow them, Beatrice said. How true were her words. Marguerite gave birth to eleven children—the greatest power of all, it seemed, but no, only six remain, two killed now by Louis. She saved Louis from death in Egypt only for him to die a much more ignominious death in Tunis. She restored France's treasury, but Louis spent every livre she saved on his ill-conceived campaign.

Even her proudest moment, the signing of a peace treaty with England after two hundred years of fighting, came to naught. Their kingdoms ceased to battle each other, but neither lived in peace. The men of England attacked the throne, plunging their kingdom into a bloody civil war. The men of France burned Cathars at the stake, plundered the Jews, and raced off to Outremer at the first opportunity. Men will never be at peace, she thinks, until they can find it within themselves.

And now Louis is dead, killed by Charles; and her queenship, too, dead at Charles's hand. Charles has taken everything from her:

her husband, her children, Beatrice, Provence. Her heart pangs. She will never see Provence again. Charles will not even allow her safe passage through his county. Her grandchildren will never know the poetry, the fruit trees, the gentle and kind people whose hearts are as warm as the Provençal sun. All that is lost to her now, because of Charles. He coerced her sister into changing her father's will, and the pope agreed. Only the pope could overturn that ruling now.

She rummages in her purse for her handkerchief and finds the letter she received this morning, forgotten until now. She breaks the seal with her thumbnail, then unfolds it. The mayor of Marseille has written to her, inviting her to Provence. While King Charles tarries in Outremer, he says, he will send an army to Tarascon Castle to secure it for her. *Should you choose to fight for your right to Provence from there, you would find many men on your side, for we have had enough of Charles's tyranny.*

Her tears subside. In the past year, as she mourned her children's deaths—Margaret, too, dead in childbirth this year—a new pope was ordained. Might he be more receptive to her petition? To change a will after a person's death is unheard of, Louis's chancellor has said. And what of the new king of Germany, appointed after Richard died last year? Might he support her cause, being in competition with Charles for the emperor's crown? She could prove a valuable ally, holding Tarascon and with an army at her behest.

Marguerite's pulse quickens. She sits up straight, the caskets forgotten. Not even God has the power to change a dead man's will. Might this new pope be wary of Charles's ambitions in Naples, Genoa, and Hungary? Might he wish to diminish Charles's power by divesting him of Provence? He would certainly grant it to Marguerite, the eldest daughter of Count Ramon Berenger and the county's original heiress.

She stands. If she regains Provence, she can help its people. The days of wine and poetry can return, and peace to that peace-loving land. At the very least, she might live out the rest of her days in Tarascon, on the banks of the tranquil Rhône.

Nothing to live for? She has Tarascon, and she has the love of Provence, and she has her own wisdom, gained after so many trying years. She can take her county back from that usurper. She will! The flavor of peaches fills her mouth as she hurries to her chambers, her letters to the mayor of Marseille and the German king writing themselves in her head.

Epilogue

Queen Marguerite of France lived in Provence, fighting against Charles of Anjou for the right to rule with the help of her nephew, King Edward I of England, and King Rudolf von Hapsburg of Germany. After Charles's death in 1285, her son, King Philip the Bold, awarded her an income from Anjou in exchange for Provence, placing the county at last in France's domain. She died in 1295 at the ripe old age of 74, having outlived eight of her eleven children—and having steadfastly refused to testify in favor of sainthood for Louis, which was granted in 1298. She was buried under the altar steps at the Basilica of St. Denis near Paris, where her tomb—unmarked—probably still remains today.

❦

Queen Eléonore of England took an active role, after her husband's death, in bringing up her grandchildren. She resided at Windsor for a time, then in various castles given by King Henry as part of her marriage dower. In 1286 she joined the Amesbury convent in Wiltshire, to which the fabled Queen Guinevere had supposedly retired after the death of King Arthur. She died at Amesbury and was buried there in 1291; her heart was buried in London. Her son King Edward I of England established a memorial for her in the Chapel of the Kings at Wesminster. Her son Edmund Crouchback became the first Earl of Lancaster and, in contrast to his mother's love for white roses, adopted the red rose as his emblem.

*A*cknowledgments

*M*Y SINCERE THANKS go to my editor, Kathy Sagan, for her encouragement, support, and terrific ideas; to copyeditor Mandy Keifetz, for her excellent work; to the rest of the editorial team at Gallery Books; to Shereef El-Talawy, my Egyptian tour guide who made special arrangements for me to see the house in Mansoura where King Louis IX was imprisoned and who drove me to Damietta to see where the crusaders landed; to Bob Spittal, for saying, when I fretted over all the things this book could be, "Why don't you just focus on the emotional lives of your characters?"; to my daughter, Mariah Jones Brooks, for listening to me read aloud and for taking such excellent author photographs; to Rich Myers and Todd Mowbray for reading early drafts and providing me with helpful comments; to Shanti Perez for allowing me to debut a chapter at the Flying Pig Reading Series; to the folks at Red Room, the online writers' community; to Lois, Linda, and the other wonderful people at Auntie's Books for their support of local authors; to Gillian Bagwell, Christopher Gortner, Mitch Kaplan, Donna Russo Morin, and Susan Higginbotham for their kind endorsements of this book; and to Pia Hallenberg Christensen, Sam Mace, Renée Roehl, Suzanne and Paul Markham, Nettie and Dan Simonsen, Amy Watson Logan, Karlee Etter, Pavarti K. Tyler, Michael Smith, Siarah Myron, Mike Petersen, Andrea Hubbard, Charity Doyl, and my many other friends and fans around the world who believe in me and my work, and help me to keep the faith.

GALLERY
BOOKS

Readers Group Guide

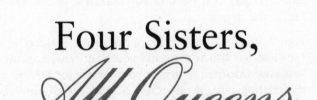

SHERRY JONES

INTRODUCTION

Four Sisters, All Queens follows the lives of Beatrice of Savoy's four daughters—all of whom became queens in thirteenth-century Europe. As Marguerite, Queen of France to Louis IX; Eléonore, Queen of England; Sanchia, Queen of Germany; and Beatrice, Queen of Sicily, all work to both expand their husbands' empires and increase the influence of the House of Savoy, they find themselves unable to remain loyal to both. Told from the alternating points of view of all four queens, the novel explores family and political dynamics as allegiances to kin and country are tested.

QUESTIONS AND TOPICS FOR DISCUSSION

1. Beatrice's maxim, which she tries to pass on to her daughters, is "Family comes first." Do you agree with this motto? Which queen best upholds this mantra?

2. In the prologue, Beatrice states, "A woman achieves nothing in this man's world without careful plotting." (p. 1) How does this statement apply to the rest of the novel? As Eléonore wonders later, is it possible for women to decide their own fate in this novel?

3. *Four Sisters, All Queens* is told from the perspective of all four queens. Which sister did you identify with most? Who was your favorite? Who was your least favorite? Did any of the relationships in this novel remind you of any relationships in your own life? If so, why?

4. "[Marguerite] had thought that, as queen, she would have control over her own life as well as the lives of others. Now . . . she thinks the opposite may be true." (p. 53) Does being in a position of leadership allow one to have more power over others? Or does it actually serve to limit control in one's own life? Have you ever been in a leadership position? What did you struggle with? What did you enjoy about it?

5. Beatrice of Savoy and Blanche, the White Queen, are both strong matriarchs with great influence over the other characters in the novel. Compare and contrast these two powerful women.

6. Discuss the different marriages and relationships throughout the book. What motivates these unions? Love, money, power, sex? In your opinion, which relationship functioned the best? Why?

7. Similarly, as Marguerite wonders, "What is the meaning of loyalty?" (p. 279) Is there any merit to remaining faithful in this novel? How do you define loyalty? Who is the most loyal person in your life?

8. Marguerite ponders the true meaning of happiness, and if it is to be found with a man or in spite of a man. (p. 280) Which do you believe? What would you choose?

9. Eléonore wonders, "[Who] cares which kingdom has more power, which kings and queens have more lands? We fight and scheme for our children's sakes and then we die, and they may lose all that we built up for them. There is nothing we can give to anyone that lasts—except love." (pp. 400–1) Which characters would agree with her sentiment? Do you agree?

10. What is the source of each character's power? From where do they derive their confidence and authority? How is power for women different from men?

11. *Four Sisters, All Queens* takes place over a period of forty years. How does each sister evolve throughout the novel?

12. Why does Beatrice force her daughters into their marriages? Did she sacrifice her daughters for her own interests, as Marguerite believes? (p. 354) Or did she truly have their benefit in mind?

13. "In this struggle to navigate a world made by men, for men, are not all women sisters?" (p. 390) Do you agree with this statement? How does it apply to thirteenth century society in contrast to present day?

A CONVERSATION WITH

Sherry Jones

When writing this novel, how did you strike a balance between historical accuracy and fiction?

Historical accuracy is very important to me, and I know it is to my readers. I research, research, research before and during the writing process, and throughout revision and editing. I keep a timeline of events to which I refer throughout. I keep a cast of characters with information about each, and I pay close attention to details regarding the culture of the era. I discovered fairly late in the process, for example, that cardinals in the Church didn't begin wearing red hats until the fourteenth century, and so I had to make a change. And yet, because the story takes place some eight hundred years ago, so much is unknown, especially about the women. I've seen conflicting accounts of the sisters' birth years, for example. We don't even have descriptions of their appearances! That's frustrating, yes, but it also means that I have ample room for invention, which is the heart of fiction.

In this novel, you cover a span of almost forty years, and write from the perspectives of four different women. How did you choose which events to include and which to leave out for the sake of the novel's pacing and length?

Four Sisters, All Queens touches on so many issues: monarchy vs. democracy, corruption in the Church, religious persecution, xenophobia, anti-Semitism, colonialism—especially in the Middle East—Islamophobia, conspiracy theories. It could have filled a thousand pages, and taken me a decade to write. The possibilities of the book, the number of directions in which it could have gone, felt overwhelming at times. When I told this to a friend, he said, "Why don't you focus on the emotional lives of your characters?" It was terrific advice. In doing so, I touched on all the themes I've mentioned above, but explored in depth those most important to this tale—those of family, in particular marriage and sibling rivalry, as well as women's power. Every scene in *Four Sisters, All Queens* focuses on the emotional lives of Marguerite, Eléonore, Sanchia, or Beatrice. Any scene that didn't do so, I eliminated.

How did you research the historical events and characters in *Four Sisters, All Queens*? Did you visit any of the European sites your characters frequented?

Yes, I had visited London and Paris, in particular Westminster, Sainte-Chappelle, and Notre Dame Cathedral, and I went to Egypt to see where King Louis, Charles of Anjou, and Jean de Joinville were held prisoner in Mansoura as well as the beach at Damietta where they landed. Mostly, however I read Nancy Goldstone's *Four Queens*, biographies of Eléonore, Blanche de Castille, St. Louis, Simon de Montfort, and Richard of Cornwall—even a biography of Marguerite written in French, which I translated very painstakingly into English! I read many books on medieval culture and studied online courses about the Church, medieval philosophy, and the high Middle Ages. I read the letters of the sisters available through the women's Epistolae project online and books on the Crusades. I listened to medieval music and read about the troubadours. The thirteenth century was such a fascinating time, and one that hasn't been written about as much as, say, the Tudor era. It enchants me.

Your first book, *The Jewel of Medina*, was about life with the Prophet Muhammad, as told by a wife. What did you learn from the experience? How was its sequel, *The Sword of Medina*, received?

I learned never to send a historical novel to a historian for an endorsement, for one thing! A University of Texas professor's overwrought response to *The Jewel of Medina* caused my original publisher, Random House, to "indefinitely postpone" publishing the book and its sequel in 2008 for fear of retaliation from radical Muslims. Her remarks to the *Wall Street Journal* characterizing the novel as pornographic caused an uproar that resulted in the fire-bombing of my U.K. publisher's home office, scaring him into canceling publication of my books. Ultimately, I found a U.S. publisher as well as publishers around the world.

I also learned that people believe what they want to believe, and I learned that A'isha lives not only in the pages of my books, but also within me. My challenge throughout the controversy—death threats, Islamophobic jeers, accusations, even body guards!—was to not be distracted by all the hype but to remain steadfast in my commitment to telling A'isha's remarkable story. My books have inspired many thousands of readers, especially women and girls (including me), with her example of courage and strength.

The sequel, *The Sword of Medina,* was not controversial. It received much critical acclaim, including a starred review in *Publishers Weekly* and a silver medal in the Independent Publishers' Awards. It tells of A'isha's life when things got really interesting, after Muhammad's death, when she was a political adviser to three caliphs and a military strategist who led troops in the first Islamic civil war. It tells, also, the story of her nemesis Ali, Muhammad's cousin. Writing from alternating points of view—first A'isha's, then Ali's—stretched my limitations as a new author and gave my readers a more complex portrait of both characters, far beyond the A'isha and Ali you see in *Jewel*.

This novel is very different from your first. What drew you to medieval Europe from seventh-century Arabia?

As usual, it was the story. I read about Marguerite, Eléonore, Sanchia, and Beatrice in Nancy Goldstone's biography *Four Queens* and felt unsatisfied when I reached the end. I wanted to know more about these fascinating sisters. What did they look like? What were their personalities like? I wanted to hear them speak, to eavesdrop on their conversations with their husbands, to feel their feelings and think their thoughts. I'd had the same experience when I'd first read about A'isha, the protagonist of *The Jewel of Medina* and *The Sword of Medina*. I felt inspired, then, to write a novel about them.

You describe yourself as an avid book lover. What are your top five, all-time favorite books?

Hilary Mantel's brilliant *Wolf Hall* is my all-time favorite book, hands down. I adore Iris Murdoch, and love her book *The Sea, the Sea*. Edith Wharton's *The House of Mirth* is the first, and only, book ever to make me cry. Tolstoy's *Anna Karenina*. And, of course, *Little Women,* whose four sisters correspond so beautifully, in order, to the sisters in "Four Sisters, All Queens."

Other books and authors I adore include Debra Magpie Earling's haunting, beautifully written *Perma Red*. I also love the books of Eudora Welty—Southern like me, she was an amazing writer, especially her use of metaphor; Salman Rushdie (a genius); Ellen Gilchrist—*The Annunciation* was a huge influence on me in my twenties; Anne Tyler, Isabel Allende, Anne Patchett, Louise Erdrich, and Alice Hoffman, to name a few.

Your path to becoming a novelist was long—you've recalled wanting to write a novel since your early twenties, but didn't begin writing until twenty years later. What inspired you to finally start writing?

Actually, I decided in the second grade that I would become a writer. I had a teacher who praised my poetry and stories and said to me, before the entire class, "If you ever become a published author, make sure to keep your name so that I know it's you."

I have written all my life. In school, as I mentioned, I wrote poems and short stories. When I was eighteen and still in college, I began reporting and writing for the Kinston, N.C., *Free Press*. I worked as a journalist at newspapers and for magazines for thirty years. All that work delayed my college degree, but I was determined to get one. In 2002, I was casting about for a topic for a story or novella to submit to the University of Montana's Davidson Honors College for my honors thesis, and I ran across the interesting fact that the Muslim prophet Muhammad had a harem with twelve wives and concubines in all. This fascinated me, and as I read more I discovered A'isha, his youngest and favorite wife and the most famous and influential woman in Islam. I would have liked to know this feisty, witty, tender-hearted gal. I think we would have been friends. She's long gone, though, so I wrote a novel about her, instead. Actually, I wrote two of them.

Do you have any advice to share with aspiring novelists?

1. The first draft, as Hemingway famously said, is always shit. Don't let writing badly discourage you. Just keep going, finish, and then revise. In revision is where the real writing starts.

2. Read, read, read. Read everything you can, of the highest quality possible.

3. Don't publish too soon. Find, and pay, a good freelance editor to critique your book, then revise again. Don't be in a hurry. Be patient. Musicians study and practice for years before playing Carnegie Hall. Olympic athletes train hard before reaching their level of achievement. Writing novels takes exactly as much hard work and dedication.

4. Don't give up. Be stubborn. Believe in yourself. If you write something truly good, someone will publish it.

5. Get a literary agent. Be prepared for this to take a year or more. Make sure your work is as good as it can be before you send it out. Expect rejection, and more rejection. Cry if you must, then get back up and query again. If your work is good, someone will represent you. A literary agent is the single most valuable asset to your career. I dedicated *Four Sisters, All Queens* to mine, and with good reason.

Your first career was in journalism and you continue to be a freelance reporter. How does your background in journalism impact your novel writing?

Writing for a living meant I wrote every single day, on deadline. As a result, I'm a prolific writer, and I never suffer from writer's block. Journalism taught me to observe details; it gave me an ear for dialogue; it taught me how to do research and it gave me lots of experience working with editors. Also, reporters are usually the generators of their own story ideas. I'm such an idea person now that I will never run out of books to write.

When the four sisters are young, they talk about which historical queens they are most like. Is there a queen of the past you would compare yourself to? What traits do you share?

I'd be Eléonore, the second sister in *Four Sisters, All Queens*. Bold, outspoken, competitive, ambitious, devoted to her family, fanciful, interested in fashion, a lover of literature and a patron of the arts—these are the traits we share in common (many of which Eléonore also shares with Jo, the second sister in *Little Women*). Unlike Eléonore, however, I'm a peacenik, while she seems not to have hesitated to send troops into battle. Indeed, she may have preferred war to negotiation. "Love is a verb."